# Between Pictures

# Between
## Pictures

### JAYNE LOADER

GROVE PRESS • NEW YORK

Published by Grove Press, Inc.
920 Broadway
New York, N.Y. 10010

The author gratefully acknowledges permission to reprint lyrics
from *Riders on the Storm* by The Doors. © 1971 Doors Music
Company. All rights reserved. Used by permission.

LIBRARY OF CONGRESS CATALOGING-IN-PUBLICATION DATA

Loader, Jayne, 1951-
  Between pictures.

  I. Title.
PS3562.017B48  1987    813'.54    87-12086
ISBN 0-8021-0013-9


Designed by Irving Perkins Associates

Manufactured in the United States of America

First Edition 1987

10 9 8 7 6 5 4 3 2 1

*for Ethel Small*

The author wishes to thank the MacDowell and Blue Mountain Colonies and the Adcock and Schaefer Foundations for making it possible for her to complete this book.

Drink leads to disaster. Cars lead to disaster. Roads lead to disaster. Sidewalks lead to disaster. Boxcars lead to disaster. 707 jets lead to disaster. Sex leads to disaster. Women lead to disaster. Little boys lead to disaster. So do little girls. Ass leads to disaster. Chastity leads to disaster. . . . Dollars lead to disaster. Even a bent dime leads to disaster. Movies lead to disaster. Dreams lead to disaster.

—G. CABRERA INFANTE,
*Three Trapped Tigers*

# Between Pictures

TODAY is the first day of the rest of your life," says my ex–great love Clement Goodbloode optimistically, peering out from the depths of a really bad hangover. I scan my similarly damaged brain for appropriate comebacks but nothing springs to tongue, so I keep quiet and sip my spritzer like a lady. Clemmy stubs out a Marlboro in what's left of his Eggs Sardou, waiting for me to say something sarcastic so he can pontificate for a while on how good he's going to be forevermore, but I've heard it all before on previous H-days and even said it myself on one or two sad occasions, I kid you not.

Anyway, I just smile in friendly nurselike fashion and fork one of Clemmy's rejected anchovies, all the while getting this large charge out of depriving him of his favorite speech. An inch short of mouth I see the anchovy's bathed in ash-flavored Hollandaise, like everything else on Clemmy's plate, and punctuate my find with a characteristic housewifey shriek.

"You're so inconsiderate," I complain, slamming my fork down noisily. "You know how much I love anchovies." But finicky Clemfish isn't taking the bait. Not just any old fight will do for Clemmy, who's grokked my strategy at last, sighs this disappointed sigh, drains his third Becks, and signals for another round. We're both being good today, drinks-wise, as is our wont after major debauches. I for one am being especially careful, since I've got a heavy date tomorrow that I want to look good for. No blotchy cheeks, bags, or piggy red eyes allowed for this extremely important three-day encounter with the current great love of my life, Walter Light, who just might take me away from all this.

But I'm not thinking about Walter now. It's Clemmy who's got my full attention. He looks so mournful, poor sweet baby: like a basset hound at a wake. He looks so disappointed—it's one of his best emotions—that I almost regret holding out on him, because I really do like Clemmy. More accurately, I love him, but don't ever tell him I said that or we won't be having any more of these cute little lunches. Love from me is the last thing Clemmy wants, or thinks he wants, or is willing to admit to wanting. I can't tell which is true and doubt Clemmy can either, but in any case we don't talk about love anymore, ever. Not in relation to each other.

I start figuring the odds on what Clemmy said, on the drecky Sixties phrase he managed to dredge from the shallows of his so-called consciousness turning out to be actually true. That's why they call them truisms, right? I sit up straight and study Clemmy like the good little student I am, head extended on the long white neck that is one of my better features, like a snapping turtle out of its shell. The evocative smell of old expensive flannel soaked in guzzled-then-sweated-out Scotch wafts across the table to reassure me. Clemmy is the same as always, I decide. Big and handsome and sexy and elegantly decrepit, his red face enhanced with a couple dozen more broken veins, maybe, a substantive number of wrinkles accrued around the eyes, but after all it's been a week since I've

seen him at least. And the eyes themselves are still good,
clear and China blue in spite of all the abuse they get in
sleazy joints like this one. And those cheekbones! Real
quality stuff. You can't buy cheekbones like that, not on
your salary.

But a girl can only do this for just so long: I mean, pay
attention to somebody else. And these shiny mirrored
walls in the Bar Car don't help. That's the name of the
dive we're currently in, our favorite New York bar actually, full of easy women and hard drugs. It's a genu-wine
antique railroad car, just like the ones Clemmy's ancestors
used to take, to Tuxedo Park or Topridge or someplace
even fancier, hauling scions and nannies and upstairs
maids and the second-best silver so they could while away
the summers in comfort with their fellow robber barons.
The Bar Car was bought, then restored by this group of
dark-skinned Spanish-speaking gentlemen who don't actually admit to being Colombian but have all the ac-
coutrements, if you get my drift, and they're making a
tidy albeit taxable bundle off their investment too, I guarantee. Still, it's all done quite nicely, polished wood and
brass and these muted fabrics that feel good on bare skin
should you happen to have some on hand. It's filled with
people like Clemmy who belong here and interlopers like
me who don't, but nonetheless here we all are anyway,
one big happy family. So many more me's than Clemmies,
of every race, creed, color, and sexual preference. Just
listen! It's a veritable Café de Babel.

These wraparound mirrors are the only modern touch.
So reassuring to peek behind Clemmy's blackheady
neck—he never uses soap, just rinses himself like let-
tuce—and see my own dear kisser loom. What a welcome
sight! My eyes flock to it like starlings. I look almost as cute
as Clemmy. Oh yes I do. Almost as well-preserved, though
it's true we both had a lot of advantages, looks-wise, to

start with, Clemmy more than me. "He's got arms like
Popeye and a face like Eugene O'Neill," I remember saying once to a girlfriend, who was suitably awestruck.
The best way to conjure *me* up should you be so in-
clined is to think of a short showgirl or starlet, a bottled
blonde, a second-rate Forties pinup whose face will one
day show vestiges of great prettiness. I have the same face
at thirty-four that I had at five, same sulky mouth and
Kewpie-doll cheeks, unlined and missing something, the
face of a Gerber baby, so essentially unmemorable that a
change of hairstyle or color is enough to cause acquaintances of many years to pass me by on the street. "My God,
Anna Kate! You look so different!" they say at these moments when I confront them. My eyes, as yellow-green
and changeable as a chameleon's skin, rescue me from
blandness five days too late. I am already in the autopsy
room, toe-tagged and dissected, by the time the eyes decide to do their stuff.

This decorative but highly forgettable face and marginally more interesting brick-shithouse body are a little too
extreme for current tastes but make a nice little package
nonetheless, a regular bundle of joy or so they tell me—
they being men, of course. Especially your average Joes
on the street, your working stiffs with dark complexions.
Delivery boys offer me rides on their bicycles. "God bless
America!" bums say as I amble by. "Lemme in there,
momma, and lock the door!" When I strut down the street
in my jazzy outfits, men fall like drunken squirrels, clutching their nuts. None of this offends me the way it's supposed to. *Au contraire,* it makes my day. Someday it will
all collapse, of course, face and body at once like a black
hole imploding, but not as long as the money holds out,
which it should do forever since I've made so much of it,
far far more than anybody expected.

Clemmy helped me make it, before we split up. We

wrote scripts together, and eventually did quite well at it, too, but our love affair ended and our partnership after that and since then we've both been between pictures: in this netherworld, this dead zone, this timeless gray place where everyone looks the same and every thought, every act, every so-called feeling runs together and turns to mud like a watercolor somebody's worked on too long. That's what happens to people who measure their lives in movies. Anyway, that's how I used to see it, before I met Walter Light.

I'll have to admit, studying our heads in the mirror, that neither of us looks quite as gorgeous since leaving L.A., which we did separately but at more or less the same time a year or so ago, I have trouble remembering why. Something to do with being taken seriously and fulfilling my so-called destiny, but neither of these seems to have occurred. I can't imagine why, can you? Clemmy and I live six blocks apart now, in the meat district, and we can't help running into each other here and there though none of it was planned, I kid you not.

I miss L.A., where the sun may give you cancer but not yet, and in the meantime a tan hides more than you'd expect. A year in New York and your vices, your impure thoughts for Christ's sake, start showing on your face, your body, everywhere. You become transparent when you want to be opaque. And everybody looks. They pretend they don't but they do, through spread fingers, like kids at a vampire pic. Studying my face, I understand why Clemmy wants to be born again, but as much as I love him and wish him the best, there really isn't any chance of that.

When I manage to tear myself away from the mirror, Clemmy is staring straight at me and grinning like an astronaut, I mean genuinely but with a little too much pep. He's grinning exactly like Gordo Cooper, not the real

Gordo, who I wouldn't know from Adam, but the actor who played him in the flick. Those bio-pics are so confusing. The actors replace the real people in my mind and no matter how hard I concentrate the real people never come back. I just can't *see* them. Point to ponder: If Buddy Holly hadn't of died, would he look like Gary Busey looks *now?*

Then something not entirely unfamiliar happens to Clemmy's face. After he makes sure I've seen him grinning, after he takes my hand and pat-pats it in this condescending way he knows I hate, after he's absolutely sure I've grokked all the connotations of him seeing me so transfixed with myself and wrings out of that little self-revelatory scene all the points he's going to get, for the time being anyhow, then his grin kind of collapses. Oh, it stays on his face, all right, but without any discernible change in expression it shifts from a Gordo Cooper grin to a Pat Nixon grin. You know the one: this frozen, pasted-on, unconvincing kind of travesty. And I realize what's caused the transformation is his eyes. Clemmy isn't looking at *me* anymore. He's looking at himself in the mirror. I can just about guess what he's seeing, too.

And there you have it, folks: Clement Goodbloode and I, hands intertwined, knees almost touching, looking like lovers for all intents and purposes but not thinking about love, no sirree. Thinking about ourselves, our little problems and vices, the state of our so-called souls. Something tells me I've seen this picture *before.*

"Is my baby a little depresso today?" I say sweetly in the domestic patois we resurrect to needle each other with, interrupting Clemmy's little reverie with himself. "A little hungo? Still drunk?" Clemmy breaks away from the mirror slowly, like a sperm whale coming up for air.

"Slack off, Porter," Clemmy says gruffly, signaling for the check as he was born to. Clemmy's the only person

who calls me Porter, which is not my last name but my
first name, my third first name if you want to get techni-
cal. I don't think they have a name yet for that.

"Promise not to laugh?" I used to say cutely before
spitting out my despised monicker, but I don't do that
now since nobody does, not in New York City, not at
Katherine Anne Porter O'Shea. That name caused riots in
Weatherford, Texas, where I was born, and stopped traffic
in Fort Worth, where I was brought up. New Yorkers
don't laugh because I might be a relative, and while I
never say I am I don't deny it too hard either, not to these
vampires, these suck-ups, these would-be slaves of litera-
ture. So now you know what ship Momma stowed away
on when she brung me into the world and has been sailing
on, come to think of it, more or less ever since.

But choices confuse, don't you think, and a name like
mine creates too damn many. Just thinking about it makes
me profane. I named myself Anna Kate when I was
fifteen, when it was clear that if I didn't take some sort of
evasive action, I was going to spend the rest of my life as
Kathy, Annie, Katie, or worse. So this made-up name is
the one I'm known by, to my mother's unabated dismay.
"Anna Kate? Who's that?" she sniffs when my name rolls
by on the credits of some movie or other. (You know how
to tell a movie person from a *real* person? They're the
ones reading the credits like they were the Dead Sea
Scrolls, yammering about who was fucking who, while the
other peons are putting on their coats. Usually you don't
find them in theaters, though. You find them in screening
rooms, like the one I dragged my mother to in Dallas.)
"Why can't you use your own name?" she said after the
pic. "Isn't it good enough for you? It was good enough for
*her.*"

Clemmy comes from a place where first names often
sound like last names because once upon a time they

were, so he calls me Porter because it sounds so . . . *normal*. To *him*. Even now it makes me feel warm when he says it. It brings back all the years he spent trying to transform me—into what, I never was sure. He really did try, though. Mrs. Goodbloode didn't raise no slackers. There were a number of things I managed to learn from him, too: how to eat in expensive restaurants every night, how to spend my days going shopping, how to talk to rich people without swallowing my tongue, that it's okay to wear jewelry with your bathing suit but only if it's real gold. I had my first Krugerrand with Clemmy, my first credit card, my first convertible, but calling your dachshund Anastasia won't make it a Russian wolfhound, no matter how often you say the name. No matter how loud you yell it or how sweetly you croon, some dogs can't change their spots and I was one of them. But I'm changing for Walter Light *even as we speak*.

"Walter's flying in tomorrow," I say with demure pride.

"Under his own steam?" says Clemmy nastily.

"Ha ha ha," I say without a trace of humor, Marlon Brando to his Vivien Leigh. "Ha-ha-ha ha *ha*." Clemmy loathes my boyfriends on principle, begrudging me any shot at happiness, however remote. Life just wouldn't be the same for Clemmy without me out there somewhere, pining away. He loathes Walter especially because Walter is perfect, with no faults to point out, no bad habits or eccentricities to lampoon, enlisting me in love-killing laughter. Walter's smarter than Clemmy, and, worse, everybody *knows* it. While Clemmy was majoring in poontang and poker at one end of New Haven, Walter was scooping up prizes at the other. Science prizes, of course, but *writing* prizes too. Poor Clemmy remembers Walter all too well. Walter doesn't remember him at all.

I've always been a pushover for boy geniuses—*real* geniuses, no IQs under 150 need apply. *The G.E. College*

*Bowl* is my favorite pornography. But I want geniuses who are well rounded, well adjusted, well . . . ha, fooled you! I'm not *that* predictable, not yet anyway. Well *liked.* Popular geniuses. Scientists who could just as easily have been great poets or great stand-up comedians, and Walter Light is the best of the breed, like a young Robert Oppenheimer, only cuter, with smaller ears. And surprise, he loves me, too. Walter Light really *could* be my guardian angel, sent from heaven to save, save, save me from the walking horrors I attract and can't shake off, from the Clemmy clones I want who invariably dump me. Nobody needs saving more than me, and if they do God help them. And that's what Walter Light means to me. Amen.

It is worth noting that Clemmy's mother was never even tempted to call me Porter. She knew right away I wasn't a relative; she *knew* all the relatives and used to introduce me, in Newport, as Annie O'Shea, hoping someone would hire me to lick out their toilets.

I've told you about my looks. The clothes I wear tend to set them off and my personality kind of goes with the territory, so maybe I shouldn't have been so surprised by the way Mrs. Goodbloode treated me. So *hurt.* I mean, it wasn't just that golden shovel I whored off Clemmy at Harry Winston's, the one he made me wear on a neck chain the first time I met his family—just a joke, he said—that made Mrs. Goodbloode peg me for a gold digger. Or the shameful secret of my ignoble birth. For I wasn't just from the wrong side of the tracks, as Clemmy and I dutifully, *stupidly,* informed his parents whilst sitting hand in hand on this hideous couch that echoed the color scheme of Mr. Goodbloode's golfing pants—I mean chartreuse, white, and navy blue—during the first of our many unconsummated engagements, but from the wrong side of the blanket as well. I remember how Mrs. Goodbloode blanched under her Dior foundation, how she went into this little swoon, seeing the presidency of the Rhode Island Garden Club, so near but so far, slip from her fingers yet again.

Mr. Goodbloode knew my father. All rich people know each other. "A bit of a sticky wicket," he said, embarrassed by my father's lack of class. Daddy's so rich now, they've almost forgotten he isn't a gentleman. "Does he never get in touch?"

"Only when he sees her on television," Clemmy answered. Clemmy loves my mother, Livia, and hates my father, Rodgers O'Shea, né *Roger*, who breezed into Pascagoula, Mississippi, on business, seduced and abandoned my innocent mother, and paid nary a penny in child support.

"She has a father, you know," my old man once said to Clemmy over the phone, having tracked us to NBC, dressing room B, where we were waiting to go on the Letterman show, by dropping Jay Rockefeller's name two or twenty-six times in an extremely loud voice. As usual, my father was drunk. Clemmy wouldn't let him speak to me, to upset me. To make me *blow Letterman*. This was in the days when we gave a hoot. I've always wondered what Daddy told those NBC operators. That Jay was going to *evict* them? "She has a father," my father said.

"Technically," Clemmy said coldly. "Technically she has a father."

"Don't you want to see my father?" I asked Clemmy during one of the old reprobate's rare visits to California.

"I want to see your father *hang*," Clemmy said. That's what Mrs. Goodbloode had in mind for *me*. As her daughter-in-law, even a Jew would have been preferable, an educated Negress only slightly worse.

Nobody believes it was nearly so awful, not even my own mother. They all think I'm exaggerating, to tell a better story. "It couldn't have been *that* bad," my mother chirps in typical Pollyanna fashion. "Oh yes it could," I answer grimly. "It could too've been that bad."

When Clemmy and I broke up, Mrs. Goodbloode could barely restrain her glee, her relief that no little Clement Fours or Clementines would be springing from my polluted loins. Clemmy got the story from his father, who looks exactly like Clemmy, only old, and likes me as men tend to do. Mr. Goodbloode told Clemmy the family manse that day reminded him of the Yale Club during FDR's funeral.

"You've got that look in your eyes again," Clemmy says. "That fuck-me beat-me love-me look." He takes my face in one big hand and squeezes it till my mouth purses up like a grouper's, then shakes it back and forth in time to his chant: "No no no no no no no no!"

"Fuck off," I say, knocking the hand away.

"No, *you* fuck off."

Lacking a suitable retort, I flee to the john, where vast quantities of cocaine console me. Aren't you glad *you* use drugs? Don't you wish *everybody* did? Before exiting I check the mirror warily. That moonstruck look is gone, sandblasted, like the graffiti on General Grant's tomb. Fortified, I march down the Bar Car's center aisle, the only aisle I'll ever march down with Clement Goodbloode.

"Bad girl," Clemmy says, scanning my face. He grabs my bag and paws through it roughly, finds what he's after, stalks off. The waiter arrives with the check. I give it back to him and order more drinks, cognacs this time. No point in sticking to spritzers *now*. When Clemmy gets back, his eyes are burning, prompting me to break into a spirited rendition of "Ring of Fire." Clemmy hands me the cocaine to shut me up.

"You did it *all?*" I say, examining the bottle Clemmy's

forgotten about emptying. I'm not really surprised, though I try to sound that way. Always the good provider, Clemmy gets up to chat with one of our friendly hosts, the one who looks like Rasputin only more well-clipped, one of the guys who are always so glad to see us, and things degenerate predictably from there.

Two or six hours later, we are still at the Bar Car with some of the usual suspects when Clemmy gets up and walks away. I love Walter Light, but Walter is so different from me, a different species almost, and Clemmy is so much the same that when he gets up and turns his back it's like somebody ripping out both kidneys. Walter is who I want to be but Clemmy is who I *am,* so why is he walking away? Could it be the vile abuse I've been spewing forth? Perhaps that has something to do with it. I've never even *heard* words like that before. Dick brain! Ha! That's a good one. Dumb ball? Strictly third grade. Where are these words coming from? But Clemmy brought it on himself, *he started it, Mommy,* by reaching across the table to fondle my tits in this proprietary way that set me off.

"Don't you get it yet?" I shrieked. "You can't have me that way! You can't do me like you do those other girls."

"Yeah, I get it," he said, without too much visible anguish. Then, mocking my resurgent accent: "Ah cain't do yew lak Ah do those otha gulls."

My ears were still stinging when Clemmy locked his hands behind his head, revealing the tops of his pale blue Brooks Brothers shorts and a few inches of golden-blond belly over that. Clemmy's getting a paunch, I thought fondly, as he pivoted his chair toward this woman on his right, this nobody, this also-ran, this second assistant editor of third-rate documentaries, and turned his charm on her full force, the searchlight charm that blinds you if

you're not prepared for it and even if you *are*, looking
back at me with this monster grin every few seconds to
make sure I get the point.

"I'm just a dog with two legs," Clemmy said on one of
these occasions, right in the middle of their conversation—which was about whether *One from the Heart* con-
stitutes (A) empty formalism or (B) pure cinema—like
Richard the Third making an aside. The woman pre-
tended not to notice, par for the course for someone who's
passionately arguing position B, though she was visibly
distressed when Clemmy's hand descended from the top
of his head in classic seventh-grade fashion and inched
down toward her breast. She didn't remove the hand, just
wriggled under it a little to see if it would go away, which
it didn't, of course, and even as I prepared to launch into
my very best *Exorcist* routine and claim the life achieve-
ment award in projectile vomiting, I could hear her little
pea brain churning: put up with him now and change him
later. Which is what they all think. I didn't like her enough
to disabuse her of this disaster-making notion, and she
wouldn't have listened in any case. Not to *me*. She was
opening to Clemmy's charm like flowers to a honeybee,
thrilled. Like she'd been blessed. And that was what *really* set me off, off, off.

"I hope I didn't ruin your little game," I said.

Clemmy shook his head. "You ruined my *life*."

In any case Clemmy's left me now—and the disappointed floozy too—to pursue some sister of a former
classmate, some Muffy or Puffy or Buffy with a big trust
fund and small tits. He goes for those bosomless wonders
when he's trying to slaughter me. But the film editor
doesn't slink away like she's supposed to. Why is she still
*here?* Oh, no. I can't *believe* it. She's trying to make
*friends!* How drunk does she think I am? There are eight
million assholes in the naked city. I'm almost as powerful

as Clemmy, and I guess she thinks if she can't be
Clemmy's girlfriend she can get almost as far as my best
chum. The *nerve* of some people. I wasn't exaggerating
when I said she was a pea brain. She sits right there with
chinny chin quivering and this brave, noble smile full of
sisterly solidarity and tries to enroll me in the Rejected
Girl of the Month Club by taking potshots at Clemmy,
whose dick she didn't get the chance to suck, and inviting
*me* to join in. Some people never learn. She goes on and
on and on, big eyes brimming concern, completely oblivi-
ous to the effect she's having. Is she actually trying to *take
my hand?*

"Shut your fucking yap," I say finally as preface to a
whole lot more. Nobody talks about Clemmy like that but
*me*. She disappears, muttering dire threats. I'll never
work for PBS, I guess. Wasting herself here, though, that
one.

"You'll go far in Hollywood, dear," I call after her mag-
nanimously. Then I wallow in self-pity, not an unfamiliar
emotion. Three or thirty minutes of hysterical boohooing
later, there's no one left at my table but this off-duty cop,
who probably figures a drunk fuck is better than no fuck
at all.

"I can't live without Clem Kadiddlehopper," I say, as if
I knew what that silly name meant, what long-canceled
radio program it came from.

"A girl like you?" the cop says with a friendly laugh that
warms me slightly. "A sweet little thang like you?
Suuuure you can." Basking in this shameless goal-oriented
flattery, I peer at my worthy companion's name tag.

"Clyde," I say proudly, like a child who's just done poo-
poo.

"What, baby?"

"Clyde, are you from the south?"

But Clyde doesn't answer. His hands, under the table,

seem remarkably busy. Uh-huh. There's some important
investigating going on down there. I reach over and grab
something big and hard, which turns out to be his nightstick, *thank you Jesus,* finally locate one big paw, and
reposition it on the table. But that won't change anything,
only postpone the inevitable. If I don't let him fuck me,
he'll probably arrest me. Then someone else will fuck me
anyway, in jail. Someone uncute, unclean, and of the
wrong gender to boot.

When I leave the Bar Car with Officer Clyde, people
throw money, whether in tribute to my performance or
in delight at seeing my backside at last I couldn't begin to
say.

"Fuck you all very much," I say with a little bow, which
results in Officer Clyde having to scrape me off the floor,
where I pocket several quarters, and a few minutes later
it's daylight and I'm bent backward across the hood of an
old Lamborghini with a giant lamprey attached to my
neck.

"It took more than one man to change my name to
Shanghai Lily," I say enigmatically. Then I remember
Lily is the name of Walter's wife. A little tear wells up and
trickles down my cheek. I wish somebody *would* shanghai
Lily, I think, wiping the pitiful tear away. Then all my
problems would be solved.

Officer Clyde looks up in a sexed-out daze. He really is
handsome, even in the sunshine. Black men look so *good*
in uniforms, and those little gold tags they wear on their
chests help a lot when you forget their names. "I thought
your name was Porter," he says politely.

"Don't *ever* call me that!" I say, doing a pretty good
imitation of a paranoid schizophrenic, but a crazy fuck is
better than no fuck at all. Officer Clyde makes these
noises that are meant to be soothing, the kind you'd make
to a horse you intend to ride no matter what the horse has

to say about it, then goes back to the business at hand. But when I turn my neck toward his mouth obligingly, I see this Flopsy or Topsy or Mopsy splayed across a double-parked limo doing a pretty good imitation of *me.*

Sometimes I forget who I'm supposed to be in love with, Clement Goodbloode or Walter Light. This doesn't happen often, only every time I see Clemmy and make the mistake of having a drink, which activates all the out-of-control synapses in my brain. This morning it hurts so much to see him humping that uptown slut that I scream something obscene in an exceedingly loud voice, loud even for *me,* which causes him to look up from what he's doing like a buzzard in the middle of a roadside feed with this disappointed but absolutely unsurprised stare that breaks my heart yet again, and at that moment the windows of ten or twenty irate and much put-upon citizens fly up all over the block. But then to my delight Clemmy looks at his fellow scion with more or less naked distaste, like she was a little . . . *overripe.* How true, how true; good eye, Clemmy dear. Clemmy doesn't put up with a lot from women. Only from me, because he loved me so much. Oh yes he did. I know because of all the women he's had to fuck to forget me. You couldn't get them in the Bar Car standing up. They'd have to be stacked like cordwood.

Clemmy straightens his clothes and stalks off. I don't know whether or not he actually snaps his fingers, but a few seconds later his new acquisition trots after him like the well-bred little pooch she no doubt is.

For some reason I can't concentrate on this sex scene with Officer Krumpke, even after Clemmy is out of the frame. Maybe it's all the joggers jogging, the workaholics on their way to work, work, work, but that's never bothered me *before.* No, there's something else, this feeling of being underwater, and not very nice water at that.

"There's something rotten in Denmark," I say. "Whut? Huh?" Officer Clyde replies, doing a pretty good imitation of a stupid Negro. "A stink," I say. "A smell, a stench. Also my feet are wet."

We look down and see this trickle of steaming piss making its way from a rag pile against the wall to a puddle beneath our feet. Fresh piss is soaking my new suede pumps, eating the shine off Clyde's black shoes, menacing his blue serge pant cuffs. Enraged by repeated foreplay interruptus, Clyde makes for the pile and lays into it with his nightstick. The bum inside wakes up screaming, his screams rouse the barely sleeping loft dwellers yet again, and all of a sudden it's raining bottles. Big ones. I'm not sure who they're aimed at—Officer Clyde, the screaming bum, or me—but one seems to have smashed the Lamborghini's windshield, which provokes a bullish roar from Clyde. It's his car. Of *course.*

Then a familiar red, white, and green coffee can comes tumbling down, end over end, like a gift from Santa. When it hits the Lamborghini's steering wheel, the green plastic lid pops off and mud-colored turpentine, redolent of bad painting, splashes the immaculate white leather seats, and soon New York's finest is charging through a door unwisely left unlocked and arresting every board-certified artist in sight. During the ensuing commotion a Yellow Cab passes veeerrry slowly, slow enough even for me to flag it down. The obliging driver stops, happy for a chance to get close to the action, I get in like none of it concerns me, exactly the way a normal person would, and pretty soon we're off. Officer Clyde gives chase—he must have seen me from an upstairs window—and he's pretty fast, too, I think, watching his progress through the grimy rear glass. But he's no match for this African cab driver, a genu-wine African this time, with whom I have a perfectly normal conversation about his homeland, Nigeria, just as if I wasn't plowed to the gills and Officer Clyde wasn't sprinting after us lickety-split like a mutt trailing the family Winnebago. I watch him get farther and farther behind until finally he gives up and walks back the way he came. Poor Clyde. Maybe there's somebody in that loft he can fuck, if he has sense enough to arrest her first.

"Nigeria's a lot better," I say, turning my attention to the driver, "since you all got rid of Idi Amin."

I utter this sentence with infinite complacency, like the well-informed world citizen I am, the democrat who discusses current events with meek or mighty, black or white, it makes no difference to *me,* and also with a little touch of pride at having escaped Officer Clyde and pulled myself together so quickly, in more or less record time. But this unexpected hush falls over the cab.

"I hope I didn't offend you," I say. Maybe he's a relative. What are those raised white welts on the back of his neck, some kind of royal tattoos?

The driver fidgets uncomfortably before spitting it out: "Idi Amin was . . . *Uganda!*"

I won't pretend I'm not taken aback, even speechless for a second, but I rise to the occasion nicely.

"Uganda be kidding!" I say with a triumphant shriek. This is one of Clemmy's favorite bad jokes. I laugh at it like a maniac. The driver looks alarmed. I don't want him to throw me out—Officer Clyde might've commandeered a squad car by now or, worse, cleaned the gunk off his Lamborghini—so I try to apologize, something I don't do with too much grace.

"Please forgive me, I'm usually not so stupid," I say with my best Miss America smile, refined through long hours of practice in front of the bathroom mirror. But I can see nobody's buying. The driver's elegant nostrils quiver,

maybe getting a whiff of the piss on my shoes. He looks
at me skeptically in the rearview, and I smile back all
ingratiatinglike, but what I said is true. You don't believe
me *either?* Did I tell you that Clemmy and I made our
reputations writing socially conscious films? No? Hey,
name an issue, we've exploited it! Seriously, a writer in a
national magazine once called us "the conscience of the
New Hollywood." It's amazing what gets into print these
days. That's one reason why we get away with so much.
Money, lots of money, is the other.

After Clemmy rescued me from the doctoral program
in Film Theory at UCLA, moved me into his house in
Franklin Canyon, and taught me how to write, and after
one of our scripts was made into this very successful,
somewhat controversial outer-space flick, things started
to move fast for us all of a sudden. Our spaceman sold a
lot of video games and lunch boxes, and every time your
kid cons you into buying one, Clemmy and I get a piece,
not the biggest piece, of course, but because of this, another script we wrote, *Oil and Water,* got made too. And
surprise, the day the picture opened there was a major oil
spill off the California coast. Millions of fish went belly up,
acres of expensive real estate were transformed into hos-
pices for oil-soaked gulls. Then an oil company whistle-
blower washed up too. That this is a close approximation
of the plot of our movie didn't hurt ticket sales in the least,
and afterward Clemmy and I were in fat city. "Goodbloode and O'Shea: Out of the blue and into the black,"
is how some clever captioneer once put it under an appropriately cheery picture. We went from Z list to B list with
head-spinning speed, took our old scripts out of the file
cabinet, dusted them off, went to Cannes, and sold them
on the beach like hot dogs. Then the money *really* started
rolling in, job offers too, though mostly we ignore these.

It's sort of like *Bells Are Ringing,* remember? Dean

Martin is this playwright who's split with his partner and
can't write anymore, he's afraid to. He doesn't know if he
can make it alone, so he spends an entire year expanding
his floozy collection. That's sort of the way it's been for me
and Clemmy. Both of us still write, we just don't write
anything *good*. We don't even try. We're *scared shitless.*
The casting in that movie is very astute, too, almost kinky,
since Dean Martin had just split with Jerry Lewis and
evidently they went through a lot of well-publicized
heartbreak and everything. But in real life, Jerry traded
Dean for a couple dozen truckloads of Marlboros and a
French visa, Dino traded Jerry for a never-ending glass of
Scotch, and everything was hunky-dory. See how easy it
is? In the movie, Dean found Judy Holliday, who loved
him, *believed* in him. Judy Holliday saved him, like Walter's saving me. So who says life doesn't imitate art?

We finally get to Gansevoort, where I live, without any
more geopolitical mishaps, and after winding our way
through the meat trucks and the white-coated men shoul-
dering bloody carcasses hither and yon, the cab stops in
front of my building, I pay my rescuer lavishly, which
elicits a sunny smile—like the song says, money changes
everything—and in the lobby I find that Fred Pitluck, the
insane dwarf novelist, has left a freshly mimeographed
turd, about ten pages long, in my mailbox.

"Not this morning, Freddy, I'm just too tired," I say
aloud in case my admirer is skulking nearby, but I don't
hear any demented snarls or cackles of crazed laughter
and conclude that Freddo's gone home to bed like a good
little psychopath. "I'll read it later, I promise," I lie, then
look both ways, unlock the inner door, and jump inside.

The elevator is off as usual. Since this building is mostly
offices, it only runs from eight to midnight and not at all
on weekends. I keep trying to get my own key but the
landlord's holding firm, figuring rightly that someone stu-

pid enough to sign a lease without asking about the elevator schedule is not a power to be reckoned with. So I take
off my piss-soaked fuck-me pumps, which almost but not
quite got me fucked, wrap them in Freddy's magnum
opus, toss the whole mess in the downstairs trash, and trip
lightly up nine flights to my New York penthouse apartment, pleased with myself for being more or less faithful
to Walter for yet another night.

When I get upstairs, wheezing and gasping, there's
even a telephone message from Walter by way of reward.
He says my name clearly twice, then the message segues
into heartrending sobs and abruptly cuts to silence. I listen to the tape all the way through but there isn't anything else to hear. I call Walter's office, though it's far too
early for him to be there, and listen to the phone ring,
ring, ring, while all the time these warning bells are going
off in my head in one-two syncopation.

"Whatever it is, Walter can tell me about it tomorrow,"
I say aloud, as if saying it will make it true, then head for
the john to do some business. Ummmm, that's better.
*Forget* Walter. I'm wide awake! I might as well do some
work. I get up to turn on the computer and find myself
on the bathroom floor, treacherous panties coiled round
my ankles. Maybe better *not* do work. Might forget how
to run my shiny new computer and erase my so-called
novel. Might be blessing in disguise, I think, as I pull
myself up with difficulty, then flush the toilet without
looking at what's in it (I don't want to know and you
shouldn't either, given that what goes in must come out).
Take off clothes, throw on floor as usual, and reach for
favorite natural sleep aid, an amino acid cocktail called,
appropriately, Lights Out!!! Ick, a roach is break-dancing
on the bottle! Lights-out time for you too, buddy. I squash
the roach with a checkbook, wipe off the gore with a pair
of dirty panties, throw panties on floor, toss a heaping

tablespoonful of Lights Out!!! into an iced-tea glass, fill with Martell since there isn't any juice on hand, stir into gluey mess, hold my nose, and chug. It tastes like hell but soon L-tryptophan is coursing through my bloodstream, my so-called brain is churning out gobs of serotonin to combat the coke that's already in residence, and in a few short minutes the coke says uncle and packs its bags and I'm doing a pretty good imitation of someone who's not worried at all about Walter fucking Light.

THERE is this phony back-lot moonlight in the Museum of Natural History, where I happened to be loitering five months ago. It spills out of the dioramas, scenes of nature in the so-called raw, the finest creations of long-dead taxidermists, artists, and lighting designers, not to mention the great white hunters who killed the pesky critters in the first place. Each has its own special unreality, capturing these lost symbolic moments, these encounters between species in the wild, which is shrinking even as we speak like an ice cube in a dry martini. When the animals are gone the dioramas will have some function, I guess.

The guys who did these could have made a mint in Hollywood, I thought, as Walter Light stalked me silently, skillfully, like Teddy Roosevelt himself. I noticed his reflection sneaking up, expanding in the curved glass.

It was Saturday and the place was crawling with women, with desperate career girls and graduate students and fine-boned librarians, dying to bloom. Walter could have had any of them, but he picked me. I guess I didn't have that fear scent on me. I was just killing time, after all, between lunch and dinner dates in the same neighborhood: hobbling around, dressed to the nines,

high-heeled and sexy and wrong for him, all wrong. I
didn't *look* needy. What a fucking joke. I was communing
with a few endangered species when Walter Light
popped the question.

"Which one do you identify with?" Walter asked, his
voice breaking a little at the end. This is not a bad line for
an amateur in Permaprest. I watched his image shimmer
between me and a snowy meadow, where a lynx was
eyeing a snowshoe hare shivering under a bush. White on
white and camouflaged, or so he thought, but just not well
enough. The hare was visible in the moonlight to the lynx,
to Walter, and to me. But the lynx will never eat, the hare
will never get eaten, and either answer to Walter's question would be too revealing, so of course I said, "The
lynx," and laughed at my bravado, which clung to me that
day like a staticky nylon slip.

Walter laughed too, and I turned and looked at him
head on: cute and square and tweedy, but with great blue
eyes, twinkling at me. He reminded me of Pat Sajak on
*Wheel of Fortune.* Pat's always so kind, so *decent* to the
contestants, even when they can't solve the puzzle. "Dog-
gone it!" he says when some poor fool hits a BANKRUPT,
and *means* it, or *seems* to. He never makes fun of the
stupid ones, like the guy on *Press Your Luck.* What I mean
is I trusted Walter. He had that kind of face. So I took his
arm and took him home and let him fall in love. Who
could fall in love with a bunny, cowering under a bush?
Walter's marriage wasn't much of an issue then, for either
of us. The surprise was that I started to love him too. And
became the bunny: afraid to be eaten, but more afraid I
wouldn't be. It's cold, out in the snow. Life is *hard.* This
is not a role I wear with grace or resignation.

When Walter is away from me, which is most of the
time, I think a lot about his wife. Lily of the sensible shoes.
Lily of the pinched face, crepy already around the eyes.

This is not just being catty. I've seen her pictures. You say maybe she doesn't photograph well? I'll think about that *tomorrow.*

Lily calls my lover Wally. Good ol' Wally. How's the Beave? Bow ties and Dagwoods and *I'm home d-d-dear, what's for d-d-d-d-dinner!* Wally. Jesus! Like a castrated sit-com Pop. My insistence on calling Walter by his given name endeared me to him immediately. Walter loves having two names, one for each of his women. It feels wicked, like bigamy. He takes Wally off with his wedding ring and puts him in his briefcase. When he gets off the plane, he's Walter. But sometimes, meeting new people, Walter forgets who he is. "Wally Light," he says, extending his hand like a friendly puppy wriggling on his back extends his pink-tipped sex.

At eighteen, when Lily married Wally, she was a smart girl and pretty, probably. Maybe even fun to be with. But now, Walter says, she has no sense of humor. She doesn't get his jokes. She undresses in the bathroom. Always has. Walter doesn't like to talk about it. Lily is no older than I am, but Lily is already old, old, old. The clichéd nature of this whole mess sorely tries my feminism. I know how Lily *got* old, of course. Typing Wally's papers and mending Wally's clothes, having Wally's children and wiping their collective nose. Creating this secure little nest for Wally to come flying home to. Leaving him free to do his work, his wonderful, important work. Walter is a scientist and Lily is dedicated to him. He is her whole life. Her Whole Life. I know this and Walter knows it even better, but it hasn't slowed us down *yet.* It hasn't slowed us down at all.

I see us driving down the highway on a clear, starry night. The top is down, it's spring, the snow is melting. I'm doing ninety, heading for California. There's this little vine-covered cottage, see, somewhere between Hollywood

and Cal Tech, where we're going to live. Mr. and Mrs.
Light *the second.* Happily ever after. Walter's dozing, his
head is in my lap. The radio's playing something by the
Righteous Brothers. And then there's this thing in the
road. I have to hit it; I have no choice. If I stepped on the
brakes we might skid and crash. There's a noise, a bump,
then an object in the rearview disappearing fast. Maybe
it's a piece of muffler or somebody's lost dog, heading for
Indiana. Whatever it was is no concern of *mine.*
    "Anna Kate?" Walter murmurs.
    "Go back to sleep," I say, and Walter does. And that
bump is Lily.
    Walter never talks about Lily as a person, as someone
with thoughts and dreams and feelings, so I don't think of
her that way either. I think of her as expendable. I never
think about Walter's children at all, except to be jealous
of them, jealous of Walter's time. I tell myself they're
smart and strong and have had more stability, already,
than most people get, far more than I had. They'll survive,
one way or the other. Lily will get custody, of course.
There will be some pain, but one day they'll accept me,
maybe even like me! I'll be their glamorous stepmom, a
punk Auntie Mame.
    Of *course* Walter prefers me. I'm smart and pretty and
independent. I have money and talent. I laugh a lot. Wait-
ers, cabdrivers, meter readers, and telephone repairmen
adore me. Why shouldn't Walter Light? I'm a little bit
famous, but less so than Walter, and this is good, sort of
reassuringly traditional. It makes us both feel more secure, since everything else we're doing is so wildly out of
kilter: me with a straight guy, a virgin almost; Walter in
hotel rooms with a woman not his wife. "This just isn't
me," Walter says, and I believe him. "I just don't do things
like this, Anna Kate," he agonizes for about five seconds,

then gets out his calendar to figure out how to do them as often as possible.

I go wherever he can meet me, given three minutes' notice. My own work is in a rut. I don't even pretend to do it. I travel light and carry cash. Walter always peels off my jeans too fast. After we make love, there's money all over the hotel room, crumpled hundreds sticking to my sweaty ass. It'll never be *me* in those American Express ads, asking Karl Malden to save me. No budgets, no plastic, no checkbooks to balance. Walter's never met anyone like me before, he says.

"No old girlfriends, Anna Kate," Walter told me in bed one night after a brief encounter with my most famous old boyfriend, Billyjim "The Twister" Thibideaux, on *Monday Night Football.* When I revealed our connection in typical playgirl fashion, Walter's face fell a thousand miles. He got out of bed and turned off the television. Walter wasn't titillated, said he didn't want to hear about it, *not another word,* then turned off the lights, got under the covers, took me in his arms, and cried.

"No old girlfriends," Walter said. "Not ever."

"Honey, if I believed in reincarnation, I'd say this was your first time around," I joked. I thought it was a *miracle.* Once I win him, Walter Light will love me forever. I'm the first thing in his life worth struggling for, or so he thinks. The first lie he's ever told. The first surprise. This makes me precious and worthless at the same time. Walter's had to work, all right, but he's never had to struggle. All he had to do really was pick everything up. He's never done business, never been corrupted by the marketplace. He's never had to lie or cheat or steal. My Hollywood stories horrify him.

"Why must you associate with people like that?" he asks.

"Walter, I *am* people like that."

"You're not, you're not," he murmurs, blind as a bat. *You* figure it out. My life is a movie Walter doesn't want to see, one he would turn off immediately if his kids were in the room. X-rated. No plot. So messy, so *unresolved.* All the boyfriends, all the traveling. He thinks I'm on sabbatical, expects the new term to start any day. Poor Walter. "This is no vacation, honey, this is my *life,*" I say. Which isn't strictly true. I'm fucking off extra these days. But for Walter it's far beyond belief, and lately it's started to seem that way to me too. This subtle change has occurred: I don't just want boring Lily's husband, I want boring Lily's boring *life.* Only Walter Light can give me normalcy. I believe this like a snake handler believes in God. You have to believe in something, with those fangs so close, right? There's no point in *not* believing. And though a part of me keeps saying, Forget it, you're too far gone for that, years too far, there's another part saying, Go for it, like the little engine that could. You haven't broken any important laws or killed anyone. Your sins are little ones so far. You're a bit greedy, true, but not *totally* rotten. This tough-bitch business is just a pose. Put yourself in perspective, kiddo, my good angel says. And I *want* to believe. Do I ever. There are times, though, when my conscience gets the best of me, when I surround myself with these DANGER, FALLEN WOMAN signs and try to give Walter Light up.

"I'll hurt you," I warned him one night, in a fit of decency that mercifully passed. "I'll hurt you and you'll hate me for the rest of your life." Walter was so tender and funny as he talked me out of it.

"I'm not a fool, or a child, or a ... a ... a ... *mathematician!*" he said. So I go to these academic conferences with him and see, between bouts of maniacal fucking, how the

old men anoint him with their eyes, with sweet dusty
smiles and feathery pats on the back. I go to his speeches
and sit in the back row and listen to the words I only
understand a third of—supermagnets . . . plasma . . . con-
tainment vessel—and watch the other physicists watch
Walter. That's what Walter is, a physicist. Don't ask me
any more because I don't understand it, but then again I
don't have to. That's *Walter*'s job. Everything I know
about science comes from *Rebel Without a Cause*. "Do
you think the end of the world will come at night?" Plato
asks Jim in front of the phony spinning stars. And Jim says,
"No. At dawn." Then all hell breaks loose and the sun
comes up and Nick Ray, the director, the *scientist*, walks
into the planetarium with his briefcase. To go to *work*.
That just about sums it up all right.

Walter spends a lot of time visiting these fusion reac-
tors called Tokamaks scattered conveniently around the
globe—conveniently for *me*. "What a great name! Who
thought of it?" I said when Walter tried to tell me about
Tokamaks in far too much detail. He also has a thing for
this multipath laser in Princeton named . . . *Shiva*.
When he's at conferences, giving speeches, his *mind*
jumps everywhere, too. He makes them laugh and think
at the same time, my genius, my Renaissance man. Like
me, he's a performer. I'm so proud of him I could bust.
If I imagine eyes on me, I get up and leave, afraid my
rapt gaze, my guilty hands, my smell, which is Walter's,
will give me away; that in each auditorium there's a
laser connecting our eyes, a hot white beam that everyone can see. But only we see it. Walter finds me wherever I sit.

One morning in a hotel room in Houston, Lily called.
I woke up when the phone rang and heard Walter in

the bathroom, talking to her, explaining why he wasn't coming home, as scheduled. What a nice surprise. For *me.*

"Hi there," I murmured as Walter came into the bedroom.

"Go back to sleep," he said softly, rustling through some papers in his briefcase. "Go back to sleep, angel. It's early." Walter sat at the little desk in his Jockey shorts with the sprung elastic, bony back exposed and vulnerable, staring off into space. I got out of bed, stood behind his chair, and put my arms around him.

"Was that your wife?" I asked. Walter nodded.

"I told her I had an important seminar today. I was very creative. I couldn't bear to leave you." Walter started to cry. Then: "I've never lied to her before. She didn't suspect a thing. She trusts me completely, and I took that trust and turned it against her and used it for us, and that was wrong. It was evil.

"Oh, maybe not *evil,*" he corrected, feeling me stiffen and pull away. "The funny thing is, it was so easy, the lying. I still can't believe how easy it was. It sounded true, even to the liar. Come here, Anna Kate, so I can look at you." Walter pulled me around and onto his lap.

"Listen to me. I met my wife when I was fifteen. She was the skinny girl with the flute. I was the skinny boy with the slide rule. No one wanted to talk to us, so we talked to each other. When we were old enough, we got married. We had children." This was where Walter's voice broke. "Lily's a wonderful mother. I've known her my whole life. My life was whole, before I met you, and now it's in a million pieces and you have the biggest piece. I'm afraid of what you'll do with it, Anna Kate. What will you *do* with it?"

"I'll cherish it," I whispered. *For a while,* I heard somebody say.

Walter said, "I've changed a lot in fifteen years." This is how long he and Lily have been married.

"Of course you have," I said soothingly. "You shouldn't feel guilty about it either, honey. Lots of people get divorced."

"Not in our family," Walter said sadly, before he took me back to bed. Less than a month after we'd met, imagine that, and already I felt him giving up. So I walked faster in my four-inch heels. I never trip. I never wobble. I'm walking the plank with both eyes open. I know where I'm going, or pretend to. Walter follows me at first. Then he starts to lead. He plans and schemes for more time. He tells more and more lies, the kind that are easily exposed, and I start to think I'm actually going to win him. I'll be Kitty to his Robert Oppenheimer, but a stable, sober Kitty. Not nude on the couch drinking cocktails at midday for Mrs. Fermi to find and write about, oh, no. Sane and creative and productive. We'll bring out the best in each other, exorcise the bad, grow old together, be happy. A real *House Beautiful* couple, one of *People* magazine's Fifty Best. Just as soon as we've dealt with the Wife.

Four months after we met, things were going so well that Walter came home with me to Fort Worth. To meet my family. A bit of a risk on *my* part. I still don't know why I took it. I told you this wasn't your run-of-the-mill roll in the hay. We flew to Texas from the Havana Film Festival, where *Oil and Water* was showing. Part of me was still there, relaxing on the perfect beaches, driving in the 1950s cars, having a *mojito* at the Havana Libre, listening to stories about how this or that American comrade got arrested, trying to spend black market pesos with Batista's picture on them at the Communist Party bookstore. Fidel himself had kissed my cheek, seeing as how I'm such a cute little *compañera,* and gossiped with Walter about

baseball. Fidel *prefers* the designated hitter. Even Walter
was impressed with Fidel, though he worried about what
the trip might do to his security clearance.

"What do you need a security clearance for, honey, to
be a scientist?" I remember saying, eyes far too wide, a
trick I learned at the Lucy Ricardo School of Logic. Walter looked troubled for a second or two, then melted and
came along.

My mother had this man living with her named Jesse
Turner. Livia isn't a great beauty. I have her features, but
smoothed out, prettied up, glossed over, like someone
made a Barbie doll out of her. I'm a white-bread version
of Livia, who is also not particularly fashionable. She's
poor, fiftyish, and overweight but has the meanest, shar-
pest wit of anybody I know. She's good and kind and
selfless, too. *How did I get* this *way?* That's a very good
question, doctor. I have room for it on my calendar in
1999.

I know it's not all that easy for ladies of fifty—even
terrific, funny ones—to find boyfriends, ladies who are not
Jackie O. My mother has an extra problem, too: her *job*.
Head bookkeeper at the Woodbury Funeral Chapel. The
only men she meets are *morticians*. I can understand her
*compromising*. But standing next to my mother, waiting
to greet us, Jesse Turner looked like something out of
*Tobacco Road*. Small and dirty and bandy-legged. Drunk.
But mostly dirty, clear through to his skin. The working
men I grew up with were never dirty unless actually working. They wore the whitest shirts you ever saw. Their pants
were creased like razorbacks. They smelled like Aqua-
velva and Old Spice. I loved to nuzzle up against them and
inhale. But when I met Jesse Turner, I backed away immediately. He smelled like a refugee from the Lone Star
brewery. He smelled like he fell head first into the vat.

"Y'know my mama's car?" Jesse said as we waited at the

baggage carousel. "Lost the hubcaps on it. Y'know how much them hubcaps cost? Huh? Forty-five dollars! That was two years ago. Must be worth fifty, sixty dollars now. Insurance'll cover it, she don't find 'em. Lost 'em two days ago. Don't know where she lost 'em!"

"If she knew where she lost 'em, honey, they wouldn't be lost," said my mother sensibly.

"Know how much them hubcaps cost?" Jesse continued as he drove my mother's old Plymouth down the turnpike. "Fifty dollars! Ha! I wouldn't give two cents for them ol' hubcaps on your car, baby. Ha! Women don't know how to take care of nothing, y'know what I mean, Walter?" Jesse turned to the back seat. "Know what I mean? Know what I mean?"

"I know what you mean," Walter said in his normal tone of voice.

"Y'know what I mean, bubba?" Jesse bellowed, fishing for a response he could relate to, a tone that was just like his. "*Y'know what I mean?* Y'KNOW WHAT I MEAN?"

"Will you calm down, honey?" my mother said.

"Yeah!" screamed Walter, getting the idea finally: This is just like the Harvard-Yale game. "*Yeah! Yeah! Yeah! I hear ya, bro!*"

I was figuring the odds on dying if I jumped from the car, which was doing eighty, when Walter calmed down. For a minute there, he was almost in the front seat with Jesse. He leaned back, relaxed, and took my hand. He smiled at me reassuringly.

"I know what you mean, pal," Walter said to Jesse, who was mollified at last, and quiet. "It's all right," Walter said. But it wasn't. "Don't worry," he whispered, kissing me on the cheek, but I did.

"You ever heard o' Watergate?"

"Of course he's heard of Watergate, honey," my mother said.

"You heard o' Watergate, Walter?"

"I've heard of Watergate, Jesse," Walter said.

"Ha! If I was a Republican, I'd be a rich man today. We's all Democrats. You ever heard o' Richard Nixon? Why you punchin' me, honey?"

"Stifle! Stifle!" my mother commanded, as if to a Kaypro on the fritz.

"If I had me a tuxedo, I could be president right now! Yeah. I tell it like it is, bubba!"

This monologue continued for thirty-five minutes, during which Jesse put away a six-pack of Coors, I fidgeted in misery, and Walter pat-patted my hand. Texas never looked so grim until the day I saw it through Walter's eyes. The low, sprawling prefab houses and factories, the chain stores and shopping malls all stood out starkly. No snow hid the spindly naked trees, the pervasive brown grass, the highways littered with carcasses of armadillos, indistinguishable from blown-out tires.

When we arrived at my mother's house, I saw that six months of Jesse Turner had almost destroyed it. Our house was once the finest on this decaying block, on the edge of the neighborhood that's still called Niggertown. Only powerless people live here, black and brown and poor white. But my stepfather, Jack Hill, was house-proud. While he lived, everything was cleaned, painted, and put away. The lawn was always mowed. Repairs were promptly and correctly done by trained workers whose wages were haggled over, then paid.

Now when something goes wrong with the house, Jesse gets one of his buddies to fix it cheap. If that doesn't work, he fixes it himself. Jesse never completes any of the improvements he starts, while the house falls down around my mother's ears. The remains of his do-it-yourself projects litter the porch, the back and front yards. Several windows are boarded over. It's as dilapidated now as the group home for the mentally retarded on the corner, or the way station for illegal immigrants on the left. Sometimes there are as many as twenty men in that two-bedroom house, eating tortillas and beans around campfires in the back yard, waiting for a truck to take them north to pick fruit.

When we drove into our driveway, ten or twelve brown men stared at us suspiciously from the neighboring porch.

"Mr. Rodriguez, have you met my daughter?" my mother said breezily, getting out of the car.

Mr. Rodriguez, who owns the joint, smiled at me with tobacco-colored teeth and tipped his straw hat politely. A pack of naked children swarmed around his feet. A tired-looking woman in a dirty apron peeked out the door worriedly. Mr. Rodriguez spoke curtly to her in Spanish. The woman went back inside.

"Mes'cuns," said Jesse loudly, pointing to the porch three feet away as if to a smelly cage in the zoo. "You know why God give Mes'cuns noses, Walter? So they'd have 'um somethin' to pick during the off season!" Nobody laughed. My mother gave Jesse a fond but threatening look. Mr. Rodriguez fingered a bulge in his pants pocket that might've been his cock or a flick knife from Laredo. Walter got our bags out of the trunk.

"Let me get those for you, Walter. You look to be a slight sort of feller," Jesse said, though he is half Walter's size. He ripped the bags out of Walter's hands and carried them up the steps like an overloaded pack mule.

The neighbors on the other side came out to look too: Mr. and Mrs. Tucker. Both of them are from the country, kind and good. Mr. Tucker drinks every waking moment, and Mrs. Tucker is what we call "simple": not quite ready for the group house on the corner, but almost. The Tuckers run an illegal business in their home, repairing small appliances. Derelict washing machines, vacuum cleaners, and the hulls of generic machines, cannibalized for parts, cover their front porch and spill down into the front yard and, when that's full, onto the sidewalk and street. These obsolete relics never quite get hauled away, though Mr. Tucker promises that a man is coming to lend him a truck "any day now" so he can take the junk to the dump. Mrs. Tucker often makes my mother a pie or does some sewing to compensate for the eyesore, but looking at the two houses, I couldn't see why she bothered. I couldn't see that much difference between them.

Mrs. Tucker waved, went back inside, and came out with a pie to welcome me home. She handed it to me with an inappropriate, nervous giggle. It was my favorite, lemon meringue. I thanked Mrs. Tucker for the pie, and all of us went inside.

I peeked into the refrigerator automatically. My mother had made a special trip to the grocery store. Bright fresh vegetables gleamed in their packages: broccoli, spinach, scallions, green beans. I closed the door softly, as if a child were sleeping inside. My mother cut the pie. Mrs. Tucker giggled.

"I fixed it just the way you like it, Katie," she said. "Real whip cream! None of that Cool Whip!" Then, proudly, to Walter: "Katie don't like nothin' artificial."

Just as Walter was about to sit down, Jesse grabbed his chair out from under him.

"You're sittin' on that ol' broke chair, Walter. Git up and let me fix it!" Jesse said. He picked up the chair and started squeezing the legs together with his hands. Jesse's face bulged tomato-red as he strained to bend the metal. "I can fix it! I can fix it! See? See?"

Jesse smacked the chair back down on the linoleum with a bang. Walter sat down in it gingerly, settled himself in, and praised Jesse extravagantly. They beamed at each other across green Formica. My mother served the pie.

We ate. It was delicious. My mother looked at Walter with bassinets in her eyes. I could almost hear them squeaking cozily. Jesse chugged his hot coffee, then fanned his mouth and grinned. His fingers left black smudges on the cup. There was so much dirt embedded in the whorls of his fingers, it would take a tiny trowel to get it all out.

"I ever tell you 'bout my mama's hubcaps?" Jesse yelled, his mouth full of pie. "Just as soon as I find the keys to my truck, I'm gonna go out and look for 'em. Where's my keys, baby?" he asked my mother. "She was drivin' somewheres—" *Ding-dong!* The doorbell! I jumped up and fled the kitchen.

"Saved by the bell," my mother said with a carefree laugh.

"She must really be in love," I muttered as I headed for our new front door, a wire and glass and aluminum horror. When it wouldn't open, because Jesse had been tinkering with the latch, he explained later, to make it harder for burglars to get in, I bumped it with my hip. The glass cracked immediately. First one tiny hairline crack, then the whole thing shattered all over me. There was glass on the carpet, and me on my knees trying to pick up the shards, as everyone from the kitchen rushed in hollering. Scooby-Doo, a giant schizophrenic bloodhound, leaped through the door frame and landed on top of me. He pinned me to the floor, licked my face, and howled. My stepsister reached through the door and opened it easily.

"What have you done to your haaa-yer?" Brandy shrieked as she pranced in, ignoring the jagged hunks of glass. "What have you done to your hair, Sissy? It looks like a goldurned bird slept in it!" Brandy's deranged familiar made a truly horrible sound, a whine of doggy devotion, dug his claws into my shoulders, and humped my knee affectionately. Everybody laughed, even Walter! Jesse pulled Scooby off me with difficulty.

From the floor, I tried to introduce Walter to Brandy but couldn't remember her new last name. What was it now? Something low-class and ugly, not Snopes or Jeeter but it might as well've been. Scooby saved the day by cutting his paw, as he was bound to. I remembered Brandy's name eventually: Skinner. Brandywine Skinner, wife of Rusty Skinner. Jesus. Sounds like a knife to gut fish with. "What kind of a guy is he?" I asked my mother after the wedding. "Oh, a bum," she said. "Same kind I got."

Later I cried in Walter's arms while he kissed the cuts on my hands, the scratches on my shoulders. Walter thought the day was great fun. Like going to Coney Island, I thought bitterly. He couldn't understand; my mother and sister were *charming*. Why was I so upset?

Because I wanted to be more normal, I guess. Before Jesse arrived, we were poor but within the bounds of decent society. With Jesse on board, we've slipped a notch or three hundred. We're lumpenproles now. Poor white trash. I wanted a normal family to give to Walter, to replace the one he'll be giving up.

"No divorce in our family. Not ever," Walter's father says every Christmas while he carves the turkey. Knife and fork in hand, he stares at his wife meaningfully. This is their family joke, but it's true, as jokes tend to be. Walter told me if he divorced Lily he'd lose the rest of his family too, parents as well as children. No divorce in Walter's family. Not ever. No need to say that none of them would ever accept *me*. It's one thing to visit with a family like mine, another thing to marry into them. In Amherst, Walter's mother does charity work on people like us. She'd take one good look and send a bundle of old clothes, maybe some canned goods too. I had nothing to give Walter but myself, I realized. And that might not be enough.

Walter got up to brush his teeth the next morning and came back laughing. Jesse had a toothbrush and razor set hanging in the bathroom, red, shaped like naked women.

"She loves him," Brandywine told me privately, succinctly. "She's happy as a clam, when *you're* not around."

Later, the planes stopped flying, which necessitated yet another big lie to Lily. We were iced in with my family for three days. The pipes froze. Two big buckets under the kitchen sink caught the runoff. Jesse insisted on fixing it himself, instead of calling a plumber. It never was fixed, not the whole time I was there. We played Scrabble with my mother and half-brother, Tommy, and the ominously titled Trivial Pursuit, which just about summed up my situation, I thought, though I never said this to Walter. We took a drive. The crumbling South Side streets were fraught with hazards, wrecked cars and frozen water mains. There was no place to go anyway. At every intersection, water gushed from broken pipes. Inside, the gas heat sucked moisture from the air. The oxygen too, Walter said nervously, afraid to sleep with the heater on, too frozen to sleep with it off. We kept glasses of water by the side of the bed, woke up and gulped them thirstily, every membrane parched as if from cheap cocaine.

One morning before dawn, while Walter was tossing and turning, too hot or too cold, I got up and went into the kitchen where my mother was writing. Recently, my mother became the oldest living person to win the American Legion's annual essay contest, writing on "What Democracy Means to Me." This encouraged her enormously. Now, every morning, she gets up at five, puts on a cassette of *Jonathan Livingston Seagull* for inspiration, and works on her novel until it's time to go to work.

"What's it about?" I keep asking.

"Oh, us," my mother always replies before clamming up. Hmmm. That's what *my* novel's about. Have I told you about the novel I'm writing? No? Maybe that's because not much of it's *written,* which is sort of a problem, but it's set right here. It's about my mom and dad, kind of a roman à clef. The first line goes like this: "My mother's house is in a valley between two freeways, and in this valley there is no true night." Pretty good, huh? Pretty good first line, for a first novel. They don't let you write like that in California. It's against the law. Only in New York. That's why I moved there. If I could only get past that first perfect sentence. If I could only think of what comes *next.*

In the kitchen, my mother was typing away happily. Not having any trouble with *her* novel. I tapped her shoulder. She patted my hand and took off her headset. I wanted to talk about Walter. I hadn't talked to her about my boyfriends in a long time, too embarrassed at how many there'd been since Clemmy, how none of them seemed to work out. But we didn't talk about Walter, or Jesse either. We talked about my father, though we didn't set out to. The subject came up because of something I said. Five stupid words, count 'em: "I make my own luck." Glenn Ford said something like that while he was shooting craps at the beginning of *Gilda,* and evidently my father used to say it too. He probably stole it from Glenn Ford, just like I did. I never heard him say the line myself. I've seen my father perhaps ten times in my life, not often enough to absorb his philosophy of life or to pick up any pet homilies or endearing paternal clichés. He left my mother long ago, stunned and squeezed dry, with his other discarded women. He left me squawling with his other needy brats. My father traveled light, onward and upward with dazzling speed, changing families as easily as he changed jobs. Those left behind were not quite right, not flexible enough to make the journey with him. I saw his picture once in *Fortune* while I was sitting in some doctor's waiting room. If not for his name, which is also mine, and his mouth—mine too, greedy and rapacious like a Hoover run amok, crowned with these gleaming choppers, these trust-me teeth—I wouldn't have recognized my father at all, so closely did he approximate the norms of his chosen class. The photograph was the size of my thumbnail, and toward the end of the magazine, not the front. The achievements noted underneath it were scant, the man depicted no longer young. I was pleased to see that my father's ruthlessness, which cost others so dearly, didn't do him that much good in the long run.

But that morning I said, "I make my own luck." Sitting across the green Formica table from my mother, drinking cup after cup of strong black coffee, I just tossed it off without thinking about what it meant. All future, no past: this was the impression I tried to convey, although I don't particularly believe the words, or see myself so harshly, as an opportunist. I've always thought my good luck was thrust upon me arbitrarily, that I was the bemused beneficiary of luck. I don't know why this phrase stuck in my mind, or why it happened to come out just then. But when I said it, my mother sat up reed straight and looked at me hard. Her whole face changed. The warmth drained out of it and out of the little kitchen. My mother looked at me as if I were a stranger, or worse: someone she had known in another life and recognized all of a sudden, some long-forgotten ghost come back to haunt her, some killer sent to finish the job. When I said those words, with my father's tones that say you can manipulate the world but never change it, with the regionless accent I affect that's also my father's, with a bitter little laugh tacked on at the end, ironic and confusing, obfuscating everything, it made her blood run cold, my mother said later. She said it felt like something walking on her grave.

I didn't know what to say to my mother after that, so I went back to the bedroom. Walter woke up and kissed me. We made love. I cried.

"It was a mistake, bringing you here," I told Walter between sobs. He didn't ask me to explain. He knew what I meant exactly.

"I'm not marrying your family," Walter said stiffly. "I'm marrying *you.*"

I couldn't believe it. "You are?" I whimpered. "Are you *really?*"

"You underestimate me so much," Walter said, a little angry. "It hurts, that you don't trust me. Somebody left you once, and now you think everybody's going to. You think all men are alike. I'm not *like* other men, Anna Kate. I'm not Clemmy. I'm not your father. When I say I love you, that *means* something. It's not just words."

I stopped crying and wiped my eyes. Walter took me in his arms. A few minutes later we went to sleep.

The next day, all of us had plenty of time to study the interior of the house. I noticed the changes in furnishings: the shelves overflowing with knickknacks; the old sturdy pieces that were broken or gone, replaced by things shoddy or useless.

"This is nice," Walter said, fingering a delicate piece of painted china my stepfather brought back from Germany after the war. "Kind of baroque."

"Huh? Lemme see!" said Jesse, snatching it away. He examined the cup carefully, then waved it in our faces. "Don't look broke to *me.*"

I went outside, a quilt over my coat, and sat on the warped porch in a rusty metal swing. I noticed for the first time how dark the street was, how there were no Christmas lights on College Avenue that year. I found that if I pushed really hard with my feet, I could still make the swing move: back and forth, back and forth. The freeways rumbled like distant oceans. Walter came out and took me inside.

S IT down, Anna Kate," Walter gurgles into the phone when I pick it up. "Are you sitting down? Are you sitting down?"

"I'm *lying* down, honey. I'm still asleep," I say, but I know there's a problem when I hear Walter's voice.

"I can't see you again," Walter says, and pretty soon it all comes out. I can't believe how classic this story is. There they were, in the *den,* watching *There's Always Tomorrow* on television. Fred MacMurray, the quintessential henpecked sap, was kissing Barbara Stanwyck and offering to leave his wife so they could run away together when Lily said, all innocent-like, "I'm glad I don't have to worry about something like that with *you.*" Walter burst into tears and fell apart. He told Lily everything: about all the hotel rooms, the phone calls, the letters; about Houston and Havana and meeting my mother.

"Did you tell her you loved me?" I ask coldly.

"Yes. I told her. I was very clear about it too, honey. She wouldn't believe me. She said it must just be . . . *lust.*"

For what it's worth—that is, *nothing*—I think the motive behind Walter's little confession was to tell Lily the truth so she'd leave him. That's what he always *said* would happen, if Lily found us out. Then Walter wouldn't have to make a decision. The choice would be in Lily's dishpan hands. She'd let him go. But *noooo.* Lily's willing to forgive and forget. Can you believe it? I can't. *Don't.* But wet-mackerel Walter's caved in to her already. It took him all of eight hours to renounce me. Now he's calling to break the news.

"Didn't you see the *end* of the movie?" I screech. "Fred MacMurray makes the wrong choice! When he gives up love, his life is *over.* He turns into one of those toy robots he makes." I take a deep breath. Calm *down.* Save it for *later.*

"At least it was a *good* movie, Anna Kate," Walter says plaintively. "It could've happened during *The Flame Trees of Thika.*"

"You should've watched it all, Walter," I say quietly. "He makes the wrong choice. That's Sirk's whole point."

"I remember that letter you wrote me from Stockholm, about the Barbara Stanwyck movie," Walter says wistfully.

*"Ball of Fire,"* I say. My life is a Barbara Stanwyck retrospective.

"Right. *Ball of Fire.* The scientist and the gun moll. I loved thinking about you and me that way. I loved imagining you in that hotel room, by yourself, watching TV and thinking about me."

"Barbara Stanwyck *let* Fred MacMurray leave," I say to Walter, who's crying in this hopeless, resigned way. "She was brainwashed. I'm *not.* She thought giving him up was right. Being with the person you *love* is what's right."

By the time I get done with this little soliloquy, I'm crying too and it doesn't take long for me to talk Walter into coming to New York on the next plane, so we can see each other One Last Time. My threat to fly to Groverton, Ohio, where Walter teaches, might have had *something* to do with it. After we hang up, I get out of bed and straighten up the loft, take a long shower, and call the liquor store for a case of champagne.

After the champagne arrives, I walk up the street to Casa Moneo for some of those homemade enchiladas Walter likes, a nice little assortment, too: potato, chorizo, beef, bean, chicken. You can't get good Mexican food in the Midwest. The enchiladas look so good, I eat one on my way home. Just as I'm unlocking the door to my building, I see Freddy Pitluck, the psychotic dwarf novelist, peering out at me from the dumpster that's become his home away from home.

Have I told you about me and Fred? Clemmy and I saw him on Fourteenth Street one day, selling chapters of his novel for ten cents a pop. Clemmy tried to drag me away, but I'd just drunk six margaritas and couldn't be restrained. Lady bountiful here insisted on buying a chapter and getting it autographed, too. Freddy was so cute. He reminded me of Rumpelstiltskin, jumping up and down in impotent rage at the people who passed him by, cursing and haranguing. I thought he was a real original, a find, a petite dish of passion-fruit sorbet who'd clear our jaded New York palates. This was before I actually *read* some of the stuff friend Fred was peddling. This was before he started following me everywhere and stuffing my mailbox with pages and pages of horrible crap. My favorite part of Freddy's novel is the beginning, when he's hiking the Appalachian Trail surrounded by secret police in bear suits. One of them, cleverly disguised as a hiker, tries to drive Fred crazy by singing "I Love a Man in a Uniform" over and over and over. It *worked*, too.

I walk over to the dumpster and kick it two or twenty times, but Freddo doesn't come out.

"I've got something to tell you, Freddy," I say. "I've left a letter with my lawyer. To be opened in the event of my death, should anything *unusual* occur. You understand?

Your name is mentioned *prominently*. Anything strange about how I go, and they're going to come and *put you away*. You wouldn't like Willowbrook," I say, then pivot the way I learned at the Fort Worth branch of John Robert Powers—BE A MODEL! OR JUST LOOK LIKE ONE!—open my door, and trill, "Y'all have a nice day!"

Upstairs, I get ready for Walter's arrival. Makeup, check. Exotic lingerie, check also. French perfume, extremely high heels, silky, lace-trimmed peach pajamas, chilled champagne, spicy food, clean sheets: check, check, check, check, check, check. Okay, Walter, you can come in now.

I figured that once Walter saw me on my own turf, he wouldn't have a snowball's chance in hell, and this is how it turns out when he finally arrives. Last night he caved in to Lily; today he caves in again, to me. Why do I *want* this so-called man so much? His clothes are off in less than five minutes, poor chump. I actually feel sorry for him, between bouts of hating him and thinking I will die, immediately, without him. Poor Walter. Poor Lily. Poor me. Our combined IQs are over 400, but none of us is all that smart. Do you think it's too late to trade some of these pesky brains for a new face? I'd like something in beautiful, this time around. I'm bored with pretty. Something with cheekbones. *Marlene Dietrich?* Too hard. Something that'll still look good when I'm sixty. Something that'll wear well. How about that one over there? *Catherine Deneuve?* Okay, give me one Catherine Deneuve. No need to wrap it up, I'll wear it. *That'll be thirty IQ points, please.* Cheap at twice the price! *Hook her up to the brain drain, boys.* Ah, that's better. Much better. Why, I never felt better in my life. My! How time does fly! I must skedaddle. Wouldn't wanna miss *Family Feud.* And how about you, ladies and gentlemen? Would you recognize your body *without your head?*

Walter's face is red and wet now. His bright blue eyes
are bloodshot, from crying and drinking and crying some
more. But he's not thinking of me, though he's naked and
in my arms. He's thinking all at once of Lily.

"Oh, God, she needs me so much," Walter's crying. Not
thinking of me at all, goddammit. This will *never* do.

"I need you too," I interject, but Walter doesn't hear
me.

"She'll never make it on her own. I'm her whole life."

"Didn't you know when you fell in love with me that
there'd be consequences?" I ask sternly.

"I never thought they'd be like *this.*"

We're holding each other tight, babbling and crying
and egging each other on, in a frenzy of sex and misery.
Walter says my name over and over with this desperate
craven longing. He used to say my name so sweetly. It was
honey in his mouth, the best poem I ever wrote. And all
the time he's saying this stuff about how he has to go back
to Lily in Groverton, Walter's inside me, telling me how
much he loves me, that he can't give me up, not ever.
There's something contradictory going on here, uh-huh.
I encourage Walter's madness and he encourages mine.

"You're good now," I whisper, "but I can make you
better. I can make you fucking soar."

It isn't hot in here but we're both wet and sticky. Our
bodies squeak together and pop apart as I sit up and reach
for the champagne bottle. All gone. Walter's drained too,
but there's no peace on his face. He curls into himself like
a maggot or fetus, only what's dying and what's being
born isn't clear. Walter's dick is the only part of him that
isn't shriveled. All the blood that should be fueling his
brain is down there instead. Like a horny toad in the palm
of my hand, maybe Walter's dick will spit blood from its
tiny eye one day and hop away, escape me, but right now
it's hard again and Walter's groping for me with this dead

blank look. I get up and go to the kitchen for more champagne.

"Anna Kate, oh, Anna Kate," I hear him murmuring from the bed. Already it sounds like a dirge. Something in Walter's body tells him that if he can just fuck me hard enough, I'll go away. Something will be solved then, wrenched out of us. It's a pure animal drive. Nothing human about it.

I open the refrigerator in the darkness and stand in front of it for a minute, getting my batteries recharged. The cold blue light seeps into me, the cheerful mechanical whir inspires. Already I am stronger, refreshed. A sturdy white Amana Kate, ready to go back and fight the good fight. Nothing human about me either.

I was so calm today, preparing for Walter's visit, I surprised even myself. I knew he was set on leaving me this time, that he came here to let me go. But properly. Face to face. Like a *gentleman*. He even brought my letters, tied with pale blue ribbons in a tan accordion file that he kept in back of his desk. He used to read my letters when he was alone in his office, after everybody else in the physics department had gone home. It tore Walter up to give my letters back. His hands were shaking as he handed them over. Then he looked into my eyes and burst into tears. The bulk of what went on between us is there, on paper. In five months, we've spent perhaps thirty days together. This is one of the things Lily can't believe, Walter tells me: the importance of words on paper.

"Remember when you asked me to trust you?" I say as I walk out of the kitchen. "Remember that day when you flew back to Boston?"

Walter hangs his head in shame. He told his entire family and Lily's, gathered in Amherst on Thanksgiving Eve, that he was going to the Widener Library at Harvard, then drove to Springfield, got on a plane, and flew to New York for the afternoon, with a briefcase of lingerie for me to put on and take off. When Walter got back to Amherst, long after the Widener Library had closed, he jogged half a mile in the snow to a pay phone, to tell me he'd gotten away with it.

"How did you pull it off?" I asked cautiously.

When Walter answered, I heard my own tones in his voice, my own well-indulged tendency to go for the easy laugh, the perfect one-liner, no matter at whose expense. "Oh, the old absentminded professor routine," he said.

"I remember everything," Walter whispers, but I ignore him.

"Remember what you said? 'What do you think I'm going to do?' " I quote, making my voice shrill and ugly. " 'Make a speech and walk out the door?' That's exactly what you *are* doing, you lousy fucker."

"Stop it. Stop it. I know it. I know."

"You're making a speech! You're walking out the door!"

Walter grabs my hands with effort. "You think I don't know that, Anna Kate? You think I don't wish I could cut off my tongue for saying that? Would that make it any better?"

"Why did you try so hard to make me love you? You really did try. You really worked hard at it!"

This goes on for *hours.*

"You know you love me," I shriek. "Say it, *say it,* SAY IT!"

"I love you, all right. I know it. I can't deny it. I love you."

"Oh, Walter. Please don't leave me. I can't stand it. I'll die if you leave me." Now, I don't think I'll ever die, not really. I've never believed that I really, actually would

*die.* You say everybody dies? What a *killjoy* you are. I
don't *believe* it. Somebody will find the fountain of youth
before then, or they'll put me on ice next to Walt Disney
and thaw me out one day in the microwave like a Hungry
Man dinner. But I say this stuff about dying anyway, for
effect. And it is . . . *effective.* For the moment, I have Lily
beat. There's nothing like a little pain to put the holy back
in sex. Nothing like a little really high drama. And while
Walter is crying again, and coming, my brain is calculating. It never stops. My brain chugs on like a NORAD computer. The task is not to help Walter discover what he
wants and how to do it, but how to make him do what *I*
want and think it's his own idea. Lily has done the same
already, but her weapons are more potent: marriage, tra-
dition, children. I have to fight dirtier than she does. I
would have Walter already, if it weren't for the children.
I know that. Walter knows it too. Lily is the only one of
us who doesn't know this salient fact.

We finish off another bottle of champagne and have a
little coke, too. I've taught Walter all my expensive tastes,
my bad habits. Such a quick, sweet study. So handsome,
too. All this pain's added character to his face. It's taken
away some of the boyishness.

"You're strong and she's not," Walter's murmuring, but
without a whole lot of conviction. "I don't think you'd like
being a mother, honey. Lily is such a good mother."

I go to the kitchen, come back with more champagne.
The cork pops like a wet fart, weak and unfestive. I drink
from the bottle and stroke Walter's white belly. Walter
doesn't look at me. He doesn't sit up as he drinks, and
uncheap champagne dribbles all over the pillow. On the
underside of his cock, in the place where I always rub him,
bright blood is welling. It doesn't heal, we don't give it
time. We used to fuck all night and break the scab and
Walter would go home to Lily and turn his back on her

so she wouldn't see. He was the one, then, who undressed in the bathroom, in the dark. This is what he *told* me. Lubricants don't help; we've tried them all. Wouldn't *you* think something was the slightest bit amiss, if your husband started carrying K-Y Jelly in his *briefcase?* It's Walter's broken hymen, this tiny wound that's been bleeding all night, but Walter doesn't seem to feel it. His face is as rigid and expressionless as his dick. We sit there for a few minutes, not saying anything. Then Walter sits up like somebody coming out of a nightmare and crawls on top of me with a moan.

"I don't care if you lie to me," he says. "Just tell me I'm your favorite."

"You're my favorite, Walter."

"Are you lying?" he shoots back immediately.

"I'm not lying," I say soothingly.

"Tell me you love me."

"You know I love you. I wouldn't be here if I didn't fucking love you."

"Don't say 'fuck,' " Walter corrects absently. "Just tell me."

"I love you, Walter."

"Are you lying?"

"Stop *saying* that!" I say, and start to laugh. Walter is doing a very tenth-rate Perry Mason, but Walter isn't laughing. He can't see the humor in the situation. But there's something in his voice that tells me I'm really *really* winning, that the balance of power has shifted from Lily to me again, for the last time.

"You'll get bored with me, Anna Kate," Walter says. "We don't have anything in common. I don't dance. I don't go to the movies. I'm not really a whole lot of fun, once you get to know me. All I ever do is work. You'll get bored and you'll leave me, and then what will I do?"

"I won't leave you."

"Yes you will. I'll leave Lily and you'll leave me, and then I'll be all alone. I've never lived alone before," he says, in this quizzical voice.

"Oh, it's not so bad. It might toughen you up." Walter rears up on his elbows, stricken. "I was *joking*. Can't you tell when I'm joking?"

"Don't joke," Walter says. "Be serious for once. Be serious about *us.*"

"Okay, I'll be serious," I say earnestly. Walter settles down on top of me with a thrust that makes me moan.

"Do you like that?" he asks, doing it again. "Do you like having sex with me?" This is such a stupid question that even Walter laughs, and some of the tension goes out of his face. He kisses me over and over.

"I love you," I say between kisses. "I'm sure. I won't leave you. You're the best man I've ever known."

"Oh, God, you're so beautiful," Walter moans, shifting into anguish again. "You're so beautiful I can't bear to stop looking at you."

"Then don't. You don't have to. *Don't.*"

"You better be sure, Anna Kate," Walter says between strokes. "You better be there. You better not change your mind."

There is some fuck-up in the circuitry then, some computer malfunction, because Walter is crying and I'm crying too and suddenly I'm not acting. I'm not thinking at all. My brains have taken a vacation and I *do* love Walter terribly, blindly.

"I have two children," Walter pleads.

"Baby . . . we can have our *own* children."

Who said *that?* Oh, God, I did, and meant it. Walter comes with a groan that tears my heart and when I croon *baby, oh, baby* it's as much incantation as endearment, a send-off for the sperm heading up inside me. Maybe one of them will make it, dodging nimbly through the clogged and abused tubes like an Olympic hurdler, and presto! Zygote! That would fix everything, all right. I really do want Walter's child. I want to be tied to him, by someone else's flesh. I'm that far gone.

And as the sperm come out of Walter, so do these incredible promises come out of me, with the same force and haste and illogic. I ejaculate promises all over him. Yes, I'll marry you. Yes, I'll be faithful for the first time in my life. I'll never even look at another man. Yes, I'll move to Ohio—*Ohio!*—so we can be together all the time. I'll have your babies, so you won't miss the ones you'll be giving up. Walter has a daughter named Gerda, such an ugly, clunky name.

"If we have a daughter, we'll name her Luz," I say dreamily. "The second one will be Lumiere."

Maybe some residual part of me is still thinking, still calculating, telling me to give Walter everything he wants as a tactic to win our little battle of the bands. But it doesn't seem that way. It seems a pure, spontaneous sacrifice, giving in to Walter. Being a faculty wife in Groverton will cripple my spirit totally. I'll run amok, behave badly, the way I did in graduate school. Smash monogamy! Remember? What a nice *ring* that has. I'll never write another decent word in my life. The Ohio Institute of Technology is too horrible to contemplate, therefore I don't contemplate it. I just kiss Walter Light. Kissing Walter is so nice, I think I can do it forever.

And while there are these vague reciprocal promises from Walter about job hunting at Columbia, MIT, or Cal Tech, in cities where I could live, I know as well as he does that this is improbable if not impossible, and in any case years away. I give up my life, Walter gives up his. A fair deal, maybe. I know it's the best I can get, if I want to keep him. I've pushed him as far as he'll go.

*Have you ever walked across a pond that's not frozen*

*quite hard enough?* Walter wrote me in November. *Every step on the thin ice makes a sickening crack that threatens to send you down into the cold dark water. There is terror in it, but when you're halfway across, it's just as sensible to keep going. Maybe the ice is stronger, or the water is shallower, ahead. Sometimes I hope, and sometimes I don't care.* As I fall asleep, I hear ice cracking.

Unlike some people, I'm never afraid to go to sleep. This is because I can control my dreams. If I enjoy a dream particularly, I have it again and again. If I don't like the way a dream resolves itself, I go back to sleep and dream it over. So in the morning, after Walter and I make love and he goes back to his hotel to tell Lily about the wedding plans, I hug my pillow tight, burrow in, and dream.

Here I am treading water in a murky swamp, surrounded by men. There's been a shipwreck, there are crocodiles in the water, and every few seconds one of the men screams and goes under. I know that I'll be dead soon too. It's just a matter of time. So I think of a little plan to save myself. I decide to become a crocodile, instead of a human being, and sink down into the water like a stone.

Down below, the reptiles regard me curiously. I sink nice and easy, moving my arms and legs as I imagine a baby croc would, coming out of an egg. I touch silt with my feet, push off slowly, break the surface, breathe, sink. It's very relaxing, this process, up and down, up and down, drifting through the water, red and green like Christmas, while all around me men are dying. The crocodiles stare, even bat me around a little with their front legs and snouts, but they don't eat me yet because they don't know what I am, family or food.

I crawl onto the roots of a huge tree, like an evolutionary missing link, making the transition from water to land for the first time. A big crocodile is chasing a man around this little plot of ground. She's walking upright on thick hind legs, huge and hideous and terrifying. The man is screaming. He doesn't notice me crawling around, intent on perfecting my croc imitation. He runs right over me, trips, falls. The crocodile devours him. She nuzzles me with her bloody snout, trusting me finally. Under her motherly gaze, I feel my body start to change. I grow a tail. My body hardens to the waist, crusting over with golden scales. I'm reveling in the tranquil feeling that comes from being covered with gold when I hear this persistent ringing noise. Beneath the security, there's the slightest taint of guilt. But not enough to really bother me. I didn't *cause* that man's death, I think, waking up a little. It was an accident. Benefiting from somebody's misfortune doesn't make it your *fault.* Or does it? I try to go back into the dream and change the ending, to save myself without killing the man, to win the mother crocodile's love without doing anything even faintly immoral, *to get myself off the hook,* but I can't, because the telephone won't stop ringing. These philosophical subtleties pervade my subconscious as I wake up, without anything being resolved, at least not to my satisfaction, and say hello groggily, cross at being foiled.

"Anna Kate?" Walter says. His voice sounds strained and far away.

"Hi there," I say in my dreamiest, sexiest wake-up voice. I could make a fortune doing telephone sex, if my luck ever really *really* ran out. Even bill collectors get quivery, talking to *me,* I'm thinking as Walter starts to cry. He keeps crying for several minutes. I have a premonition that these few seconds, between waking up and hearing Walter cry, are the last time in a long time that I'm going to be happy.

It's about Lily. Of course it is. You knew that. Sure you did, Einstein. You're smarter than me. You fucking well better be. Lily, who I had forgotten about completely, except to assume that she would eventually be all right, since everybody gets divorces. Lily, who I figured would be happier in the long run, since nobody wants a husband who loves somebody else. Lily is in the hospital. Not at the Center for Continuing Education for Women, getting a scholarship for advanced studies in linguistics, which used to be her chosen field. Not at the McFleecum Employment Agency, getting a fulfilling new job. Not running for Congress. But *noooo.* It seems that while Walter and I were kissing and crying and fucking and planning our little lives, Lily was on the phone, calling Walter at his hotel, eager for the blow-by-blow on how he'd dumped me, calling him over and over and over. When she got no reply, Lily assumed the worst, I mean the truth, and ingested a goodly quantity of pills, a nice little selection too. And while it is true that the number of pills she took was fewer than I might take to get loose on a particularly debauched night, it is no use telling that to Walter. He believes that she meant to die of her misery, her love, our sin. She didn't, though. Of *course* not. Walter's the one who's damaged—irrevocably, I think.

"Do you understand *now* why I can never leave her?" Walter says in this mean, sarcastic tone I've never heard before that lacerates me. As if Lily's act had proved him right on some hotly contested point in Debate Club. *"Do* you? *Do* you? *Do* you?" Walter screams, losing control again.

"Yes," I whisper, barely able to talk at all.

"Well, that's great. That's just *great,*" Walter says in the same voice, which changes without missing a beat to this desperate sort of pleading. "She can't live without me, Anna Kate. You *can.* You're *strong.*"

Oh no I'm not. I'm not, I'm not, *not,* NOT, I want to say

but don't. He wouldn't believe me anyway. I just wish to God for once that I wasn't the strong one, that I was the one in the hospital eating steam-table food off a plastic tray, watching *The Price Is Right* while everybody else picks up the pieces.

"I don't love you anymore," Walter says. "Do you hear me, Anna Kate? I don't love you, and I hate myself."

As I sit there listening to Walter scream and cry, listening to him hate our love, the fight goes out of me. I nod into the phone as if Walter could see me through the wires, trying to think of something to say to comfort him, loving him all at once with a selfless love I don't recognize or know what to do with. I don't want Walter to die of this. I don't want it to kill him. He would do it scientifically, if he decided to take his life, like a good little genius. Not like Lily, I think, hating her. Walter would measure the pills correctly, or walk in front of a train, or blow out his brains with a steady hand and a well-oiled gun.

"Perhaps . . . it's for the best," I say. Walter seizes this platitude like a life raft.

"Of *course* it's for the best."

A few seconds later he's gone. Just like that. It's over, and so *fast,* as if it had never been. Lily's won him back and there's nothing I can do about it. I could try to kill myself too, I guess, but what if I fucked up and succeeded? I can just imagine Walter, shuttling back and forth between us, from hospital to hospital, going broke. I have to hand it to Lily. I really do. She played all the cards in her hand.

Oh, sure, I write a few more letters. Eloquent ten-page literary-type essays. One-page tear-stained pleas of screaming anguish.

"Get a lobotomy, *get it!* GET IT!" I scream at Walter on the phone. He calls all the time, at least once a day. *He's*

worried about *me,* ha! I tell him I'll get him the name of
Frances Farmer's doctor.

*I know you believe my life, from now on, will be a
disaster,* Walter writes. Very good point, honey. Lily will
make it one long act of contrition. Better run down to
K-Mart and pick up some shin guards, some pillows for
those pretty knees. *You must not wish this for me.* As if
*my* wishes made a difference.

But it's all sort of perfunctory, all the calls and letters
and weepy conversations and keeping Walter up-to-date
on the Jean Harris story. It's like throwing starfish back
in the ocean, the way I used to do on the beach with
Clemmy. You hope that one out of the thousand you find
along the waterline will turn out to be alive, find the
bottom, hang on and live, then thank you in its brainless
way for your efforts on its behalf. But I know I can never
win Walter back with words. That my words and Lily's
act are not equivalent. That all the beached starfish are
dead.

As you can imagine, this is a little hard for me to take.
I'm not a good loser, and there's nothing to fall back on
except the bed, which is surrounded by champagne bottles and week-old newspapers. The sheets still smell like
Walter's corny aftershave. I can't bear to change them.
Maybe that's why my dreams are so out of control. The
erotic dreams I used to love turn into nightmares in mid-
fuck: Penises grow warts when I touch them, change just
before entering me to knives. I have one recurring nightmare that begins with Walter and me lying in bed, safe
and cuddly, sleeping like spoons. Walter wakes up and
turns to me with this happy smile, but when he sees who
it is in bed with him, that it's *me,* he starts to cry. The tears
eat into his face like acid. Walter screams and claws out
his eyes.

This dream always wakes me up. I stay woken up after

it for days. I discover that if I drink enough I don't have any dreams at all, so I drink, pass out, wake up five hours later and feel my liver pump-pumping, get up and drink some more. Drugs help too. I ask total strangers for Valium and eat them like M&M's. The liquor store delivers. So does my dealer, who says he's worried about me, after pocketing my cash.

"Don't be," I say brightly. Worried about his *ass*. The next time Jimmy comes, I manage to be dressed. Other than that, I hardly get up at all, except to piss and to take these long hot showers, which fail to make me feel cleansed of anything.

This is quite a change from the other breakup scenarios of my life. I used to work my best after I'd split with someone. I would cry and scream and beg to keep them, if they were doing the leaving, and beat my head against the wall, thinking I had made a life-threatening mistake, but after they were gone, really and truly gone, the mourning period would be exceedingly short. Not feeling things makes it easy to eschew holding grudges, and I never had any doubt after a while that I was better off without the person in question. This shows the essential shallowness of my character, my lack of affect, one or seventy-six people have told me. I thought I was *lucky*. There would be this period between breaking up and feeling insecure about not having enough boyfriends when I would work, work, work, putting all the energy that usually goes into men into writing. Though these periods never lasted all that long, I value them greatly. I started our spaceman script the morning Gary Cavanaugh, a black-haired gray-eyed Irish lout that Clemmy picked out for me at the Formosa—one of my many illiterate drummers—left me.

Gary Cavanaugh, though, was smarter than most. "You love me, but I don't love you," he said sensibly at five in the morning. We were fighting in the bathroom when I blacked out. When I came to three hours later, we were fighting on the Santa Monica Freeway. No need to say who was driving. It was *my car.* After I kicked Gary out in some desolate spot and crawled home to Clemmy, I started wondering why I bothered going on at all, which led me to wonder if other people ever regretted their actions the way I always did, which led, by some circuitous tortured path in my brain, to the question of whether or not the American Revolution was really such a good idea. Then this big bright light bulb turned on in my head. Might other people wonder about that too? *People from outer space!* I outlined the entire script that morning, wrote the first twenty pages, and went to sleep. When I woke up at sundown like a good little vampire, Clemmy was downstairs reworking what I'd written. He was so engrossed he hardly noticed when I put my arms around him and kissed the top of his greasy blond head. The sixteen-millimeter film cans he uses for ashtrays were overflowing with fresh butts, denoting a productive day. Clemmy never asked what happened to Gary. Neither of us mentioned him again. You might say that breaking up so painfully—*dangerously*— with Gary Cavanaugh was the beginning of our so-called success.

I keep expecting the same surge of energy to appear now, but it never does, as if the power's been shut off permanently. I don't feel myself getting distanced from Walter. I can't convince myself I'm better off without him. I keep expecting him to walk through the door. I imagine what he would say, how harshly I would punish him before taking him back, five seconds later. I haven't loved all that many people. The fucked:loved ratio is shockingly immense. And Walter doesn't help. He keeps those cards and letters coming in. He wants to be forgiven, the asshole. Secondarily, he wants me to be all right.

"What do you expect me to do, Walter?" I sneer, hating him. "Cut my wrists all over your secretary's desk?"

"Anna Kate—"

*"I'm* not the one killing myself around here! *I'm* not the one getting the lobotomy! That was somebody *else's* discarded mistress."

Walter is so sad and silent and stoical. So resigned. Typical telephone conversation:

Walter: "Hi, how are you."

Me, nastily: "Great. Just *great.* How's the little woman?"

Walter, cautiously: "Oh, fine."

Gently: "And the kids?"

"Fine, too," Walter says as I start to cry. What about *our* children? Long silence.

Softly: "Walter?"

Tenderly: "What, my darling?"

"Tell me you love me."

With great anguish: "Oh, Anna Kate . . . I love you. You know I love you. I'll love you all my life."

When Walter Light's not making me hate him, he's breaking my fucking heart. I can't seem to get better, with this going on. I can't seem to move *on.* I finally ask Walter to stop phoning. He does. *I can't fucking believe it.* Instead of taking the good advice I saw Bette Davis give herself when *Mr. Skeffington* was on the tube a few days back, i.e., "It is unwise to seek admirers when one is falling to bits," I'm so angry I decide to get up and reacquaint myself with some of my former boyfriends, jettisoned when I met Walter. Hey, Bette Davis didn't take her own good advice either, and everything turned out all right for *her.* She found a blind man to love her! Oh, lucky, *lucky*. I excavate the phone and call one of these second-string reptiles, Nigel Featherbone, *a Jewish prince from South Africa*. Bisexual, too. Think about *that* for a minute. Think of the subplots! The twists! *"There's a killer on the road, his brain is squirmin' like a toad."*

What's that you say? Why didn't I run for my *life?* Let's put it this way: If there are two men standing on the corner, and one of them is single, has just won the Nobel Peace Prize, has a million dollars in his briefcase, a house on Fishers Island, an eight-inch cock, and is dying to visit Harry Winston's before taking a trip with someone special to Mustique, and the other one is a diseased, married junkie with open fly exposing pitiful limp wienie and filthy hand extended for change, which one do you think I'll pick? Hey, wait a minute! Not so fast! First I have to know if the junkie is *cute*.

Nigel Featherbone is *extremely* cute, unfortunately. There's something about his dark, stocky body that appeals to me, even if he doesn't do much with it that's interesting. For the past few weeks he's been leaving these pathetic messages. His wife, Odile, with whom I once had a brief bathroom flirtation, has flown the coop yet again for parts unknown, there's nobody else within three blocks to distract him, so wouldn't *I* like to get together, for old times' sake? Nigel's so common in his arrogance. Even the dull men, the poor, the unfamous, think they're Warren Beatty these days. Catch us if you can, they warble, then flee like foxes down our holes, drunk with their own desirability. We watch them put on their tennis clothes and feel their sperm on our thighs and laugh at them, and ourselves, for being there, next to these worthless thugs. They never ask why we're laughing. They *know*. Men like Nigel will never make me cry, the way Walter Light did.

Despite or because of this, I make a date to see Nigel at Raoul's. Old boyfriends are handy that way, like clothes pushed to the back of the closet. Some of them you pull out and they fit you fine. They make you proud of your good taste way back when. Some are comfortable if unexciting. Then there are others you take one look at and think, How *could* I? What possessed me to get into *that?* More to the point: How could *that* have gotten into *me?*

I should have known Nigel was a close encounter of the last kind while I was getting ready for our date. When I turned on the blow dryer two fat roaches came shooting out along with the first *whoosh* of hot air, like cannonballs, and landed on my head, provoking a flurry of little screams, hysterical stomp-stomping, and a genuine mad dash to the liquor cabinet for solace. But instead of taking that as a sign of something and crawling into bed like a smarter girl would've, I got back in the shower, rewashed my hair, and wielded the disgusting dryer yet again, after first shaking it vigorously to dislodge charred roaches. I even manage to ignore another roach I found, embalmed in a bottle of Develop 10.

A few minutes later and here I am at Raoul's, only an hour late. Raoul's, where one of the waitresses is a French chrome dome whose entire left ear is tattooed off-black. Very appetizing, Monique. Looks like you're decom*posing.* Nigel's overjoyed. He suspected I stood him up, but when I tell him the roach story he forgives me soon enough, though a woman at an adjacent booth drops her fork with an audible clunk and runs her fingers through her hair with gusto.

Nigel directs rock videos for morons and used to love me in his own twisted way but hates me now for not loving *him,* though if I *had* loved him he would've stopped loving *me,* but despite all this we have a good time as civilized people will, eating rich food, drinking, chattering away. After dinner we meander down to the Bar Car, but it's strange here tonight. It's gotten all yupped up! Eavesdrop on a few conversations. You'll see what I mean. Is it books they're talking? Music? Movies? Only if they're in one of those *businesses,* believe me, and then they only cover the money angles. These mercenaries could care less what they peddle. But there's not even much of that dirty business talk tonight. They're all talking real estate. Jesus H. Christ! These people don't even fuck, except for rent-controlled apartments, and only then when they're about to go co-op.

Nigel doesn't notice the yuppies. He's gotten a little yupped up himself. In fact everyone I know's gotten yupped, except me. All over town acts are being cleaned up, disparate selves are being pulled together. I'm the only holdout. Even Clemmy's caught the bug. I try to buy him a drink, but he's on the wagon. He's drinking tonic and bitters and chatting up some lady producer. He even has on one of his grandfather's suits. This depresses me, for some reason. Lucky Nigel's brought me lots of coke, dissolved in a Dristan bottle.

"How's that sinus condition, Anna Kate? Any better?" the bartender says wryly as I take a discreet snort. Nigel doesn't do drugs himself. He *never has.* This gives him a somewhat mythical status. The coke has a sweetish taste and after the second hit, I feel my sphincter muscles loosening and this warm impending gush welling up and bolt for the toilet just in time. Nigel's not doing drugs handicaps him somewhat in the informed consumer department. Mannitol, I think, as my dinner runs out of me. Ex-Lax for babies. Somebody pounds on the door.

"Don't take all bloody night!"

"Fuck off," I say cheerfully, but I'm done for the moment and start pulling up my panties. Then I see that they're stained with something, not shit, but with dark blood that should have been Walter Light's baby. I start to cry and can't stop. No amount of door pounding, not by

Nigel or Clemmy or the Bar Car owners, will dislodge me from the bathroom. Someone breaks down the door finally and stuffs me with pills, then washes my face, wraps me in a white cashmere coat, picks me up in his arms, and takes me out through the kitchen.

The bed I wake up in smells like murder. I smell it before I see it: the butcher shop where Uncle Elmo worked. Sure enough, when I open my eyes, there's blood on the sheets; it's an abattoir, all right, and I'm in the middle of it. I check my body for wounds but don't find any. The gore must belong to someone else. When I scramble out of the bed to look for the body, head pounding ominously, and feel wet warm rivulets run down my leg I remember where all the blood came from and I'm not afraid anymore, just hideously embarrassed. But the person whose bed I soiled doesn't seem to be around. I manage to locate a bathroom without bleeding on his carpet. I wonder what to do next, then notice an unopened box of Super Tampax waiting for me on the sink.

Back in the bedroom, I notice everything is the same pale shade of blue except me and the blood: blue walls, blue carpet, expensive blue sheets. Like the boxer shorts Clemmy buys at Brooks Brothers. I wrap the top sheet around me, open a sliding door, walk onto a tiny balcony, and try to figure out where I am. The river's where it should be, but I must be pretty far uptown. I can't see the Maxwell House sign or the old Hoboken railroad terminal. To the left there's a bridge, but I don't know which one. Then my feeble mind makes the impossible, logical leap: it's the George Washington, only in the wrong place. If hell is being on the wrong side of the river, then I'm in Weehawken, maybe even Fort Lee.

Back inside, I decide to get dressed. But where are my clothes? Naturally I look on the floor first. Given the con-

dition of the bed, that seems the logical place to look. But
my clothes aren't there, in the usual twisted heap, bra
tangled in still-buttoned blouse, panties wedded to hose,
everything inside out. I finally find them neatly folded on
a chair, arranged in the order of putting on again, shoes
aligned beneath. Everything's there except my panties,
which I remember seeing in the bathroom. Sure enough,
there they are, clean and slightly damp, hanging next to
the shower curtain. Somebody's washed them, certainly
not me.

Maybe I *am* in hell instead of New Jersey, I think, as I
venture into a living room the same cool shade of blue. On
a glass coffee table in front of a beige sectional couch,
*Playboy* magazines are neatly stacked. The magazines
are in order, with April of last year on the bottom and the
current issue, February, on top. Their corners are square
to the table's edge. On the other end is a similar pile of
*Psychology Today*s. Maybe not hell. A nice clean mental
hospital! At least that makes *sense.* I've finally been committed, as predicted, and massively dosed with Thora-
zine, which explains why I feel so awful.

Next, the kitchen, where I find hot coffee in a Krups
contraption and croissants in the warming oven. In the
breakfast nook, a place for one is already set. Beside the
plate is my purse, fifty dollars, the business card of a car
service, and a pile of junk mail addressed to occupant
telling me exactly where in New Jersey I am. No note.
Nothing personal from my unseen provider. I'm starting
to feel like *Beauty and the Beast,* the Cocteau version, but
the door to the hall opens silently when I try it. I decide
not to leave right away, to poke around for clues, but
there aren't any. No letters to read, no journals, no pre-
scription bottles in the medicine cabinet. It's like nobody
lived here at all. In the bedroom closet, in the pocket of
an immaculate white linen suit with a German label, I find

some matches from the Reggae Lounge. Could my rescuer be black? All the records in the hi-tech cabinet are
classical, which, in my experience, militates against black-
ness. Side seven of Alban Berg's *Lulu* is on the turntable.
I get this queasy feeling, looking at it. Did we fuck to
Lulu's death scene? Maybe that explains why he didn't
mind the blood like most men do. The bed really is a mess,
all right. I strip it and throw the sheets in the washing
machine with some of that new protein-based detergent
and the stains come out, just like on TV. The mattress is
stained too, so I do exactly what any other girl would do
under the circumstances. It's not easy, it takes at least
twenty minutes. I turn over the mattress, then remake
the bed.

While I'm waiting for my car, I flip on the stereo. *Lulu*
is one of the only operas I know. This film professor at
UCLA, my boyfriend before Clemmy, made me buy it
because T. W. Adorno, his hero, wrote the liner notes. But
I could never concentrate on the music. I kept seeing
Louise Brooks in the silent picture: the way she looked,
the way she bounced around. She said more about Lulu
in two seconds of screen time than Alban Berg does in
four hours. I think about how the movie ended, how the
only time Lulu gives something for nothing it kills her,
how Louise Brooks wound up selling lipsticks at Macy's,
how Lulu sat in Jack the Ripper's lap.

M Y little adventure in New Jersey sends me crawling back to bed for succor, but a few days later, my mother calls at Clemmy's instigation and tells me, not gently, to get myself up.

"Why don't you do somethin' healthy once in a while, instead of shut up in there, a-crawlin' and a-festerin'?" my mother says, paraphrasing her favorite line from her favorite movie, *Oklahoma.* When I fail to laugh the way I'm supposed to, my mother gets down to business: "You did a bad thing, honey, taking that woman's husband, and now you have to pay the piper."

"Men aren't like fruit on a tree, Momma. You can't just come along and pick one."

"Ha!" my mother says.

"You can't take somebody that doesn't wanna be took," I persist.

"You don't really believe that, do you, sweetie? Why, I never saw a man less able to look out for himself than Walter."

"You're saying what?" I ask coldly.

"I'm saying he was easy pickin's, Katherine Anne! And that you knew that and, knowing it, you shouldn'ta

picked. It was beneath you. You should've thought for
both of you and done what was right."

"He wanted to change his life, Momma."

"He *said* that, because that was what you wanted to
*hear.* He wanted to make you happy. But change, really
change . . . I don't think so. Some people *like* being the
way they are. They don't all want to be like *you,* all fire
and storm and drama. Take me, for instance. I couldn't
live like you any more than a pig could fly! Just thinking
about it makes me want a nap. No, Walter just wanted a
little adventure. Something to look back on fondly, in his
old age. If he really wanted to change, he would've done
it before he met you. Not *for* you. You never change for
anybody. You change for *yourself.* So get up, darlin'. Get
a move on," my mother says cheerfully. "To hell with the
poets! Nobody dies of a broken heart."

"Oh, really?" *Just watch.* "Since I don't have a heart to
start with, Mom, it's pretty sure I can't die of a broken
one," I say, stabbing my poor sweet mother in the back
yet again. Long hideous guilt-soaked pause, during which
I refuse to apologize.

Then: "Why not remember the *good* things, Katherine
Anne? Why only remember the bad?" But there really
isn't any answer to this, and a minute or so later my
mother hangs up.

Why *is* it I always remember the bad things? They just
seem to stick in my mind. When my mother said that
thing about hearts, I couldn't help but remember this
other thing she said once. I didn't *want* to remember it.

She said, "I bore two children, and one of them was
born without a heart." Imagine that! *Now* do you understand why I was so mean to her? I heard my mother
confide this once to Mrs. Tucker, who was visiting. My
mother might have had a really bad day, I don't know. She
might not have meant it. But as I stood outside the kitchen

door and listened to her recite those words with this weary, hopeless inflection, I could tell she'd said them before. Oh yes she had. And I knew which child she was talking about, too. Don't you?

Once my mother sent me this printout of a computer game she played with my stepsister Brandywine. The program was called "Mindprobe," and on the basis of a bunch of yes-and-no questions it purported to give you an analysis of your *true character,* okay? My mother answered the questions for me and my little brother Tommy, then sent me the happy news: Both of her children were named Gandhi, all right, only one was Mahatma and one was *Indira.* My favorite line in the three-page single-spaced character analysis, which wasn't that far off the mark, was this: "Ms. K.A.P.O.'S. is not bothered by confrontation, provided she wins." After getting that Mindprobe printout, I stayed drunk for a week.

I was about ten, I guess, when my mother said that stuff about me not having a heart, and though the words stung momentarily, they didn't really hurt. I knew my mother was right. I couldn't cry, not ever. And it was soothing, somehow, to think my problem was *biological.* From the time my mother married Jack Hill and took me to the big city, away from the soft bosoms of my aunts, the unconditional love of my uncles, the safe small country town where I was born—from that time, when I cried all the tears I had to shed, no one could drag a tear out of me. Jack Hill would wallop me and I'd just stare at him, all glassy fish eyes. This threw him into a rage and he'd beat on me some more until he got too tired to lift his arm. Then he'd plop down on the old sprung couch, too stunned by my stubbornness to continue, something ruined about his eyes.

You might call it passive resistance on my part, or you might say as my family does that I exacerbated the situation. I would sit at the table all night rather than eat my liver, or whatever it was that didn't tickle my picky palate—*Not good enough for you, Miss High and Mighty?* The liver would get cold and congeal on the plate, and it would appear again the next night, and the next, a tactic Jack learned at the Joan Crawford School of Parenting. This would go on until the liver would get really smelly and everybody would sneak these glances at it and turn green. All of them would be nervous wrecks except me and Jack, who knew what was coming. Counted on it, even: my mother breaking finally and screaming face down on the conjugal bed, *"I'll* eat the goddamn liver! *I'll* eat it! *I'll* eat it! *I'll* eat it!"

Because this was what the thing was about, anyway. About him and her, and the unindicted co-conspirator, my dad, whoever *he* was. I didn't know yet. We had never been properly introduced, seeing as how Rodgers O'Shea wasn't interested in meeting *me*. I wasn't famous enough! I had never even been on television. But in those days I sort of stood in for him anyway. Our family squabbles weren't about discipline or obedience. They were about the duck in the henhouse, about my poor mother's sin, for which I provided evidence to convict like the fingerprints on a cadaver's thigh.

For talking back, my mother would get slapped around a little. Not too hard. Just enough to Show Her Who's Boss. *A man's gotta be king in his own castle.* And then the Boss, the *king,* would get tarted up and go out. He was never so happy as after beating my mother, when he'd dress up and go to this dive he favored on the Waco highway, Guys and Dolls, which was full of his ex-wives. He'd bathe carefully and put on his cheap suit and black shirt and white gangster's tie and drench himself with Old Spice and slick his black hair back with more than just a little dab of Brylcreem.

My mother would sit in the bedroom, crying. She's never had any trouble with tears. She's so softhearted that after twenty years with the Woodbury Funeral Chapel she still cries over the dead whose records she processes, whom she persists in thinking of as people instead of remains. The one job she refuses to do, backed up by the entire female office staff in an unprecedented show of spunk, is to call the widows and orphans and dun them for cash. The vice-presidents, all men, do that job themselves, though they grumble about it some. But the grumbles don't have any depth to them, my mother says. The women's little revolt only served to bolster their ingrained belief that women should never be promoted to management positions, because women are too softhearted.

After Jack's new Oldsmobile pulled out of the driveway in a most leisurely fashion, all of us would crawl out of our holes. Maybe someone would get real brave and turn on the lights. My mother would wipe her eyes and pull herself together for our sakes, then take us to the Dairy Queen for dip cones and Dr. Peppers in her battered Corvair. If my stepfather failed to score at Guys and Dolls, he would come home about three and jump my mother's bones. It was a small house. We heard them struggling through the walls. His terms of endearment, used to break down my mother's resistance, were highly original. "One more slice off the loaf won't hurt," Jack would argue winningly. "Why feed the cow and buy milk too?" is another suave line I particularly remember. My pillow failed to muffle these battlefield noises. And the next night there would be something less wretched to eat for dinner. Meat loaf, maybe. My mother would look younger, dewier, more submissive. And life would go back to what passed around our house for normal.

At some point I condescended to *pretend* to cry, just to

keep peace in the family. When Jack wasn't looking, I would spit on my fingers and rub my eyes and boo-hoo real effectively. But this performance never fooled my mother. When I finally did cry for real, at age thirteen, she practically got down on her knees to thank Jesus for the miracle. God's agent was my stepsister Brandywine, who hated me deeply and not without cause. I scattered paper dolls and marbles on the floor of our bedroom and failed to pick them up, especially after Brandy had just cleaned. When she wanted to take my Gene Pitney records to a party, I rented them to her for ten cents a pop. If she needed to borrow some of my carefully hoarded allowance, I charged her interest. Twenty percent. I also did this to my mother. Do you understand *now* why I've done so well in Hollywood?

One day Brandy's dark brown searchlights, scanning for weakness, homed in on my bangs, of which I was inordinately proud. And we all know what pride goeth before, don't we? Brandy's instincts were really good that day. Those bangs were perfect, a little too long everywhere, but especially on the sides. Cher bangs. Not the Cher of Cher and Greg or Jack LaLanne commercials, not the I-won't-go-out-of-the-house-with-a-pimple Cher of kitschy TV specials. Not *her.* I mean the Cher of pre-paunch Sonny, of elephant-legged pants and paisley and "I Got You Babe." I even filed my nails like she did: square.

"Let me cut your bangs," said Brandy. "They're too long."

"I *like* them long."

"Come on, I'll just trim them a little. You don't wanna go around looking like an old *sheep dog.*"

I distrusted Brandy, because she hated me and I knew it, but still I had the deference of small dog to big. And Brandy, at seventeen, *did* look really good, I'll give her that, as good as she possibly could seeing as how we were so impoverished and her father was this fanatical lapsed Baptist who wouldn't let her wear makeup. He'd catch her wearing lipstick and smear it all over her face, then beat her. After it was over, she'd run to him sobbing, "Daddy, Daddy, I'm sorry, Daddy." She was the one *bleeding,* and she was the one *apologizing,* as if Jack Hill had a *right* to beat her. She still has this jagged scar from one of his early morning attacks. We were listening to Paul Harvey when Jack threw her against the venetian blinds. Brandy's elbow split like a pomegranate and ran down the wall. Jack was too cheap to take her to the doctor for stitches. He put a Band-Aid on her and sent her to school. When the blood soaked through her blouse, the school nurse called my mother. Brandy went to the emergency room. Jack grumbled about that bill for *weeks.* I can see the ugly scar now, peeking out from Brandy's Ship'N'-Shore blouse, ruining her efficient brown arm. *Snip, snip, snip.*

"I'll just take a little off here," Brandy said, trying hard to radiate sisterly love. "Oh-oh. It's not even now. Just a little on the left."

I don't want you to think Brandy was innately evil. She wasn't. Somebody *made* her that way. Her mother was a German war bride, the perfect victim for Jack. Helga could yell her head off and no one would come, because no one could understand her. No one ever came to save Helga. One night Jack lit her hair with his Zippo lighter. He didn't like her schnitzel, I guess. Then he took the kids to Grandma Hill's, while Helga was writhing on the floor, blond hair in flames, learning a little history lesson, the one about the crematoriums. Brandy told me this story one night under the covers when I was eight. For years I had nightmares about my hair combusting spontaneously, maybe while I was doing problems in long division.

One minute, you'd be sitting at your desk chewing a pencil, the next minute your hair would just *go up.*

"A little bit more off the right, I think." A few minutes later Brandy stepped back and handed me the mirror. I looked like a Lhasa Apso clipped like a poodle by mistake by some deranged apprentice at Le Dog House. Fear of going to school, of dwindling popularity, overwhelmed me. I didn't notice I was crying until I saw my mother, Aunt Faye, and Aunt Zelda hugging each other and jumping up and down, like teenage girls at a football game. Even Brandy didn't hate me, all of a sudden. They liked those crocodile tears so much I've incorporated them permanently into my repertoire. The lesson I learned that day was so dramatic, in fact, that at times I even believe it myself: It's better to have a broken heart than no heart at all. Maybe that's why I can't get over Walter. By breaking my heart, at least he proved I *had* one.

I think about how the heart moves three beats behind the brain and hangs on to these skimpy threads of belief. Love comes crashing out of it like an elephant through the forest, knocking down the trees that are its natural defenses, risking everything, bellowing its need. Love goes down this ancestral path that isn't even there anymore, exposed and bewildered, and sticks out its trunk tentatively, hoping for sympathy, a peanut, a kind word as the pygmies move in for the kill. The elephant in the clearing, obsolete already, who has destroyed, accidentally, an agricultural project funded by the Ford Foundation, is still looking for someone to protect it when the first little arrow strikes. And that's what *I* think about, when I think about love: an elephant on its knees.

A week into March, I get up again, this time for good. There's nothing else to do. It's boring in this bedroom, and *rank.* The bed and I are quite chummy, like Velcro strips, but I manage to tear myself away long enough to turn off the television, pick up the phone, and get on with my so-called life.

Most mornings, I try to work on my novel. That is to say I get up at eleven, turn on the computer, and read what I've already written. Hmmm, pretty good, I think. Then I turn off the computer and pour myself a drink, if it's not too early—but it must be cocktail hour somewhere, right? I curl up on the couch and read other people's novels and sneer. Huh, I can do better than that! I think uneasily, not really believing it. Even the crummiest popular novel intimidates. After lunch, I have heart-to-hearts with my girlfriends and complain about how miserable I am and how I can't work. They're all a little sick of listening to me by now. Not many of them have the luxury to whine and pine like I do.

Sometimes I even do a little business. This consists of calling my accountant, Maury Goldleaf, for an update on my finances, and letting my agent, Emma Gomez, read me the riot act. I owe her that much. I've been kind of a disappointment to Emma. She thought she was going to make lots of money off me, after Clemmy and I broke up and she took me on as a client. She thought I had every chance of becoming a highly paid screenwriter, of raking in those big buckeroos. She never took my post-Clemmy problems seriously. I *warned* her. She thought I was *joking.* Poor Emma. My very existence baffles the hell out of her. I'm worth serious dollars now. Why don't I bend over and *pick them up?* I *have* managed to crank out some treatments of dubious quality and quite a bit of script doctoring, so I haven't been a *total* loss. But I got bored with that after a while. Offers come in, I turn them down. I keep waiting for these great new ideas to arrive en masse for a party in my mind, but none of them ever shows *up.*

"How's the novel coming?" Emma asks.

"Oh, fine. Just fine."

Emma swears in Spanish. She senses the unprofitability of my literary ambitions and hopes I'll get over them soon so I can get back to *serious* writing, the kind that makes money. For *her*. I'm not Emma's biggest client, but I'm not her smallest one either. That's why she hasn't given up on me yet.

In the evenings I go to screenings, clubs, and parties. I drink. I drink too much. I drink *far* too much. Everybody I know drinks too much, except the people who take too many drugs, and usually they drink too much too. We are all, most of the time, either getting drunk, drunk, or hung over. And every time some asshole asks me what I'm working on I say, "Not a whole hell of a lot," real bitter, and have another couple dozen cocktails.

On weekends I take the subway to Coney Island, to the aquarium. The whales smile like sweet fat Buddhas. The sharks are toothy, prehistoric and evil. Things look the way they *are*, at the aquarium. I find this comforting. I love to watch the two Belugas, their skins all white and ripply against the glass. They float or play or sleep; I stare at them and smile. I start to think they recognize me when I come.

Sometimes the female swims alone along the bottom of the tank, rubbing herself against it, spouting cloudy jets of milk. The male doesn't look at her then, he doesn't move at all, but his penis peeks lazily out of his body, testing the water, white and whiplike. I've never seen the whales make love. People fuck, whales make love. That's why every quarter I write a fat check to Greenpeace. Their cowboy tactics slay me. Ram that fucking whaler!

And speaking of fucking, I do a lot of that, too. I can be quite charming when I put my mind to it, and pain gives a vulnerable cast to my eyes that some men—the Ger-

mans, especially—find appealing. A warm body in bed
helps. Even a cold one helps a little. I'm afraid to sleep
alone, a good excuse for excessively whorish behavior. I
try to spend time with men like me, selfish and charming
and arrogant, on the surface at least. Who knows what
goes on in these men underneath? Whether or not they
wake up screaming in the dark? Whether they're as terrified as I am? Not *me*. I don't want to know anything
about anyone. I pick them up and discard them. They
pick me up and discard me. No one thinks too much about
this process, about what all this meaningless fucking and
fucking over *means.*

I take a lot of drugs, of course, proud of being an informed consumer, the kind who buys in bulk. We use
drugs to simulate the feelings we don't have for each
other. But my body is strong, with good Irish pauper
genes. My moderate self-abuse, still under nominal control, is nothing compared to the plague or the potato
famines, to the stinking holds of the ships that brought my
clan to America. I take drugs to forget about Walter. Or
try to. You mustn't think I've forgotten about Walter. Not
for a moment do I stop comparing him with the thugs I'm
with. So Walter was a wimp in the end, a folder. At least
he did what he thought was right, while right is a concept
that continues to elude me. I never want to mess with
decency again. Given the company I keep, this is an easy
goal to meet. We use each other's bodies, then hold them
like Teddy bears. Sleep is a problem, for all of us.

"Take some downs," I'm ordered crossly, as I toss and
turn in somebody's bed, still awake from too much coke.
But I avoid barbiturates, see Monroe in the Seconal bottle
winking, Dorothy Kilgallen tap-tapping on the glass.
What's that they're saying? *Wise up, toots?* They certainly
are trying to tell me something, all right. Downs are the
only drugs that scare me. One minute you're sitting on

the commode, changing your Tampax and thinking about trying this new moisturizer, the next minute a bunch of strange men are dropping ashes on your carpet and there *you* are, outlined in chalk, not able to do a *thing* about it. I toss and turn, instead of taking the proffered downs. I won't be invited *here* again.

But no matter. There are plenty of men to choose from. The pool of applicants for the job of being my boyfriend is truly immense indeed. How come? you might well ask. She's not *that* cute, not *that* rich. A sweet little fuck, true, but *look what you have to put* up *with*. Most enlightening, pal. I couldn't have said it better myself. But you've forgotten one thing, the thing Emma could get *mucho dinero* for, if only I'd condescend to work. What have you forgotten? You've forgotten *fame*. A few weeks ago the Academy Award nominations were announced. Can you *believe* it? Nobody ever said virtue was rewarded; that's why it's its *own* reward, right? People like me *need* Academy Awards, so we can have even more boyfriends! Enough fame and I guarantee, sisters, you don't even have to go to the health club.

I was a little surprised, though, when Clemmy told me about it. We were nominated for a script we wrote four years ago that was developed, then put into turnaround, by two different studios before it finally got made by these indie producers, backed by a consortium of New Jersey dentists. It's sort of a roman à clef, about our sordid relationship, but funny. This is when we thought we were the new Valerie Curtin and Barry Levinson. Clemmy wrote his lines and I wrote mine, a technique we stole from somebody, I forget who, and the script wasn't great, just good. But the movie they made of it was *horrible*. Really! And nobody owes us any favors. We don't even *live* in Hollywood.

"What's the catch?" I asked Clemmy on the phone.

"No catch. Only . . . Rodolpho's dying of AIDS." Rodolpho directed the picture, *Last Chance for a Slow Dance.* You know Rodolpho. The ancient neo-realist genius? Lured out of retirement, he really did a job on those dentists. "They couldn't give him best director because he so clearly wasn't, or best *picture,* for God's sake, so they gave him *us* and two best supportings," Clemmy said.

"So if we win, we make a speech about the great Rodolpho." Rodolpho, the pig who butchered our script.

"Don't stay up all night writing it, Porter," Clemmy said nastily. "Don't strain your little brain. Don't even consider it. Nobody cares *that* much about Rodolpho. And if they did, it'd be one of the Best Supportings; Kerry Graham was actually good. If I was directing, *I'd* use her."

"I just bet you would."

"Anyway, Rodolpho won't last till April. I saw him last week at Columbus. He looks like he's already dead."

"What were you doing way up there?" I asked suspiciously. Clemmy never goes north of Fourteenth Street, except for screenings, and if he does he stays on the East Side, where the Yale Club is.

"Taking a meeting. Remember meetings, Porterhouse?" Only Clemmy would name his girlfriend after a steak.

"So are you going?" I asked.

"Where? To hell? With Rodolpho?" Clemmy said with a mean chuckle.

"I'm sure he'd enjoy the company, honey," I said, laying the molasses on thick, "but I was *referrin'* to little Oscar's big night. Are we going, and if so, are we going together?"

*"I'm* going. Not sure with who. Definitely not with you."

"Okay," I said, not really that surprised. A date with an Oscar nominee, even for Best Original Screenplay, could be a big treat for some lucky nobody. Clemmy will be able to parlay it into some extremely dirty business, two or six hundred times, between now and April.

Let's see, who can I get to go with *me* to the Oscars? Who, among the possibles, would really get Clemmy's goat? Must be more famous, more powerful, richer, cuter. Must be bigger, too. Clemmy *hates* being towered over. Difficult. Clemmy is pretty big. There's only one possibility. Did I do anything terrible to him recently? Don't remember, but that doesn't mean much. Is it the off-season? Yes, it is. Has spring training started? Maybe, but he won't be there. He never even bothers to pretend to go. So I pick up the phone and call the proud possessor of my maidenhead, Billyjim "The Twister" Thibideaux, in Biloxi, Mississippi.

How did a marginally cultured degenerate type like me ever get mixed up with a genu-wine American hero, you're probably asking yourself right now. With America at his mercy, why would Billyjim Thibideaux, two-time All-American, Heisman Trophy winner, Super Bowl MVP, and the NFL's leading passer for three years straight ever even bother with me? Simple. He's my cousin. Incest is so . . . all-*American*, don't you think? Billyjim and I think so. So dirty. So much *fun*. Billyjim thought so *long* before it occurred to *me*, seeing as how he's five years older. All those summers we spent in Biloxi, while Billyjim was bouncing me on his knee, tilting back rocking chairs to look up my dress, slapping me playfully on the butt, walking in on me in the bathroom accidentally on purpose, and trying to get me to play doctor in the garage, he was thinking about it.

By the time we actually did it, I was already fifteen. Old enough, in Mississippi. Wouldn't wanna let her rot on the vine. And if Billyjim hadn't gotten me that summer, somebody else might've. My first true love Sam Allen had been trying for over a year, with some minor successes chalked up despite my terrified resistance, but my mother thought he was much farther along, so in order to save me from sex with Sam, which would have led to pregnancy, shotgun marriage, rats and roaches and dead dreams, the works, my mother bit the bullet for the first time ever and called my father for help. Could I come to him in West Palm Beach for the summer? I thought this was a *wonderful* idea. Daddy declined with regrets. New wife to break in. Full social calendar. He didn't think I'd fit *in*. So Momma packed me off to Mississippi, where I would be *safe*. Poor Mom. She never imagined her favorite nephew could be such a *skunk*.

"Take off them red pants, Texas," he said one night on the beach. It didn't occur to me to say no. Cousins marry. It happens all the time, doesn't it? It does in *English history*. It's not like doing it with your *brother*. See where this is leading? It never crossed my mind that we wouldn't get married. I assumed we would. We'd done *it*. IT! That Billyjim had done It with half the women in the states that field teams in the Southeast Conference was a fact he prudently withheld from me.

I was too ecstatic at nabbing Billyjim to cross-examine him about all those nights he was gone, to ferret out the truth like a smarter girl would've. I was too full of *myself* to notice *him*. Saving myself for the right man had worked, actually worked! I couldn't get over it. My mother was right. Holding out against Sam's onslaughts had paid off. No need to go off to college *now*. I would have success and respectability the *right* way, the female way, without the unseemly displays of ambition I was prone to. I would have it all the *American* way, through a *man*. I would become one of those football wives you see on TV watching their husbands, every tear, fear, and cheer on display for the world. That would be *me* one fine

day not too long from now, I thought, hair teased high, lips
painted red, eyebrows plucked into perpetually aston-
ished crescents, on *television.* Mr. and Mrs. Billyjim "The
Twister" Thibideaux. Anna Kate and Billyjim "The
Twister" Thibideaux. I would pop out lots of little Bil-
lyjims, enough for a whole offensive line, and everything
would be okeydoke. I would do *my husband* proud. Oh
yes I would. I would yell louder than those other wives.
After all, I had experience. In junior high school, I was a
*cheerleader.*

"You? You were a cheerleader? I don't believe it!" some
Doubting Thomas said one night in the Bar Car, a very
unwise move.

"Wanna bet?" I said sweetly. I named an outrageous
sum, the loudmouthed fool in question extended his hand,
and I proceeded to get up and do a team-spirited version
of "The Hello Cheer," the one you do to welcome the
visitors, when you're the home. *"Hello, Tigers, we're here
to say / Hello to you in a special way! / We're startin' out
with this welcoming cheer / Just to let you all know we're
glad you're here! / H-E-L-L . . . O! Hello!"* The Bar Car
aisle wasn't really wide enough for a good jump, the kind
where you touch your foot to your elbow, which was lucky
for me since I'm not in the shape I was *once,* but anyway
I won my bet. Another idiot once bet me I couldn't hook
both ankles around my neck at the same time, but I won
that one too. All that sex is good for *something.* There I
was, *sitting on a bar stool. . . .* I remembered that part a
second after I got my limber limbs in place, held out both
hands—*ta da!*—then toppled over like a Joe Palooka doll.

I expected to marry Billyjim. Was I counting my chick-
ens? I was counting my *bridesmaids.* I'd have to have
Brandywine and the cousins. Couldn't avoid *that.* But if
I had twelve, that left eight spots to fill. What a great
chance to reward loyalty, to settle old scores! I made lists

of all the girls I knew in my notebook, ranked and re-
ranked them endlessly, then crossed them off one by one.
Teresa Skelly, my best friend, definitely, though that
would be a problem, because Teresa's family was poor,
even poorer than *we* were. She wouldn't be able to buy
the dress. Boy, oh, boy, I thought, what a dummy! No need
to worry about money ever again. Billyjim would be
drafted by the pros. We would be rich, *rich,* RICH! *We*
could buy Teresa's dress. Already I was spending Billyjim's money. Spending men's money comes naturally,
for some reason. Lucky, *lucky.* Problem solved, move on.
Debby Francis? No way! Remember that time in seventh
grade, Debby, when you didn't invite me to your birthday
party because I'd stolen your boyfriend Roger Early, the
JV quarterback? Remember what I did? I had *my own*
party. All the *boys* came to *mine.* On to costume design.
Let's see . . . the ribbons on the bridesmaids' dresses would
be pink, yellow, blue, or green. And these would match
*the best men's carnations!* How I Spent My Summer Vacation: planning my wedding and learning how to fuck.

   After I went back to Texas to start tenth grade, Billyjim
and I wrote. I wrote twenty-page letters; he wrote post-
cards, with pictures of motels on them. Motels with swimming pools. I found this glamorous. That was how *we*
would live when we got married. We would stay at Holi-
day Inns and Travel Lodges *all over the country.* It went
on like this for months, but nobody in the family was
seriously worried. They didn't imagine things had gone
that far.

   "Puppy love," my mother said serenely. Better than
doing It with a boy my own age. If she'd known I'd done
It with Billyjim, he wouldn't've been long for this world.
Every night I slept in one of Billyjim's jerseys. I wrote his
name on my textbook covers and dropped it whenever I
could. My popularity soared, though all the boys were

afraid to date me. No matter. I wouldn't have *lowered* myself.

The climax of my little life thus far came when Ole Miss played Texas in the Cotton Bowl that December. Aunt Joan, Uncle Melvin, and cousins Adele, Ora Mae, and Evelyn came to stay at our house. We drove to Dallas. It was freezing cold. The adults sipped rum toddies from a thermos. I couldn't see Billyjim the night before the game; his coach wouldn't let him go out, or so he *said*. But right before the kickoff, I kissed him for luck. Ole Miss lost, Uncle Melvin got so drunk we had to stop on the turnpike for him to throw up, but that night I was on the *Texas News*. The *Texas News!* Everyone gathered around to watch, not expecting to see anyone but Billyjim, losing ignominiously, and then there was me, kissing him.

"It's Katherine Anne! Look!"

"Why, honey, you're on *television*."

"Don't she look *cute?*"

"I think she looks *fat*." This would be Brandy, jealous enough to cut my throat with her fingernails. Poor Brandy. She had gone to Kilgore Junior College to be a Rangerette, so *she* could be the one on television, then found herself an inch too short for the squad. Behind my mother's chair, I stuck my tongue out at Brandy. I could afford to. I was famous! This was an omen of things to come, though none of us knew it at the time. All our lives, Brandy would do everything right and I would do everything wrong, but who would get *famous?* Who would be on *television?*

Except for my mother, who always expected the best, everybody in my family expected the worst for yours truly. I'd die in a cheap motel room with a needle in my veins and a red neon sign clicking on and off over my syphilitic body saying Dew Drop Inn, or get carved like a turkey by one of my boyfriends—the number is thought to be infinite—driven berserk, poor slob, by my obstinacy, promiscuity, and nose-in-the-air high-class bitchiness. *"Jesus, judge, I had to do it, she was stubborn as a gol- durned mule."* "That's all right, son. I get your drift. Thirty dollars or thirty days." I should have at least picked up some incurable disease, like Saigon Rose or herpes, or had bastards of my own—*like mother, like daughter*—or numerous messy abortions.

But I had none of the above. Despite doing everything wrong, doing it far too soon—drugs, sex, politics, like a premature antifascist, always in the vanguard—there was no retribution, no witch hunt. Not for me. No day of reckoning before that big committee in the sky. I got away clean. I got away with everything. I got away from Texas with a big scholarship and went to one of those fancy schools I saw on *The G.E. College Bowl*. But when I got there I found out the team captain was a junkie, dead before I even got to meet him. Is it any wonder I'm fucked up? You say that's no *excuse?* With Texas safely in the rearview mirror, I got taken up by a series of rich boys who tried to teach me how to behave and a series of professors who tried to teach me how to think. They groomed my brain like a bunch of gorillas. During one of these romances, I got scholarshipped to film school.

"Film school? What years? I don't remember you from film school," some studio hack or indie praiser is always saying suspiciously.

"That's because I was in the wrong department, in *the- ory,"* I chirp. Some people find my lack of foresight *en- dearing.*

Poor Brandy does everything right, but to no avail. The phone rings. It's some friend or cousin, the TV's turned on, and there's Katherine Anne, *Anna Kate,* again, on David Brenner this time. Don't she look cute? my mother says. *I think she looks fat.* Brandy's had my tombstone

ready for years. It says, KATHERINE ANNE PORTER
O'SHEA, SPINSTER, GETS HER COMEUPPANCE.

It is worth noting that another member of my family
also appeared on television. "I'm in show bid'ness too,
just like Anna Kate!" my brother Tommy allegedly said
when he called Brandy from California one summer. He
hitchhiked out there between high school and the army
and got picked for *The Dating Game* as Bachelor Number
Two. Despite being cutest, Tommy lost. He blames his
accent.

Billyjim got married the next summer to somebody
else, a Virginian with skin like gardenias, a rich daddy,
and a way of twisting men around her little finger that I
didn't have yet and never would have to such an *extent*.
Instead of hating her the way I'd planned to, I fell in love
with her. I wanted to *be* her. That Billyjim would prefer
Carmella to me was something I never questioned. She
took to me, too. We drank cherry cokes together, went
shopping for clothes. She treated me like a kid sister,
never once mentioned my affair with Billyjim.

Then something strange happened. It started at a fra-
ternity party a week before the wedding. I was rummag-
ing around in this guy's record collection and at the back
of the stack found an album I'd never heard of, by Pete
Seeger. I put it on. The first song on Side One was "We
Shall Overcome." Pretty song, right? In *Mississippi?* In
*1968?* Our host ran over and started screaming. He was
the one who'd really fucked up, of course. It was *his record.* He should have hid it better. Instead, he tried to pin
its very existence on *me.* Carmella picked up on this little
ploy right away.

"She didn't know what it was! Why blame it on her?"
Carmella said, putting her arm around me. "She's just a
kid."

When our host unwisely went on with his tirade, Carmella called him a nigger-lover. His face went white, but he didn't say anything. He *couldn't.* Why else would he have a record by that *outside agitator,* Pete Seeger, if he wasn't a nigger-lover? People got up, put on jackets, slunk out. I wanted to tell the guy whose life I'd probably ruined the awful truth: that I was a nigger-lover too. Already I'd gotten fired from one job, checking groceries at the Piggly Wiggly, for letting my friend Calvin Washington, a slight, bespectacled, homosexual Negro, take me home. The next day, the manager, E. O. "Bud" McAfee, marched me into his office and fired me. Even if I hadn't done anything *wrong*—he wasn't saying I *had,* he knew I was a *nice girl;* what was wrong was letting them into the schools in the first place where they could meet nice girls like me— Piggly Wiggly employees, trusted public servants, people who handled *food,* had to avoid even the *appearance* of wrongdoing. Of nigger-loving.

Then Mr. McAfee told me about this time he was at Fort Bragg, getting ready to go to Korea, and there was this big nigger in his platoon and one day they were running an obstacle course, and part of it involved slithering, on your back, under a barbed-wire fence, and that night back in the barracks, the nigger was on his bunk crying. *What was wrong with him? I'll tell you what was wrong, girlie. His thing was so big he couldn't get it under the barbed wire without tearing it all to shit, but he went on under anyway. He was that dumb! He let us look at it finally, to see how bad hurt he was, and honey . . . it was* AS BIG AS A NEWBORN BABY!

Mr. McAfee stopped and took a deep breath. Do you know what a thing like that would do to a *white girl?* he said. But Mr. McAfee, I wanted to say, Calvin's is only three inches long, I saw it at Possum Kingdom, and anyway he doesn't want to put it in *me,* but I didn't say anything then or in Mississippi either. The National

Guard was quartered a few hundred miles away, true, but not close enough to prevent a lynching. And if anybody had had the slightest inkling of what a nigger-lover I would one day become, of how frequently and with what enthusiasm I would love niggers, even Billyjim himself couldn't have saved me. *Au contraire.* He would've been right along with 'em, stringing me up.

Carmella took me and a fifth of Wild Turkey outside. We all got in Billyjim's shiny new Corvette, a gift from a grateful alumni association, with his nickname, Twister, on the plates.

"Let's drive to New Orleans," Carmella said, and I said sure, if I could *drive,* and pretty soon we were on the road doing ninety, a hundred, a hundred and ten, drinking Wild Turkey from the bottle, laughing our asses off. I remember being at the wheel, and Carmella's hand on the back of my neck. I remember how good her hand felt, how *gentle,* while Carmella talked to me about men, gave me all this good advice about them. She told me that a good-looking woman could get anything she wanted from a man, as long as she didn't let her *thing* do her *thinking.*

"You let him do it to you, didn't you, Katherine Anne?" I nodded, ashamed. "I thought so. That was a mistake. You should've *held out.*"

Carmella raised her left hand, fluttered her fingers, and grinned. Her diamond glittered green from the dashboard lights. So *that's* why Billyjim was marrying Carmella, I thought before I blacked out. She was the only girl in America he couldn't fuck.

When I woke up I was in my bed at Aunt Joan's, fully dressed. I stood up and fell over. Thus began my very first hangover. Not an auspicious occasion. Hello, hangover! H-E-L-L . . . o! If I'd known then what I know now, about how many times we were going to meet and in what *circumstances,* I wouldn't have bothered getting up at all.

When I finally crawled to the bathroom and took off my clothes, I discovered my bra was on inside out. This was my first, most spectacular blackout. Will anyone who knows what happened to Anna Kate O'Shea on the night of August 7, 1968, please call this toll-free number?

I never saw Carmella alone again. A week later she and Billyjim got married. Three years later, they got divorced. Billyjim's been married twice. Never to me. By the time he finally came around to wanting me, I was already famous and didn't want *him.* I was too proud, which is probably too bad. We're a lot alike. Billyjim isn't humble, like a hero ought to be. I saw him one day on television, being interviewed by Howard Cosell. Howard was needling him about this interception, trying to get him to justify it. To *explain* himself. As if Billyjim "The Twister" Thibideaux had to explain anything! To anybody!

"Yeah, I threw it. So what?" my cousin said finally. He got out a pack of Luckies, lit up. Then he blew smoke in Howard Cosell's face, endearing himself to me permanently, me and six million other thugs. We saw each other again for the first time in years, when Billyjim caught my act on *Johnny Carson.* (This was when they thought Clemmy and I were the new David and Leslie Newman. But *no more.* We've been *found out.*) My cousin saw me on the tube and came out to the Coast to look me up. We hit it off immediately. Our clothes were off in less than ten minutes. If we hadn't been at Spago, our time would've been halved, but there's always a line there for the bathrooms.

Back at Clemmy's house, Clemmy being conveniently out of town, Billyjim fed me Percodans like I was a cute blond squirrel. We stayed in bed for days. I took him to parties and introduced him to movie stars, most of whom he fucked and one of whom, an Alabama girl, feisty, he married, then divorced. Whenever I go to a film festival and Billyjim's free, he likes to come along and hang out. He loves the way movie people talk. He says it's like going to a foreign country. He loves me a little bit too, I think.

"Hi, Texas," Billyjim says when he hears me drawl his name. Will he be my date on Oscar night? "Why, cousin, I'd be tickled pink."

I hang up the phone triumphantly. This is gonna fix Clemmy's wagon, but good.

IT's a cinch no one's gonna throw me a party to celebrate the good luck I most assuredly don't deserve, so I decide with the recklessness that's become my trademark not to just slink out of town like a whipped pup but to go with a bang instead: to have my own party before the impending L.A. junket, which I'm already dreading. I invite all the people I've been avoiding these past months, too embarrassed to admit to friends, let alone enemies, even one more romantic failure.

The party comes off well. I drink just enough to be witty and sparkling, not enough to be sloppy, unconscious, or mean. I manage to hit that spot where liquor makes you prettier before it makes you ugly, like Jean Rhys said on *her* way down. I tell a few friends I'm not seeing Walter anymore, in a lame attempt to justify the bad behavior that's made the predictable rounds, and my girlfriends, who are fiercely if not deeply loyal, tell me I'm better off without him, that Walter was too boring, too *straight,* without realizing how much that word dates us, how the ultimate Sixties insult has lost its meaning.

"What would you do with him if you got him?" my girlfriends snort derisively.

"Oh, maybe have him stuffed, like Roy did Trigger."

"You'd be bored to death in six months."

The truth is, they don't know I'm hurting. They have no way of distinguishing Walter from the sleazeballs that preceded him, and I have no way of explaining without sounding like a jerk.

But this is different! I could say, imagining their skeptical looks, the giggles that would threaten to sally forth.

It's hard, these days, to be girlfriends. We loathe each other's boyfriends, perceptive for others if not for ourselves. Though we try to look on the bright side for the hapless girlfriend's sake, this optimism vanishes the second the fool in question is out of sight. We dissect each other's men, clamp them down on cheap glass slides, stain them Venetian blue, examine them. We lampoon and type, categorizing by age, class, color, and handicaps, physical and mental. We do entire routines, killingly funny, on their predictable peccadilloes. We trade these dogs like baseball cards, when we can remember who they are.

"How's Harold?" I might ask my girlfriend LaDonna.

"I don't know. I'm seeing Beauregard Cutter now. But I ran into Harold at Tower Records. Harold really likes you, Anna Kate. He said to tell you hi."

It's hard to keep the men straight, they come and go so fast. Often they overlap us, moving from woman to woman in a social group until we are all gone through, snapping at each other in chaos and confusion. They use our cynicism against us, disarm us with passion so complete that we are veritably struck down.

"Carolyn's a wonderful girl, but *you* . . . oh, angel!" some worthless slob is bound to say before lunging at you across the couch, while Carolyn is in the kitchen whipping up his ten-course birthday dinner. Of course, you can never tell this to Carolyn. Carolyn would never believe you, and if she did, *you'd* get the blame. *You must've done something to . . .* provoke *him. You know how you are.* Uh-huh. So does *he:* so quick to say "I love you," to just toss it off. Their lies are so extravagant, so elaborate, so unlikely, that they *must* be real. Right? *Right?*

I'll buy you a co-op in Manhattan. *At Christmas, we'll go to Jamaica/Guadeloupe/Casablanca.* I'm taking you to Nantucket, to meet my grandmother. *I'll be there on Friday.* I'll see you at the Odeon at twelve o'clock, and there better not be another man there. *I'll be there in December for sure, I promise.* I'll make it up to you, if not this weekend, then shortly. *I think you'd be perfect to direct my movie.* I've never loved anyone the way I love you. *You should be in front of the cameras, not behind them.* You're the only woman I've ever even considered marrying. *I'm living with someone, but I don't love her.* We're breaking up. *I have to stay with her tonight. It's business, baby, business.* I didn't want to hurt you. That's why I lied. *I'll never leave you.* I'll always love you. *What do you think I'm going to do? Make a speech and walk out the door?*

Our little hearts flutter proudly, while the bullshit drips like wax down a candle. That's why I trusted Walter. His values were so *different.* I never found out, after a half hour's idle chatter, that he'd slept with the second cousin of my forty-sixth boyfriend. I never heard, in reference to Walter, the dreaded remark, "Uh-huh. He said the very same thing to me. In exactly those words." So who *can* you trust, if not Walter Light? The answer lumbers toward me like an ax murderer: nobody, nobody, nobody. There are a lot of nobodies at my party tonight. Nobodies disguised as somebodies.

In the bathroom, I rashly tell two or thirty people about what happened to Lily and why I have been lying low. The story spreads like crabs in a commune. Why I told it

I don't know. It's a new piece for the mosaic of my horrible reputation. My killer metaphor, literalized at last. It increases my glamour, this brush with somebody else's death. The men cluster round like flies to rotten meat. One of them's brought a bottle of my favorite champagne. I don't want to share *that*. I take his arm and steer him into a corner.

"So what are you doing in New York?" I say conversationally to this one-picture director, expecting to hear some boring business story, to nod politely after the bottle is finished and move on like a good little hostess, but he looks at me kind of shyly and clears his throat and launches into this tale about how he's flown here just to see me and wanted to tell me, before he left the country, exactly how much he admired me. How I am the girl of his dreams. Uh-oh. Another flaky loser. The whole thing is so farfetched I don't even bother to be polite. We met at a party a year ago, and talked for at least three minutes. I can't even remember his name.

"Can you believe this guy?" I say to my friends in front of him, telling his story and jeering. But Eben van der Post—he's had to tell me his name about five times—just stands there like a little soldier, taking it.

It's not me he's fallen in love with, of course, though if I were fat and ugly he might have had difficulties. He's fallen in love with my work. The body attached to the work is incidental, not to mention the so-called soul. And this is a very creepy feeling. When Eben looks at me, his pale blue eyes make me nervous. I can't stomach adoration. I like to be kicked around, if the truth be known. To be taken down a peg or three. Before Walter my head was as big as a goddamn basketball, in serious need of deflating. Lately it's been dribbled far too much, true. Maybe that's why I feel this tingle of warmth, this little bit of response to Eben what's-his-name.

" 'One should never meet a person one admires,' " I tell
him gravely, quoting Toulouse-Lautrec in *Moulin Rouge,*
which I saw one day when I was catatonic and absorbed
like a Bounty brand towel. " 'What they do is always so
much better than what they are.' "

Eben manages to keep a straight face at this pretentious
malarkey for about as long as I do, and after we laugh
together I start to like him even more. After all, he's able
to take all the kidding I bombard him with, to take the
consequences, in public, of his impulsive romantic act,
and I'm a sucker for gestures like this. I like his bravado
though I can't take it seriously, could not ever take seriously someone so easy to obtain. He just stands there
while I eviscerate him. Is this strength or weakness? You
don't know *either?* With his long ash-blond hair, his California tan, and Hawaiian shirt, he stands out like a prince
among the spiky-haired New Yorkers. Eben looks healthy,
like someone who doesn't spend his days collecting bed-
sores. Like a Golden Delicious apple, ready to be gobbled
up. We, to tell the truth, look strung out and maggoty. A
little bit wormy. Used up. Men like Eben don't throw
themselves at me every day. I start to think maybe my
luck is changing, changing back to the way it was before
I met Walter. That Walter Light was just a fluke.

I go out on the roof about midnight, with Eben and
some other party animals. Eben puts his arm around my
waist. I watch the Maxwell House sign blink on and off:
GOOD TO THE LAST DROP. Ummmm, *I'll* say. I want to
perform an unnatural act right away, but it wouldn't be
proper for the hostess with the mostes'. I never fuck at
parties, and if I do I never come. Eben takes me into the
shadows and kisses me sweetly, then pulls out the ubiqui-
tous vial.

"It's not coke," Eben says, after I've already taken two
big hits.

"Oh?" I say, immediately paranoid. "What is it, smack? I'm not wild about spending my evening throwing up."

"It's Ecstasy." Eben takes the bottle and does a few spoonfuls. "MDMA."

"Oh, Ecstasy," I toss off breezily. Ecstasy and me. "Am I gonna see God?" Eben laughs. What a laugh the guy's got, pure Daisy Buchanan. Full of money, just like Scotty said.

"I hope not. It's very mild." Eben squeezes my hand, looks into my eyes, kisses me again. Beam me up, Scotty! "I'll be with you all the time," Eben says, then hands me the bottle. I do two more big snorts, to show him I'm not afraid, then pocket the vial, but I don't like it when people give me strange drugs. Did Eben give me the Ecstasy so I'd *have* to be with him? So I wouldn't have a choice? His hand, on my waist, doesn't feel as good as it used to. When he nuzzles my neck, I don't respond at all. Bad move, Eben. And so unnecessary. I don't leave Eben right away, but I already know I'm going to.

Let's see, what are my other options? I've already explored, *exhausted,* most of the possibilities. In fact, there's a whole slew of my old boyfriends here tonight. I always invite as many as I can. There's Jerry Marx, who I met in Washington when I was plugging *Oil and Water,* a funny, handsome Brit, brimming with positive energy. But I made kind of a faux pas with Jerry earlier this evening. He said, "Hi! Remember me?" I said, "Sure. You used to work for Ralph Nader." And he said, "I *still* work for Ralph Nader." Whoops! Probably still spells America with three Ks. There's Clemmy, of course. Can't risk Clemmy. Nigel Featherbone's here with his wife, Odile, but he still isn't speaking to me after that scene I made at the Bar Car. In fact quite a lot of people aren't speaking to me these days, though they don't have any trouble guzzling my liquor.

They aren't forgiving me in the morning, the way they used to.

Is there anyone here, besides Eben, who doesn't *know* me? There's a pretentious but not unattractive German cinematographer, Stefan Ratt, who came with my agent, Emma Gomez. He might be a possibility. But *noooo.* Emma seems to be in love with him. Poor Emma. Her starry eyes depress me. One look and I peg him for a crumb. But Stefan is witty, there's no denying that. Wickedly, compulsively witty. He tells us snide stories about the German filmmakers, trying to build us up by tearing them down and planting himself firmly in our camp. We know he'll go back to Germany and tell similar stories about *us,* in order to ingratiate himself with his fellow Huns, so we laugh at his stories but don't tell him any back. We don't give him our cards or ask for his. So each anecdote gets a little more desperate and cruel and pointed, like Stefan Ratt's little chinny chin chin, as he fishes for an exchange of intimacies, for a response that's committal.

All of us are admiring the skyline when Stefan starts to talk about a film that he probably didn't really work on by Wim Wenders, whom he probably doesn't really know: the one where the woman blows out the lights on the Empire State Building like they were candles on a birthday cake. The Ecstasy's coming on, I'm feeling cool and invincible, so I toss my head and lean over the edge of the building very theatrically and blow for all I'm worth. Two seconds later, the lights on the Empire State Building go out, which doesn't surprise me at all.

Eben is looking at me open-mouthed: *What was in that bottle anyway?* Herr Ratt practically comes on the spot. I tell him to make sure to tell his buddy Wim about this little scene the next time he sees him. I remember Wenders slighting me one night at a bar in Munich. Maybe he was tired or shy, but there's some sense of tit for tat.

"Tell him you don't need to direct to work magic," I say, since I've never been allowed to, but the reminder is unnecessary. Stefan Ratt will eat schnitzel on this story for weeks.

Emma takes my arm and looks at me wistfully.

"You're worth ten of that little shit, Emma," I whisper as we go inside. But Emma doesn't really hear me. She's a little older than I am, shorter and fatter. She's thinking about what it was like when she could do magic in public. Wondering whether she'll ever be able to again. She's maybe thinking of going back to the health club, or buying an ounce of coke and snorting away twenty pounds, then going to that doctor in Buenos Aires to get everything tightened up. How much does a total tune-up go for these days? Maybe when she sees what a prick Stefan is, he won't be able to hurt her, I think, so I let him imagine there is some chance with me. But this is just an excuse. I love playing these games with men like Stefan. I'm so *good* at them. I always *win.* I like putting Stefan Ratt where he belongs, under my thumb. He can keep Eben what's-his-face company.

Stefan wants to show me East Berlin, but I have already been there, and stifle a theatrical yawn. Eben wants to take me to the Harvard–Yale game. The gold drips off him, the easy upper-class assurance, as he offers this treat to the plucky working girl, the pizza parlor waitress from New Haven who scooped up Warren Beatty while Natalie Wood was in the loony bin. I'm sure he's splendid in the grass, but I have already been there too, with Clemmy. With Mr. Goodbloode and his fellow merchant princes. What a fucking bore.

"There's nothing you can tell me about rich boys I don't already know," I say, smiling sweetly. I've already learned, from several sources, that Eben is a toilet-seat heir from Grosse Pointe. "Have you ever been to Havana?" I ask seriously. "They really *need* toilet seats there."

Pretty Eben is a little confused. He doesn't understand what he's done wrong. Ecstasy is the love drug, right? Why aren't I acting more loving? Toward *him?* Poor Eben. I decide we need some kind of auto-da-fé, scrape together the dregs of the party, and organize a trip to Hellfire.

The Hellfire Club is a short walk from my loft and would undoubtedly be my local bar if it weren't so hard to find. I always get lost when I try to go there, which can be damaging to your reputation when a bunch of the usual suspects are following you meekly through the meat district, spiking bloody wax paper and ruining their shoes. These particular suspects—Eben, Emma Gomez, and Stefan Ratt—are starting to get a little cross, in fact, are starting to wonder how cool I really am. Have I really been to this notorious dive as claimed, or did I read about it in *New York* magazine?

I'm about to start making the excuses that will fail to save my face when I see a couple of local yokels who just might be heading to Hellfire themselves. What is it about them that makes me think this? Could it be the black leather that covers them both from head to foot, the bullwhips dangling from their chain link belts? What about those boots with the cleated soles? Maybe it's that they're both six feet tall, weigh in at two twenty, have bald heads, and are women. In any case we give them plenty of room when they pass us going the opposite direction, then exchange complicitous looks, turn around, follow them half a block to an unmarked doorway, and go in.

The gentleman inside the mesh cage at the entrance

takes twenty-five dollars each from outraged Stefan and blasé Eben, who pays with a hundred and leaves his wallet open just long enough for me to get a good look at its brothers and sisters. My, what a large family, must be Catholic dollars. I start thinking about getting Eben to stay in New York an extra day or two, so he'll have a chance to visit Harry Winston. Mustn't miss *that*. Poor Harry would be heartbroken. The cashier gives Emma and me the once-over while we try to look stern and forbidding without cracking up, then stamps our hands and waves us in casually.

"Chicks free," he says.

There's smoke billowing out from under the doorway he points to, bright red smoke that's pulsing in an unreal fashion. Too much Ecstasy, I think, hardening my heart to Eben even as visions of diamond earrings dance in my head. Then the door opens from the inside without any visible human intervention, I see the room really *is* filled with pulsing red light and smoke, and in we go, clutching each other's hands like Our Gang at the dentist's.

A few steps inside, and this place doesn't look so bad. Nothing to worry about. Just your everyday hellhole. The pair we followed are lollygagging at the bar, having frozen margaritas and a chat. I take orders from everyone and sashay over. Nothing to be scared of *here*. I smile at one of the women, who smiles back in a perfectly friendly, nonthreatening way, despite an absence of eyebrows. What an overrated joke this place is. Guess what? I read about it in *New York* magazine.

I pay the bartender an outrageous sum for the no doubt hideous house brands that are all he has on hand, but when I try to pocket the change, I forget how tight my jeans are, like hot-dog skin, and manage to drop most of the money on the floor. Now, normally I wouldn't bother

to bob for quarters on a barroom floor crawling with filth,
but these drinks were so expensive and promise to be so
*bad* that I don't want Hellfire to have even a penny more
of my money and peer down into the vile red smoke.

Oh, shit. *Ooooh,* shit. I've never actually seen filth
crawl, have you? There's a man down there. He's wearing
a dog collar, *très* unchic, and licking the boots of the
woman on my right, who's gabbing away with her girlfriend about getting elected to her co-op board just like
nothing untoward was happening. Just like some pathetic
creep in a dog collar wasn't slobbering on her boots.

"Do the soles too," she says casually. Must have read
Diana Vreeland. Only nouveaus fail to do the soles too.
Oh, no. He's doing the *soles* too. The woman notices me
staring at her canine companion and smiles her charming
smile again. "Lose something?" she asks. I manage to nod,
my mouth wide open. The woman spies my forgotten
change, then kicks dogboy in the face affectionately.
"God, what a boor you are, Simon!"

Simon looks up from his shoofly pie, face caked with city
grime and God only knows what else, but he's too drunk
with pleasure to fetch. "Give the nice lady her *money!*"
the woman commands, kicking him again. Simon moans
deliriously. This could go on all night! Dogboy finally lo-
cates the change and offers it up, panting obsequiously.
Down, boy! I take the quarters out of his hand delicately,
trying not to touch his unclean flesh, and nod my thanks
to his owner.

"It's so *hard* to get good slaves these days," she says, and
goes back to her conversation. I scoop up the drinks and
scamper off. Things don't get much worse than this, but
they don't get a whole lot better either. We down our
drinks in record time, like camels at an oasis. When I trot
back to the bar for more, Fido has finished his mistress's
boots, and is giving the spit-shine treatment to her girl-

friend. The conversation now is about g.f.'s new Filofax and what a difference it's made in her life. I refrain from joining in, though I have an important insight to contribute: *If you can't remember it, it isn't worth doing,* which is a variation on another perverted proverb invented by me, *If you don't remember it, it didn't happen.* What? You don't agree? You say everything counts, every bit of it? Ho hum. I could sit down for a real yakfest with these two, but sitting down might inspire dogboy to love me up with his tongue, and *my* boots are suede. Better not. Best skedaddle back to my merry band of pilgrims with armloads of double Scotches, which disappear more or less immediately. Then Emma grabs my hand and drags me to the bathroom.

There's a line, of course. All New York City bathrooms have lines. You might stand in them but we stand *on* them, a much more powerful concept, don't you think? Like pinning down a rattler in Tony Lamas. A well-dressed man is sitting outside the ladies' in what looks like a tenth-grader's desk. Does it cost money to *pee* here? That would be a new twist. But *noooo.* We find out his mission when we near the door.

"As long as you're going to relieve yourselves anyway, why don't you give me a little relief too, girlies, and do it on me?" he says in the self-confident voice of a door-to-door Bible salesman. When we decline to buy, *contribute,* he gets surly. "Why not? What does it matter to *you* where it goes?"

A big black woman on line behind us takes him up on his offer and they go off arm-in-arm to the back of the bar, where all manner of atrocities are said to take place. When he picks up the desk, I see it's got this hole in the seat, like a king-sized potty chair. Emma goes through the door ahead of me and comes out immediately, her face pea green.

"My God, I can't go in *there!*" she says, shuddering convincingly. "I've had it. I'm leaving."

"What about Stefan?" I ask, as if her answer really made a difference.

"Oh, you can have him if you want," Emma says, sounding like she really means it. "I don't feel particularly sexy, after this." But *I* do.

"Just as well," I say.

"Oh, I don't know. Stefan's not so bad," Emma says, this little smile creeping into her face. I really love Emma. "If you love her so much," a mutual friend once said coldly, "why do you keep stealing her boyfriends?" *Hmmmm.*

"Oh yes he is," I say. "He is too so bad."

"Oh, I don't know," Emma repeats, completing the groundwork for what's become our favorite routine. "He's not . . . THE BOYFRIEND WHO CAME FROM HELL!" I join her, screeching, for the punch line, which once fell from Emma's lips in an unpremeditated fashion, in reference to some long-gone crumb. We thought this line was so killingly funny and would be such a great title for *something* that one night, in the throes of a coke-induced delirium, we actually developed it into a treatment. See, it's about this television show, sorta like *Queen for a Day* except the way you win is to tell an atrocity-packed story about the world's most horrible boyfriend. Then this all-girl video crew goes out and *tapes* the boyfriends so the studio audience can judge for themselves, and . . . well, maybe you had to *be* there.

Nothing ever happened with *The Boyfriend,* but I wrote a spin-off using the futuristic television game show concept called *Where's My Line?* that, surprise, had a drug theme, and I'll tell you something even funnier. Not only did I write this little abortion, which took less than three grams to progress from offhand remark to finished treatment, but Emma sold it, too, *for more money than my mother makes in an entire year.* Who ever said life was supposed to be fair? It never got out of development, of course—this was just before Richard Pryor became national spokesman for the Ignited Negro College Fund—because eventually it crossed the path of someone at the hapless studio in question who *didn't do drugs.* And that's what *TV Guide* had in mind when they said "Cocaine Is Ruining Our Movies," in case you were too cheap to pop for the sixty cents.

"Get some work done," Emma advises at the exit, thinking of her ten percent, true, but of me, too. I crumple up her good advice and toss it in my mental wastebasket, then go to find Stefan, who's now legally mine, transfer of title completed, poor sap, and Eben too. Neither of them ask where Emma is. They don't seem to notice she's gone. They are deep in some boring business conversation as befits their gender when I propose a tour through the back room, to liven things up. I step between them and take both their arms. Hmmm, *this* feels good. I like the sandwich effect. It always makes me feel nice and powerless, being between two men. Maybe I should come to Hellfire more often, everyone's getting so loose and chummy, what with all the visual stimulation. Taking them both home would eliminate the boring choice part. I look up at Eben, who smiles back in perfect understanding. He's been thinking about it too, I bet. They do anything, any time, anywhere, in California. *Some* people do. Gee, I'm homesick.

One glance at Stefan Ratt, though, shatters my nice little sex fantasy. The closer we get to the back room, the more Stefan looks like Jimmy Cagney in that gangster flick being dragged in for execution. Cagney was just pretending to be afraid, of course, on account of Father Pat O'Brien convinced him to save some other poor boy from a life of crime, but Stefan isn't faking, he's q-q-q-quaking, hanging on for dear life, hoping the governor's gonna give him a reprieve, but the phone in this joint's out of order, permanent-like. Say your prayers, Jimbo. In we go.

My, it certainly is dark in here. And what's that smell? Not very nice. Yuck, it's dripping down from the ceiling. You don't have to be the brightest light on the porch to figure out what goes on up *there.* Wish I'd brought my umbrella. They should sell them at the door. Have to drop that one in the suggestion box, ask for points. Oops! Poor Stefan, he forgot to duck. A big fetid drop just landed on his bald spot.

Oh, look, you guys, at all the exhibits! Just like the dioramas at the Museum of Natural History. They look so . . . *lifelike.* I could almost swear that one moved. Gosh, there's one right out of my own little dirty mind! How did they know I was thinking about *that?* Looks like *she's* having fun. Not too cute, though, any of them. Nobody here's too cute but *us.*

What's that elderly gentleman doing? Taking off all his clothes? Not a pretty sight. Kinda puts you off your feed. What's he getting up on? It looks like the table in the gynecologist's office. That's right, gramps, your feet go in there, uh-huh. But it has the same kind of things for your wrists, these little buckles and straps. Somebody has to help him close the last one. He's sitting up straight, legs spread. Nothing's happening. Did somebody forget to throw a switch? What's he waiting for? Oh. That. Where's the exit? Are we going into another room?

"Those were just amateurs," Eben says. "Customers. These are the pros." How does Eben know all this? I wonder. He leads me, and I lead Stefan, over to a roped-off spotlighted area, where a woman in a leather Merry Widow and eight-inch platforms is whipping a naked man in stocks.

"Ow! Ow! Ow!" the idiot actually goes each time the

whip falls lackadaisically. The woman is vodka-fat, with
track marks behind her knees. The whip-ee is fat too, but
healthy looking, with rosy skin and a curly blond mop, like
one of the Fabulous Furry Freak Brothers. I look up at
Eben and roll my eyes to show him I'm not impressed,
then notice Stefan's gone this sickly blue color. He sits
down and puts his head between his knees.

"Don't they have clubs like this in Berlin, capital of
decadence?" I say nastily. Eben laughs, which he can
afford to do, seeing as how he's won point, game, set, and
match. Stefan sits there a minute, then stands up and
gives me a kiss, and a very nice kiss it is too. I give it an
eighty-five, Dick. One more sad longing look—nobody
does regret quite like the Germs—and Stefan says he'll
see me again, in Cannes perhaps, and disappears into
smoke.

I know I shouldn't have been so offended at the proprietary way Eben put his arm around me, the confidence
with which he let his hand graze my ass. To the victor the
spoils and all that, and no one's more spoiled rotten than
me. You know what they say about bad apples, too. Maybe
I could recruit some local talent here to complete the
little triangle I had in mind. But *noooo.* One might catch
something . . . *catching.* I'm tired of always being in the
vanguard of everything, including new diseases. *Thwap!*
*Thwap! Thwap!* Point to ponder: Can you get AIDS from
dirty *whips?*

"Can't they do any better than that?" I say to Eben,
pointing at the so-called sadist, who's obviously not enjoy-
ing her work. "Fire the casting director, *I* say."

A tall black woman next to us catches my eye. She
winks—who do they think they're kiddin'?—then walks
suddenly, decisively up to the stocks, grabs the whip from
the fake *maîtresse,* who is too stoned to stop her, and
brings it down hard on the fat man's buttocks. She hits

him six times. The sound of it charges the ions in the air. Then she shrugs her shoulders, grins at me, throws down the whip, and walks out. Twenty men follow her, drooling all over themselves. By the time the soft blond man in the stocks turns his head in joy and anticipation, the woman is gone. His erection wilts as suddenly as it blossomed.

I take Eben's arm and press against it with my breast. But there's one more little exhibit to visit at Hellfire. Here it comes. Another diorama. A black man in a robe. A monk? No, a sorcerer. His robe has these little embroidered moons and stars on it, gold thread on purple satin, very classy. Very nicely done. But where's the sorcerer's apprentice? Over there on that slab, like a corpse at the morgue, waiting to be dissected? Uh-huh. That's her, all right. Now the sorcerer's putting on his hood, very Darth Vader. A real mistake, big guy. Ruins the whole effect. Now he's lighting a candle, a big black candle. The woman starts to moan. *What's he doing with that candle?*

"Get me out of here," I say to Eben, like Jezebel after the debacle of the red dress.

"Why? What's wrong?" His voice drips condescension.

"Just get me out of here," I say. As we move toward the exit, the woman starts to scream. A real scream this time, folks. The first real scream of the evening. Practically everyone in Hellfire leaps to their feet and rushes over. Eben pulls me through the crowd and outside into cold air. I lean against the building, crying helplessly. Three or four people pass and stare at us curiously, wondering whether to intervene, but when they see what club we're in front of, they figure I'm just spillover from the floor show and walk on by, happy to not be me. *Whatever it is, she probably deserves it.* No question about *that.*

"What was it about that scene that upset you so much?" Eben finally asks, when I'm more or less under control. Taunting me earlier would've been no fun at all. "You

watched the rest of it without batting an eye. What bothered you?"

"You know what bothered me."

"I want you to explain it. Explain why it bothers you
more to see a man torture a woman than it does to see a
woman torture a man."

"Who elected you to the thought police?" I ask, looking
at my feet. "I don't have to explain anything."

"Of course you don't have to. Don't you want to?" Eben
waits. I take a deep breath. I guess I do want to, after all.
I don't want him to think I'm so laughably inconsistent, so
transparent. Such a jerk.

"Okay. The man getting whipped could be a banker, or
a general, or the head of the New York Stock Exchange.
When he comes here, he's giving in to his weak side, the
side that never gets a chance to come out. Okay? He has
real power in the real world." Eben nods, actually interested. "But the woman—" I shudder, remembering the
hot wax burn her body.

"Go on," Eben says gently.

"When the woman comes here, she's acting an exten-
sion of her life. She has no power to start with, and she
doesn't even want what little she's got."

Eben smiles, walks over, and hugs me, which starts me
crying all over again. Why is he being so *nice?* "You're
really so smart," he says. I am? *That* was easy. "I knew
when I saw your work that you were smart, but then
when I met you I thought maybe it was all Goodbloode,
that you were just the girlfriend who got her name stuck
on everything." I nod. Lots of people think that. "Then I
met *him*—"

"Just like peas in a pod," I say. Eben shakes his head.

"I didn't know what to think then. Did you two hire
some chimpanzees to write all those scripts? Then tonight. All those games. Poor Stefan."

"He deserved it."

"Nobody *deserves* it. You're so smart. Why do you act so stupid?"

"I don't know," I admit. "If I knew maybe I could stop."

"Have you tried therapy?" Eben asks, in the smug tones of the already-analyzed. I shake my head. This is the kind of question I usually turn back with a vicious joke, but tonight for some reason I answer seriously.

"Clemmy and I went to couples therapy once. This guy was primaling in the next room, which made it kind of hard to *relax.* At the end the therapist said, 'I don't know if this relationship can or should'—emphasis on should—'be saved, but I want to see you both twice a week.' " I laugh a shaky laugh. This is one of my favorite stories. Clemmy tells it differently, though. I've heard him. He loves to tell it in front of his new girlfriends, to convince them we've gotten over each other, so much so that we can talk rationally about the past and all the rotten things I did to him. Not about the rotten things he did to *me.* Of *course* not. When Clemmy tells the story, he doesn't mention the primaling part, or the twice a week. He talks about how the therapist said it was okay to be jealous of my infidelities. He claims that hearing this freed him up so much we never went back. Clemmy actually *believes* this story. Hey, Goodbloode! Wanna buy a nice bridge?

"What happened then?" Eben asks.

"Clemmy fucked the therapist," I toss off with a giggle. Eben doesn't laugh.

"That's *terrible,*" he says. I shrug, uncomfortable with all this honesty. So this is what Ecstasy is. I don't find it all that . . . *ecstatic,* being so honest. Eben's face is so full of concern it embarrasses me.

"I told you you should never meet people you've admired from afar," I say miserably. "It's always such a let-down. Martin Short may want to meet Pat Sajak, but *I* don't. I don't want to be disappointed."

Eben kisses the top of my head and pulls me close. "You haven't disappointed me at all," he says. "You're terrific." I *am?*

"Do you want to come home with me?" I say, feeling a lot better all of a sudden.

"Not tonight," Eben says with a grin.

"If not tonight, then when?"

"In November, when I come to take you to the Harvard–Yale game."

"November! That's six *months!*"

"Waiting makes it better, Anna Kate. More special." I look at Eben skeptically. "Try it sometime and find out."

"I can wait if you can," I say, cross at being so callously deprived of him, now that I'm starting to like him so much. Maybe *he* could take Walter's place in my little hearty heart heart.

"I'm looking to the future," Eben says, kissing me again. His kisses are making me dizzy. "Didn't you ever read Daniel Moynihan?"

"Benign neglect," I manage to regurgitate from Intro Poli Sci. "Blame poverty on the poor." Maybe if I grab him *here* I can change his mind. Ummmm, that feels good. No problems in *this* department. All out for penises. Third floor!

"That's just part of it, you little knee-jerk leftist." Eben takes my hand away from his crotch and kisses it, then licks between my fingers. "You only remember what you *want* to remember."

"Everybody does that," I say.

"Just because everybody does it doesn't make it right."

Eben sounds just like my mother, poor chump. I wondered why he hadn't made another picture, after his first one was so good. Clear as a bell now: Eben's *honest.* A rare commodity in Hollywood, about as valuable as a house on the San Andreas fault.

"There's also something about present-oriented and future-oriented behavior," Eben is saying. "If I take you home and fuck you till the cows come home, in six months you won't even remember my name." Eben grabs my shoulders and pushes me against the wall, not gently. "What's my name, Anna Kate?"

"Huh? What?" I say, doing a pretty good imitation of Officer Clyde at his worst.

"What's my name?" Eben repeats. I consult the old mental Rolodex. *Category: men's names. Subhead: Dutch.* Something with a V. Vandiver, Van Gelder, Von Genkel. Something with cereal?

"Van der Post," I say finally.

"Very good. I want you to remember it," he says. Then he takes his hands off my shoulders, puts them on my ass, and pulls me into him. I try to stifle the moan this elicits, fail.

"Talk about games! Who taught *you* to play?"

"There's a lot about rich men you *don't* know," Eben says, kneading my ass. "You know Goodbloode, but I'm not sure it's wise to generalize from *that.* Just because they're named it doesn't mean they *have* it." Whatever you say, darlin', only keep puttin' quarters in the Magic Fingers. "They're not even really rich, just well-to-do." Why Clemmy got less than a million when he turned twenty-one! "Part of being rich is being future-oriented, not present-oriented like a sweet, greedy child," Eben says, stepping back. *Oh, noooo.* "And that's why I'm not gonna fuck you tonight, Anna Kate." He puts my hand on his cock, which is throbbing nicely. "Not because I don't want to."

"Okay, I get it," I say, taking back my hand myself this

time and folding my arms in front of me for protection. "I have to wait."

"You have to wait," Eben agrees.

"Okay. I guess that's fair. But I don't like it. I don't see the point. And I'm not gonna make you any promises, about what might happen in the meantime."

"I'm not asking for any."

"You might not *like* some of the things that happen," I say threateningly.

Eben grins, nonplused. "I might not. You might not like them either, angel." Why do men always call me angel? It's like calling a stewbum moneybags.

"What about you?" I ask suspiciously. "Can *you* wait six months for *me,* or are you gonna let some rich girl scoop you up?"

"I've waited a year already," Eben says. "It took me that long, to make up my mind. Besides, I've got a lot of work to do. Don't you?" I shrug. "I don't have any interest in rich girls, not even if they used to be poor girls. Think about it."

"Okay, I'll think about it. Is the lecture over, professor?"

Eben nods. "Want me to get you a cab?"

I shake my head, give Eben another kiss, a special gutter concoction of my own that leaves *him* gasping this time, and saunter off toward Gansevoort, swinging my hips like the self-confident career girl Eben thinks he's in love with and wants to make a tad more perfect, just like everybody else who's ever loved me. A wee bit *better.* No major changes, oh, no. Nothing that couldn't be accomplished with a total brain transplant. "They fall in love with Gilda and wake up with *me,*" Rita Hayworth once said about this phenomenon. I couldn't've put it better myself. Good thing I'm not as famous or beautiful as she was, or I'd really be up shit creek.

Some of the things Eben said were true, though. Maybe I should write a script for Eben to direct. Under my tutelage, he could be successful, probably. I could teach him how to lie, at least how to *pretend* to. Maybe I should make Eben proud of me instead, I think, as I approach my building, keys in hand. All at once I hear footsteps behind me. Maybe Eben's changed his mind! But when I turn around to look, there's nobody there. The footsteps stop. When I get to the door I hesitate. It's Saturday night, I've got drugs and money. There must be somebody who'll love me just the way I am. Maybe I'll walk to Fourteenth Street, flag a cab, head downtown, and find him.

The next day, give or take a week, I taxi out to JFK for my flight to Oscarland.

I always used to feel at home in airports. There's something comforting about their uniform look, their rituals. You put your luggage on the conveyor belt. You walk through the electric eyes. Your jewelry sets off the psycho detector sometimes, but it is always all right. You point out the offending piece, which obligingly beeps. You wait in the waiting room. That's what it's *there* for. You get on the plane and think about dying. You don't die. That's the way it *used* to be. But today I see too many men who remind me of Walter, jeans too loose, shirts with too-short sleeves, in these awful E-Z Care fabrics. Their wives buy their clothes for them. That's why they're always so ugly.

I bought a shirt for Walter once, to tide him over while his suitcase took a Caribbean vacation. It was a Calvin Klein, nothing fancy, just a subtle, deep blue plaid that brought out his eyes, with a dark blond streak in it that matched his hair. Walter never looked better in his whole life than he did when he wore that shirt. He had to iron it himself, when he wore it in Groverton, since it wasn't wash-and-wear. Lily wondered a lot about that, he said.

She's probably cut it up for dishrags. She probably smelled my perfume on it: White Shoulders, Evening in Paris, My Sin.

Today these Walter-like men are everywhere. Some of them carry children, little gurgling wreaths of garlic that keep me at bay. Others have leaky pens, encased in plastic pocket protectors, dangling from their Permaprest shirts. Their cheap vinyl briefcases are open on their laps, their jackets beside them, corduroy or tweed. Elbow patches. Wedding rings glinting like crosses in the sun. Walter couldn't stand to watch himself touch me, with *his* ring on. It didn't seem decent. *Decent, Gilda? That's a strange word, coming from you.* I never saw Walter's ring, until the night he came to leave me. He cried when I pointed it out and put it in his briefcase.

Some of these men are with their wives, who are what I imagine Lily to be: cold and thin and capable. They snatched up their boy geniuses early, before they had a chance to meet anybody better. Get those puppies young! They're easier to housebreak before they learn how to think for themselves. The wives stand there, pouting, not appreciating what they've got. At twenty or forty they all dress the same, in these awful matronly clothes, in this so-called timeless style, I mean no style at all. When it's cool, they wear navy blue acrylic sweaters with polyester blouses underneath. Peter Pan collars. Why are they called that? Peter Pan wore a jump suit! Skirts too short or too long. Supp-hose. Dr. Scholl's sandals. These little worried frowns, etched permanently on their faces, get worse as the flight fails to be on time. They blame their husbands for this hitch in their busy schedules. Adults from the cradle, they never laugh, or kiss in public. *Oh, yeah, well if you're so smart, why aren't you rich?* I am rich. *Well, if you're so rich, why aren't you married?* That's a very good question. I'll think about it *tomorrow.*

It's not that some of the wives aren't beautiful. They
are. Far more beautiful than I am, but with the sexless
beauty of nuns. They live for Another, for the husbands
they've chosen so carefully, while I was sitting around
with my thumb in my ass, waiting for somebody to choose
me.

Our flight gets called finally. We troop into the plane.
Over America, drinking indifferent champagne, I think
about my latest close shave, my personal brush with the
banality of evil. I didn't tell you about that. It was *très*
banal. It was evil *aussi*. I don't remember all of it, or
maybe I just don't want to. Clemmy always used to accuse
me of that. Maybe I just can't bear to. I'm not sure I'm
ready to talk about it yet, but I can tell you one thing: It
was all my fault, as usual. I brought it on myself. At least
I'm *consistent.* I was walking home and—

Ah, saved by the bell, the *dinner* bell. My Veal Fuselage
is here, and this is definitely Not Dinner Table Conversation. Clemmy taught me that one. "That's en-dee-tee-
cee," he's sure to say, wagging a freckled meathook in my
face, whenever I launch into some tasteless story or other
in front of all the wrong people, the ones who don't know
how to take a joke. "No no no no no no no no!"

I forget all about evil and dig into my petro-meal. I was
kind of nauseated the first time somebody told me the
shake I was quaffing at McDonalds didn't have any milk
in it, just *oil,* and if you drop it on the sidewalk it doesn't
melt. I never eat there now, and if I do I drink something
healthy, like Pepsi Light. But when I'm on an airplane I
just shovel it all in. I've tried to get rid of that poor person's habit of accepting everything that's offered as long
as it somewhat resembles food or drink since who knows
where the next meal's coming from, but I haven't been
able to yet. I can't cut the mustard in the nouveau riche
department. In places like Elaine's or the Russian Tea

Room, where Emma drags me sometimes on business, I squirm and fidget and complain with ill-disguised bad grace, like a child forced to visit her maiden aunts on a sunny day and listen to them talk about their hysterectomies and about all the people they know who have died and how lovely the funerals were and how badly the groundskeepers are tending the graves. It's a boredom mixed with fear. Fear of *not* being bored. Of taking it all seriously.

But take a gander at the lady next to me in the three-piece gray pinstripe: *She's* not having any trouble cutting it. She's ordered one of those special meals that the organized people get, the ones who care about polluting the sacred temple. A peek at my Boeingburger and she goes quite green. It's never seemed quite right to me, ordering a special meal. I used to feel the same way about flying first class, but two or twenty-three encounters with the wretched refuse in steerage cured me of *that* little affectation. There are people back there who should never be let out of their *neighborhoods.*

Once I rolled my car in Topanga Canyon. That was banal if not particularly evil. A Velvet Underground song was playing when I went over and out. Oh, shit, I thought, drunk as a skunk. *Ridiculous.* But appropriate. A few seconds later the car was crushed as if by Godzilla himself and I was standing beside it laughing like a hyena with nary a run in my hose. Two pretty Vals, drunker even than I was, stopped and took me home, before the police came. I didn't even have to go to jail. "I wrecked my car," I told Clemmy, shaking him awake. "Don't worry, honey, I'll buy you a new one," he said. Then he went back to sleep. And the next day he bought me another car, even nicer than the one I totaled.

Things like this don't happen to other people. Other people have wrecks and lose their pretty faces. Old boyfriends, hardened cases, serious fun-havers get arrested and change their ways. "The best deals are made in AA," they tell me smugly. "All I want to do now is get married and settle down." But on me, escaping death has the wrong effect, the opposite effect from the one it should have. I didn't die, therefore I'm terminally lucky. I can continue to press my luck: walk under ladders, thumb my nose at black cats, steal other women's boyfriends. They'll forgive me. Wouldn't *you?* I didn't die. Hmmm, that's interesting. I can get away with even more than I thought.

I s this a joke, or what?" I say angrily to Billyjim, after he leads me to our bungalow at the Cha- teau Marmont. Billyjim looks perplexed.

"I thought you liked the Chateau, honey. You always used to."

"Oh, I do. I do." Poor sweet baby, he really didn't know. I almost don't have the heart to tell him the truth, but Billyjim loves a good laugh. "It's just that they've put us in the John Belushi death suite, cousin. Did they give you a discount or charge extra?"

"I do declare!" Billyjim says, then laughs a laugh that almost, but not quite, drives away the ghost who's lurking nearby, cracking some pretty good jokes of his own. "Want me to get us a new room?"

"It's okay, cuz," I say bravely. "Everybody has to die somewhere, I guess." Billyjim gathers me up in his arms, swings me round and round, carries me into the bedroom, and pretty soon I forget all about John Belushi dying on the floor next door. That's what kissin' cousins are *for*. A few days later, we get up and dress for the Oscars.

After months of intensive shopping, I've decided to wear this tight, low-cut black silk gown that an East Vil- lage designer made especially for me. It has a very full,

three-tiered net overskirt, spangled with these bright-col-
ored plastic and rubber toys: horses, cows, goats, soldiers.
There's a headpiece like Julius Caesar's to match it, with
the same little toys mounted on the leaves of the wreath.
Over that, I'm wearing the fox flings that Clemmy bought
me in Vienna: one coral, one royal blue, with rhinestones
for eyes. We call them Mr. and Mrs. Fox and think of them
more as pets than clothing. Lingerie, high heels, elaborate
makeup, carefully set hair, and I'm ready, in less than four
hours! So . . . what's the verdict? Is this class, or what? It
doesn't take Billyjim quite so long to dress. He's wearing
a tuxedo and his face. And *away* we go.

What a good idea it was to come with Cousin Billyjim!
All those flash bulbs popping! All those cameras whirring!
*Over here, Twister! Just one more, Billyjim!* With so many
movie stars to choose from, movie stars are a tad *overex-
posed,* don't you think? But everybody wants to see my
cousin, and doesn't he look *good.* Very Greek god. He's
grown a beard since last season, which is newsworthy.
With his crisp black curls, he looks like Kris Kristofferson,
only stupider. You can't see how cute he is on *Monday
Night Football,* what with that helmet covering his face,
that padding, that sweat and dirt, so tonight should be a
treat for all you football fans out there, you ladies in the
audience too, and if he has some flamboyant blonde on his
arm, some nobody, well . . . so *what?* You say that's his
cousin? What a *nice* boy he is. Good to his *family.*

Since I'm probably not gonna meet Mr. Oscar tonight,
up close and personal, I use this little occasion to reestab-
lish myself, celebrity-wise, and a very good job I make of
it, too: smiling at all the right people, remembering everybody's names, looking cute, cuter, cutest as I introduce
my famous cousin to one and all and even induce him to
sign a few autographs. *For my daughter.* Uh-huh. Maybe

I can parlay this into a guest spot on *Saturday Night Live* or take over Vanna White's job if she decides to trade up.

Oh, that look on Clemmy's face when we sat down next to him! It was really priceless. If I could have shaved that look off and framed it, I would've. So angry. So hurt. So *outclassed*. Billyjim's the only man in the place bigger than Clemmy. Between them, I feel petite, delicate. Absolutely protected and secure. I lean into one of them, then the other, never able to let even one man escape my grasp, no matter how many I have on hand already. Clemmy's trotted out one of the heiresses from his stable, and a nice little thoroughbred she is, too, very Princess Grace. At first she's all aquiver over meeting Billyjim—even rich people watch *Monday Night Football*—then aghast when she realizes how drugged we are, then appalled, because Clemmy's joining in too.

"How *could* you?" she actually asks, provoking a merry, unstifled laugh from me, right in the middle of the thank-you speech for Best Supporting Actress. Kerry Graham, who was in what might have been our movie, if the late great Rodolpho hadn't directed it—*decapitated* it—didn't win. Poor Kerry. Did I tell you Rodolpho died, just like Clemmy said he would? He did, last week. Of an overdose of street urchins. Poor Rodolpho. Nobody's gonna say thank you to him. Not tonight. Rodolpho: gone, forgotten.

"Everybody she thanked was someone she fucked," Clemmy whispers of the winner, a bit of a dim bulb.

"Everybody except her mother," I say with pert giggle. But wait a minute! It'd be exactly the same for me, if I was up there. *Which you won't be.* Remember the speech Pia Zadora gives in *The Lonely Lady,* when she wins *her* Oscar for Best Original Screenplay? She makes this scene about all the people she's had to fuck, to get to the top. I found this speech hilarious. I didn't have to fuck a single

person to get to the middle, not even one. Imagine that!
Clemmy didn't either. Neither did Billyjim. *Au contraire.*
That's why we all get along so well. We *wanted* to fuck
them. *We did it for fun.* When the heiress leaves in a huff
after Best Documentary, Clemmy takes off his hostility
like a too-heavy coat and the three of us proceed to get
very chummy indeed.

There could be real trouble if Clemmy and I win against
the odds and have to figure out how to take that long walk
to the stage, as blitzed as we both are, without falling flat
on our faces on worldwide satellite hookup. The evening
drones on, measured in Percodans, swallowed dry. An
appropriate way to go, I think: choking on a Percodan at
the Academy Awards.

I get a little weepy when they trot out the old movie
stars, always the best part, then indignant when they
honor some strikebreaking fascist producer who gave
Mussolini's son the star treatment in Hollywood after he
got through bombing the Ethiopian spear chuckers back
to the Stone Age. But nobody else is gnashing their teeth.
Am I the only one here who studied fucking *history?*
*What about Mussolini* JUNIOR? I barely refrain from
screaming. Billyjim's hand over my mouth helps a lot in
that regard. I start crying again, but that passes quickly
like most of my emotions. All these emotions are just
flickering across my face tonight, like fireflies. Where do
all these emotions come from? It's like squeezing a black-
head and seeing pus shoot out all over your mirror. Where
did all that come from? you think, dabbing the crater with
peroxide. How did all that get inside of *me?*

If it weren't for the camera panning our seats for reac-
tions when our names are announced, and staying on us
a long time on account of Billyjim being my escort, and
me remembering to wave and say "Hi, Mom," when I see
the red light flashing since I know for sure I'm not gonna

get another chance to, the whole event of our nomination might have just walked on by. What's that you say? Who won? Who *cares*.

After that part's over, I figure I can relax, curl up on Billyjim's shoulder, and have a good snooze. I'm very good at just nodding out: at dinner parties, during violent arguments, at the wheel of speeding cars. "You look like an angel when you're asleep," a number of people have told me, including Walter Light, Billyjim, Clemmy, and my mother. "What's there, to make you say that?" I asked Walter once, knowing as the words left my mouth what the answer would be. *It's what's not there*, I thought miserably. "It's what's not there," Walter said.

Clemmy and Billyjim wake me when it's over. They put their arms around me and get me out without any serious mishaps. In the limo, they pour coke down my nose to revive me. Maybe they use one of those funnel things the Frogs fatten geese with. Anyway, I wake up. Where *am* I anyhow? Who are these two large white men? Oh, Billyjim and Clemmy. What a nice surprise! What a *treat*. I kiss them both sloppily. Billyjim hands me my evening bag. I get out mirror and makeup to salvage what's left of my face. Billyjim and Clemmy talk football. The limousine driver reads *Vanity Fair*.

When I'm done, Clemmy says, "Welcome back to the land of the living." I grin sheepishly. *Guilty, guilty, guilty!* Clemmy taps on the glass. The driver puts down his magazine, turns on the engine, and pulls away.

"Where are we going, anyhow?" I ask. "Are we going to Spago? To Irving 'Swifty' Lazar's?"

Clemmy shakes his head. "We weren't *invited* to Irving 'Swifty' Lazar's."

"We weren't? Why *not*?" Clemmy stares at me balefully as if I were a giant white slug mysteriously transported to his side, to be borne until the arrival of the exterminator, blessedly soon, one could only hope. I turn to Billyjim, who like most former poor people hates being left out of anything, and say winningly, "Don't worry, honey. I'm sure we *would've* been invited, if he'd known *you* were in town." Instead of Spago, we go to the Reconsider Lounge on Sunset, which used to be our local bar. The regulars—gaffers, grips, wranglers, location managers, and burned-out writers—never knew what to make of us. The script girls, ex-starlets, and former old ladies of long-forgotten rock stars would look at Clemmy hungrily and bide their time. In his grubby flannel shirts with the missing buttons, Clemmy never did look rich, and I never did look *smart.* "You carry your brains like a secret weapon," Jimmy Shapeshifter, the pigtailed Navaho bartender I used to sleep with, enhancing my madcap reputation, once said perceptively. Tonight everybody's got our number, though. They've been watching us on television.

"Uh-oh, here comes trouble," somebody says loudly as I sashay in, Clemmy and Billyjim in my wake. I make my way down the bar, kissing all the men I know, never less than a second too long.

"Whatcha up to?" says Jimmy.

"No good," I say.

An old stewbum I haven't seen in over a year picks his head up off the bar with effort, sees me, and smiles sweetly. "You still here, princess?" he says. "What time is it?"

Billyjim, a trifle agitated, makes a beeline for the phone to call a very important somebody—the coke's almost gone, maybe the Percodan too—while Clemmy steers me to a backroom table, where he gives me a lot of good advice about my so-called career and how this is a good time to revitalize it, which I don't plan to attempt, and tells me a pointed tale about Nigel Featherbone and how he's been spreading that story about the Bar Car bathroom far and wide, and how Clemmy's had to defend me from him more than once, most recently at a bar in Locarno *in front of Rex Reed,* and how it took some serious schmoozing to keep a lid on that one and the next time he sees Nigel he's going to ram his teeth down his throat if he so much as mentions my name, none of which I want to hear.

"I can't be your champion forever," Clemmy says by way of finale. I look at him skeptically, then roll my eyes.

"Champion, schmampion," I say.

"You have the worst judgment of anyone I know. Why do you let men like Nigel Featherbone *near* you? He's a nothing, Porter. A nobody. He's not worth your *spit.*"

"Stop it! You sleep with millions of women!"

"I don't like to be criticized for my lifestyle."

"Neither do I!"

"But I never do anything *wrong,*" Clemmy says. He doesn't even fucking laugh.

"Why do you tell me things like this? You know it just depresses me."

"I thought you'd want to know what people are saying."

*"Why?"* Long pause. "You can tell me one thing," I say finally.

"What?"

"You can tell me who took me home that night."

Clemmy slams down his glass. "I can't believe you, sometimes. Don't you *know?"* I shrug. "Or do you just not want to?" I stand up but Clemmy grabs my hand. "Look around," he says.

I sink back down and scan the room nervously. There's nobody here I recognize from that night in the Bar Car, nobody I connect to the condo where I woke up. "What do you mean?" I say nonchalantly.

Clemmy laughs. "Why, your knight in shining armor's

here. Your rescuer. Your *savior.* " Clemmy looks at me all
of a sudden with what just might be love. Then, sadly:
"Why is it some dames always fall for gangsters?"

It takes me a minute, but I manage to feed him the lines
he's fishing for, from *The Big Combo:* "It doesn't matter
what a man *does.* If he's a cop or a killer. What matters
is how he makes love." Clemmy nods once, then looks at
me with a tortured smile. "Let's forget it, honey," I say,
loving him back all at once. "Let's just have a good time,
you and me."

But Clemmy doesn't want to have a good time. He
wants to talk about money and how mine isn't gonna last
forever like I thought it was, how our royalty payments
are starting to shrink inexorably and he knows I'm not
saving a penny, am I? He says I can't keep living the way
I have been, that I have to think about it sometime and
now's as good a time as any, while we're in the public eye,
and what a good idea it was to bring Billyjim even though
he didn't like it at first but it did get us a lot of extra press,
and on and on and on. God, I love Clemmy. He really does
try to look out for me. But I hate talking about money. It's
so fucking boring. Making money *work* for you. Making
money *grow.* Money should grow on *trees.* Finally, I get
a bright idea, an ancestral memory it is, really. I get up off
my chair and sit down on Clemmy's tuxedoed knees, rub
myself up against him, and kiss him hard, to shut him up.
Kissing Clemmy is soooo niiiice. *Yum.* He has such a dis-
tinctive smell, not all gussied up.

"Don't get any ideas, Porterhouse," says Clemmy
fondly, patting my rump roast through the cloth.

"Don't worry, honey. I haven't had any ideas for years."

Billyjim comes out of the bathroom then, eyes glitter-
ing, trailing a nasty piece of work indeed, Euro-trash judg-
ing from his skin and teeth, albeit an impeccably,
expensively dressed one.

"Nice tux," I say, fingering the snowy material. The stranger smiles. A dealer? Billyjim seems so glad to see him.

"Dinner jacket," Clemmy corrects absently, then pulls me closer, bouncing me on his knee like a protective uncle. But he doesn't invite Billyjim and his friend to sit down and makes a point of talking only to me. After a few awkward minutes, they slink away. Almost immediately, Billyjim comes back alone. Clemmy frees me, I get up, take their arms, and lead them to the bar. Billyjim and Clemmy look so *good* together, big, handsome, muscle-bound all-Americans. I may have bad judgment, but I have exceedingly good *taste.* They match each other shot for shot and talk about baseball. I smile vacantly. Jimmy Shapeshifter puts down his bar rag and grabs my hand.

"Dump the bookends, princess," Jimmy says. "Come home with me. Haven't you noticed? They share one personality between them." Jimmy looks at me so intently, I can almost read his thoughts. Let's see . . . he wants to bedeck me with silver like some albino Pocahontas, then ravish me in his hogan, on bearskin.

I pull away with effort. "How's Loretta?" I say sarcastically, yanking one of his pigtails. "How're the kids?" Jimmy comes out of his trance, smiles sheepishly.

"I taught her everything she knows," Clemmy is bragging. He puts his arm around me possessively, forgetting entirely who it is he's talking to, that Billyjim's the only boyfriend he can't one-up. "At the Goodbloode finishing school!"

"You finished me, all right."

"I taught her everything she knows," Clemmy repeats, ignoring me.

Then Jimmy leans across the bar and puts in his two cents worth: "Uh-huh, Clemmy. You sure did. The good, the bad, and the ugly." Billyjim roars. Clemmy looks

perplexed, then genial all of a sudden. I didn't realize
before just how drunk he was, but his eyes are real killers.
He sits down and takes off one massive shoe, then puts a
beer bottle in his mouth like it was the barrel of a shotgun
and pretends to pull the trigger with his big toe.

"Do I still love you?" he demands, the bottle in his
mouth, talking around it.

"No," I say. "Stop that."

"Do you still love me?" I don't say anything, but a fat
tear trickles down my face. Clemmy pulls the trigger.
*"Kaboom!"* he says.

Billyjim takes the bottle out of Clemmy's hand. I run to
the john crying. Two English girls are at the mirror making up their eyes.

"He wanted me to fuck his dog, I think," one of them
whispers.

"Blimey!"

I wipe my face with a wet paper towel, take a deep
breath. "But . . . was the dog cute?" I say.

Emma Gomez walks out of one of the stalls. I guess she
wasn't invited to Irving "Swifty" Lazar's either. Emma
looks angry when she sees me, a tad intoxicated too, and
before I can apologize for what it is I've done wrong she
launches into this tirade in the gutter Spanish she learned
in the barrio. She had to ride the bus from Beverly Hills
to *get* there, true. But *still* . . . I figure Emma has plenty
of reasons to be mad, so I just stand there hanging my
head and looking contrite while she rattles on about what
I did, which began the night of my party, after the Hellfire
Club. I'm a little hazy about all the details since I was
somewhat polluted, but I do remember that I came home
alone, without Eben, and was just about to go out again
and find someone to love or fuck me when, imagine,
somebody grabbed me!

The mugging part of it was pretty frightening, with a

thin deranged albino warthog and large rusty tetanus-
laden knife involved. Then things started to *escalate.* He
took me into the lobby and told me to take off my clothes.
What he actually said with big festering grin was, "Take
'em off, cunt." I kind of froze then, wondering if I was
going to die, if getting dead would be a leisurely process.
You can choose death or ooga-booga; remember the joke?
Okay, death, the missionary says. Death then, says the
cannibal chief. Death . . . by *ooga-booga!* Then I noticed
that the mugger's left hand, the one with the knife, had
a smudgy death's head on it, just like mine. I started to
laugh and couldn't stop. Everything made sense. I
brought it on myself as usual. Like a good little mad dog,
he followed me home from Hellfire.

Then I remembered this evasive tactic I read about in
some self-defense manual or comic book. I turned my
back on the mugger, unzipped my jeans, pulled them
down around my ankles, bent over, put my head between
my legs and screamed, "Surprise! Aren't girls unpredict-
able?" I didn't really get a chance to test the *efficacy* of
this particular maneuver, because this reptilian monster
from one of my nightmares came out of the shadows at
the back of the lobby.

"Do you *see* it?" the mugger said desperately. He
probably afraid he'd lost his mind since a few minutes
earlier he'd taken the Ecstasy out of my purse, stuck the
whole bottle in one scabby gray nostril, tilted back his
head, and snorted the entire thing. I pulled up my jeans
and turned around.

"See what?" I said coldly. The mugger dropped his
knife and fled. Freddy Pitluck took off his Godzilla mask.

"Secret police," he said, and spat.

Freddy saved my life. He was afraid if he didn't, *he'd*
get the blame, because of that letter I said I wrote to my
lawyer. What's the big deal about the truth, anyway? It's

lies that keep saving my ass. I tried to thank Freddy the
*usual* way, was looking forward to a rare new experience,
in fact, there are so few of them *left.* I once went out with
a dwarf in London who had all the positive attributes of
Clemmy only squashed, *compacted,* but when we got to
my hotel he gave me a dry kiss and said, "Sorry, ducks,
you're not my type."

"What can I do for you, Freddy? To thank you?" I asked,
once we were safe in my apartment.

"Not *that!*" Freddy hooted. "I never drink water from
a dirty glass!" Hmmmm. There's something about me that
just doesn't appeal to dwarves. Freddy got a manuscript
out of his backpack and dropped it in my lap. "Here! This
is what you can do for me! This is how you can thank me!
Read! You have contacts. I want it *published.*"

I didn't have much choice. I sat down and read Freddy's
so-called novel while the author perched on top of the
couch behind me. Whenever my interest in the six hundred or so pages of his rantings and ravings flagged,
Freddy kicked me in the back with his tiny shoe. I finished
his book, then put it in an envelope with a cover letter to
Emma that was as noncommittal as I could possibly make
it, with Freddy over my shoulder, reading every word. He
took me to the post office and watched me mail the package. I tried to call Emma, to warn her, to say it was all a
joke, but she was out of town and by the time she got back
I guess I just forgot. But Emma's exhausted herself finally.
She's even speaking English. She gives me a big hug and
sloppy kiss. All's forgiven. Or maybe she's just being practical.

It isn't until we're out of the john that I realize it wasn't
Freddy's book Emma was yelling about. It was what happened earlier, with Stefan Ratt. Emma thinks I fucked
him. It hurt her feelings. Why do people tell you it's all
right to do something when it's not? Why didn't she tell

me it *mattered?* What's that you say? Would it have made any difference if she *had?* Oh. So *that's* why she didn't say anything.

There are a lot of sexual vibes in the air when we go back to the bar, a lot of four-way snuggling, a lot of eyes that meet portentously, but I'm too skunked to pay proper attention, to instigate anything. I know Clemmy likes that sort of thing or says he does and I've always wanted to try it too but tonight's been too full of excitement already, so, an innumerable number of drinks and pills and tootskies later, we pile in the limo and head back to the Chateau.

Oh, sure, there may have been a certain amount of low-level petting in the limousine, and a bit of melo-dramatics on my part when we were safely back in the death suite, and I warbled a few verses of "Put the Blame on Mame," since they're all going to anyway, then peeled off one long black glove very theatrically and locked my hands behind my head and said in my very best Gilda voice, "I never *was* much good with zippers." But after that, nothing much happened but a little more lackadaisi-cal nuzzling. We were all too tired, too out of shape, for any serious aerobics, after that buildup, and the buildup is really the best part anyway, don't you think? Bed is usually more of a technicality, one we've all been through before. I have anyway, haven't you? Ho hum. *Sex.* Clemmy and Emma leave, Billyjim crawls into bed beside me, and both of us fall asleep immediately. And if there are things in that suite that go bump in the night, rest assured, brothers and sisters, we don't hear them.

"Rise and shine!" my mother chirps at some ungodly hour. Then: "So which one are you gonna marry, Kather-ine Anne? Billyjim or Clemmy?"

"I wasn't planning on marrying anybody," I say finally. *Except Walter Light.*

"I always liked Clemmy," my mother says. "I couldn't tell you *why* exactly." We both laugh. Clemmy's visit to my mother's ended less than twenty-four hours after it began, with Clemmy drunk in a bar which he refused to leave, except by force. Clemmy loves my mother. He thinks she's good. (That's why he got so drunk, or so he says. She's so good he was *embarrassed.*) Clemmy often muses on this fact, as preface to a lengthy discourse on why I'm *not* so good, like my mother. "Well, do you think maybe you and Clemmy might . . . you know . . . get back together?" my mother says.

"I don't think so, Momma," I say sadly. My mother laughs.

"How 'bout you and Billyjim?"

"You know I can't marry Billyjim! We're first cousins!" I say. My mother laughs *again,* goddammit. Does she know *everything?*

"Being cousins hasn't stopped you doing all those *other* things you've been doing, the past nineteen years," my mother says primly. She knows everything. "And since Billyjim already has the twins, and you've never even wanted children, I don't see why being cousins should prevent you from *marrying.*"

"You know everything, huh?" I say. My mother doesn't even answer. Of course she does. "From the first?"

"We figured it'd work itself out, if we didn't interfere, and we were right!" she says gaily. *Everybody* knows everything. "Do Billyjim and Clemmy get along?"

"Uh-huh."

"I figured they did, by the way ya'll were sittin', all chummy-like."

"Oh, God," I say.

"Don't get bent out of shape, Katherine Anne! We thought it was *cute*. Maybe all *three* of you—"

"Gosh, Momma!" I say.

"Don't you 'gosh-momma' me! I can't help it. You have to admit, darlin', they'd keep you *busy*."

"They certainly would," I say truthfully.

"Why, they'd run your tail off!" *Fuck* it off's more like it.

"I'm not sure either one of 'em'd go for that situation."

"Why, that's just because they don't know what's good for 'em! I never understood the monogamy thing, anyhow. Like I've always said, one woman's enough for *any* man, but one man's never enough for any woman."

"You've always *said* it, but you've never *done* it."

"Oh, I leave that to you, honey. You do the living for both of us."

"You know what I think sometimes, Mom?" I say wistfully. "I think I should have married Billyjim when I was sixteen and had his babies, even if they did turn out like Prince Charles, and avoided all this so-called living."

"Ha! You might've, but it never would've took. Even when you were a little baby, Katherine Anne, you never could stay put." Then: "Your father called." Of course he did. He saw me on television.

"What did the old reprobate have to say?" I ask guardedly.

"Oh, he wanted to know all about you, of course, and then he told me how awful his *other* children were, and how they only call when they want to borrow money."

"God forbid!" I say with a triumphant cackle.

"Yes, indeedy! Then he told me about Judy's volunteer work at the unwed mothers' home." Identical mean-spirited chuckles. Judy is my father's fourth wife. "And then he said he was coming to Dallas on business, and did I want to meet him for a drink at Trader Vic's." I groan. "Wait, I'm coming to the good part! *Then* I told him I was living with someone and *I wasn't interested.*"

"Wow."

"That's the first time I've ever said that to him, Katherine Anne. All the other times he asked, I just made excuses, but today I actually said no. No! Can you believe it?"

"How does it feel?" I say cautiously. My mother laughs like she doesn't have a care in the world.

"Great! It was great! I feel great!"

"Have you finally stopped loving him, Mom?" No response. Say *yes.*

"Well, that's difficult to say. I still love the man he was, the same way he loves the girl I was, but those two people are dead. Let 'em rest, I say. Can you imagine the look on his face if I did show up? Forty pounds more than he bargained for? The surprise he'd get?" My mother laughs merrily and I join in.

"It'd almost be worth going," I say finally, "just for the look on his face."

"No, I think I kinda like leaving it like this," my mother says. "Your father is the only person in the world who still thinks of me as that twenty-year-old girl. Except for me, of course. She lives in *me,* but so do a lot of other people. She's the only me he's got. You hate him, I know, but I don't, honey. Not enough to ruin that memory."

"He saw you when you were thirty-five," I say, cross at my mother's unrelenting goodness. He saw her at Trader Vic's, with me. They drank cocktails with gardenias in them. When my father was done impressing me, and my mother was done sobbing, I had enough gardenias to make a lei, and enough disgust for both of them to last for years.

"Oh, yes, but he probably doesn't even remember that," says my mother. "That was just a woman in a hotel on a business trip. He's got that woman confused with all the other women he's had. When he talks to me, it's that girl he's talking to. The one who knows all his secrets. Your father is a very lonely man, Katherine Anne. Instead of hating him, you should feel sorry for him."

"I'm not that big a person, Mom."

"Oh, but you will be. Then you'll see that your old mother was right. Why do you think your father's been married so many times, honey? Because he doesn't want anyone to know his secrets. When they get close too, he finds a fresh, ignorant girl to charm."

"Sounds like you're talking about me."

"No, I don't think it's the same with you, honey. You *want* people to know you. You just don't give them long enough. You give up on them too quick. You're impatient. Your problem is that you want everything too fast. In that respect, you *are* like your father. Things that were hard, you always gave up on, even if you were good at them. Like your violin—"

"I wasn't that good, Mom."

"—and your metal sculpture—"

"The boys wouldn't let me use the acetylene torch."

"You should've fought them, dammit! You should've made them! You stuck to writing because it was easy for you." *Not anymore.* "There's the easy way and there's the hard way. But sometimes the easy way's harder on yourself."

"Like the tortoise and the hare, huh?"

"Oh, *winning!* Winning isn't everything. Look at me, just a lazy old mud turtle, pokin' along. But I'll get there, sweetie! I'm not really sure where yet, but *somewhere.* What's the point of going, if you don't enjoy the trip?"

Then: "I think you'd like nothing better than to have somebody know you, Katherine Anne."

"I don't know, Mom," I say. "Clemmy got to know me. After that he didn't like me much."

"Not like you? Open your eyes! Clemmy *loves* you, not that he'd ever admit it. I can see it when he looks at you. Anybody can."

"You think everybody loves me."

"Of course! Why wouldn't everybody love my daughter?"

"I can think of lots of reasons."

"Pshaw! I can't think of a single one."

"You're such a Pollyanna, Mom," I say crossly.

"Well, sometimes I think you're a . . . *dis*-Pollyanna!" she counters.

"You've been reading John Gardner again."

"What does it matter who thought of it first, as long as it's *true?* What ever happened to Hayley Mills anyway, after she married that dirty old man? Whether Clemmy loves you or doesn't is beside the point. He'd act just the same, irregardless. Clemmy's like your father, Katherine Anne. It isn't you he doesn't like, it's himself. Has Clemmy ever gotten close to anybody? Ever? No matter how perfect a girl was, Clemmy'd find some fault in her that made her not worth loving. When you say you'll get close, only you've got to find the perfect person first, what you're saying is you're afraid to get close, *period.* Of course, some people—like Jack Hill—are just plain unlovable. But Brandy loved Jack."

"That's because she's exactly like him," I say. When my stepfather finally died of an overdose of wickedness, Brandy was the only one who mourned, the only one, really, who didn't fucking cheer.

"Right!" my mother says. "There's somebody for everybody in this world."

"Well, if there's somebody for everybody, not all of them can be for me, right?"

"Maybe." My mother laughs. "I'm not saying you're right. People like us, with big hearts, why, we can love just about anybody, given the proper encouragement. That's why when Mr. and Mrs. Buttinsky criticize me about Jesse, why, I tell them to just butt *out.* Jesse has his faults, but there's not a mean bone in his body, and who's to say he doesn't deserve to be loved, just like anybody else?"

"Not me," I say.

"And there you have it," my mother concludes. "Whew! How'd we ever get off on that? I know you've got better things to do than sit around all day, yammering with your poor old mother."

"Not really," I say truthfully. "How's everybody else? How's Brandy?"

"Oh, fine. Brandy just loved your dress last night. She told me to make sure and ask you—"

"—how much it *cost?*" we drawl together before launching into our Jack Hill memorial call-and-response routine:

"Pasteboard cradle," I say.

"HOW MUCH DID IT COST? HOW MUCH DID IT COST?"

"Silk-lined casket!" my mother shoots back.

"HOW MUCH'D THAT SET YOU BACK, BUBBA?" Then:

"Is Billyjim there?" my mother asks. "Put him on, honey. I wanna put the fear of God into him!" I go into the bedroom and wake Billyjim up.

"My mom's on the phone. She wants to say hi."

"She knows?" he says.

"Honey, *everybody* knows." Billyjim puts on a robe, sits by the phone.

"Howdy do, Aunt Livia!" he says with false heartiness.

I watch Billyjim nod into the phone while my mother reads him the riot act, wondering what might've happened if we'd gotten this phone call in some motel when I was sixteen. I would've been one of his ex-wives, if that had happened. After a while, Billyjim hands me back the phone.

"Did she tell you to make an honest woman out of me, cousin?" I say as he walks away, looking chastened. "No chance of *that.*"

"I almost forgot to tell you the most important news!" my mother says after we reconnect. "Remember I told you that Professor Tomsich wanted me to apply to one of those writers' colonies?"

"Uh-huh." Professor Tomsich is her creative writing teacher. "So what happened?"

"So I got *in* is what happened! Can you believe it? I'm going to Yaddo for six whole weeks, starting in September!"

"That's wonderful news, Mom." Yaddo never accepted *me.* Snooty Yaddo turned me down *twice.*

"Oh, it is. It is. I'm sorry to tell you today, when you got such bad news." What bad news? *Oh.*

"We never expected to win, Mom," I say truthfully. "So we weren't disappointed." This Yaddo thing is something else.

"Maybe they'll put me in the very room where Katherine Anne Porter herself stayed!"

"Momma," I say, preparing to rain as hard as I can on my mother's parade, "did you know that Katherine Anne Porter denounced her best friend to the FBI as a Communist because she was jealous over who got the best studio at Yaddo?" Long pause. I feel like I've just run across a beautiful lawn at dawn, kicking the tops off of mushrooms.

"No, dear," my mother says sweetly. "I *didn't* know

that. But if it's true—and I'm sure it is or you wouldn't repeat it—then she must've had a very good reason." Shortly after that my mother and I hang up. "I love you," we both say, and mean it. Then why can't I be happy for my mother, instead of jealous? Why can't I be tickled pink? Why can't I be a *bigger person?*

Billyjim is singing show tunes in the shower. I go back to bed, feeling sorry for myself for being such a louse. Billyjim crawls in with me and takes me in his arms.

"What's wrong? Homesick?" Billyjim says. I nod. What a liar I am too. Billyjim has an unfamiliar look on his face. Could it be . . . *thoughtful?* "You know, I was thinking, maybe your mom wasn't wrong."

"About what?" I say listlessly.

"About *what?* About us getting married, Miss Potato Head!" I pull out of my funk immediately. Could he possibly mean it? Yes he could. He's got stars in his eyes! For me!

"It's taken you kind of a long time to pop the question," I say cautiously. "If you *are* popping the question."

"Oh, I don't know. It was just a thought. We don't have to decide right away. But if we're still gettin' along, after all these years, we must be doing something right," he says. Or *wrong.*

Billyjim kisses me, then dresses and goes out to some business meeting. They want him to endorse a new cologne. I get dressed too, finally, thinking about my mother and how we got to be so different. Wanting to *be* my mother, I go to the Safeway on Sunset and locate, with great difficulty, some instant mashed potatoes, the kind we used to eat together at home. Walking through the aisles to the cash register, I carry them tucked under my arm like some women used to carry Kotex. Even the grocery checker is hip enough to snigger as she bags the box.

"For the maid," I say haughtily. Back at the Chateau, I cook the potatoes, but even smothered in butter, they taste horrible. I scrape them into the garbage, toss the box in after. There's no one I could possibly give them to without losing face.

BILLYJIM and I pass a few pleasant weeks in the death suite, eating and drinking and fucking and taking the odd meeting here and there, but we don't talk about getting married again. What we talk about is another tax-deductible romp somewhere foreign. Did you think I was paying for all this globe-trotting, all this drugs and sex and sloth and going to the movies *myself*? Surely you jest. When tax time rolls around, do you help your poor old Uncle? Then surprise, buddy. *You're* the one paying for it. Somebody's writing off every cent. Hey, it's business, right? Uh-huh. *Monkey business.* Another jaunt's on the agenda too, because yesterday I found out that the very last script Clemmy and I wrote together, *The Penetrator*, is finally a finished film. And, surprise, it's supposed to be very, very good, because this unknown actor, Bucky Cream, took a role that was written as a *Terminator* parody, only with sex, and turned it into something special. He put all this humor in it, all this pathos, all the tragedy you see in Fifties films like *I Married a Monster from Outer Space* where the alien can't love but is smart enough to see that not loving is deprivation rather than strength. So without having a heart technically, the Penetrator grows one, sort of like the Tin Man did, and falls in love. *The Penetrator* promises to be very big, and Bucky Cream is already hard at work on another picture, Royce Browder, the director, no relation to *Earl,* tells me when he calls to try to talk me into repping the flick at Cannes.

Royce and I spent three weeks together, holed up in a motel in Lake Placid, while I did rewrites on his second picture, a remake of the classic teen pic *Ski Party.* Only instead of James Brown and his Famous Flames busting in on this bored bunch of snowbound white kids, we did it with Twisted Sister and some Young Black Republicans! Nice, huh? You say you've never even heard of *Ski Party '83?* That there's a conspicuous gap between *Ski Party* (the original) and *Ski Troop Attack* in your *Guide to Movies! Movies! Movies! on TV?* Very good eye, pal. That's because it never got released. Royce and I spent all those weeks in Lake Placid for nothing. Except *money.*

We've both come a long way since then, *uh-huh,* but when I hear Royce Browder's gravelly voice, a whole flood of memories comes welling up. I remember all those long nights working, then fucking our brains out in the Jack Daniels Motor Lodge—Royce figured that would keep me out of trouble—then going to the A&P for provisions, never failing to stop and pour endless quarters into a contraption called the Fun Chicken, which squawked at us, then laid eggs with prizes: one day a rubber snake, the next day decals of Marmaduke, or a gold plastic ring with the sphinx on it. I remember how Royce, a filthy, funky dude under his tweeds, tried to make me actually *lay* one of those eggs for him, like the girl in the Oshima flick, you know the one I mean, the very very sexy one about erotic obsession, my favorite subject. They're in this teahouse and she sucks the boiled egg up inside her and lets it out again and her boyfriend eats it very delicately, with chopsticks. Royce wanted me to be his Fun Chick, but I demurred. What if it got stuck? The thought of explaining my imitation of a Fun Chicken to the emergency room squad at Lake Placid General was enough to dissuade me from performing this mildly degenerate act. Royce and I had a lot of fun together, before he went back to the wife and kiddies, just like they all do.

Hey, should I go to Cannes or not? Do I have anything better to do? Billyjim doesn't. Does Clemmy? Why not make it a party?

"I'm working, Porter," Clemmy says in his usual hostile fashion when I ask about his availability. "I have a *job*. Remember *jobs?* You better. And *fast.* " Clemmy tells me he's doing rewrites on Verity Low's new picture *Horse Opera,* which has gone through three lowly scribes already. Verity, a small but flawless redhead, asked for him personally. Clemmy leaves for Mexico tomorrow.

It's true that Clemmy's a great rewrite artist, but then again so am I. Why didn't Verity ask *me* to come to Mexico? Even now, in my somewhat reduced mental circumstances, I have this little reputation as a film saver. I can turn out reams of zingy dialogue in trailers from Tucson to Timbuktu with only the tiniest bit of coke to grease the wheels and a big fat check for inspiration. I can look at two scenes that aren't working and conjure up exactly what's needed to link them, to make them both play without a lot of costly reshooting. I set these little gems betwixt base metal, like an alchemist, and they radiate meaning in all directions, turn shit into gold. Why didn't Verity call me? She's supposed to be my *friend.* After all, I introduced her to Billyjim, her third husband. Then I remember that the nights are cold, down Mexico way, and that Verity's producer, director, and co-star are gay. I can't save Verity the way Clemmy can, in the cold nights department. So I call Verity in Mexico, to thank her for coaxing Clemmy back to work.

"Oh, I would've called *you,* cousin," Verity lies, "only I heard you were too busy over at the Chateau, shacked up with that old shit-ass Billyjim." Everybody knows everything. Don't ever let them tell you they don't. After I give Verity a blow-by-blow of my affair with her ex, editing out all the time I spent with him while they were married, of course, and after Verity asks me a few indiscreet questions about what Clemmy's like in bed and whether it really is true what they say about men with big feet, and I tell her just enough to whet her appetite without being disloyal to Clemmy, at least I don't think so, since Verity's gonna find out for herself soon enough, then Verity says she has a little something for me, too: her suite at the Martinez, in Cannes. She won't be using it. Then Verity gives me a few cousinly words of advice about how I should try to keep Billyjim under control so he won't have to go to that clinic in Switzerland for another blood change.

"It takes everything out of him when he has to do that," Verity says. "I don't think it's *natural.* Plus, you never know whose *blood* you're gettin'! I don't want him to take any more risks with his health. Take care of him, okay?" I promise to try, though taking care of Billyjim, drugswise, when he doesn't want to be taken care of is a little like stopping a NIKE missile run amok. A little bit like trying to take care of *me,* come to think of it. "Take care of *yourself,* too," Verity says, plucking the words out of my mind. How much does she know? Everything, probably.

I find out later that nobody who's anybody's going to Cannes. My invitation there confirms this appalling fact. Something to do with Libyan terrorists. I vaguely remember Libya from my post-Walter stint in the sack. Libya kept interrupting *Gilligan's Island.* I remember *that.* Libya made me quite cross.

While I'm mulling over this new development, this slight, Lily Light makes this grievous tactical error. Not content to just sit back and savor her little victory in silence and get on with her miserable life, Lily decides to chortle a bit, to rub my face in shit via this awful letter that arrives care of Emma's L.A. office.

I examine the envelope carefully, when I'm alone, in no great hurry to get at the contents. It's this very gentle beige, embossed on the back with Lily's name, which is Walter's, and their address in Groverton, Ohio. The paper inside matches, and there's this dodo bird on the front. Looking at Mr. Dodo, I get a lump in my throat. Could Lily actually have a sense of humor? Her notepaper really slays me. It's not stationery like mine, thick and engraved and expensive, but notepaper. Half-sized. Made for writing thank-you notes to other faculty wives and letters to the teacher. I feel superior to Lily's notepaper, but touched by it, too. It causes a strange sort of forgiving feeling to sweep over me, an affection for Lily. I really do want to like her. What a surprise that would be. But then there's this truly awful letter.

*I am at the kitchen table waiting for cupcakes to come out of the oven,* Lily begins. *This afternoon, Jason will take these cupcakes to school to celebrate his seventh birthday. As I sit watching the goldfinches at the bird feeder, I think of you, Anna Kate. I hope someday I won't think of you at all.* Lily goes on to talk about how goodness has triumphed and evil's vanquished, hallelujah, and would I just kindly drop dead now, please. Thank you. She talks about how happy she and Walter are going to be for the next twenty years. The ones without me in them. Even *Stalin* had the grace to stop at five. *We will travel, eat, kiss, bicycle, canoe, go to the movies. We will talk and make love and even play golf with a new intensity fueled by this terrible time. I certainly hope we never see you or your brand of "love" again. It was selfish, thoughtless, wrong, and evil.*

Those quotation marks around the word "love" make me want to put Lily's hand down the garbage disposal and turn it on, like the bad guys did to William Devane in *Rolling Thunder.* I wouldn't have any qualms about that at all. I wouldn't even charge. I'd do it for fun. It's those quotation marks, more than anything else, that drive me wild, like the ones around "singer" in *Citizen Kane.* Remember all the trouble *they* caused, all the opera houses Kane built for poor Susan Alexander, just to take those quotation marks away? What movie do you think this *is*, Lily, one of those revenge pics they show to our dusky brethren on Times Square? Those guys *need* revenge. They're losing. You *won.* Don't you get it yet? This is *Brief Encounter!*

Walter makes this tactical error too, of course. In fact he's been scattering them all over the world. Eventually they all get forwarded here. When people see you on television, like Walter and Lily did—cf. *The other night, after Jason and Gerda were asleep, we witnessed your disgusting performance*—they know where to send your mail. There is jewelry, lots of jewelry, all of it in my colors. Lapis lazuli and turquoise and opals, always set in silver, not in gold, which probably has some deep psychological significance that escapes me at the moment. Jewelry Walter says he bought before we broke up and couldn't bear to throw out. There are a few pathetic notes and one long, tortured twenty-page mea culpa, written in the language of Lily, full of her words, her values, her morals. If language is the mirror of the soul, I know I've lost him. Sayonara, Walter. Don't say it hasn't been fun.

The worst of Walter's letters confirms something I always suspected: Lily's suicide attempt was more or less a sham. She admitted this. Of course, it makes no difference *now*. Walter will stay with her anyway. He's so weak, I don't even want him back. I sit by the pool, looking at these pathetic tokens. I read the letter from Lily over and over, hating her more and more. So smug. So unnecessary. She went to such trouble to write it, to compose it, to recopy it neatly on her notepaper, with no mistakes, no erasures. She took such trouble to address it properly, to print, in the lower left-hand corner, PLEASE FORWARD. That Lily's letter was written with Walter's knowledge, his *compliance,* since she couldn't have addressed it any other way, is the one thing I'll never forgive him for.

But I hate Lily so much more. I used to feel sorry for her, back when we were pulling the old wool over her eyes, but now I really hate her guts. All my ill will flows in Lily's direction. Since I can't write anything decent of my own, I decide to use my not insignificant if dwindling literary powers to write Lily a letter. I know she is a prude, a real Cotton Mather–type New England Puritan, so I throw in a lot of cunts and cocks just so she'll be sure to know Walter and I weren't talking physics in all those hotel rooms we stayed in. I try to remember every indiscreet thing Walter ever said about her: what she does in bed, what she doesn't do, what she said at this or that significant moment, stuff about the kids, intimate family things I know far too much about. But most of all, I write about sex, something I do with great aplomb, not to mention relish. I talk about the taste of Walter's come like I'm giving a consumer report on a new flavor at Baskin Robbins. Lily rubs my face in cupcakes, I rub hers in come. Exceedingly mature, on both our parts. I want Lily to know I wasn't just some slut Walter porked a few times. *I was the love of his life.* Sorry, Lily. But, hey! You were first *runner-up.*

The letter makes me feel a whole lot better. Especially the part where I address it: Mrs. Wally Light. I wish I could say I didn't mail it, and show some class here. But *noooo.* Off it goes.

About a week after I debase myself with the letter, Billyjim wangles a trip to Cannes on Sterling Johnson's Learjet, but when we get to the airport, we find there's only one empty seat, not two. Billyjim insists that I take it, though I don't want to. I don't know any of these people, studio flacks and second-rate starlets, and they don't know me, don't know who I *am.* They want to hobnob with Billyjim "The Twister" Thibideaux, not with little Miss Nobody.

"Please, honey," I say as Billyjim stows my luggage and prepares to get off the plane. "Let me stay with you. Let's go together, on a commercial flight." But Billyjim won't hear of it. *Pay* for a *plane ticket?* Not on your life. He can hitch a ride with somebody else I don't know in a couple of days.

After Billyjim gets off the plane, I sit alone and drink, wondering if maybe Billyjim didn't plan this to get rid of me, if maybe he doesn't have another girl back in the death suite. Before the plane leaves, I get off and make a call. A woman answers. Of course she does. She has a sweet southern accent, the kind I used to have before I went to college up north and took all those elocution lessons, so people wouldn't think I sounded like Lady Bird Johnson. "It's my daughter, the Yankee!" my mother says sometimes when I call, wounding me inexplicably. But Verity still has her accent, and she's a major star. Just listen:

"Hello? . . . Hello-*oooo?* . . . Is anybody there? . . . Hey, pervert! Cocksuckah! I'm talkin' to *you!*"

I try to get back on Johnson Sterling's airplane, but a

coked-up teenage actress has taken my seat. I haul my
luggage out of the plane. Nobody helps me. I go back into
the terminal, stand in line, and buy a one-way ticket to
France.

It's a long way to Europe from California, and since I was
so disorganized I couldn't get a first-class seat. When I
change planes at JFK, I find I'm on this low-rent discount
airplane that sounds like a lawn mower and threatens to
disintegrate any minute. I can't sleep at all. I'm *terrified*.
I have two white wines with dinner, but the Riesling
doesn't relax me. I'm thinking maybe some cognac will
help. I have a bottle in my bag from the Duty Free, ever
the practical traveler, but am too tasteful to just pop the
bottle and pour a shot in front of the flight attendants,
who might stop me, and the other passengers, who would
surely type me a lush. My seat's too revealed to do anything subtle, since it's the least desirable seat, the one at
the front, next to the toilets, and a long line of people are
standing next to me, bored and restless and fidgety, need-
ing to go, their eyes looking for something, anything, to
distract them from the pressure in their bladders that
threatens to break through at any moment and embarrass
them hideously. The line moves slowly. People bump into
my knees and grunt apologies, or don't. I won't expose
myself to *them*. So I devise this little plan to go into the
toilet with my flight bag and open my bottle of cognac and
pour some booze, quite a lot, in fact, into my empty coffee
cup very discreetly. Then I can come back out, get drunk,
and maybe sleep. A foolproof plan. But first I have to stand
in line for the toilet.

Before I can get up, the door to one of the cubicles
opens and a woman comes out. She's been the "friendly
passenger" all through the flight. You know who I mean.

The one who finds out the names of all the stews and calls them by these names as often as possible, to set up this chummy false comraderie.

"What's the movie again, Brian? Is it in English? Mavis, be a dear and get me a coffee when you get a chance? Oh, no hurry!" A friendly person, but it's this nervous, phony friendliness. She probably doesn't have a friend in the world, seeing as how friendly she is with strangers. She keeps finding excuses to go up to the front of the plane and stand around and gossip, even talks the crew into letting her make an announcement over the PA.

"You may not get your first-choice entree, folks, but I guar-an-tee, it'll all be good!"

She carries this off with panache. I tell her she may have a future in broadcasting, but she just looks at me, hurt, blinking furiously, not getting the joke. I don't know how to apologize. She sort of reminds me of Lily Tomlin without a sense of humor. That she was the passenger who made a stink because she didn't get her favorite seat—*mine*—is something, three hours into the flight, I've almost forgotten about. Then the toilet door opens and out she comes. She stands directly in front of me, doesn't go back to her seat, just looks around all hostile-like, waiting for someone to notice that it was *her*, not me, in the toilet chugging booze. I can see her poison of choice, Regal Scotch, protruding from her blue canvas handbag, seal undone, a picture of Edinburgh Castle on the label.

Her once-sweet face is mottled and red, her eyes are darting guiltily back and forth, her mouth is working silently. She's like a barroom bully, waiting for someone to insult her so she can pick a fight, but no one does. No one notices her except me. Her bravado collapses a little after a while. Nothing bad has happened. She can relax, or so she thinks, so she leans against the door of the second

toilet for just a second, head lolling loosely as if she's about
to pass out. When the door behind her opens inwardly,
she's thrown off balance and almost falls on a little blond
girl, seven or eight, who jumps nimbly out of her way,
then stands there staring. The woman's face snaps into
that Lily Tomlin smile about three beats too late to pull
anything off. A middle-aged German pushes past her and
curls his lip at her smell. The woman stumbles again. The
German curses. The blond girl backs down the aisle. She
never takes her eyes off the woman and neither do I. Then
the woman turns and stares back at me all of a sudden.
She's caught, and I'm caught too, watching her. And
though I try to project sympathy, empathy, with my eyes,
I can't think of anything to say.

The woman digs into her handbag energetically, looking at me all the while, eyes narrowed into hot little slits,
daring me to look away. The old stare-down game. I never
could win it, not with women anyway. And I'm sure, all
at once, that there's a gun in that handbag, that she's
slipped it past all the metal detectors.

Embarrassed to cover my eyes, I dip my head toward
her, stare at my lap, and wait to be dead. I see a path in
my brain like a deep red tunnel, with snapshots pinned to
the walls. My mother. Walter. Clemmy. Carmella. A dog
I had that died. My Aunt Faye in her coffin, with pancake
on her face like putty where the cancer ate through. A
poem I wrote for one of my boyfriends, Morton Saper-
stein: "I stabbed your mother with tarnished needles," it
began. All the brash triumphs, tacked on the walls of my
brain like grocery lists on the refrigerator, secured by
magnetized Snoopys.

When I look up five seconds later, the woman is still
scowling, still staring, and filing her nails with the file she's
located in her handbag. Whittling herself to marrow. The
skin around her nails is chewed off, just like mine is. I

unbuckle my seat belt, pick up my Duty Free bag, and get
in line for the toilet. In Cannes, where I end up, there are
castles, but I don't visit them.

A German friend once told me that Americans sound like
geese gabbling, and sitting on the Carleton terrace with
some of the usual suspects, I stop listening for content and
start to see what he means: *Boobus americanus.* I sit here
with my acquaintances and ogle the stars, the hottest di-
rectors and coolest blondes of the moment, such as they
are, given the desultory state of Cannes this year. Do they
really have more fun than we do? I can't believe it. I had
more fun when I was seventeen or twenty, really and
truly a nobody. I get up, stroll back to the Martinez, and
submit to yet another mindless interview about *The Penetrator,* since nobody else is here to do press. Australian
Broadcasting today. Some fun. Then another drink. Oh,
well, at least the weather's nice.

In Cannes, people talk to me about work. I try to
change the subject gracefully, but it's difficult. This town
right now is about work and work only. If I don't want to
work in pictures, I shouldn't be here at all. Even I can see
that. Even I am not *that* far gone.

"The only thing I'm writing these days is checks," I
quip, knowing as the words leave my mouth that I should
shut up. People laugh, but tepidly. The joke isn't all that
funny, seeing as how it's true. I shouldn't be parading my
lack of desire to work in front of people who will notice
it, remember it, and use it against me later. I shouldn't be
acting superior about *not* working, as if I'm above it. I
didn't win the Oscar, after all. I lost. How can anyone be
so traumatized by so little success?

But as long as I have money, I don't *have* to work. I call
my accountant, Maury Goldleaf, to make sure, and though
he criticizes me gently, I can tell I'm not really in serious

trouble. Clemmy was wrong as usual. I can probably spend a few more years wallowing in my misery and making jokes about it. But in the midst of all these eager beavers giving good meeting, pushing their projects and themselves, thinking about nothing but work, work, work, I start to feel a glimmer of ambition. I start to feel a tiny bit like my old self.

Then this idea develops in my pea brain for a picture, a cheap little picture I might be able to write myself, without Clemmy, maybe even direct. I'm ready for that, I think. Maybe it's the fear of directing that's immobilized me so badly, not just my little disaster with Walter. While I was sinking down, down, down, into the muck of self-pity and the slime of true love lost, I read a lot of books by women like me, hoping I could find out, vicariously, just how far down is, without actually having to go there myself. I read books by women who went this route before: drugs and sex and liquor and self-immolation. One of these women, who pushed herself over the edge, obsesses me: Melissa Reed. She killed herself faster, more finally, than I am doing. She's dead now, really and truly dead, not just flirting with death, and all she has to show for her life is a bunch of letters. No novel. Not even a script. She was only a few years older than I am now when one of her sleazy boyfriends killed her.

I rent a typewriter in Cannes and bang out a treatment based on Melissa Reed's letters. I don't even bother to buy the option—a rash, unprofessional move—so sure am I that no one else has thought of this project, that no one will try to steal it from me. The three days I spend writing the treatment are the best ones I've had since Walter left me. When it's done, I take it to this producer I know who likes me, Heinz Hunnertmark, a Berliner who looks remarkably like Albert Einstein. Heinz has always wanted to do a project with me, or so he *claims.* He also claims to be a leftist. He claims to have studied Critical Theory. He claims to know several members of the Baader-Meinhof Gang personally. He even claims, when making deals with *actual* leftists, to give ten percent of his ill-gotten gains to the Greens. Even *I'm* not stupid enough to believe that.

I go to our breakfast meeting at the Majestic wearing a white suit like Mark Twain's, looking smashing, tanned, confident. Heinz greets me warmly, kisses me just a little too long, then decapitates his boiled egg neatly with a knife, puts the removed top shell at the bottom of his egg cup, and eats. He chews every bite fifty times, then gets down to business.

The sex-with-twenty-year-old-beachboys part sounds good to him, and Mexico is cheap these days, and colorful. But death by blunt instrument? Too depressing. Besides, it's been done before. Remember *Mr. Goodbar?* The book presold the picture, and it still wasn't a very big hit. Heinz has all the figures in front of him. The fact that the killer is unknown, unsympathetic, is a big problem too. No mystery to solve, no retribution. Perhaps I could change the ending? No? Oh, well. . . .

"I love your work, Anna Kate. Call me when you've got something new," Heinz says. "But remember, baby, the bottom has dropped out of the political film market. No one wants to see serious movies during a depression." Then Heinz invites me to stay in his suite awhile, for fun and games, but just until his wife shows up and not a word to anybody. That Hunnertmark really puts the germ back in German. Rather than rejecting him with some witty retort about my busy social life or alluding to his notorious lack of sack know-how—or taking him upstairs and fucking his brains out—I decide for some reason to *talk* to Heinz, to tell him why I've stopped sleeping with married men, how I've changed, since Walter, but this self-

consciously cheeky attempt at honesty never overcomes
the intense artificiality of its premise. Heinz looks at me
like I was a specimen in a jar and not a very interesting
catch at that, one he would just as soon flush. He cuts me
off finally, exasperated by my obtuseness.

"Oh God oh God oh God oh God," he says, grabbing
hunks of his wiry gray hair and pretending to tear them
out by the roots. "Everything with you is always so serious,
baby. You always make such a big deal out of everything."

I choke back one or two pitiful tears. Heinz Hunnertmark could care less about knowing the truth. The truth
does not have Alan Ladd, Jr.'s home phone number. The
truth does not know the maître d' at Spago. The truth is
the first wife of an industry player who inexplicably failed
to hire a good divorce lawyer. If Heinz were working the
room at Elaine's, he would pass the truth right by, and my
wish to know this unfashionable person makes me the
tiniest bit passé.

When Heinz gets up to go to another meeting, I notice
that his place is spotless. Mine is a mess of bread crumbs,
egg yolk, and spilt coffee. Heinz is right, of course. Lies
*are* neater.

For some reason this rejection finishes me. I don't have
the guts to take the treatment to anyone else. Work? Ha!
See what happens to you when you *work*. It only briefly
occurs to me that my treatment might have been rejected
because I didn't work hard *enough* on it, or because
Heinz had no intention of dealing seriously with me in the
first place and just wanted to leverage a zipless fuck, before I get back to the serious business of feeling sorry for
myself. Billyjim still isn't here, to entertain me. He didn't
come in a couple of days, he hasn't come in a week, he
may never come. Who else can I get to distract me? I call
Eben van der Post and get his machine. I call Royce
Browder. His wife answers. Finally I call my mother.

"Come back to Texas and do *my* job," she shrieks over the crackling phone lines after I unload on her awhile. My weepy self-pity really cracks her up. She thinks I'm on top of the world, the luckiest girl she knows. Every time I go on a trip, my mother gets out her world atlas and marks the places I've been with gold stars. She can't understand why I'm not happy. "Come on home, honey, and I'll go to Europe *for* you. How would all your boyfriends like that?"

"They'd like it just fine, Mom," I say, but they wouldn't. All my boyfriends are terrible snobs. All of them are rich, or have been, or will be.

"You know who the real oppressed people are?" Nigel Featherbone said one day, when we were trying to decide whether or not to get up one afternoon or to stay in bed and fuck and order out Chinese. "The people who have to get up in the morning."

"Five o'clock, eh?" he'd say merrily as we left an afternoon movie for a crowded New York street. Then it would begin, like a nursery school chant: tormenting the workers. "*Here* come the *workers* on their *way* home from *work.* Did you have a hard day, madam?" he'd say into the face of some exhausted middle-aged lady.

"Must you, Nigel?" I'd beg, pulling my coat high around my face.

"Oh, I must. I must. How about you, sir? Bad day? Boss give you trouble?"

"Fuck off!"

"I'm bloody glad *I* don't have to work!" Nigel would scream, invigorated by these encounters with the toiling masses, of whom he is not one.

All my boyfriends think I exaggerate my class background, for effect. I call one of the worst of them in Paris and get a nice surprise. All my chic Parisian friends are arriving, en masse, for an extended house party. Nicholas de la Rue flies down the next day and kisses me as if it were only this morning we'd last kissed, not over a year ago, as if our affair hadn't degenerated into one more horrible scene, as if nothing bad happened. Maybe nothing *did*. I pack a small bag and move into his mother's villa and return to partying with a vengeance, as Lily would say, fueled by these terrible times.

During the five years I lived with Clemmy, we developed this pattern of binge and purge, binge and confess. We'd do the most awful things we could think of, to ourselves and others—for people did tend to get in the *way*—then apologize profusely, spend a few days atoning, and go back and do them over. After a while, we exhausted most of the usual sins people commit and had to get really creative, to top each other. Most of it I can't remember, thanks to my highly evolved skill at blacking out. Whole huge chunks of my life are gone, millions of brain cells stir-fried. Clemmy stayed at least marginally conscious but forgot the unpleasant things *he* did, in a somewhat calculating manner, so that our mornings, or afternoons, since that was when we got up, often went something like this:

"I did what?" I'd say groggily. "I didn't!"

"Oh yes you did," Clemmy would insist. "You got right down on the curb and put your arms around that bag lady and kissed her. You were feeling each other's titties, right on Santa Monica Boulevard."

"No!"

"Yes!"

"Naked?" I'd ask. Clemmy thought carefully.

"No, through the cloth. If you could *call* it cloth. Then you gave her all your money." Hmmm, that sounds right. Clemmy and I are always giving somebody all our money; that is, all the money we have *on* us.

"Oh, well. Was that before or after you shook your dick at that barmaid who wouldn't serve you?"

"I never did that."

"Oh yes you did, honey. You said he was thirsty. You took him out and gave him a little drink."

"Of my own drink, or somebody else's?" Clemmy would ask. I tried to recall.

"Yours, I think."

And after all the tales were told, the juiciest parts saved, by Clemmy, for last, savored and strung out and relished, Clemmy would moan, "I feel sick, honey," and I'd get up and cook him something spicy, if there were groceries, or go to the phone and order out Chinese. During most of these misspent evenings I was the worst, atrocity-wise, though this was not always the case. I did the worst little things, Clemmy did the worst *big* things. I kissed scummy drummers in front of him, true. He took heiresses to Ireland. Ultimately, Clemmy did the very worst thing: He stopped loving me. But you already know all about that.

Our lovemaking, after these bouts of abuse, was very nearly perfect, blood vessels swollen, every nerve close to the skin. We got up, ten minutes before the last good restaurant in L.A. closed down. We rested a lot, trying to recover our health. We worked sporadically.

A few days later, the whole cycle would start over. The point is, we always forgave each other. I thought I'd met my match, someone I could show my real self to, someone who was just as bad as I was, who would love me despite or because of this, who I didn't have to lie to, at least not much.

But Clemmy was always going through these massive self-improvement campaigns. He was always trying to be *better.* I wanted us to improve too, but slowly, less dramatically. I wanted us to drink and fuck around less, to work more, but gradually. Clemmy couldn't do that. It was all or nothing, on the wagon or falling down drunk, monogamy or Mr. Wu's Outcall Massage Service, *Send up a six-pack please.* I'll say this for Clemmy: Nobody ever called him Mr. In-Between. And every time he went on one of these cleanup campaigns and failed to be stronger than dirt, Clemmy blamed me for pulling him down.

I'm not sure what caused this pattern, or why it was so much worse when we were together than when either of us was with someone else. As for me, I think it had something to do with going to the AA nursery when I was a kid, playing with the children of the other alcoholics and listening, through the door, to our families testify. In my family, it was Uncle Elmo who fell off the wagon. He fell off it over and over. His sister-in-law, Aunt Zelda, would drag him to AA. She had the power to do this. She owned the family business, a small country store where Uncle Elmo was the butcher.

I used to visit Uncle Elmo at work, behind the butcher block. The meat cleavers and knives hung all around him, gleaming from racks that came down from the ceiling. Uncle Elmo stood there in his bloodstained apron. When I toddled through the door, his gray eyes lit up, and he'd stop what he was doing at the sight of me, put down his knife, wash his hands very carefully, take off his apron and give me a kiss. I always waited for him to perform this ritual cleansing. I never just jumped into his arms. I can still smell Uncle Elmo's kisses: a blood smell, mixed with Vitalis.

After that kiss I played in the store. My favorite object was a big yellow salt lick, bigger than I was, with totemic powers. I circled around the salt lick warily and approached it as if it were alive. Finally I ran up quick and touched my tongue to it and tasted the rough salt like ambrosia. Then someone—my aunt or uncle or perhaps some neighbor—was sure to say the magic words: "She's just like a little heifer." And all at once I *became* that heifer, galloping and mooing up and down the aisles, smelling the groceries like field flowers. "Why, lookee there," they'd all say. "Look at that baby. She's just like a little heifer." Those are the magic words I said on my roof, the night I blew out the lights on the Empire State Building.

But there was this little worm in the idyllic apple of my childhood, this occasional problem at the grocery store. As often as once a month, my uncle would be different when he came to work. He'd come in perhaps five hours late. He'd hang up his hat in the usual place and reach for his apron and get ready for work like a man under water, thinking hard about the ethics of every step. His eyes would move twice as fast as his body, looking like something was lost. His Adam's apple would crawl up and down like a small pet rat. He'd forget to tie his apron, and on either side of him the limp white strings would dangle in blood-soaked sawdust, threatening to trip Uncle Elmo up and send some shouldered carcass flying into the pickle barrel with a joyous, incriminating splash.

This part of the day, leading up to something, never lasted all that long. Aunt Zelda would go behind the meat counter with the strangest look in her eyes, sad and angry at the same time, but always more sad than angry, and a little wistful too. Maybe she was thinking of her own dead husband, Elmo's brother, R.D., who was rumored to have died of drink, driving his pickup, liquored up. Before Uncle Elmo could sharpen his knives, Aunt Zelda would stop him.

"I think you'd best get along home now, Elmo," my aunt would say firmly. "You're drunk."

There was never any arguing with this statement of my

aunt's. My uncle would look at her for a few seconds, considering what she said very carefully, rolling it over in his mind, then would nod politely, just once, as if he was glad she'd pointed it out to him, as if he hadn't noticed the being drunk himself, but now that she'd mentioned it, he guessed it was pretty well true after all. Then he'd take off his apron and leave the store, tipping his straw hat politely as he shuffled out. The customers would avert their eyes, ashamed for him. This was a dry county, a Godfearing one. Drinking to excess was considered a serious problem, not just a disagreeable by-product of everyday life, a social necessity almost. That my uncle consumed less alcohol in his entire life than I have so far—than most of my friends who live so-called normal lives have—should be, by now, apparent.

After my uncle left the store, not going home but to a bar he favored on the Fort Worth highway, my Aunt Zelda would pick up the receiver of the old black wall phone and turn the crank energetically.

"Marguerite! Marguerite!" Aunt Zelda would yell. She always yelled into the phone. After all, she was bridging distance. "Marguerite! Could you get me Gus Biederkampf?"

Gus was a German butcher, now retired, who had settled here after being interned in a POW camp thirty miles away, during the war. He became a butcher in my Aunt Zelda's store soon after Uncle Elmo got drafted. Gus didn't like to butcher anymore, which was understandable. He had his own farm now, his own chores to do. But Gus owed a lot to Aunt Zelda, and there was still something of the enemy alien in him, an eagerness to please which Aunt Zelda never failed to take advantage of. In an hour or two, Gus would be over. My aunt put the phone back in its cradle, satisfied.

Aunt Zelda always waited until my uncle was out the door before making this call to Gus Biederkampf, though she could have saved herself, and Gus, some trouble by making the call at 6 A.M. when Uncle Elmo failed to show up for work. She never did that. She wanted to be sure. She didn't want to embarrass him. He could have been in a car wreck, after all. But her delicacy, if that's what it was, didn't save Uncle Elmo's face. The minute she put in the call to Gus, the whole town knew the story—if not from Marguerite the telephone operator then from Gus himself or his wife, Mary Ella, or just from seeing Gus, who owned property, cutting meat like an exiled king— and go out and spread the word: Elmo Desplanes is drunk again. Elmo Desplanes got liquored up. At three in the morning, after the bars closed, Uncle Elmo would creep into our little garage apartment. Sometimes he and Aunt Faye fought. Not always. The following week, my uncle would go back to AA. Our town wasn't big enough for its own AA chapter, so we drove forty miles in Aunt Zelda's new Pontiac to the one in Mineral Wells.

"Pass 'em, Zelda! Pass 'em!" I'd urge, jumping up and down on the dark green upholstery. Despite my encouragement, my aunt never drove over forty. The cars streamed by us.

Meetings were held in a building that looked like a cattle barn and might have been that at one time. Bales of hay were piled outside it, but these were just for decoration. The building was used for square dancing every night but Wednesday, when we took it over. There my uncle testified, sweet and embarrassed, never really sure what it was he'd done wrong, while I played with the children of the other drunks. They formed an alternative social group for me, different from nursery school or neighborhood. They seemed more exciting, wilder, older.

They stole their fathers' cigarettes, nickels from their mothers' purses.

But when Uncle Elmo was about to fall off the wagon, he wouldn't want to go to AA. When Wednesday night came, he was nowhere to be found. This was the tip-off, for us, that he was about to tie one on, the aura that comes before an epileptic's seizure. Waiting for Uncle Elmo to come home, and realizing he wouldn't, her face put on and purse packed up, her Pontiac outside gassed and ready, Aunt Zelda's face would get set and stony. Aunt Faye would chew the lipstick off her lips. My mother would hide in the kitchen, trying to stay out of it. I was always the first to break the silence. When I realized Uncle Elmo was AWOL, a big howl would spill out of me. I'd stomp my little feet and cry in frustration and Aunt Faye would come over and pick me up and rock me, her fine teeth spotted with scraps of red skin. I didn't care at all about Uncle Elmo's drinking. I wanted to play with my friends. The following week, I'd start on Uncle Elmo three or four days in advance. You might say, manipulation-wise, that I cut my teeth on poor Uncle Elmo.

"I want AA," I'd pout to my uncle at every opportunity, sticking out my wet lower lip against him. I nagged him mercilessly for hours. Not even playing horsey would shut me up. "AA, Uncle Elmo! AA!" I'd demand imperiously, joining the chorus of female disapproval against him even as I bounced up and down on his knee. Most of the time, Uncle Elmo stayed sober. We'd pile in the Pontiac and drive to Mineral Wells, while Uncle Elmo thought of whiskey.

Every few months, AA had these socials which Uncle Elmo called "Cokers," because that was all there was to drink there. They'd play Hank Williams records and people would dance close, their children darting between them like butterflies.

"That music does make me powerful thirsty, ma'am," said a red-faced old dirt farmer mournfully, depositing my mother at our table after a dance.

My mother, whose sweet lips liquor never touched, responded politely. "May I get you a Coke, Mr. Dupree?"

One night my mother fought with Dusty Sherwood. Maybe he tried to get fresh, I don't know. Maybe he tried to hold her too tight. All I saw was the end of the altercation, when my mother pulled away from him, her face on fire.

"If I was a man, I'd blister your britches," she hissed.

Dusty Sherwood laughed. He weighed two hundred pounds, all of it muscle. He was the biggest thing in sight, twice as big as my mother, and not unattractive for all that. He picked her up effortlessly and held her in the air, big hands almost spanning her waist. She fought him for a minute, then stopped and looked down. I saw something pass between them, some current of attraction. I saw it in my mother's eyes for about a second, the pleasure at being lifted taking her completely by surprise. My mother was twenty-three. No one had touched her in five years. She was on the *man* wagon, the *love* wagon. Then the pleasure just drained out of her, as quickly as it came, replaced all at once by this killing despair with which there was just no arguing. My mother's mind had these faulty circuits in it, these demented crossed wires. All feelings concerning men or sex or pleasure led inevitably, in my mother's mind, to my long-gone father. Daddy stood at every synaptic juncture, holding a suitcase with a sign on it saying WELL-TO-DO OR BUST over this arrow pointing straight up, waiting to hop on the gravy train, making my mother miserable, keeping her from loving anybody else. Dusty Sherwood didn't recognize the look, but I did and

started to bawl. Dusty put my mother down. She picked
me up automatically and walked away without a word,
thinking about my father and those nights in Pascagoula
on the grass.

Dusty Sherwood followed her, bewildered. When he
stood in my mother's path, she steered around him like a
rock in the river. He followed in her wake a second time,
but not a third. He was still trying to figure out what to
do when Mrs. Hill intercepted us. She got up from her
chair with difficulty, and propelled her great bulk toward
us, took my mother's arm, and led her over to this old bull
fiddle in the corner.

"Play, child," Mrs. Hill said.

"Lord, Miz Hill, I can't play!"

"Cain't never did nothing," Mrs. Hill said firmly. Already my mother was putting me down, moving like she
had no choice. She picked up the shredded horsehair bow
and stood behind the fiddle. When she drew it against her,
her skirt hitched up far enough so that Dusty Sherwood,
across the room, licked his lips at the sight. My mother had
legs like a Las Vegas showgirl. Dusty started to come over
for a better view of them, but thought better of it when
he caught Mrs. Hill's good eye. Her other eye was glass,
as shiny as a crow's.

"Play 'Turkey in the Straw,' " Mrs. Hill commanded.

Valiantly, my mother sawed. She had taken cello lessons
in high school, so she knew the principles. The music
sounded horrible, but my mother got better with every
stroke. She had a picture of the music in her head to go
by. She knew what the music was supposed to feel like,
when it traveled through her and into the fiddle. She
knew what it was supposed to sound like when it came out
the other side. All her life, if nothing else, my mother
knew how to fantasize. When we walked down country
roads, she'd have conversations with the landscape, the

animals: "Good morning, Mrs. Tree, Mrs. Footbridge, Mrs. Boulder. How's the weather, Mrs. Black Snake? Mrs. Swamp? Mrs. Stump? Getting enough sun, Mrs. Turtle, Mrs. Water Moccasin?" Mrs. Hill tapped her foot while my mother played, satisfied.

Three months later, my mother married Mrs. Hill's son Jack, a middle-aged auto mechanic who lived in Fort Worth. Jack had recently divorced his third wife, Helga, after committing her to the asylum at Wichita Falls. We would've been happier on Dusty Sherwood's farm, but my mother didn't want to risk anything like *that*. *You* know what I mean. My mother wanted to stay on the wagon. She said she did it for *me*.

In Cannes, I decide my problem isn't the falling-off-the-wagon part of these cycles, but the getting on the wagon in the first place. The wanting something better. The complaining about being so wretched. The feeling guilty. The problem isn't fucking up, but expecting to do anything else. I start to accept the deranged personality I was born with, or maybe created. What's *your* opinion on nature/nurture? Does heredity make a difference? Does anybody give a fuck? I decide to stop expecting so much of myself, in hopes of being less frequently disappointed. I concentrate on bingeing, take the pledge on purge.

I learn about smack from the chic Parisians. At twenty, already they're as old as death. Dragging centuries of dark perversions behind them, dragging lies and compromises, the fruits of their dubious civilization, they don't have much of a chance to start with and they never take chances in any case. Many of them, like me, have talent, which militates against happiness but not insanity. Our talent makes us interesting, but it doesn't protect us. We do smack all night and sleep like puppies in a pile for the Moroccan maids to find in the morning.

The French are so sophisticated, I don't know what to make of them. I have never been to so many parties, or met so many men who are bisexual. I am always, always, putting my foot in it here. I feel constantly out of my league. Every time I say something direct, something that requires a yes-or-no answer, I feel like a rube from Iowa or, as we used to say in Texas, from Bum Fuck, Egypt, before I knew what a bum fuck was, before I had ever been invited, by a film festival, to Egypt, all expenses paid.

Nicholas, who owns the villa where I'm staying, is kind and gentle and complex, also small. When he's on top of me it feels like nobody's there at all. He says he only falls

in love with women, but spends most of his time chasing
men. For the first time, this doesn't worry me. I'm resigned to getting AIDS, along with everybody else. Surely
it's only a matter of time. With Nicholas and the heroin,
I move effortlessly into the high-risk group, female, where
I belong. I go straight from barbarism to decadence without stopping at civilization, just like de Toqueville predicted. I find this doesn't bother me at all.

Despite his lack of stature, Nicholas treats me like a
little girl, which doesn't bother me either. I no longer
mind if men patronize me. I don't *want* to be taken
seriously. It's far too much responsibility. When Nicco
takes me to parties, I talk to the girlfriends of the other
powerful men, just as if I were a girlfriend too. Just as if
I'd never accomplished anything. So much *easier* that
way, don't you think? Nicco is happy to let me talk about
shopping and the exchange rate with the other decorative
bimbos. He only remembers my place in the world when
someone else points it out, and even then he doesn't quite
believe it, though that's why he reacquired me. There had
to be *some* reason. But I'm not acting right! Nicholas
thinks I'm conning him. I'm not acting like a famous person should. If I'm somebody, why am I hanging out in his
villa, instead of on the Croisette? Why aren't I introducing
him to movie stars? What's *wrong* with me?

"Tell them about when you were on the Johnny Carson
show, Anna Kate," Nicholas commands before a roomful
of skeptical Frogs. "Tell them how Johnny put a bottle of
champagne in your dressing room."

"I was on the Johnny Carson show," I say listlessly.
"Johnny put a bottle of champagne in my dressing room."
I tell these stories with such a lack of conviction that even
I start to doubt them. Maybe it happened to somebody
else, after all. Maybe somebody *really* famous hired me as
their stand-in, and I just don't know it yet. My very exis-

tence depresses my new French friends. Why should anybody struggle, just to wind up like *me?* I'm a neon sign
flashing *It just doesn't matter.*

Every few days, I sit down at Nicco's desk and look at
his typewriter. I put a sheet of paper in it, type a few
phrases, and sigh to myself about the difficulty of the
French keyboard. I sit there for an hour or so, then close
up the typewriter and make myself a drink. Does this
sound familiar? Nicholas *told* me to make myself at home.
Even so, I'm always sure to make up some anecdote, some
tale about my so-called work, so my *chéri* won't think I'm
becoming a slothful parasite, therefore uninteresting, and
kick me out. By eight o'clock, I usually pull myself out of
zombieland, aided by drugs, of course. By eight, I'm witty
again, and sparkling. I'm Anna Kate O'Shea—*ta da!*—who
debuted so auspiciously such a short time ago.

Most evenings, we go clubbing. We start at these clubs,
which are always the same clubs, barely distinguishable
one from the next. We start somewhere and end somewhere else, moving from club to club like a school of
gaudy fish. All the chic clubs in Cannes have imported
these New York doormen to insult their would-be clien-
tele in the hippest possible way. You can be picked over
in Cannes right now, *right this minute,* by the same high
school dropout who wouldn't let you into Nell's last week.
Some *vacation.*

After clubbing we sleep, then wake up and eat something rich and tasty and go out again to parties at somebody's home. The best parties, the serious parties, are at
people's houses. The *very* best parties are at our place.
Since I moved back in with Nicholas, the intensity and
frequency of the parties has increased dramatically, or so
I'm told. Both Nicholas and I flirt outrageously. He uses
me to bait these traps he sets for other men. I go along
with them to a point, but I don't really follow through, or

participate, which annoys him. I like my sex in private, intense and dirty, old-fashioned. I refuse to let other people watch me do things, or watch them, or pretend to be excited about things that happen in groups, with the lights on. The truth is most of these people don't attract me. They're too civilized. I'm longing for some ex-Marine, some Bud or Spud or Pud to take me in his tattooed arms and ravish me in the back of his pickup, then swing me up on his Harley, the one with the sticker that says HOGS R US. Will somebody please fish me out of this frog pond? You say I'm in so deep, it'll take *meat hooks?* Very astute of you, sir, and now that you mention it I think I'll stay right where I am.

One night I woke up and found two people fucking in our closet, trampling my best shoes, crushing Nicco's expensive suits. This casual assault on our property made me angry. I got out of bed and kicked them out. Usually this doesn't happen.

If I'm tired and want to sleep and can't get rid of the person whose elbow is in my back, who is moaning too loudly because Nicco is using his or her body, I take a pillow, blanket, and book to the maid's room and sleep there. Our maid, Farida, sleeps out. In the afternoon when we all get up, we have Bloody Marys together, made with spicy Polish vodka with buffalo grass in the bottle. If the person in question is very pretty, very witty, we have smack. I never inject myself with anything, though. This isn't because of any residual instincts of self-preservation, but because I can't find a vein. Even when my arm is tied off, my veins are hardly there. I eschew needles. My friends call me a baby for it. There is something childish, for them, also wasteful, about snorting heroin instead of injecting it. They feel I'm holding back, which makes them nervous. But no amount of peer pressure will cause my veins to bulge for the needle. Not even a tiny bit.

If my veins were like garden hoses and popped out nicely on demand, I would be in big trouble, I think, watching Nicholas shoot up last night's boyfriend with our house works, newly sterilized by me in the dishwasher. The bright blood blossoms in the syringe, then vanishes. The model from Marseilles leans back, relaxed. Serious, serious trouble.

Friends call us in the middle of the night sometimes, come over, take our stash. They say they'll pay us back but they don't. They think we're rich enough to help them out once in a while. Their dead eyes scare me, but not enough. I yawn, cut another line, and snort it. Nicholas watches me and pouts. Lucky we're rich enough to afford this wasteful indulgence: my adamant refusal to shoot up.

As I lick the mirror, I think about a story I heard last night about a designer who couldn't get any more smack out of the bottle, and wanted more, and couldn't find anyone to bring her any, and was found later, by friends, rolling on the floor, chewing the bottle, trying to suck smack out of the glass. Drugs do strange things to people. Some people get so desperate they lick the coke out of each other's noses. Drugs make even close friends into horrible liars. Let's take a typical case: Your best friend's bought a quarter ounce of coke—buying in bulk is so thrifty, don't you think—and she wants to sell off just a wee bit to you, to do you a favor, or so she says, so you go over to her place to try it.

"This is really great stuff!" she'll say, pumping you up psychologically before you sample the mixture of baking soda, Novocaine, and ground aspirin she's bought sight unseen and is trying to unload on *you*. You can *afford* it. She *can't*. "Almost pure rock!" she says.

"Gino told me he didn't even touch it, just tapped it very lightly."

Does she really think this coke is *good?* you wonder miserably after trying it, too embarrassed to call attention to what might be bad taste instead of greed. Does she really think this coke is *coke?* But you buy a gram of the awful stuff, which she's already bottled for you and cut even more, herself, with Extra-Strength Tylenol. Perhaps she puts the so-called pure coke on top and hers on the bottom. By the time you've excavated those final layers, you might not even notice. And when you get home and haul out the scales, you find she's given you short weight, too! Oh, well, if you do up the entire so-called gram of so-called coke, you'll probably get a buzz of *some* sort. At least it won't *hurt* you. It'll cure your *headache.*

The next night, you'll be out together and agree to split yet another gram, and your friend will finish her half long before you do, since you're being prudent for once. Such a waste of time and money.

"I had to turn on Jeremy D'Entrement, in the bathroom," she'll say, hand out for your half. "Mine's all gone," she'll say, as the cab pulls up to your door, and immediately do up the entire bottle. If you're lucky, when you get upstairs, you might be able to scrape out one more line. Being prudent, drugs-wise, never does anybody any good. You never get the leftovers anyway. Frugality doesn't save you anything. Might as well do up everything you've got, as fast as you possibly can, so nobody else does. You can *always* buy more. That's what we do in France, only, because South America is so far away and Turkey is so close, we buy smack, to be neighborly. We go to parties, snort smack, and throw up. *Très* festive.

Oh, now and then some cocaine does come in, by diplomatic pouch, from Nicaragua. Such *politically correct* coke. Doing it makes me feel so virtuous, I think I'll do

some right now. Hey, don't give me that look, *compañero,*
*compañera.* Even Reagan gets it right once in a while.

The night *The Penetrator* opens I abandon my own party,
which is full of my peers, all of whom are congratulating
me, seeing as how I've finally gotten a movie made out of
one of my scripts that isn't just successful, it's actually
good. I flee my own party, where everyone is giving me
such good advice, as well as the A list, B list, and C list
parties, and improvise an intimate Z list party at Nicco's
villa that promises to get seriously out of hand. On the way
up there from the Croisette, Chipper Donaldson, a street
musician from Wilmette, Illinois, tries to make me in a
taxi, but he's so cheap I just can't see it. Chipper never
picks up a check. He never has the correct change for
anything. He has more luck with Dixie Credit, a gossip
columnist for the *Toronto Star* who knows the royal family of Monaco personally.

"You're really quite dishy," Dixie says to Chipper,
touching his cheek, and indeed he is, a sleek and well-fed
rich boy. Even while slumming he's bursting with health,
like a fat pond leech.

"Yeah, don't you just want to take me upstairs and fuck
me to death," Chipper says. Dixie grabs him by the tie and
calls his bluff. Things get somewhat raunchy from that
point on. Pretty soon, Chipper and Dixie are in the bedroom and the rest of us are upstairs, trying to peek
through the keyhole.

"Touch her leg, touch it," Nicholas says to me later.
Five of us are on the bed by then. Dixie is still naked,
though bashful Chipper's pulled on his pants. "Touch her
leg," says Nicholas. "It's so soft."

I do. It is. How would *you* like to be Dyke for a Day?
Dixie winks at me. We are both unregenerate heterosexu-
als, obliging the men with a little visual treat. Why do men

want to see women make love? Why do they force it on us, over and over? The best answer wins a weekend in the sack with Anna Kate O'Shea! Please enclose a recent photograph with your entry. Also some blood.

And speaking of photographs, Nigel Featherbone's here. He's got a video camera with him to make these tapes for his fellow throwbacks in swinging Jo'burg. When I was with him, he made tapes of *me,* some of them not too discreet, all of which I wiped the minute he was out of sight: Anna Kate O'Shea Dressing; Anna Kate O'Shea Doing Illegal Drugs; Anna Kate O'Shea on the Toilet Changing Her Tampax With a Killer Hangover. You get the picture. Nigel's loaded with equipment, he keeps shooting events that most of us here would just as soon keep private, if you get my drift, and finally someone calls him on it. This French producer, whose wife is a moderately big star, very politely walks over to Nigel and asks him to erase the group portrait he's made of them and a couple of *needles.* What's that you say, Nigel? No? Nigel says no one will ever see the tape, I feel compelled to point out that this is a lie, and a few minutes later the camera is smashed to smithereens and Nigel has a cut on his head that needs medical attention. Bye-bye, Nigel. Sorry you couldn't stay longer.

Dixie and I beat a fast retreat from the carnage. The last heterosexual girls in town grab a bottle of champagne and lock themselves in the bathroom. Outside, the petulant men protest. They want to watch. Their puny, bisexual shoulders crash weakly against the door. Finally, they go away. We rub each other's feet and try not to drown, but this is as far as it goes. I think it's important to eschew at least one perversion. I only kiss women in public and only when I'm drunk so that not much can happen and whatever it is I don't remember it anyway. How will I get my genius baby if I become a Lesbian? With come in a turkey baster?

By the time Dixie and I are dressed and downstairs, there are all these new guests in the house. Oh, goody, Dagmar's here! Dagmar, our dealer. She sells smack from a boutique in one of the swank hotels. Silk scarves, jewelry, and heroin, for not too many francs at all. Dagmar is funny and stylish. Of course, she makes house calls. She doesn't look like a junkie, more like a New York rock and roller. She makes being a junkie less threatening. More glamorous. Almost logical. With her flashing black hair and chunky jewelry, her ropes of acid green and yellow rhinestones, Dagmar is the junkie we all want to be. Has Dagmar brought anything tasty? What do *you* think? A quick trip to the bathroom and then back downstairs.

A gigantic medium from Martinique is telling fortunes. His massive henchman grumbles. We are too few, too drunk. The trip has been a waste, financially. And there are no big stars here, not even a single one. Nicholas is in the downstairs john, getting a blow job, his favorite pastime, from this sound editor from L.A., a really talented guy, all right. Once, when I refused to suck him a minute longer, Nicholas said, "Darrell Truesdale said my come would taste like honey, if I stopped smoking." "But you didn't stop smoking, did you," I replied crossly, batting his dick out of my face like it was a large white fly. When I see Nicholas and the sound editor, all I can think of is AIDS, which despite my earlier bravado I don't really want to get. That's what Nicholas and I broke up about the first time. I decide, on the spot, not to sleep with him again.

There are straight couples in the garden and gay boys in the kitchen, a whole group of them introducing each other to their cocks, which all have cute names here in

France. And I am being pursued by a street musician from Manchester with bad teeth. I have no intention of fucking him, and tell him so, over and over.

"That's awright," Johnny says sweetly. "It don't matter." I go upstairs, take off my evening dress, and put on a *Rust Never Sleeps* T-shirt and jeans. I take off all my makeup. I'm tired, but there's no place to sleep. Nicholas and the sound editor have joined a group grope on our bed.

When I come back to the garden, Johnny is waiting for me. He rubs my feet and tells me how beautiful I am. He's beautiful too, with his mouth closed. He wants to get into pictures. He wants me to get him a *screen test.* Poor Johnny. By three o'clock, there's no longer any reason *not* to sleep with him. Just say yes. But there aren't any beds, it's too late to find a taxi, and I don't want to go to his scummy hotel by the train station. So we take a bottle of Scotch and the keys to another house on the estate that's being remodeled. There's no electricity, no sheets on the bed, but I find some candles in a drawer in the dining room. I look there because my mother had the same kind of buffet, albeit a copy, before Jesse Turner traded it for a broken air conditioner and a six-foot plywood cross with Christmas lights on it, and this was where she kept her candles. I open the drawer. Hello, candles. H-E-L-L . . . O! I light one, then find some blankets.

On the bed, the light is really wonderful: first the candlelight, then the dawn. If I could only stop worrying about getting some strange lumpen disease, I would be having a wonderful time right now. If only Johnny would stop talking, the sex in this bed, in this light, would be transcendent. He's so sweet and skillful inside me, tender and huge and inexhaustible. He really seems to like sex with me, to be inside, on top. All the things I like, with *one woman at a time.* If only he would stop talking! I think

I'll go crazy if I hear one more word about prison or the orphanage. I've had a horrible life too, I want to say. But Johnny would never believe me—looking like I do, acting like I act. I've done my little job of assimilation far too well. Johnny's life is much worse than mine in any case, and the bad parts of it don't seem to be over. Johnny doesn't seem to have much of a plan for ending the horribleness of his horrible life. Instead of making me sympathetic, his stories just make me mad. I don't want to feel sorry for him, or to feel guilty for *not* feeling sorry. I want to fuck him, but I don't want to help him. I wonder if in some essential way I've become a man, like Margaret Thatcher. Then I go to sleep.

In my dream I'm back on a bed in the main house, this time with Clemmy. We're making love, it's slow and gentle and sweet, we've gotten back together somehow and we love each other again. I can't believe how good it is. Then a whole bunch of people troop into our bedroom. A big blonde in a fringed cowgirl suit plops down on the bed, with cotton candy hair and tits like nose cones and a big round mouth, permanently pursed for sucking. She looks like one of those inflatable dolls you buy on Times Square, only alive. Clemmy and I are still touching under the covers, but under the weight of all these people our feelings leak away. We stop touching, sit up.

"I hear you're a great writer," the blonde coos, sticking her bare foot in Clemmy's lap and wriggling her toes.

"I'm a writer too," I say, trying to put myself between them, but the blonde ignores me, intent on making Clemmy's cock grow under her foot.

"I'm hungry, honey," he says appealingly. I get up obediently and go into the kitchen.

When I get back, all the blonde's clothes are off except this leopard-skin Merry Widow. Clemmy has just finished tying her up and is showing her pornographic pictures.

Looking over his shoulder, I see they're pictures of me.
Facing the camera, legs spread, I bear an uncanny resem-
blance to the late great blond bombshell Barbara Payton,
as I remember seeing her in a still from this porno film
made shortly before her death, reproduced in some grimy
paperback bio. Payton, once the most beautiful woman in
Hollywood, was naked in the picture, slack breasts in
hands, flabby thighs spread, a drunken smile on her face,
teeth missing. Somebody cropped the picture coyly, just
above cunt level, which transformed it somehow, made it
less pathetic and more obscene. Barbara Payton was forty
when she died. I look very much like Barbara Payton
*already,* I think, dreaming logically for once in my life. In
a few more years, if I don't watch it, I'll look *exactly* like
her without the consolation of having once been beautiful.

Staring at my photos, the blonde laughs derisively. Enraged, I dump a plate of pork and beans on her head. The
beans eat into her skin. The sweet brown sauce sticks to
her flesh like napalm.

"This was my fault, not hers," Clemmy says, looking at
me sadly as smoke from the blonde drifts up toward the
skylight overhead. Her skin is crisping up nicely, like Pe-
king Duck.

"Yes, it really was your fault," I say to Clemmy. I don't
seem to be able to stop crying, looking at Clemmy's sad
face, and I'm still crying when I wake up.

"I had a nightmare," I say to no one, to myself, to
Johnny's dick, which is still at face level. But Johnny
doesn't wake up. His sleep is deep and primitive. His
hands are wrapped in my hair. Every few minutes they
open and close convulsively. In his sleep, Johnny moans
like a dog chasing rabbits.

I wake up again to the sound of French workmen laugh-

ing. Outside, they're rebuilding the foundation of the
house. One of them peeks in the window, then beats a
quick retreat, embarrassed to find me with come on my
face at four in the afternoon. But Johnny shows no signs
of leaving. He seems content in this house without electricity, in this bed without sheets. It's probably quite a
treat for him, in fact. He pulls me on top of him and makes
himself at home. I want to go shopping in Italy today, eat
*fritto misto* and drink red wine, buy cheap cosmetics and
expensive shoes. I want to stop in Monaco with Dixie
Credit and find out whether or not she really knows
Prince Albert. I don't want to pay Johnny's way, so he can
go with me, or find him here when I get back. I give him
two hundred francs to get a hotel room, about the price
of a pair of Keds at Kinney's. This is the first time in my
life I've ever given money to a man. One more taboo shot
to hell. One more little erosion in the self-respect department. I would give him more money, lots more, if he
would get his awful teeth fixed. I wonder, idly, what he
would look like then, in a tuxedo.

"Do you know what the first words I learned in French
were?" Johnny asks suddenly, curling back up into the
fetal position.

"No." I sit down beside him and stroke his bony spine,
his coccyx. "Tell me."

*"Je souffre."* I don't say anything. There isn't anything
to say. "I suffer," Johnny translates. *"Je souffre* means I
suffer."

"I know," I say. I finish dressing and leave. I go to Italy
with Dixie. I buy a three-hundred-dollar pair of black
suede boots. I have a wonderful time. We stop in Monaco
on the way back, but Prince Albert is out of town. A few
nights later, while I'm playing roulette in Cannes, I see
Johnny at the casino. I'm winning when he arrives, I have

a pile of chips in front of me, of different shapes and colors. But when Johnny comes over and kisses me, too drunk too early, laughing too loud, and stands behind me while I bet, and wraps his skinny arms around me and presses his hipbones into my ass, my good luck deserts me. The chips go quickly. My luck immediately begins to change.

THE next day the festival ends, the used and the useless decamp along with my Parisian playmates, Billyjim arrives without explaining where he's been, and I move back into the Martinez. We spend a number of days getting reacquainted, high on champagne and Percodan, which Billyjim carries with him by the hundreds. It's so easy for athletes, especially with knees like Billyjim's, roadmapped with operations, to get painkillers. At the end of our first day back together, Billyjim gives me the most expensive present I've ever gotten, a necklace with TEXAS spelled out in tiny diamonds. Although we don't discuss it, I have a hunch my cousin's trying to make up for the fact that we're not getting married and never will. All that talk he did about marriage is making him feel guilty. The prospect of not marrying Billyjim yet again makes me almost as sad now as it did the first time. I figure I deserve the rocks.

One day Cousin Billyjim is going down on me as boys tend to do, but I guess I don't show the proper appreciation or something. All I can think about is the mess my life's in, about the treatment nobody wanted to buy, about how I'm never gonna be anybody's little wife, about

Walter Light. Why don't you save me, Walter, like you promised? I'm starting to stop functioning in bed like everywhere else, but I don't seem to be able to do much about it. I just lie back and watch it happen, like TV in a foreign language and me too lazy to change the channel.

It can't be too satisfying, trying to make a corpse come, but Billyjim does his best, I guess. After a while he notices my zombie eyes and crawls up to where my face is and says, "What's the prob, Bob? Tech credits lousy?" The day that Billyjim "The Twister" Thibideaux read his first issue of *Variety* was a black one for the English language.

*"Au contraire,* sweetie, tech credits superb," I say, mimicking the lingo.

Billyjim pats my flank like I was a tired old horse and listens to my tale of woe, nodding sympathetically at the appropriate moments. I always try to keep things light, with Billyjim. I never tell him the serious things. But tonight—or is it daytime? It's dark in *here,* so let's call it night—tonight I do. I tell him about cousin Anna Kate and that sneaky skunk Walter, and Billyjim holds me tight and agrees that I should always get everything I want, including other people's husbands.

We do some more Percodan. It really is the best drug. I have missed it, hanging out with these French junkie poseurs. An American drug, I think patriotically, as it starts to hit sweetly. Percodan chemically induces a close approximation of real feelings as I recall them. Things seem sharper, more poignant, like having your nerve endings sandpapered. The conversation drifts back to me and Walter and Lily, who didn't even have to have her stomach pumped. I have Lily's letter in my bag and read it to Billyjim. By now I do Lily pretty well, though I have heard her voice only once, thin and prissy, when I accidentally picked up a phone in some hotel room.

*"I certainly hope we never hear from you or your brand*

*of 'love' again,"* I read. And then I say, real melodramatically, "I wish she'd just die, *die,* DIE!" and cry a little bit
more, angry that she hasn't, just to accommodate me, me,
me, and Billyjim holds me tight and shushes me and
makes love to me and it's better this time. Through the
pain and the Percodan, I'm feeling something. I'm feeling
that it's almost over. That the tears with Walter's name on
them have just about all been shed.

A bucket of Dom Perignon arrives with leering waiter
in tow. Billyjim calls it "Dee Pee." It took me years to
figure out he didn't mean Dr. Pepper. The waiter is staring so hard at me, decently draped with sheet, that I can't
resist a little theatrics and smile a prim madonnalike smile
as I let the sheet slide. The waiter's mouth drops open. He
blushes an appropriate cunt pink. Billyjim is laughing so
hard, the bozo doesn't even wait for his tip.

Later we go to the Blue Bar for a little nourishment, and
something strange happens. Nigel Featherbone sporting
a king-sized Band-Aid, sits down at our table, pretending
to be friendly, but he's still pissed off from the party at
Nicco's. I can tell. He thinks I should have stood up for
him when that French producer got on his ass. I know
Nigel's mad all right, and trying hard not to show it, but
I don't know *how* mad until he accidentally on purpose
upends a champagne bucket, brimming with water and
ice, on my lap.

Leave well enough alone, Nigel, I'm thinking as Billyjim and the waiter try to dry me off, to wring out my
bedraggled fox boas. But *noooo.* As smirking Nigel leaves
the table, he actually *flicks his lit cigarette* at me, as if he
were hoping it was gasoline in that ice bucket and the
spark of his Gauloise would set me on fire. Billyjim gets
the point then and goes for Nigel with a mad bull's roar.
Nigel is so surprised that anyone would actually use force
against him *yet again* that he just stands there, doesn't

even try to run. Billyjim picks him up and shakes him like
a dog worrying a rat, then slams him up against the wall
two or twenty times, until Nigel loses consciousness. His
Band-Aid slips, and I see he's had to have stitches, quite
a few in fact, sewn with heavy black thread, like Franken-
stein's. Somebody pulls Billyjim off him finally. Some *bodies*.

"Come on, honey," I keep saying, trying to drag Billyjim away. I've got the maître d's jacket on over my wet
dress and Mr. and Mrs. Fox in a shopping bag. "Please,
baby. He's not worth your *spit.*" I get Billyjim out, before the police come. I hope Nigel isn't too close to
death, I think idly, as we amble down the Croisette. I
wonder what I did, to make him hate me so much. I
don't remember doing anything that bad to him. I didn't
love him, true, but then again I don't love a lot of people.

We cross the street and walk along the waterfront. Billyjim stops to scan a yacht for fellow evolutionary detours.
I meander on. I sit on a bench and look at the ocean.
Billyjim walks toward me with a goofy grin, then breaks
into a trot and holds out his arms. I get up to meet him
and open my arms too, so we can hug like the couples in
those old Clairol ads, but when we're a few steps apart, a
screeching gull swoops down and drops the carcass of a
lobster between us on the dock.

"That was sure enough weird," Billyjim says in a shaky
voice, as we gingerly approach our little gift from God.
Yep, it's a lobster all right. A bright-red *cooked* lobster.
The gull probably plucked it from a restaurant terrace or
snatched it from a millionaire's yacht.

"Sure was," I agree, equally rattled. I tuck my hand into
the crook of Billyjim's arm, trying hard not to think about
the red and dead lobster, and haul him back to the Mar-

tinez. After a few Percodans, we both calm down. And an untold number of minutes later, Billyjim says there's this friend of his he wants me to meet.

Now Billyjim has a lot of sleazy friends, Mafia types, though no one knows whether they're technically Mafia or not. They look the part from the distance I always keep, and Billyjim fancies himself one of them, but he's not. He's big and strong but far too kind to really fit in. In America, he's careful about being seen with these villains. Already he's had one or two problems with the Football Commissioner's office. (He told them to bite his ass, as I recall.) But in Europe, he's less cautious about the company he keeps. He rubs himself like a kitten against their gangster glamour, as impressed with these thugs and hired killers as most people are with Billyjim himself. They have the best drugs, he has the prettiest women. It's kind of a trade-off. Nothing friendly about it.

And it seems one of these lowlifes caught my act and thought it was just too cute for words and wants to meet me, you know. Up close and personal. I don't remember what I did that impressed itself on his feeble mind. Probably settling a few scores with the male half of the species by taking some poor joker apart in front of my deranged cronies, who sat there egging me on, no doubt, handling me like a prize cock. Whatever it was I did was effective though, for somebody, and as a favor to Billyjim I say sure, call him up. Though I am pretty sure by now where it will lead, given the Percodan, which is good, mainly, for Only One Thing.

So Billyjim phones this guy, who must have been sitting somewhere, just waiting. He answers the phone immediately. The conversation is obscenely short. His name is Bruno, and I learn just before the door opens that the introduction wasn't a request: It was more of a command.

And pretty soon he's standing there: the man with the knife in the shower.

A girlfriend of mine once said that love can survive any-thing except fear, by way of explaining to a group of skeptical women why she was leaving this Guadeloupean fakir who could levitate when he fucked and cure her cramps by thinking nice thoughts her way. She was ter-rified of him. And I wanted to say, but didn't, afraid of being thought abnormal, that for me it's just the opposite. Except for my hike with Walter down that dead-end path, fear, for me, is no impediment to love. Fear is the precon-dition.

Outside, children play on the pearly beach. I can hear their laughter. It drifts through the window and floats across the bed, diminishing, when it gets to me, like a circus leaving town. Bruno closes the window and draws the shade. In the dark I recognize him: the Euro-trash in the white tuxedo from the Reconsider Lounge.

Up close, the first thing I notice is his skin, the kind of skin that denotes raging adolescent acne, treated by a quack dermatologist. Not the pasty Swiss-cheese faces that poor boys learn to live with after years of crater zits and Clearasil, but skin that's been peeled once too often— with chemicals and sun lamps and radiation, maybe— sandblasted down to muscle over bones like shattered glass.

Thick purple lips. Narrow blue eyes too close together. Heavy black brows. Hair bleached almost white. The smile is real horror-show stuff too, bespeaking a diet of cadged Hershey bars and Luckies during those Wonder years. Very . . . *European,* as gray as the rubble Bruno probably crawled out of. That Bruno hasn't had his bad teeth capped only calls attention to the work done else-where. He's the built-up runt in the Charles Atlas ads, expensively suited, freshly coiffed and ready to strangle the lifeguard.

Bruno is so different next to Billyjim, who always fights fair and sometimes loses, if the odds are wrong, but gracefully, clapping the winner on the back. It's Miller Time! Bruno would palm a stiletto just to get his point across. Need I say that he is just my type? That he's German only ices the cake; every woman loves a fascist, right? The brute, brute heart? *And that's why I fell for . . . the Leader of the Pack!*

We all do some more Percodans and drink some more champagne, a mellow golden glow in our glasses. The lines Bruno cuts are golden too, as thick as pencils. A little moist and lumpy, so smack, I think, and know smack when it hits: no quick cerebral rush, just a hardball straight to the stomach. And then there's this scramble for the toilet. Billyjim tries to be a gentleman and let me go first—"It don't make me no nevermind, cousin," he says graciously—but he can't hold it back. He throws up the good champagne and the half-digested tabs of Percodan, and as usual I stand in front of the bowl with my finger down my throat trying to puke like a big girl, but I can't. Something in me is always holding back, holding it down, while my friends troop out of the bathroom, empty and refreshed, ready to pour in more.

But the heroin is smooth today. The rumbling in my stomach subsides. When we get back to the bedroom, Bruno is sitting on the bed, smoking something dark and foul. Room service has already been and gone: icy champagne, but only two glasses. The bed is a long, long way from the bathroom, and I give getting there my full attention. The Frog on TV follows my progress. He gives a blow-by-blow account to the hecklers at ringside.

"Are you talking to me, you fucker?" I say out loud, De Niro to his Montand. "Are you talking to me? There's nobody else here." Halfway there, I lose Billyjim to a chair. His eyes roll back. Prospects are poor for a Thibideaux comeback. I almost turn and go to him, but Bruno's snake eyes stop me. I freeze like the Brownie manual says, but Bruno strikes anyway, and the fear hits me then, in tandem with the smack. A one-two punch. My knees buckle and I go down. Bruno catches me and pulls me to him for the count. Then his clothes are off too, and I'm counting his scars.

Some men can't fuck on heroin. Sex is no substitute for the thrills they can manufacture in their fast eroding brains. But Bruno isn't like that. The smack doesn't seem to affect him. He's big and hard, body covered back and front with silky dark hair. I don't like hairy men usually. They are too grown up for me, too adult. But I'm in no position to act on my aesthetic preferences. I start to respond. Bruno is so different, with his hair and scars and ugliness, his lack of conversation. He's like another species entirely. Like an animal, I think, as my arms go around him. I stroke the hair on his shoulders, electric against the grain.

The whole thing is so dirty, in fact, that I get enormously excited. I guess Bruno thinks I really like him, or It, since I am groaning and scratching him with such abandon. Bruno himself is completely controlled. There's no sign of pleasure in his face. Not even a tiny moan escapes him. He's a scientist completing an experiment successfully, running his cute white rat through a maze. When I come he takes both my hands and holds me down effortlessly; then he comes himself, hard and fast, banging into bone, hurting me a little but not enough to make me want to be anywhere else. His expression never changes. His eyes never leave my face.

When I squeeze him out and roll him off me finally, there are long black hairs all over my body and an odor like wet dog in the air. Bruno grins at me like a little boy, his mouth full of too many teeth.

We do a couple more lines, coke this time. Billyjim is next to us on the bed, up on one elbow, watching. I don't know how long he's been there. He could have died in that chair. I wouldn't have noticed at all. I almost wish he had when I see the smirk he's fighting, so *pleased* with himself. He's delivered the goods as ordered to Bruno, and the goods seem content, so no harm done. And a new batch of drugs, too. Free. What could be better? They toy with me casually, making sure not to touch each other. Not fags: two buddies on a double date. Bruno even says a few words. I'm surprised to find that he speaks English well, though what he has to say isn't particularly earth-shaking. Our conversation isn't exceedingly literate, but it has its intermittent charms. The leading players do their best with the shabby dialogue they've been given, the motiveless parts they've agreed to play.

I don't know exactly how long we stay in our three-character riff, in this dreamy sensual fog. I'm in no great hurry for this frivolous time killer to be over. Between these two enormous guys, these monsters, I feel ridiculously feminine and protected. Drink some more champagne. Eat a few more Percodans. Have another slow orgasm. Fondle the house nuts. A study in saturation? Maybe. But it provides moderate moment-to-moment amusement. Then Bruno says something that sets me off, when all he wants to do, I think, is *get* me off.

"I make you happy, baby," he says, his English, like my French, derailed in the present tense.

"You can't make me happy," I say crossly, reckless enough to take his metaphor literally. He's just a man like a thousand others. Why should I be afraid? "You can distract me—you understand 'distract'?—but you can't make me happy. No one can do that but Walter. Not even *you,* cousin," I say to Billyjim, sure all at once we'll never get married.

Bruno laughs at my little-girl bravado and chucks me under the chin. But his teeth are set in a sharklike snarl. Should I kill her now or later? Some heavy chin-stroking required. But I don't pay any attention. I'm thinking about Walter all at once. *Shit.* That's in-ner tor-ment!

"The little lady's blue because her boyfriend went back to his wife," says Billyjim disloyally. "The b.f. walked." My cousin giggles. The story really seems to interest Bruno, though. He is captivated by the clash-of-cultures part. He loves Walter being a famous scientist, like Werner von Braun himself.

"You think he is pure, do you?" Bruno says. He's not stupid after all. That's exactly what I think. "Better than us. Not corrupted. You think you take him away from his wife and get yourself a husband who is . . . how do you say . . . ?"

"Housebroken?" I say.

"Pussywhipped," Billyjim counters.

"The first is more what I mean," Bruno says. "Like a *teckel.* You think this Walter will never leave *schietze* on your rug. Life is not that simple, Anna Kate. You will never be happy."

"I would be."

"I know you."

"You don't know me at all."

"I know your work." This surprises me enough to shut me up temporarily. "You *make* the myths, baby," Bruno purrs, running his tongue over my nipple. "Don't start to believe them yourself."

It really is kind of amusing, I think, giving myself to Bruno's tongue. A real groaner. Here I am, demonstrating the Kama Sutra with two drug-soaked thugs and pining away for some dork scientist, just like Barbara Stanwyck did in *Ball of Fire.* I remember Barbara telling her gangster boyfriend about this encyclopedist, Gary Cooper.

"I love him because he always buttons his coat wrong," Barbara said. "I love him because he wears those funny shirts with the boiled collars." Permaprest. Walter wears Permaprest. "I love him because he doesn't know how to kiss, the jerk." The *jerk.* The *jerk.* The *jerk.*

For the first time I start to laugh at my situation. I see the humor in my dumb-cunt romantic self. Anna Kate the Girl Scout, always trying to improve, to win those plastic medals. All she needs is a Good Man's Love. How stupid can you get? I should have taken a Dale Carnegie course, or gone to AA or Betty Ford or est. I always thought I would've made a good Rajneesh. All that sex, yum. I really look good in red. Too bad there *aren't* any more Rajneeshes. Rajneeshi? They would've done me as much good as Walter Light. I can't seem to stop laughing. It really is funny. Bruno is laughing too.

"You want this physicist so much, I give him to you," he says, abandoning my nipple. I visualize Walter gift-wrapped: Anna Kate, Anna *K-K-K-Kate,* he's calling pathetically from some deserted beach. Under a tarp, Walter's naked and handcuffed, the *Mission Impossible* theme is playing on a ghetto blaster next to him, and in the distance there's Bruno in a speedboat watching through binoculars. I walk toward Walter. The motor starts. I look up, see Bruno drive away. Under the tarp, Walter struggles futilely. He's moaning and calling me, really afraid now. Helpless. All mine.

"In a few weeks," Bruno says, "I go to Toledo. On business. It is not far, Groverton. I will deliver your obsession to you. Free of his leash."

Bruno fumbles through my address book, the looseleaf

kind with little slips of paper in it. He tears out Walter's address and looks at it for a few seconds with this sly grin on his face, very theatrical, memorizing it. And then he eats it. He actually eats it! This cracks me up completely. What a great anecdote this will make after judicious editing. Just the right size for a postcard, with a picture of the Grand Palais on the front and some Libyan terrorists drawn on with red Magic Marker.

Bruno kisses me again and pulls me on top of him. He has a nice fat cock with a big purple head, the same ghastly purple as his mouth. As I ease myself onto it, I hear the familiar squish of K-Y on cock behind me. Billyjim's thinking no doubt of my cute little asshole, which he has never been allowed to visit. He grabs my waist with one hand, uses the other for exploration. I can feel one short fingernail through the jelly, then two. Then I don't feel the individual fingers, just this insistent pressure. Billyjim bends down and licks me where his fingers have been, something he didn't learn in Biloxi, Mississippi.

My eyes must have rolled out of my head because of Billyjim's tongue. Some moan of pleasure must have greeted this slippery new intrusion. I'm starting to enjoy it, enjoy it a lot, when Bruno sits up so smoothly and gracefully for such a big man that I'm hardly aware of his movement. One arm is around me, pulling me close, while the other very quickly and casually backhands Billyjim, whose skull slams into the padded headboard. Bruno doesn't want to share me with anyone. He doesn't want to coordinate his rhythms. No joint ventures for *him.*

Poor Billyjim, I think, pitying him his lost illusions. He's sitting against the pillows, with this goofy look on his face, blood trickling out of his mouth. Sacked. His dick is still in his hand. He watches it shrivel, wondering what the hell it's there for, then looks up and laughs—with all that Percodan in him there's no way he can be feeling any actual *pain*—then wipes off the blood, and wriggles his jaw. I laugh too, a tentative phony laugh, but Bruno isn't laughing. He's forgotten Billyjim completely, dismissed him like a slug on a path he's walking down in a hurry. And just about then it dawns on me that Bruno offered me something of value. Not Walter, tied up in Christmas ribbons, but something he can really give, a sort of post-fuck present, more precious than smack or diamonds: Lily's death. It's so nice that Bruno will be in the neighborhood. He won't have to make a special trip.

This is drug talk: exciting, but I don't take it seriously. I've had these conversations before. When I was fifteen, I used to plot my stepfather's death with my first love, Sam Allen. Stripped down to our underwear in his mother's bed while she was out shoving sheets through the mangle, we'd hold each other and kiss and talk about killing Jack Hill, who had sort of molested me at one point. Not a serious attack, I eventually learned, after hearing horror stories from friends and strangers, there wasn't any *penetration*, but it was effective. Yes indeedy. I was terrified of sex, a real basket case. I know it's hard to believe *now*, but I'd lie in Sam's arms, miserable and frozen and crying every time he tried to make some sexual advance, unable to fuck the boy I loved, the boy who loved me, because of this abortive attack by my stepfather.

Sam channeled his frustration into these elaborate plots of vengeance and justice. We were both convinced that Jack deserved to die for various crimes against humanity, humanity being Sam, my mother, and me. Besides satisfying my own desire for revenge, I figured I would play Honest Abe to Mom's grateful nigger. Why she never freed herself, on her own, was a question I didn't ask. So Sam and I talked about how it could be done: rabid German shepherds, hit-and-runs, artificially induced pneumonia. It had to look like an accident so we wouldn't get caught. If we did I would go to women's prison and get raped by diesel dykes with broomsticks, which would probably keep me from pledging a good sorority.

Self-defense was the best option, so Sam bought me this cute little flick knife. We couldn't afford a switchblade. I slept with it every night, under my pillow, hoping Jack would try something so he could die.

"Just stab in hard and pull up, baby," Sam said, demonstrating. Eviscerate was what he meant. I didn't know the word yet. But my stepfather seemed to have a second sense about all this, or maybe the first assault was some kind of drunken accident. Maybe Jack mistook me for my mother like he said. Anyway, he never touched me again.

It might have been better for me if he had. I could have been editor of the prison newspaper at Alderson, like Sam's big sister, Irene Frankfurter. Irene and her husband, Big Al, were arrested after they killed a motel clerk in Durant, Oklahoma, and for some undisclosed reason decided to put his body on ice, *in the trunk of their car.* Very good thinking, Irene and Big Al. It *was* hot that day. They were nabbed when somebody noticed their car dripping . . . *pink.* Big Al, whose parents were rich, copped an insanity plea, though he was the one who'd pulled the trigger. Irene, driving the so-called getaway car, got life for Murder One. If I'd killed Jack, I could've been like Irene, or learned—early enough for it to make a difference—that I am not a killer. But it never happened. So Sam started having talks with this three-hundred-pound sleazeball, this certified lowlife, Bubba Kincaid.

Bubba Kincaid was reputed to be a hit man, but he'd never been convicted of that. He'd been convicted of rape, assault, pimping, armed robbery, dealing smack, and a few dozen other things. Sam and I thought he was fabulously cool. He treated us like a couple of real cute pups, me especially. We were thrilled to be near him, to hear the stories about Leavenworth and El Reno that made me blush before I understood them. Bubba thought I was a living doll too, so when he got wind of what Sam and I had in mind, he made us this offer—made it to Sam, not to me, of course, since Sam was my owner, my *keeper.* I didn't have any say in the matter. He would kill Jack Hill, in exchange for the privilege of popping my cherry. He knew that Sam and I had no money and must have felt it was a fair exchange, even generous on his part.

"Death don't come cheap," I heard Bubba say often. But of course it does. Some people even do it for *fun.* Bubba didn't know about my little sex phobia, though, sex with *anyone,* even my smooth androgynous boyfriend, much less with a big hairy lug like him. So after weighing very carefully the question of whether or not to kill Bubba for besmirching my honor, Sam decided, prudently, to live, and for all I know is living still. Eventually I let him fuck me, seeing as how Billyjim already had, though I didn't tell that part to Sam. I let him think he was the First. We were so poor we used Saran Wrap for rubbers. And after that we stopped talking about killing Jack. A few months later, we were planning other things, like robbing Fort Knox with these psychotic ex-Marines who wanted the gold to finance the Revolution. Jack Hill died by himself, without any help from me.

Men have promised to kill or die for me several times, but none of them have. And now here's Bruno, a big unsavory lout, offering a blood-red valentine to the prettiest girl in the class. It's just empty words floating in the afternoon air, promising dubious returns, with limited offshore appeal. But it's exciting, this little flirtation with death. If I can handle this man, I can handle anybody. I've picked a winner this time. More to the point: A winner's picked me.

Bruno is completely intent on me now. I can feel my body getting lighter and lighter, like a cartoon balloon with a hole in it. I can almost hear the air rushing out of me, a loud farting sound, spelled *pfftt*. I feel myself floating, hovering above the bed. There are a thousand fingers down there inside me, a thousand sweet lips sucking as I rise into the air. I know Bruno must be lifting me, but there's no sensation of being lifted. It's like a pas de deux with Nureyev. I feel I've risen on my own, like sweet cream through milk, like shit to the top of the bowl. And I think about Faust and the bargain he made with the devil. I really do have a good education, even if all I ever use it for these days is entertaining myself when I'm blasted. I've always seen the devil dark and lean, with a beard and scepter and cloven hooves, but tonight he's blond, and I'm wondering idly if I've sold my soul or something, sort of rolling the idea around in my brain. But I haven't given up anything, or made any promises. There's no bargain. It's all on one side. A gift. An offering. Of course, I could reject it. I could tell him no. But it's all talk anyway, and then something is ramming into me hard, harder, hardest and the image of Faust shatters in hair and sweat and come. And I would be a liar if I said I didn't enjoy it. All of it. All of it. All of it.

I N a car, on a mountain pass, I'm having a conversation with my mother. She's driving the
Volkswagen bus that's taking me to Oregon,
where I'm about to start college. Everything is wet and
lush and verdant. The intense green foliage and blue sky
distract me from what my mother is saying.

"Everybody loved you, Katherine Anne," she tells me.
"I loved you, your aunties loved you, Grandpa loved you,
Sam loved you, Clemmy loved you." When the bus goes
off the highway and sails over the blue river a million
miles below, my mother is still talking calmly. "I never
saw such a pretty baby."

"Remember those little panties she had?" Aunt Faye
pipes up from the back seat, from the grave. "How many
rows of ruffles did they have on 'em, Livia?"

"Seven!"

"And who ironed them?"

"Oh, I did!"

"She was the prettiest baby," my aunt reminisces. "But
she wasn't spoiled, was she, Livia?"

"Oh, no! She was never spoiled." They go on talking,
but I'm not listening anymore. I'm wondering how I can
get myself out of this one, how I can cheat death just one

more time. The bus takes such a long time to fall. Why couldn't Jessica Savitch get out of the car? I think, as my eyes pop open. *Once an anchor person, always an anchor person.*

Bruno knots a dark silk tie with butcher's hands. Sunlight drips over his skin like butter on an English muffin, filling in the little scars and grooves, smoothing them. In the morning light, he's almost handsome. He notices I'm awake and comes over to the bed, sits down and kisses me gently. Automatically, my arms find his neck.

"Did you have a nice time, my little shiksa?" Bruno asks in a playful voice. I smile, nod. Bruno smiles back sweetly. "Did I hurt you?"

"A little."

"Good. You deserve to be hurt. Do you like to dance?" I nod again, too tired to speak, part of me still drowning in the van with my mother. Bruno takes both my breasts in his hands. "I thought so," he says, pinching my nipples lightly. "When I come to New York, I take you dancing. We go to the Reggae Lounge. Okay?"

"Okay," I murmur, responding to him, my skin like it's just been boiled. Maybe my skin will slide off under his hands like the peels on blanched tomatoes.

Bruno's left hand drifts down my body lazily, creeps under the sheet, reopens me. I come almost immediately. His free hand covers my mouth. When he takes his hand from my mouth, I kiss it. I kiss it like a calf on its way to being veal will suckle the fingers of the farmer pinning it. Desperate for a pat, a kind word in the dark, the calf will lick the hands that bolted its hooves to the floor as if they were the udders of its vanished mother.

When I wake up again, Bruno's gone. There's no one here but Billyjim, snoring raggedly and drooling pink on the pillow. There's nothing to tell me it wasn't a dream but these long fine hairs sticking to my body, this wet dog odor, and a thin liquid flood that runs all the way to my knees when I stand. I taste it with a finger: as sour and sharp as vinegar.

In the shower, I feel myself to see if anything's broken, but I am whole, if a little used up. One more slice off the loaf, like Jack used to say. They broke the mold, after they made *him*. There are a thousand little cuts inside me, as if from leprechaun razors, a few dozen bruises on my thighs. I get out of the shower and look in the mirror. As predicted, my pretty face has gone to hell.

As I'm getting dressed, Billyjim wakes up with a groan, grabs me, undresses me. When I kiss him, I can feel his loose tooth with my tongue. Billyjim pumps away, but after a while he stops and looks at me and says, "Shit, baby, I feel awful." We laugh, uncouple. I take another shower and dress.

Back in the bedroom, the zoo smell is as strong as ever. It makes me slightly nauseated. Or maybe it's just the desire for smack. I feel this unaccustomed craving for sunlight and air and head for the door mumbling something vague about my destination, but Billyjim barely notices. His eyes are riveted to the TV, which is still on from the night before. His shaky fingers dial room service first, for Bloody Marys. Then Dagmar.

"Hiya, babe," I hear him say. "How y'all are?"

And after this sordid interlude, I have a pretty good idea of how far down is. As I walk out of the Martinez, I notice I've forgotten my sunglasses, expensive ones this time, from Ted Lapidus, with gold and purple frames. So many pairs of sunglasses left in rooms I don't want to go back to. I'll have to buy another pair of sunglasses, I guess, and there are no cheap sunglasses in Cannes. Remember

that when you pack. But first I need some food. Bouillabaisse, I decide, and German beer, so I head for the
Little Carleton, where the Dutch distributors hang out
during the festival. But everybody's long gone. I don't
see anybody I know, except Stefan Ratt, remember him?
But Stefan pretends not to remember *me.* Imagine! He
doesn't want to give me any more kisses, I guess. Nobody
cuts anybody any slack.

I eat the strong fish soup with garlic paste, read the
*Herald Tribune* and think of Jean Seberg, scooting around
Paris in her Jeanne d'Arc do, T-shirted, prematurely
punk, Belmondo in her wake, her flat midwestern accent
slicing through layers of Gallic shit: "New-York-Her-ald-
*Triiii*-bune!" Exactly what kind of creature is this, *s'il
vous plait?* Just one more Daisy Miller, dead now, too. I
don't want to see Billyjim again, not for a while, because
of something I noticed on the Croisette, blinded by sunlight. I noticed my hands were shaking, too.

After bouillabaisse and the paper, I feel a whole lot
better. I decide I'm being silly. If I'm going to leave Billyjim, even for a while, I need Mr. and Mrs. Fox, my
passport, and money. I go back to the Martinez and let
myself in. At first I don't see Billyjim, but the light's on in
the bathroom so I open the door. I see him then, all right,
on the bathroom floor, big body contorted into pretzel
shape and everything the wrong color.

"Cousin?" I say softly, going over to him, though I can
tell from here he's already dead. "Cousin?" Part of the
needle is still in his arm, the syringe broken off when he
fell. My feet crunch glass into tile. I kneel down. All at
once my knees are bloody. Is that me on the floor, cradling
his big head and sobbing? Is that me kissing his ice-cold
face, begging him to wake up, telling him to please do it
for *me,* telling him how much I love him, have always

loved him, all my life? I never noticed all those gray hairs before. Did my cousin's hair turn gray, the moment he died? He must've been so *afraid*.

I don't seem to be able to get off the floor, to take Billyjim's head off my lap, to call somebody. By the time I do it's dark outside. I pull the curtains, turn on the lamp, and dial my mother's number.

"Was it . . . *drugs?*" she asks when I tell her that Billyjim's dead. "Well. We always knew it would happen. We just wondered which one of you it'd be. Who'd be the one to go first."

"I wish it *was* me. It should've been."

"Don't you ever let me hear you say that!" my mother orders. *"Learn* something."

"Okay. I'll learn something. Just help me figure out what to do next." I tell my mother the gory details, that Billyjim's in the bathroom just like Lenny Bruce. That I don't want to have to answer any questions or spend any time in filthy French jails. "This room is in Verity's name and she's in Mexico. Billyjim's always had lots of girls. If I disappear before they . . . *find* him, they won't be able to pin anything on *me.*" Then: "I can't believe I just said that, Momma. I can't believe I'm so heartless. I must be out of my mind."

"Don't think of it that way, Katherine Anne. Billyjim wouldn't want you to suffer either, for something that wasn't your fault." It *was* my fault, though. Oh yes it was. *Miss Scarlett, in the bathroom, with the syringe.* "There's *his* reputation to consider, too. And your Aunt Joan and Uncle Melvin and the twins," my mother says. Don't forget the *team.* "Let me make a few calls, darling. Can you wait there?" I say I can. My mother hangs up. I take a blanket out of the closet and cover Billyjim with it, then turn off the TV, take off my clothes, and get into bed.

Did I ever tell you about the letter Billyjim wrote me,
when he decided to marry Carmella instead of me? It was
the only letter from him I ever got. I read it so many times
that I know it by heart, eighteen years later.

*Dear Texas,* my cousin Billyjim "The Twister" Thibideaux wrote. *I have hurt you and I am sorry. You will
finish high school and then go to college the way your
mama and my mama both want, and that will be for the
best. Better than marrying an old man like me!* Billyjim
was twenty-one. I was sixteen. Then: *Carmella and I invite you to our wedding on August 15th. I have told Carmella all about you, and she wants to get to know you and
love you as I do. This is no bull! So please be there. I will
always remember you with love and be, your favorite
cousin, B. J. Thibideaux.* Then he appended a little P.S.:
*"Sweet thang, don't let any other man do you the way I
did. I said it was all right, but I* LIED. *Wait for that ring!
For one who wants only the best for you, your sorry
cousin, BJT.* Then: *P.P.S. We had fun, didn't we?* Oh, we
did, cousin. We sure enough did.

I stop worrying about saving my ass long enough to call
Verity. First she starts to cry, then cuts the tears short and
flies into a rage.

"You should've looked out for him better, you lousy
bitch," Verity says when she's able to talk. "You should've
taken care of him. Where were you? Out fucking somebody else, while he was there dying?"

"I was eating a bowl of bouillabaisse," I say.

"A bowl of bouillabaisse. Well, isn't that appropriate, for
such a *pig.* You'll never work in this town again if I can
help it," Verity actually says.

I laugh so loud and long that I guess Verity gets the
point, all right. Then I say gratuitously, "It don't make me
no nevermind, cousin," but after the words are out of my
mouth I remember who said them last, and in what cir-

cumstances. I remember he's back in the bathroom again, not just throwing up but *thrown* up like a bad oyster; the control I've mustered for Verity's benefit goes out the window finally and I start crying these helpless pathetic tears. Then Verity's apologizing over and over, she's so sorry, she had to take it out on somebody, she should've warned me about the needles, she knows it wasn't my fault and will I ever, *can* I ever forgive her?

"Cousin?" Verity says, voice brimming concern. "Katherine Anne?"

"There's nothing to forgive," I say truthfully. Then I ask her how Clemmy is.

"Oh, wonderful. A nightmare. You know how Clemmy is."

After we hang up, my mother calls, frantic that something's gone wrong with the plan she's devised for saving my ass. But *noooo.* No prisons for *me.* No facing the music. Just another chorus of "Skip to My Lou." Aunt Joan and Uncle Melvin have been contacted, and Billyjim's coach. Not his NFL coach, who's more of a bureaucrat, but his *college* coach, the one who could've been governor of Mississippi if he'd wanted to, instead of Ross Barnett, but he didn't. You know who I mean: *Coach,* the one who'll take care of everything. Nobody wants another athlete drug scandal. Coach is going to start making calls right now.

"Is the DO NOT DISTURB sign on the door, sugar?" my mother asks.

"It *always* is."

"Did Billyjim put it there himself?"

"I can't remember."

"No matter. Your fingerprints aren't on file anywhere, are they? Just get your things together and get out of there. Do you think you can do that?"

"I think so, Momma."

"Coach doesn't think it'd be wise for you to try to leave the country. Too conspicuous. Do you have a place to stay? Not a hotel. With *friends.*" Nicholas?

"I think so."

"Be brave, my darling. Tomorrow, Coach is gonna call the front desk and ask them about Billyjim and say he hasn't been able to reach him and so on. By the time they find him, everything will be . . . " my mother trails off, not knowing how to say it. "Tidied up," she finally gets out.

"Can't I even come home . . . for the *funeral?*" I whimpered.

"Well, we discussed that. Coach thinks not. We don't want anybody seeing you and puttin' two and two together. You just stay *put* for a while, Katherine Anne. Just be quiet, and stay put. Okay, baby?"

"Okay," I say listlessly. My mother warns me not to use the phone again, then hangs up. I take the blanket off Billyjim, fold it up, put it back in the closet, wash the blood off my feet and knees. I put on my blazing white suit, go down to the lobby, and call Nicholas in Paris. Can I use the villa for a few days?

"You know where to find the key, *chérie,*" Nicholas says. "I miss you, Anna Kate. I kiss you. *Je t'embrasse.*"

I pack my bags. I check everywhere for my things, even behind the doors. I pluck bleached-blond hairs out of the drain, off the pillow. While I'm packing, the phone rings, but I don't answer it. I wait inside the door until I hear people in the hall, then rush out and join their party. An Italian man flirts with me, picks up my heaviest bag, and offers to get me a taxi. Camouflaged, I leave the Martinez on his arm. I get in the taxi, slam the door, don't take the card he presses on me. The Italian curses angrily. He calls me, I believe, a brainless cunt. Very good eye, signor. Then I realize I've left Mr. and Mrs. Fox in a shopping bag under the bed and start to cry. The taxi pulls away, burning rubber. I take my sunglasses out of my purse and put them on. I don't look back.

At Nicco's villa, I don't read the papers. I don't use the telephone, except to tell my mother I'm fine, that nobody should try to find me. I visit Nicco's lawyer in Cannes. He draws up a power of attorney, which I send to Clemmy, though I don't think he'll need it. All the good scripts we wrote together have already been sold. There won't be any more big checks to endorse. But just in case, I sent the paper off and try my very best to leave the world as I know it.

*Learn* something, my mother said, and I try. First, I try to conserve whatever vital organs I have left. A few million brain cells have gone belly up, no doubt about that. Lucky I had so many to start with, for it was the heroin that was making me sick, not just angst or the bordello smell of the bed, but addiction, pure and simple. There are no D.T.'s, no gibbering hysteria. No pink elephants for me. I'm not far enough gone. Don't you find that *funny?* All these places to fall, but I never do. I never even fucking slip. It's such a joke. I teeter on the edge of lots of abysses, but I never quite seem to dive into any. Fancy that. You say you *don't* fancy it?

"I'm not afraid for you, Anna Kate," somebody once said, as I was blubbering and he was walking. Royce Browder, I think. "You always land on your feet." How true. But there's so many kinds of landing on your feet. Some people land in shit-filled Bowery gutters, but I always seem to land on a soft, perfumed pillow. There always seems to be maid service, a pair of Italian shoes to step into, and a man with a wallet full of money, waiting to take me to dinner, wherever I land on my feet. Why do you think this *is?*

Although it's summer, I sleep with a lot of blankets.

Their weight holds me down. I sleep. I don't dream. I sit in the garden all day wearing bikini bottoms and a T-shirt, watching my legs get brown. I read mysteries, drink iced tea, and practice my French on the maid. I have no reason to leave the garden. No one but Nicholas knows where I am.

Nicholas is so discreet. All his good breeding comes out. He's read about Billyjim, of course. Was it a heart attack? Brain tumor? And so *young.* He figures I'm going through some kind of mourning period, so he never bothers me about it, never asks me to talk. Eventually, Nicholas finds a new girlfriend. When he comes to the villa, he stays with her in the master bedroom. I move into a small room in the back. We are perfectly cordial. There are no more parties.

Farida, the maid, thinks I'm charming, for an American, probably because I never have men over and I wash my panties in the bidet myself instead of leaving them for her to do, scattered on the floor like pastel flowers. And I tip her well.

Nicholas's mother lives in a bigger house on the estate, the one where I took Johnny the night of our Z list party. All the construction is finished there now, and I see Madame de la Rue in the distance every morning, working in the flower garden, gloved and hatted. Sunlight never touches her skin. She reminds me of my aunt Zelda, her skin like gardenias under old-fashioned bonnets, picking peas. Madame de la Rue nods politely and leaves me alone, resigned by now to her son's strange taste in friends. But one day I write her a note inviting her to tea to thank her for the use of the guest house, and she accepts, and that goes pretty well. I have half a bottle of wine every night with dinner, sometimes a little more. For some people, this might seem a problem. For me, it's a solution, the only vice safe enough to retain.

Once coming home from the market I see Dagmar, our dealer. Dagmar is dragging this little girl along who must be her daughter from the way she treats her. The kid isn't walking fast enough to suit my old pal, who's moving down the street like a rummy with two dollars in change and the liquor store a mile in the future. Dagmar's face is white under her tan and fastened on some object in front of her, some still-elusive goal. She's on her way somewhere real important, it seems. I feel a mean chuckle starting to happen. Could this be Dagmar, like any other peon, searching for an angry fix?

*"S'il tu plait, maman,"* the little girl is crying, but Dagmar pays no attention. She keeps yanking the kid by the arm and cursing her without much conviction. None of us knew that Dagmar had a daughter, and there's something nasty about it. About being Dagmar and being a mother. Something with a bad smell. In the sun, without makeup, Dagmar's face is dull and baggy. The black clothes, which made her look so glamorous at night, in the morning only make her look old. Little drug-induced pimples radiate like stoplights on her chin. And I know, even without x-ray vision, that behind her Ray-Bans Dagmar's eyes are so bloodshot that no amount of Visine will ever get the red out.

What will I do if Dagmar notices me and stuffs my hands, unasked, with fat, juicy grams? Will I have an obligation to *execute* her? But Dagmar is too busy tormenting her daughter to pay attention to me. We've never seen each other in daylight before. I look different too, I guess. Dagmar goes down the hill at a gallop, trying to control her feet. I climb up slowly, deliberately, with fresh bread in a white net bag. *And there you have it.* Don't you?

I'm not writing yet. Of course I'm not. I'm too afraid to even think of writing. I'm fine during the days, but the nights are hard. The nights which used to be my element.

I hallucinate demons in the shadows, sit up on one elbow and watch them creep along the wall. I see monsters on the lampshades and killers in every pile of dirty clothes. The Persian rug is a snake pit. Like a kid, I sleep with the light on.

Oh, I do have this one bad night when I get into the cognac and get tarted up and head down to the Croisette on automatic pilot, like somebody else is driving me, but I don't go home with any of the dogs that hit on me. I don't hate them either, with that mean vengeful hatred that used to make me want to hurt them, to make them feel something, then throw it back in their faces, to turn their kissers into ashtrays. I don't feel anything for them at all except this vague politeness as I sit on the Carleton terrace, sipping my Seabreeze like an alien. Like the friendly little spaceman I created so many years ago, come down to study the natives. And later, in a moment of pure drunken clarity, I study my face in the Majestic bathroom: tanned and toned and rested. One night of liquor is not enough to undo that look. I walk out, without saying goodbye to anyone, and catch a taxi home.

"I sleep with you? *Pourquoi pas?*" says the fat taxi driver imploringly. "Sleep alone, no good!" My philosophical calm extends even to him, although he chatters on in this vein all the way up the hill, begging and cajoling, trying to charm. I don't tip him, however. I have never seen such a sad face. "*Et pourquoi? Pourquoi?*" he begs, handing back the five francs reluctantly. But he understands, all right.

Inside the villa, I get out my suitcase. At the bottom of it are pictures of me and all my boyfriends. I realize that I've been without boyfriends, since Billyjim died, longer than ever before in my life. Since I got cute at age thirteen and snagged Roger Early, the JV quarterback, I've never been without a boyfriend or seven. It's been almost three months. What an appalling fucking thought.

And *heeeere* they are, folks, all the old familiar faces. Remember "Ball Busters on Parade," in *Carnal Knowledge?* What would you call *this* crew? Oh yeah. "The Boyfriends Who Came from Hell." Here's me and Nicholas at these parties in Paris. In Nice. In Cannes. Surrounded by these people, these almost friends, but not quite. Looking bored and elegant in our one-of-a-kind clothes. Looking red-faced and squinty-eyed and stoned. Looking like we're having a good time. I guess we were at that. On a shopping trip to Italy, Nicholas leans against me like a little boy. I am still surprised by how short Nicholas is. I can't get used to him being so short.

Here's me and Nigel Featherbone in New York, the night we first did it, before he went back to his wife Odile. He's pint-sized too. If I had to subtitle this chapter of my life, I would call it "Short Men With Big Bananas." My hand is on his shoulder. I'm smiling, proprietary. I've just taken possession of him, or so I thought, and Nigel is still in shock. Behind coke-bottle lenses, his eyes are wide. Who *is* this pushy broad? We've just done coke in the mayor's bathroom. Here's me and Jerry Marx at a Greenpeace benefit, back when I was trying to save the world. Jerry's so alive, so committed he almost bounces. I've always thought he was too energetic to be English. Of course he *is* Jewish, but that's no excuse. Nigel Featherbone is Jewish too. He has about as much energy as one of King Solomon's concubines. He was meant to be carried on sedan chairs, by eunuchs. No chance of getting AIDS from *them.*

Toward the bottom of the pile, there's an old picture of me and Clemmy, taken in London at the opening of *Oil and Water.* I was answering questions after the picture.

Clemmy was supposed to be there too, but he never showed, and just as I was bending over so I could hear this question from the famous dwarf actor whose type I wasn't, I smelled old sweat socks soaked in Scotch and heard irregular footsteps and before I could straighten up felt this hand on my ass and there was Clemmy, breath strong enough to carry coal with.

"Hi, baby," my ex–true love Clement Goodbloode said as he goosed me. The photo was taken just before I slugged him. But that wasn't the night I hit him with the bottle. The night I thought I killed him. That was some other night. There is no picture anywhere of that.

Here's a faded Polaroid of me and Billyjim taken on the beach in Mississippi. I have his jersey on over my bikini. Billyjim has on bleeding madras shorts, the plaid already beginning to disappear. His arm is around me. The biggest grin in the world is on his face. I'm very grave, though, very full of myself, taking the responsibility of being Billyjim's girlfriend quite seriously, thank you. Just not seriously *enough*.

Of Walter and me, there are no pictures. We never went to public gatherings to be photographed. In my world, he was just another nobody. In his, I didn't even exist. I have a picture of Walter alone, though, clipped out of *Scientific American.* He's wearing a bright red sweater and a funny self-conscious grin. Walter isn't used to being photographed. He doesn't know how to make it look real. I went out the day I got that clipping and bought myself a sweater the same shade of red. I thought the sweater would make me feel happy, even when I wasn't, that it would make me feel closer to Walter. But when I wore it under my red cashmere coat, I felt like a runaway fire truck, careening down the block. Was it just the color that made me feel that way, or the innate wrongness of doing anything, however trivial, to tie myself to Walter, to build these bridges between us, as fragile as origami storks?

I still don't know. I do know it's important to process one's shit instead of just throwing it against the wall and letting it slide down, then calling the maid to clean up the mess, or pulling the handle and flushing. But flushing's so much *easier.* Remember the four Fs? Find 'em, fuck 'em, flush 'em, forget 'em? And I didn't apply them just to romances, but to everything I touched: friendships, partnerships, projects, family. Flushing or forgetting, through the usual forms of exorcism: new work, new drugs, new men. I kept trying to flush Walter down, but he kept coming back up. Now Billyjim's doing the same thing. There's shit all over the bathroom floor, but the toilet keeps gurgling. All the shit from all the sewers of my life is starting to come out too, in sympathy. It's like a Mexican bus station in my so-called mind. Do you have that dream? You've gotta go, do number two, but the toilets are all clogged and there aren't any doors, no paper, everybody's watching, coed bathrooms, bloody Kotex, and you in a miniskirt with no underwear? Does this sound familiar? Does everybody have the same dreams? How about the teeth dream, do you have that?

"Let me tell you about my dream," I once said to this professor of film theory at UCLA, prior to trusting him with my worst night terror: all my teeth falling out in my hand like pearls.

"I suppose there's nothing I can do to *stop* you," George said wearily. Then: "Typical castration dream." Funny, I thought it was about my teeth falling out. I thought it had to do with this story Aunt Faye told me when I was ten, about biting into an apple and losing a bunch of hers. All her teeth were gone by forty. It runs in the family. There's nothing to keep our pretty smiles anchored. If it weren't

for money, I'd be losing mine too. Even now my lower
teeth, the ones nobody sees, are runty and close-packed,
like a Pekingese. Aunt Faye kept her teeth in a jelly glass.
I thought that's what my dream was about. But *noooo*.
Everybody has the same dreams, like everybody has the
same first husbands. It's more economical that way. Very
astute production management. Remind me to give that
guy a call, when I get *my* movie together. Right now I
could use a little professional handling, because the
plumber isn't answering, the Roto Rooter man's on strike,
and Drano's no good, except as a late-night cocktail. I
remember another thing old George said once: *"Your
father is the structuring absence."*

I make a big fire in the fireplace. Into it I throw all of
Walter's letters to me and my letters to Walter. I throw
all the photographs of all my boyfriends into the fire, and
Lily's letter too. I have a glass of wine and watch everything burn. In a surprisingly short time, it's over. I haven't
even finished the wine in the glass. The next day, I book
a flight to New York, pack my clothes, give the keys to
Madame de la Rue, who kisses me on both cheeks and tells
me to come back any time, and I say I will, then taxi to
the airport and catch another plane.

As I reacquaint myself with my apartment, still filthy and
stinking from the last party I had, I am thinking of this
conversation I had with a bass guitarist from Toledo I met
on the plane and shared a cab with, Kaz Pataki.

"What kinda dogs do you like?" he asked before I
dropped him at the Gramercy Park. "Big dogs? Little
dogs?"

"Not little dogs. Too yippy."

"That's how I feel," he said.

"I like basset hounds," I said. "They always look so sad
and funny. Basset hounds have fur like velvet."

"Basset hounds are all right," Kaz said finally. "Basset hounds are fine. They have great barks."

Maybe I should get a dog, to keep me company. Kaz wants to do that *himself.* He said I was the greatest thing since Wheaties. But he is far too sweet for me, too honorable. It's like in *Rancho Notorious,* where Marlene Dietrich meets a nice guy, far too late. "Go away and come back five years ago," she says. That wouldn't do Kaz any good. Go away and come back when I was *five.* He really was cute, though, I have to give him that, with long ash-blond curls and high, arrogant cheekbones and Chinese-y blue eyes slanting up to heaven. But once you get over being obsessed by rock stars, once you've had a few of them, moderately famous, you never go back to that type again. Even the smart ones watch TV all day. All of them have drug problems. Kaz probably lives on cocaine and peanut butter sandwiches. He probably never eats anything but thirteen-year-old groupies. *The Dukes of Hazzard* is undoubtedly his favorite show. But he did have a great smile. I thought I might take a chance. We have a lot in common, too. Kaz used to be poor. Like me, he scrambled out. But when we passed Staten Island, he said, "That's where I want to live, if I move here. I want to have a house and a dog and lots of babies." *Uh-oh.*

There's plenty of time to decide about Kaz Pataki, who kind of looks like Lee Van Cleef in those Sergio Leone pics. He gave me a tape of his band to listen to. Maybe I can do the video, I think happily, as I start going through the mail the super's left in front of my door. That'd be one way to start directing.

It's hot in here, stuffy. I get up and open the windows, then sit down at my desk and examine the postmarks on the letters. The ones from Groverton go straight into the trash. I think about Kaz Pataki and getting a house in Staten Island and a basset hound with fur like velvet, but

I don't think about it much. Mostly I think about all the sentences and paragraphs in my suitcase. Did I tell you I started writing again? I did. The other night, after I burned all those pictures and things. I'm ten pages into my novel, the one about my mom and dad. I finally got past that first perfect sentence. I wrote it in *longhand*. I'm turning the computer into a plant stand.

I turn on the phone machine, which I haven't listened to since I left L.A. There are about eight million outdated messages which I don't bother to write down. Then I hear Walter crying all of a sudden. I can't understand what he's trying to say, he's so hysterical. Is this an old message, inexplicably unerased? Walter's crying so hard he gets beeped before he gets a word out. Gonged. Then another message, he's in control. Stony calm. Will I please call him back please. Then another weeper. This seems to go on for hours. Then there's a message from my mother, saying Walter's trying to reach me. Fuck Walter Light for calling my mother! How dare he! She sounds really worried. There are messages from Emma. Walter's called her too. Then messages from about thirty of my girlfriends he's called. For a while I think the messages from and about Walter are petering out, but here come another whole slew of them. Walter's called everybody I've ever introduced him to or mentioned. He really does seem to need me for something. He really has been trying hard to find me.

Finally the tape runs out. The messages are over. Outside, the sun is completely up. There's a smell in here of fresh-killed meat. This place used to be a slaughterhouse, and the blood smell is in the walls and floor. No matter how many times the floor is sanded, varnished, and sealed, no matter how many times the walls are spackled and painted, the smell always comes back. I rented this loft during winter when it wasn't so strong, but then last summer, just before I met Walter, it came on full strength. The heat reduced the blood like stock. This summer, it's more concentrated still, and the lilies I found with my mail are just the right grace note, as sweet as the Vitalis I used to smell, just before my Uncle Elmo kissed me.

The telephone rings. Of course it does. The surprise isn't that my sins have caught up with me. The surprise is that it's taken so *long.*

"I hope you're happy now, baby," the familiar voice says without any preliminaries. Then Bruno laughs. I put the phone down gently, shaking like a Chihuahua in a stranger's lap. I dial Walter's number. Then I'm back in a cab with the same old bags. I remember too late that it'll be cold in Ohio, that these are the wrong clothes, that I should have packed something warm instead of these cottons and evening gowns and high-heeled sandals and bikini bottoms, instead of this brothel gear, this lace-trimmed underwear, these red silk stockings with black seams.

On the flight to Toledo, the woman next to me talks and talks. She doesn't notice I'm not listening, that for the last half hour I've been applying mascara to the same glassy eye.

"You young girls really amaze me," she says cheerfully. "How can you do that on a plane? And with that little compact! I need my magnifying mirror. Every day. Gotta have it. Lord, I'd poke my gosh-darned eye out if I tried to do what you do." The lashes on my right eye are as thick as rubber hoses. "You young girls really do amaze me. My lands! You know, my daughter, she's just the same way. I think you must be just like my daughter, honey." I hope not, for *her* sake. "She just goes and goes! A toothbrush and a lipstick and she's gone! I was forty-five before I got out of Akron. Do you travel a lot?" she asks. When I fail to answer this direct question, she really looks at me for the first time, her face aglow with sympathy. "Honey," she asks, "did somebody die?"

I manage to nod, and she takes my hand and doesn't talk for the rest of the flight, except to ask if I'd like a drink, but I wouldn't. There's no point in having a drink. A drink wouldn't do me the least bit of good. And this low sob rises up out of my throat. I try to strangle it but it just keeps coming, slow and sour and lazy like vomit. I can see Walter now, in the den, waiting for me, his head in his hands, all crumpled up. I imagine his eyes. There's no way I can ever meet them.

Across the aisle, there's a coed in her very best clothes, going off to college probably, young and shining, hair all clean. Even in this ugly light she glows, no lines anywhere. She's bouncing up and down in her seat, trying *not* to bounce, to look adult, knees hooked over her cheap blue suitcase, so eager for life it's almost killing her. I stare at her with my feral eyes, my ghastly smile. She catches its chill and shivers.

Lily was buried three weeks ago. What was left of her. For of course after Bruno hit her with his big car he must have backed up calmly and hit her again just to make sure, his killing as thorough as his sex.

I'll charm Lily's son. He's young enough to be charmed with cookies and kindness. He'll love me eventually, as most men do. But the daughter will be a different story. She'll hate me without knowing why. Her instincts will be right. She'll smell the guilt on me. But her father, her brother, her teachers, her shrinks will say her instincts are wrong and this will make her crazy. And I'll get a bleeding ulcer, looking at them and not being able to say, Yes, I did it. I'm guilty. It's all my fault. I did it. Oh yes I did.

The lady from Akron pats my hand all the way to Toledo. The plane floats down. The lights of the city twinkle on and off seductively. I think of Kaz Pataki as I get

closer to his home. I could call, I guess, but this is something I couldn't even begin to explain. He might try to
save me. Can't risk *that*. The airport lights wink perfunc-
torily, because I am already caught. The wheels touch
down gently. The plane taxis smoothly to the hangar. I
don't even *like* kids. I *am* a kid. *Aren't I?*

"Did you kill my cousin too?" I ask Bruno inside the
terminal. "Because I don't think I could live with that."
Bruno shakes his head.

"He did it himself," Bruno says, and I believe him
though I don't know why. Then he takes me in his arms,
gives me a wet purple kiss, and tells me how everything's
going to be.

GERDA began a new career tonight: sleep-walker. About 11 P.M. she padded downstairs in her red footie pajamas with the white bunny tail with an absolutely blank look on her usually expressive face and sat down on a chair in the den. Three feet away, Walter didn't notice her. He'd already finished most of a fifth of Jack Daniels and was passed out cold on the couch. Never wake a sleepwalker, right? They'll lose their soul. So I guided Gerda back upstairs to her bed, where she lay, eyes wide open but, I suppose, asleep. After a while Gerda's eyes closed, her breathing changed. She sighed once, rolled over. I went back downstairs, took Walter's shoes off, and loosened his tie. Walter really looks handsome, now that he's so dissipated. He's more of a man. I could go for Walter Light in a big way, probably, if I weren't married to Walter Light.

As I left the den, I heard Walter mumbling. I used to pay attention when he talked in his sleep. I used to think his sleep talk was a clue to something. I put my ear right down there and listened in. Once I heard him say, "Here come the Jap kamikazes!" Another time he said, "I don't know! I don't know! What do I . . . so beautiful. *I shouldn't.*" The last time I eavesdropped, Walter said,

"Tell Lily . . . mail letter." Was there a word I missed, in the middle? *Not?* Sleep talk is highly overrated, don't you think? I stopped listening to Walter's weeks ago.

I turned off the television and lights, then went into the kitchen and made cookies shaped like witches' hats, black cats, and pumpkins for Jason to take to school on Halloween. As I wait for the cookies to come out of the oven, I think about Lily. The kitchen still has all her things in it: recipe file, red plaid pot holders shaped like roosters, drawers full of rubber bands and used aluminum foil, generic green beans and plum tomatoes, magnetized alphabet on the refrigerator door. I tried to pack these things up once and give them to Goodwill. Gerda caught me and held her breath until she turned blue.

Once I found something that Lily left behind, at the very back of one of the cabinets, hidden by some stale spices and unused cookie jars. I was so rattled, I went into the living room with it and woke Walter up.

"What the hell is *this?*" I said, shaking him awake, brandishing a Miracle Whip jar with tiny holes punched in the lid, full of dead and dying cockroaches. "What the hell *is* this, Walter?"

"Oh, Lily hated roaches," Walter said, coming awake. "She said she hated sharing the house with vermin."

"So instead of squashing them like a normal person, or calling the exterminator, she put them in here?"

"I guess."

"Why?"

Walter shrugged, yawned. "Oh, revenge."

Knowing Lily had an ugly secret didn't make me feel any better. I went back in the kitchen with the roach jar, not knowing what to do with it. Walter followed me. The prehistoric, armored insects made a metallic noise, an audible series of clicks.

"This is what my nightmares look like," I said, staring at the jar.

"Don't look, then."

"Oh, there's something kind of fascinating about seeing your nightmares when you're awake."

"Uh-huh."

Walter took the jar out of my hands and put it down on the kitchen table. Then he sat me down next to the jar, pulled up my skirt and rolled down my panties, smiling to himself at his own nasty wit. Before he buried his face in my crotch, Walter looked at me slyly, to make sure I got the point. When he bent me backward on to the table and knocked over the blue and white jar, Walter cursed. I heard the heavy glass make contact with linoleum, but the jar didn't break. The metal lid stayed on. Walter's shoes came off, then his pants. The jar rolled for a long, long time. It banged into the refrigerator as Walter entered me.

"The rewards of physics are glacial and few," he said.

The roaches rustled like dead leaves.

After the cookies come out of the oven, I decorate them with orange and black spreckles. I pack them in a Red Cross shoebox lined with used aluminum foil, each layer of cookies separated by used wax paper. I go upstairs, brush my teeth, take two Seconals, and sleep.

"Marco!"

"Polo!"

"Marco!"

"Polo!"

"Marco!"

"That's enough, you kids," Walter says from behind his newspaper.

"Polo," Jason whispers, looking at me. I smile encouragingly. Gerda, who has Lily's little pinched face, slams her orange juice glass down hard. When Jason turns to look at her, she shakes her head. Jason blushes and digs into his Froot Loops.

"One egg or two, honey?" I ask. When Walter was in love with me, he wrote me a little note about this radio commercial for the National Egg Association. The plot is that this woman's been out jogging and she comes home and her husband has cooked her some delicious *eggs*. Walter said the actress had a voice like mine. Hi, honey, she said to her husband breathlessly. The egg commercial made Walter think of me. It turned his brains to butter, Walter said, just like I did.

Walter holds up two fingers. I melt butter in Lily's copper-bottomed pan. I make the eggs. Walter eats them. I sit down to lukewarm coffee. The kids stand as one and bundle themselves up. Walter gets up too and puts on his coat. I hand Jason the cookies. He doesn't say thank you. Walter puts on his muffler and opens the door. The kids rush through it, then get in the car. I hand Walter his briefcase. He goes outside. Nobody kisses anybody good-bye.

It takes me about an hour to do the housework. By nine o'clock the breakfast dishes are washed, the beds made, the furniture dusted. Every few days, clothes are washed, ironed, and put away. On Saturdays I vacuum, but not today. Today I think I'll ... watch *television*. What a good idea! It's so educational, don't you think? You don't agree? It's taught *me* lots of things. It's taught me how to be a *parent*. If it wasn't for television, I kid you not, I'd be in very hot water indeed.

Walter hasn't helped. He's been kind of ... ineffectual, if you want to know the truth. Kind of a basket case, for the past several months, a *lightweight*. What a lousy joke *that* is, seeing as how it's true. No, things haven't gone that well for Walter since Lily died. The trip we took to

Cuba kind of came back to haunt him. It's got something to do with his security clearance, with these projects he was working on for the Defense Department. *Was.* He still has his job, he has tenure of course, but *still* . . . no more promotions, probably. No department chairmanship. Nobody at the Ohio Institute of Technology was happy about Walter's little adventure in Commieland. No more filching data from the Tokamak and giving it to the Defense Department so they can make bigger H-bombs. No more using that research on lasers to help Uncle Sam blast planes out of the sky. Walter got excited despite himself, talking about it. "Like hitting 'em with a giant hammer!" he said gleefully. Those are only *some* of the pies Walter had his fingers in. So much for pure science. But *no more.* Walter's been *found out.*

"Why didn't you tell me you were working on things like that?" I asked.

"I didn't want to upset you," Walter said.

Having me here hasn't helped Walter salvage his career, not to mention his so-called life. Sort of the other way around. Having a strange blonde in the house less than a month after Lily's mysterious death didn't do a whole lot to squelch those rumors. Even marrying me didn't help. What a pathetic scene *that* was. You know what? I'm gonna spare you that pathetic fucking scene. It all came down around Walter's ears anyway. For a while, he was even under investigation, but that's over now. When the police came round I played my part with panache. Everyone assumes Lily walked in front of that car, without any help from Walter. They'll find the driver eventually, or so they *think.* She tried it once before, right? Since I arrived in Groverton, the reason's been pretty clear. And Walter hasn't exactly risen to the occasion. Adversity hasn't brought out the best in him. Once I heard two coeds discussing Walter in the sauna. One of them said he *used to be* the best professor she'd ever had.

I'm lucky Groverton's got cable. Walter didn't want to get it. He was afraid it might corrupt the children, but I put my foot down. Oh yes I did. We've got cable now, and a lockbox, too, though nobody ever seems to hide the key. I don't know what I'd do all day if it weren't for television. You'd almost think they had me in mind, too, when they figured out the sched. I make myself a Scotch and soda, go into the den with the drink, some copper polish, a navy blue plaid rag and a bunch of Lily's pots, and get comfortable. I take off my wedding ring. Walter and Lily wore plain gold bands, but not *me*. Maybe you think I'm gonna watch the daytime soaps, but *noooo*. The soaps are too complicated. I can't figure out who's related to who or why they act the way they do. Behavior that appears to be perfectly normal is invariably accompanied by ominous music, which lets me know I'm missing something. The soaps are a real washout, but never fear, it's time for *The Brady Bunch!* I learn a lot about being a stepmom from *them*. Then *Bachelor Father*. All these families have maids, have you ever noticed? Or Oriental houseboys. Oh yes they do. The Greggs have Peter Tong, to take care of Kelly, but Kelly really isn't much trouble. The Bradys have Ann B. Davis. In the afternoon, she's on *Love That Bob*. The Baxters have Hazel, for whatever that's worth. Brian Keith has Sebastian Cabot, for Christ's sake! Don't you think *you* could be a good stepparent with Sebastian Cabot around to give you advice? On *The Courtship of Eddie's Father* they've got Mrs. Livingston, who's Japanese and *wise*. My God, there's Tippi Hedren! Hi, Tippi! Remember her, Melanie Daniels, the heiress who liked to jump in fountains, getting her comeuppance in *The Birds?* Is that Jodie Foster too, pre-Hinckley? It is. So young. So *short*. Television certainly is educational.

Uh-oh. Here comes *The Farmer's Daughter*. It's about

motherless children and widowers, true, but it's also a
little bit scary seeing as how Inger Stevens committed
suey, right after Marilyn Monroe did. She figured if *Marilyn Monroe herself* didn't have anything to live for, Inger
Stevens, the farmer's daughter, sure the fuck didn't either. Marilyn had this sign pinned to her bra, the one she
slept in at night so she could go braless during the day,
that Inger Stevens read. What did it say? *It just doesn't
matter?* This sours the program somewhat. I can't listen
to Inger's perky, confident advice to the lovable brats in
her charge without thinking of my own Seconal bottle,
my own cabinet full of booze, *ja. Ja.* Katy eventually
marries the congressman and becomes a stepmom, just
like me. Maybe *that's* why Inger Stevens killed herself.
Definitely too scary to watch. Lucky *Dennis the Menace*
is on another channel. Better have another Scotch and
soda first, take a load of pots back to the kitchen. My, don't
they look nice. There's nothing like copper, if you've got
the time to polish it, like I do.

There aren't any stepparents or surrogate mothers on
*Dennis the Menace,* but Dennis is a lot like Jason, he's
really smart, *mischievous.* You can tell Mr. Mitchell is
smart too, like Walter. Those glasses are a dead giveaway,
not to mention the pipe. *Dennis the Menace* is realer than
*The Brady Bunch.* Those Bradys are nothing like Lights.
They're always so cheerful, so quick with a good one-liner,
a clever gag, or at worst a pout. They never hold their
breath until they turn blue. They never sleepwalk. They
never wake up screaming, like our kids do, or yell "I wish
you'd just die, *die,* DIE!" at Florence Henderson. They
never call Florence "Mommy" accidentally, like Jason did
one night at dinner, then clamp their little hands over
their little mouths, trying to take the word back, looking
at her like she was a roach in the soup bowl while pitiful
tears stream down their faces. They never cry at all, those

Bradys, those self-assured midgets. They're more like I
was, when I was a kid: fucking little *monsters.* Whew!
How'd we ever get off on *that?*

On *Father Knows Best,* Cornel Wilde wrecks his car in
Springfield and comes to dinner at the Andersons while
it's being fixed. Jim sells him some new car insurance.
*Donna Reed* is strange. First they have two children, then
three. Their third child follows them home from a picnic!
I hope that doesn't happen to me and Walter. Today Bea-
ver gets thrown off the school bus and has to write a note
to get back on. Wally helps. What a great guy that Wally
is. *Ozzie and Harriet* makes me sad, what with poor Ricky
being gone and all. So sad I think I'll have another Scotch.
Glass replenished, I change the channel and come in on
the middle of *Make Room for Daddy,* which really knocks
me for a loop. It's about Danny's agent, a confirmed bachelor with this playboy pad and a gong to summon the
houseboy. I used to know lots of guys like that in Hollywood. Danny's wife, Kathy, tries to fix him up with this
bachelorette, a real knockout in evening clothes, and she
*fixes sports cars, too.* What a liberated show this is, huh?
But after all these speeches about how great it is to be
free, all this familiar cynical dialogue, it turns out that
everybody really wants to be married. Like the career girl
says, you can't cuddle up to a pair of pliers. But before the
plot resolves itself, everything gets so confused that Rusty
doesn't know whether he's a boy or a girl. The episode
ends with *Rusty in drag!* Wow! What a great day of TV
viewing *this* has been. Now it's time to get the lead out,
whadda ya say? It's time to go swimming. I rehang the
pans, put my weddding ring back on, get into some of
Walter's sweaters, and stumble out to my '72 Lincoln.

I used to swim at the OIT gym, but this got a little hard
to take. Too healthy. Too much optimism. Too many
chances of going into the sauna and hearing gossip about

myself or meeting people who used to know Lily. I love to take saunas after I swim, to bake out all the poisons. Liquor works so much better when your body is clean. Then it hits with a sweet, effective rush, like acid rain in a silver lake. But Lily had a lot of friends. Pretty soon I stopped going to the OIT gym. It's amazing how cold saunas can get. *Brrrr.*

I found an old YWCA across the Michigan border, outside of Blissfield, and this is where I'm heading now. It's rundown, falling apart, and full of old women who take their meals in the little cafeteria and play bridge and Mah Jong in the lobby. They don't know what to make of me, at the Y. I'm the youngest person there, except for the lifeguards, who are PE majors at OIT. But the old ladies got used to me after a while. Mrs. Harris, who runs the place, positively loves me. She thinks I'm a sign that the Y is making a comeback. I don't have the heart to tell her what an atavism I am. I try not to give her any false hopes. The place is doomed, no doubt about it. My stumbling on it, as much as anything else, confirms this sad fact.

The pool is small and the temperature regulator doesn't work. Either the water is icy or as comforting as a warm bath. The facilities are not too clean. There are soggy cigarette butts stained with drugstore lipstick in the rough concrete showers. Hairpins and pieces of soap clog the drains. There are more than a few roaches. I find one or two sluggish roaches every day in the basket where I keep my towel and shampoo. I shake them out of my bra placidly. They wake up and crawl away. The facilities suit me to a tee. When I look at the naked bulbs on the ceiling, I see halos around the lights.

I swim for a few minutes' sanity, to keep from cracking up. The blue water helps, the murkiness of the deep end as I approach it, my awkward turn, and then the light pouring in through thick frosted windows as I near the shallows. On my back, I pretend I'm in an Esther Williams movie, making patterns on the water for the camera to see. I like pretending to be part of a pattern, since I don't belong anywhere anymore. And though my body is harder than it's ever been, with all this swimming, I am far less pretty than I was once. I look in the mirror, and surprise, whatever it was that used to make me pretty is gone, like last week's garbage.

Twice a week, I get a massage from Agnes, a two-hundred-pound masseuse from the Bronx. She works in the nude, lathering me all over with eucalyptus soap, scrubbing me with a stiff brush. The first time I got up on Agnes's table and tried to tell her what to do, to not be too rough with my left foot, sprained that morning on one of Jason's toy trucks, Agnes honked, "Don't tell the doctor how to operate!" Then she fixed my foot. I never tried to tell her anything after that. I always tip Agnes well, for the effort she makes to animate me. I'm really looking forward to an Agnes massage. I step on the gas. The Lincoln shoots forward.

When I get to the Y, all the ladies are milling around the door, which is closed tight. As I walk toward the entrance, I see that some of them are crying, leaning on each other for strength. All the doors have these little seals on them, like the kind you put on Christmas packages, only these say DO NOT REMOVE. No one does. And in the middle of the door is this big sign that says CLOSED BY ORDER OF THE MICHIGAN BOARD OF HEALTH. I get back in the car and drive home.

Information in Blissfield has Mrs. Harris's number. I ask, as discreetly as I can without raising any hopes, just how much money it would cost to get the Y up to code. A would-be lady bountiful, I figure I can kick in a few thou. The money, which still trickles in, isn't doing anybody any good. Mrs. Harris starts to cry. The sum she mentions is

staggering, twenty times my entire net worth. Saving the
Y is a job for Mrs. Ford, Mrs. Dearborn, Mrs. Chrysler,
Mrs. Pontiac, but I don't know any of these worthy ladies.

The children come home with Walter. I feed them
Kraft Macaroni and Cheese, which is about all they'll
eat besides Hamburger Helper and Franco-American.
Then, with a sense of excitement even my presence can't
quell, they put on their Halloween costumes. Gerda is
She-Ra, Princess of Power. Jason paints his face blue: a
smurf. Walter bundles them up and takes them trick-or-
treating. I turn on the porch light, pour candy into bowls,
and wait. But nobody comes. Word must have spread
through the neighborhood that a big bad witch lives in
*this* house, that there aren't any treats here, only tricks.

Once I hear something at the door and go outside.
Somebody's thrown an egg against the house, a fertilized
one, too. I find embryonic chicken sliding down the wall
and start to cry. When I hear laughter behind the hedge,
I stop, wipe my eyes, then go back inside, get a paper
towel, and clean up the mess. I throw the Halloween
candy in the trash.

The kids come home in high spirits. Even Walter is
smiling. I haven't seen him smile in months and months.
The kids go upstairs to bed. Walter tucks them in, then
comes downstairs without saying a word, face hard and
stony again like always, gets drunk, and passes out.

In the kitchen I call Eben van der Post in L.A. Remember Eben, the toilet-seat heir from Grosse Pointe? Maybe
*he* can introduce me to some Michigan philanthropists.
But Eben is no help at all.

"It takes *years* to worm your way into those circles,
Anna Kate," he says, annoyed that I would ask him for
that kind of favor. He won't even give me his mother's
home phone number. Infatuation only extends so far.
"Swimming pools for senior citizens aren't exactly what

I'd call sexy charities," Eben sneers. He is really annoyed with me, annoyed especially to learn that I am living in Ohio and married. That I didn't wait for him the way I promised. He thought I was calling to confirm our date for the Harvard–Yale game.

I wash the dinner dishes and put them away, take off Walter's shoes, loosen his tie, and turn off the downstairs lights. Gerda's reading Proust or Stendhal or Nietzsche or something under the covers, while Jason's sneaked into Walter's office. The computer's on. Also the modem. Jason's playing a game called "Adventure" via Compuserve. He does this almost every night. I caught him last month when the Compuserve bill arrived, a truly formidable sum. I hid the bill from Walter, then paid it immediately. I figure it's the least I can do.

I go into Walter's office shyly and ask Jason how he's doing. He tells me he's just killed a Wumpus, whatever that is. I look over Jason's shoulder at the screen. Right now he's carrying: set of keys, brass lantern, small bottle, batteries, Persian rug, and an emerald the size of a plover's egg. So far so good. I kiss the little adventurer on the top of his golden head, which he lets me do since Gerda isn't around to see, and tell him not to stay up too late, and Jason says he won't. We say good night, I go into the bedroom, put on a *Live Fast, Die Young* T-shirt, take two Seconals, brush my teeth, and sleep.

A week later, Yale beats Harvard, 14 to 3. The Blissfield Y stays closed.

Bruno comes to visit every couple of weeks. Come on, you knew that. You didn't think he just went up in smoke? You didn't think he went to all that trouble and just *left me alone,* did you? Oh, no. Bruno's around, my provider, my *savior.* He wants to keep tabs on his little experiment. Like Ricky said about Lucy one day, "I caught the redheaded mouse in her own little trap." Bruno visits the rat lab every few weeks, to fuck me and to gloat, also to do business. He's trying to bring jai alai to Michigan, along with a couple dozen other villains. I meet them in Detroit over steak house dinners, open my mouth only to smile or chew. That's why Bruno's here so often, or so he *claims*. He doesn't come just to torment me. The first time I lied to Walter, to spare him, and got away with it. But the second time Walter caught me.

"You betrayed me! You betrayed me!" Walter screamed, jumping up and down and waving his arms like Rumpel-stiltskin—like Freddy Pitluck, come to think of it. I haven't thought about Freddy in a while. Walter was so comical I had to laugh.

"Come on, Walter," I said. "What the hell did you expect?" There's nothing between us now except guilt, and Walter doesn't know the half of it. He's changed so much I don't even recognize him. When Bruno comes, I don't say anything, just tell Walter I'm going and go. Walter has somebody else too, I think, a graduate student in philosophy, Marjorie Main, who took care of the kids before Walter tracked me down. Marjorie was a great friend of Lily's. Jason and Gerda worship her. When Marjorie comes to visit and I open the door, the kids jump straight into her arms. They run past me like I'm not even there. I asked Marjorie, when I met her the first time, when we were still speaking, if she was related to *the* Marjorie Main, the movie star, but Marjorie just turned this blank look on me and said, "I think not." *I think not* Can you believe it! Marjorie Main doesn't even know who Marjorie Main *is*.

Walter and I tried for a month or so to get back together, I mean *really* together, but there just wasn't anything there. Though I used all these little endearments when I spoke to him, refined during my years with Clemmy, every word hardened the second it left my mouth. The words were tight black marbles, condemning Walter. Writing him off. All the things that used to be so lovable about him aren't. It's over, it's gone. Everything he does or says is wrong. Walter's being drunk all the time didn't help, *doesn't*. He can't fuck anymore—that time in the kitchen when he got turned on by the roaches was an exception—but he's heavy into *reading* about fucking. He carries *Killing Lust* in his briefcase now, instead of lingerie and love letters. I've looked. One night he even wanted to *tie me up*. Not Walter, oh no, I thought, as he stood over me, brandishing Gerda's jump rope. Anybody but Walter, I thought, before I let him. Tying me up didn't help Walter at all in the erection department. His pathetic knots didn't even hold. He should've reread the Boy Scout manual. I don't love Walter, he doesn't love me. I'll leave eventually, when Walter and Marjorie get it together. But not on my own. Walter's making the decision this time. I'll leave when he tells me to, not a minute before, unless *Bruno* tells me to. Then I don't have any choice.

Guess who *does* love me? You're right, it's Bruno, the big dumb doofus. I figured that out the last time he breezed through town. It was around Thanksgiving. I called my mother and asked her how to make the turkey, and she talked me through it all right, like ground control in Phoenix talked some grandmother through a landing, after the pilot croaked, up in the air. When the turkey was finished it looked really good, but my mother forgot to tell me to take out the little bag they put *in* the turkey, to hold the guts in. I guess she assumed I'd figure that part out myself. Walter discovered the gut bag when he carved. I thought it was funny, tried to turn the whole thing into

a joke like in the old days, but the steaming paper bag
made Walter too sick to eat, or so he claimed. Gerda and
Jason too. Maybe they were sick already. I was, seeing as
how there wasn't a whole lot to be thankful for. Either
that, or they'd already eaten dinner on the sly, with Marjorie Main, a.k.a. Ma Kettle.

   After the kids were in bed, Walter was passed out, and
Thanksgiving dinner was safely in the trash, I called my
mother again and cried. Before that, though, Jesse told me
about the nifty decorating he'd been doing. He repapered
the living room, and just to make everything extra nice he
took the leftover wallpaper and *papered all the lampshades, too.* Now everything matches. Nice, huh? Finally
he put my mother on. Without too many preliminaries I
broke down completely. My mother gave me the usual
line about how strong I am, then said, "If the situation's
making you that unhappy, honey, why, you'll weasel out
of it somehow."

   "Thanks a lot," I said sarcastically. "That's just what I
wanted to hear."

   "You can take the *truth,* can't you, honey?" Long silence.

   "Why does everybody always say that to me? 'Anna
Kate's the strong one. Anna Kate's the one in control.
Anna Kate's the one with willpower.'"

   "They say it because it's *true.*"

   "'Since Anna Kate's so *strong,* let's walk all over her.
Let's see how much she can *take!*'" I finished dramatically. My mother laughed.

   "That's just the way it is, sweetie. You *are,* that's all. It's
a responsibility you have to accept. Other people can't
stop themselves from falling apart, no matter how hard
they try. They don't want to crumple, but they do. They
want to be strong, but they aren't. No matter how bad
things get, you'll always bounce back." My mother

laughed again. "Be glad you're strong, honey. It's a hell of a lot better than being the opposite."

"I wonder," I said dreamily, thinking of a nice clean mental hospital. Nothing to do there all day but weave baskets and watch TV, drugged to the nines. The only problem is, I'm not crazy. Not *technically*.

"Don't wonder," my mother barked, shattering my nice little fantasy. "Just trust your old mother." Then my old mother gave me the lowdown on her trip to Yaddo, where she met and vanquished the fabled Yankees and heard the third syllable of her name pronounced for the very first time. "Imagine that! Live-ee-a! Wonders never cease!" My mother's novel is almost finished. She still won't tell me what it's about.

The day after Thanksgiving, Bruno came. I drove to Detroit and visited him at the Ren Cen, where he likes to stay. "Ren Cen sin," I quipped in the elevator on the way to his room, but it was Rin Tin Tin he wanted. Afterward, we went to all these used bookstores, Goodwills, flea markets, and garage sales, so Bruno could look for old 78s. He's a big jazz and blues fan, my Bruno. He loves charming old black ladies and getting valuable records for fifty cents a pop, when they're asking a dollar. Bruno would be great in Hollywood. Then we went back to the Ren Cen for more sex, more Sekt, more humiliating talk about how things were going between me and Walter.

Most of the time I forget about Bruno being a murderer. He doesn't *act* like one, but then I don't really know what a murderer's supposed to act like. In bed, Bruno's kind of old-fashioned, actually. He doesn't like anything weird or degrading. He doesn't even like blow jobs, imagine that! One day when I descended toward his cock like a cow to the barn at sunset, Bruno said, "Don't bother."

"Don't *bother?*"

"What's the matter, baby? Is that one of your . . . special-ties?"

"Don't talk to me like I'm a whore!"

"I'm sorry," Bruno actually said. "My penis is an iron rod. I cannot really feel it."

I crawled back up into Bruno's arms and kissed his big purple mouth. *I'm sorry?* I tried to understand the significance of this new development. Does it make any sense to *you?* It was when Bruno apologized, of course, that I knew for sure he loved me. And who's to say Bruno doesn't deserve love, likc anybody else?

CHRISTMAS walked on by without Walter and me particularly noticing it. Jason and Gerda went to Massachusetts, to their grandparents', but Walter and I weren't invited. No divorce in Walter's family. No unexplained suicides or hasty, ill-conceived remarriages to bleached blondes, either. Walter drank, I watched television. We stayed out of each other's way. Bruno's coming for New Year's Eve, the day after tomorrow. It's funny how I've started to look forward to his visits. He's sort of all I've got. I guess that explains it. I'm more of an au pair girl than a wife, and these days Walter's gone more than he's home. He never stays out all night, though. I wonder how it's going between him and Marjorie. I wonder if he's popped the question.

I know something about Marjorie. She's only got one breast. I started going back to the university gym, after the Y closed, and one day she walked into the sauna and I saw it: no left breast. Just a fat dark scar where her breast should have been. Marjorie sat down right next to me before she noticed who I was, then picked up her towel and walked out without speaking. I guess she showed *me* who was crippled, all right. I guess she showed *me* who was handicapped.

Tonight Walter leaves after dinner and doesn't come back. I do the dishes and put them away. I watch television. I have several cognacs. I go upstairs, brush my teeth, take two Seconals, and sleep.

The phone rings. It rings and rings. I can't quite seem to wake up and answer it. Finally I pick it up, I think. Everything's a little hazy, it could be a dream but since I don't dream anymore, it must be real. It's Bruno. He tells me to pack my things. He tells me it's all over. He tells me he's coming to take me away, that I've suffered enough. He tells me he loves me. I cry and cry. Do I take another Seconal? I think I do. The phone rings again, but this time I don't answer it. And then someone's kissing me. It's Walter. What a surprise. It *must* be a dream. Walter looks so handsome in his very best suit. "Sweet angel. My sweet blond angel," Walter says between kisses, his face red and wet the way I remember it, the last time he came to leave me.

A little while later Walter's gone. My mouth is so *dry*. I reach for my water glass but there's something else in it: bourbon, ugh. Where did that come from? I never drink it, and if I do I don't enjoy it. It tastes like Texas, like bad high school memories. Tonight I just chug it down though—I'm so dry—but most of it spills on the bed. And the next thing I know I'm under water. My T-shirt's soaked. I'm in the shower, it's cold and I'm drowning and Bruno's in there with me, getting his suit all wet, holding me under the spray. I try to get away, but I can't. My mouth's full of water. I choke, spit it out, and start scream ing.

"WHAT ARE YOU DOING? ARE YOU TRYING TO KILL ME? WELL, GO AHEAD! JUST GO AHEAD! SEE IF I CARE!" But Bruno's not killing me. I figure that out soon enough. He's not trying to kill me, he's trying to *save* me. He turns off the water and lifts me out of the shower.

"I'm sorry. I'm sorry. I'm so sorry," he says, peeling off my wet T-shirt, drying me. But for *what?* Bruno wraps me in a fresh towel, picks me up, and carries me out of the bathroom. There's something vaguely familiar about this gesture, but I can't quite put my finger on it yet. Or maybe I just don't want to.

"I'm near. I'm always near. Lovely dreams are coming," Bruno says, smoothing my damp hair back from my forehead.

He tucks me into bed tenderly and sings songs to me in German. I recognize one of Bruno's songs from an Elvis Presley movie. Elvis sang it to Juliet Prowse, but I don't know what any of the words mean. And then Bruno forgets who I am. He gets me confused with some other soggy cupcake, and a big bright spotlight goes on in my head, like the one in front of Grauman's Chinese Theater. You can see it all the way to Anaheim. Bruno forgets who it is he's talking to, who he's singing to so sweetly. He calls me by the wrong name. I don't bother to correct him.

"My white rose. *Mein Weissengel.* My tormentor. My joy. My hangman's noose. Be kind to me," Bruno says.

"I must look like shit," I say, because this is what Bruno wants. He looks at me gratefully with tortured eyes. I've got his number, all right. The things that fly out, when you open Pandora's box! People find their angels in the strangest places. I should know. Bruno called me Lulu.

"Have you ever been to . . . *Sacramento?*" he says dreamily. "From the air, it is covered with flowers."

When I wake up again, I feel like death warmed over. Bruno's asleep beside me—on Walter Light's bed! I spring up, head pounding, and stagger downstairs. It's morning. It's New Year's Eve. Walter's blanket isn't on the couch.

There's a note from him, though. Walter's gone to Amherst, to see his parents, who don't want to send Gerda
and Jason back. He hopes I'll understand. He has to think
of the children first. He *thanks* me for trying. *I love you,*
Walter's note says. *I always will.* I dial Marjorie Main's
number, but there's no answer.

Whew, that was a close call, huh? You know what I did
with the rest of those Seconals? I threw them in the trash,
I really did. Do you think Walter left that glass of booze
there accidentally on *purpose?* I never expected something like that, but then again I wouldn't put it past him
either. Maybe Walter's learned something from history.
Maybe he wanted to make me a *real* little angel. Maybe
Walter's not such a lightweight, after all. Anyway, there's
no need for Seconals now, because Bruno's here, loading
my bags into his Cadillac, full of the same summer clothes
I had when I came. I haven't bought any new clothes at
all, in Groverton. I've been wearing Walter's. I've worn
Walter's clothes every day for months. Except for shoes
and underwear, everything I have on right now is Walter's: moth-eaten Yale sweatshirt, L. L. Bean pants rolled
up at the bottoms, brown tweed jacket with suede elbow
patches, rolled up at the wrists. If it wasn't for the white
cashmere coat Bruno's thrown over me, they probably
wouldn't even let me in the Ren Cen.
   One day I went into Walter's closet looking for something new to wear and found that blue plaid Calvin Klein
shirt, the one I thought Lily cut up for dishrags, way at the
back of the closet. I took it downstairs and ironed it in the
kitchen. I put on the shirt, dug a pair of good jeans out of
my suitcase, brushed my shaggy hair for the first time in
weeks, put on lipstick, and looked in the mirror cautiously. Hmmm, not bad, considering. At dinner, Walter
didn't even notice. You may suspect I've been unfair to

Walter in the dialogue department, but I haven't. Walter never says anything. That night, he didn't speak to me at all, except to say "Pass the butter." I went into the kitchen, took off the shirt, and cut it up for dishrags. Just the other day I used a piece of that shirt to polish one of Lily's copper-bottomed pots. Goodbye, Ohio. Don't say it hasn't been fun.

We're going to a party tonight, but first I have to shop. Detroit doesn't have the selection of shops I'd like, but what's nice is how concentrated the shopping district is. You've got everything in one place, right in the Ren Cen. You don't even have to go outside. Then you have the packages sent up to your hotel room that overlooks the river. That's Canada over there. Hello, Canada. H-E-L-L . . . o! After that, I go back downstairs and find a beauty parlor in one of the department stores. The manicurist can't do much with my hands. Her best hot oil treatment hardly helps. That copper polish really did a job on them. But my hair looks great, sans roots. With new hair, new clothes, new shoes, new makeup, I look familiar, you know? Who do I remind me of? I almost look like— wait, let me guess—I almost look like Anna Kate O'Shea! Hey, you know what? Now that I'm out of Groverton, *I feel fucking great!* I forgot how much fun it is to go shopping with other people's money. Bruno's being so sweet. He came into a bundle recently. He really made a *killing.* He just put a big wad of the stuff in my purse, told me to have fun, and took off for some business meeting. I don't want to know what kind.

Being a gangster's girlfriend isn't such a bad thing to be, is it? It happens all the time in Jackie Collins novels. It happens in all those *film noirs* I saw back in film school. I wrote my M.A. thesis on *le film noir.* I never imagined it would come in so *handy.* You usually don't get to apply graduate school to real life. But now I know just how to

behave. I know exactly how to be a gangster's girlfriend.
And it isn't such a bad life. I kind of like it. It's dangerous,
sure. I *guess* it is. But for Bruno. Not for me. *I'm* not one
of those gold-hearted whores, like Linda Darnell or Marlene Dietrich. You'll never catch *me* stopping a bullet for
some man, so Deborah Kerr can sashay off with him and
straighten him up. A gangster's sort of like any other busi-
nessman. He's away a lot of the time. He brings home lots
of money. He puts it in my purse and tells me to have a
good time. Are *you* having a good time? I am. I'm having
such a good time I can't fucking believe it. Free at last!
Free at last! What about Bruno? What *about* him.

Bruno comes back, kisses me absently, dresses. We get
in his Cadillac and drive to Grosse Pointe. In Germany,
where there aren't any speed limits, we'll have a BMW
and drive very fast indeed. In the Cadillac, I tell Bruno
about my day at the mall. He doesn't say much back, just
shoves his hand under my new suede skirt and strokes me
above my new stockings, outside my new silk panties,
while I babble on and on. It's been so long since I talked
to anybody. I have lots and lots to say. I feel like I've just
woken up from a nightmare, and I have to tell it before
I forget what it was about. I have to tell Bruno my nightmare about Groverton. It used to be a good dream, but
then it came true! That was the nightmare part. I
dreamed I married Walter Light and had to take care of
his children, and they hated me and Walter hated me too.
"You don't know what it's like, getting up there every
night, when the whole audience doesn't *want* you," I
actually say. I almost forget who I'm stealing from: Susan
Alexander in *Citizen Kane.* That's what *her* bad dream
was about. That's why she took *her* pills. Everybody has
the same dreams, good *and* bad. I have to talk about
mine, before I forget it. I don't know why I'm crying, it

wasn't *that* bad, was it? Oh yes it was, it was *too* that bad.
Walter Light was too *the boyfriend who came from hell.*

When we get to Grosse Pointe, Bruno takes me in his
arms and kisses me. "I'm sorry, Anna Kate. I'm so fucking
sorry," Bruno says, really upset.

"What are you talking about?" I say coldly. I calm down
immediately, take out my makeup bag, and fix my face.

"Dear, do you know what a pinko is?" the faded blonde
with 45-inch nose cones asks me several hours later. Rita
and I took to each other at once. We spotted each other
like long-lost sisters. The Percodans helped, of course. The
champagne. But what it is, really, is that our lipsticks
match. Our nails are polished the same shade of frosted
peach. Now Rita's talking about Havana, when the pinkos
came:

"We were on our way to a cockfight. Everywhere you
went, there were soldiers in the cars with machine guns.
Oh, Havana was a lovely place then. All the men in their
uniforms. Back then almost every Cuban man wore a
uniform. Oh, it was exciting! Mr. Indelicato had a helicop-
ter, to fly us back to Miami. There was this colonel we used
to pal around with, he said if I get a shortwave radio and
call you, *langostina,* will you come back for me? I said
sure, but we never did hear from him again, did we,
honey?" Mr. Indelicato, who owns the joint, is with us
now. He comes up to Rita's chin almost, gives me the
once-over coolly.

"No, we never did," he says.

"I wonder what happened to him?" Rita says vaguely.
"You know why he called me *langostina?*" I shake my
head. Rita laughs and pats her ass. "Big!" she says. "The
langosta carries all its meat on its back!"

"Me too," I say.

Rita says, "Is the Riviera still there?" I say it is, and full of Russians. The Cubans have a name for them that means *smells bad.* "What about the Hilton?"

"It's the Havana Libre now," I say. Mr. Indelicato nods and moves away gracefully, to greet some new guests. He's Bruno's partner in the jai alai business. We're in his study drinking champagne. There are pictures of Mr. Indelicato all over the walls, with jockeys, boxers, gamblers, pool sharks, presidents. Mr. Indelicato's at the top of the gangster heap, and Rita's come along with him for the ride.

"Can you still see all the lights, from the tenth-floor bar?" she asks.

"When I was there there weren't many lights to see, and the windows were dirty."

"That's a shame," Rita says. "A dirty rotten shame. What I wouldn't give for a *mojito* right now! Who took you to Havana. Bruno?" I shake my head. "I went for the first time in 1951," Rita says. "I took the United Fruit Company boat from New Orleans. It cost seventy-five dollars. I remember the way they pulled all of my underwear out at customs. All the customs men would gather around each suitcase and take each article out and comment on it, oohing and ahing. Only when it came to me, I thought they weren't going to let me in the country, because my underwear was too shabby! I stayed at the Sevilla-Biltmore, which was the second-best hotel, after the Nacional. They took one look at me, just off the banana boat, and put me on the south side, next to the Polar Beer Company sign. This neon volcano erupted *beer,* and it had a clock on top, and this little polar bear on a bicycle would ride around the clock every fifteen minutes, striking a gong! How cute, I thought, until it was time to go to *sleep.* Every fifteen minutes with his little hammer: *Bong!*

*Bong! Bong! Bong!* And then in the morning the street
vendors would start, so it would be *'Fruta bomba! Hela-
dos!' Bong! 'Café!' Bong! Bong! Bong!* The circles under
my eyes must have made me look older, which turned out
to be a blessing, because they hired me at the Tropicana
right away. And then I met Mr. Indelicato and got away
from that goddamn bear!"

Rita's the first real gun moll I've ever met. She's wearing a transparent nylon blouse, true. You can see her bra
through it, but it's an *expensive* bra. I wouldn't mind
looking like Rita when *I'm* fifty-five. Bruno comes by
briefly, kisses me, goes off to talk more business. Rita looks
at him thoughtfully. "How much do you know about that
young man?" she asks.

"Oh, everything," I toss off. Rita looks alarmed.
"Enough," I correct.

Chuckling, Rita takes me by the hand and leads me into
her bathroom, still reminiscing about Havana. She tells
her stories so well that she almost loses me, as if her life
was a well-loved novel, read at an impressionable age. I
start to drift off and tune her out. Rita rummages through
the drawers, finds what she's looking for, and sits down on
the toilet.

"This used to be my scent, right up to 1959," Rita says,
handing me a little bottle: Noche Cubano. "Go on, sniff,"
Rita commands, and I do. The bottle's empty, but there's
still the faintest odor.

"Violets," I say. Rita smiles, pleased.

"That's right. When I think of Havana, I always smell
violets." Rita takes my hand. "I love your polish. In
Havana, the women painted little red rims around their
cuticles. They all had Great Danes. I used to think their
hands were bleeding, from being pulled around all day by
those great big dogs."

"Fidel Castro kissed me, when I was in Havana."

"Goodness! I hope you washed your face!" I hear Bruno calling me. Time to go to another party.

"I really have enjoyed this," I say honestly.

"Me too," Rita says. "I don't have many women friends, to talk to."

"Neither do I," I say.

Rita stands up suddenly, kisses me on the cheek, and whispers, "There's something about your Bruno that's not quite right. If I were you I'd watch my ass, *langostina.*" I say I will. Rita pulls away and stares at me hard. Her tired blue eyes look so troubled. "I mean it. You've still got a lot to learn."

"I don't have much time left! I better learn it quick!"

"I guess you better!"

"I can take care of myself. Don't worry." Rita looks at me kindly.

"Bullshit," she says.

"Where to now?" I say brightly to Bruno in the car.

Bruno tells me we're going back to the Ren Cen. "I have to see Mr. Indelicato. Alone."

"Can't I come?" I say cutely. Bruno shakes his head. I see Mr. Indelicato and a bunch of his henchmen pile in a limo and follow us out of Grosse Pointe, into Detroit, through the slums where Bruno searches for old records. He's so unafraid of the *natives.* He thinks they're *exotic,* that it's fun to be blond in a slum in a Cadillac. Once I told him a story about Heinz Hunnertmark getting kidnapped by these Rastas in Jamaica. Heinz kept telling the Rastas that he was on *their* side, that he was a Marxist, that he knew Michael Manley personally, not to mention Jimmy Cliff himself, but the Rastas just kept saying, "De money, mon! Give us de money!" and finally Heinz had to, a *lot,* but Bruno just laughed when I told him this story. It didn't

really penetrate. At first I figured that was because Bruno
was armed. A guy like Bruno, you'd expect him to carry
a gun, right? But he doesn't. I've watched him undress.
When he's out of the car, haggling with some poor old
black lady, trying to save twenty-five cents, I've searched
it pretty thoroughly. It's not guns that make Bruno not
afraid. I don't know what it is.

When we get to the Ren Cen, Bruno parks me in the
bar. He heads up to our room for this meeting with Mr.
Indelicato, while I have a number of drinks, then drift out
into the lobby, looking for trouble. Oh, my God, who's
that over there, waiting for the elevator? Could it be? *Oh
yes it could.* It's Patti Smith, in the flesh, holding Fred
"Sonic" Smith, who used to be an MC5, by the arm. Fred
and Patti are married now. They live in Detroit *all the
time,* by *choice.*

Who's that coming in the door? Another rock and roll
idol? Ted Nugent? Shit! And *more* MC5, Amboy Dukes,
even Stooges! There must be a party somewhere in the
Ren Cen that all these ex–Detroit rockers are going to,
and I'm going too. Oh yes I *am.* Whose name can I drop,
to get me in? Oh yeah. Mine. I pull out my compact, check
my lipstick, and sashay over. Bob Seger's there, too.
Hmmmm, he looks so accessible, so friendly, so . . . *hairy.*

"Haven't we met somewhere before?" I say to Bob
Seger with winning smile. Seger's polite but wary. Am I
really a fellow famous person? But a *Rolling Stone* editor
recognizes me, I get the right kind of introduction right
away, and pretty soon everything's great. We're all chatting away amiably. The elevator comes down. Alice
Cooper's inside it, to take up the guests. It's his party. The
guy from *Rolling Stone* asks me to stick around for a
second. He's waiting for Iggy Pop. We can all go up together. I let him drag me into the bar and give me coke,
which I bend down under the table to do. When I

straighten up, I see Iggy Pop's crotch is three inches from my nose. I tear myself away from the sight with difficulty.

"Lost an earring," I lie, though mine are on my ears. Iggy doesn't do drugs anymore. He's clean as a whistle. Talk about *survivors.*

"Jim Osterburg," Iggy says, extending his hand, and a very nice hand it is too, for a short guy, with big square nails and impossibly long thick fingers. I get a rush in my stomach that I suppose must be lust, relinquish the hand reluctantly.

"You clean up nice, Jimmy," I say flirtatiously. Iggy laughs. The editor pays the check and we head for the elevator, but once it comes down the operator won't take us up because Iggy and the editor aren't guests at the hotel. I am so I can take them up with *me,* but only to my *floor.* The moron won't take us to the penthouse unless Alice Cooper himself comes down again, and there isn't any way to sneak up, either. There aren't even any fucking *stairs.*

"I'm Iggy *Pop,* " Iggy says a number of times, but the operator's not impressed and Iggy's too pissed by now to find a phone and call Alice Cooper. While the elevator descends, I rant and rave. It's one thing to keep undesirables out but clearly we're somebodies. Can't the operator see that? No. He can't. Iggy gets out without a goodbye and heads for his limo, trailing my fantasies like stardust. The editor asks whether or not he'll see me again. I tell him I don't know, he rushes off after Iggy, and I go upstairs to pout.

In the suite, Bruno's having some kind of conference with Mr. Indelicato. Harsh words are being exchanged. It sounds like Bruno owes Mr. Indelicato some money. Something's gone wrong with their little deal, it seems. A *lot* of money? Search *me.* Bruno gives me a worried look when I clomp in noisily, lower lip dragging the ground.

Three or four members of Mr. Indelicato's charming en-
tourage are loitering here too, drinking our champagne.
I go over to the little refrigerator, pull out a bottle for
myself, pop the cork, eat a number of Percodans, plop on
the bed, turn on the TV, and file my nails in bored gun-
moll fashion. The Times Square show's on, as usual. Everybody looks like they're having fun back *there,* and a few
floors away all my culture heroes are having a party which
I was even invited to, shit. But I can't *get* there. Fuck this
hotel, I hate it. Now it's midnight. I walk over to where
the men are arguing, kiss Bruno hard on the mouth.

"Happy New Year, baby," I say.

"For this, I'll take off a thousand maybe," says Mr. Indelicato with a smile, indicating me, taking me totally by
surprise. A friendly rug peddler, willing to cut a deal.
*This?* I back off a step, alarmed. The gorillas close in to
watch. Their practiced eyes appraise me quickly, calculating my current market value, which is depreciating even
as we speak. I edge toward Bruno, who drags hard on his
cigarette. A quick glance at his cruel face reassures me.
His thoroughbred nostrils flare with distaste at this intru-
sive whiff of commerce.

"She is not for sale or barter," Bruno says with weary
Old World politeness, tapping an inch-long ash onto the
floor. My little heart flutters proudly, but the friendly rug
peddler is gone.

"BULLSHIT! BULLSHIT!" Mr. Indelicato roars suddenly, the spittle flying in little glass beads from his
mouth.

Bruno says, "You do not understand, my friend," this
worried tone creeping into his voice. "She is not a whore,"
Bruno says, but that worried tone worries *me.* I'm just
beginning to wonder what that worried tone means when
Mr. Indelicato fixes his red eyes on me and rips my blouse
down the front with one quick motion. The silk is still

vibrating from the assault, kind of hanging there in shreds
shivering gently when Mr. Indelicato wags a stubby digit
at Bruno.

"You uppity Kraut bastard. It's *you* that don't understand."

My arms are crossed over my breasts, corpselike, as the
terror envelops me like a shroud. It floats down so gently
I hardly feel it. Through the thick black gauze, I can
barely see Bruno's face. None of this has anything to do
with *me*. It has to do with Bruno, who steps forward to
protect me. We look at each other for a long, long second,
Bonnie and Clyde before the shit hits the fan. I can still
see the quick, choppy shots. His face. Her face. The gentle
shy glances, sutured at the eyeline, just before the bullets
rip and rend. He never meant, after all, to put me in any
danger.

Mr. Indelicato is smiling too, but the drool is still glisten-
ing on his chin, and before Bruno takes two steps forward,
one of the gorillas cuts him off. Bruno blocks his first
punch, gets in one of his own. He moves quickly, power-
fully. The gorilla grunts with pain. Maybe everything will
be all right after all, I think, when a hard punch to the
stomach doubles Bruno up completely. The gorilla is
chuckling with derision as he chops efficiently at Bruno's
neck, exposed and vulnerable, then knees him in the
groin. Bruno goes down. His eyes are wide with shock and
surprise, locked on mine, apologizing. The second gorilla
moves in. It's over, and so *fast.* Not like a movie at all.

"It's okay," I whisper, even though it isn't, forgiving
him now for everything, even the things that haven't
happened yet. But Bruno doesn't see me. Both of them
are kicking him now. One of them aims at his head like
a punter kicking a field goal, but holds back a little at the
last minute to prolong Bruno's agony. Something breaks
with the kick, but not Bruno's neck. He's still moving, still

alive. While the gorillas mangle Bruno, Mr. Indelicato
watches with ill-disguised glee, grunting at each blow.
One calloused hand moves over my breasts mechanically.
"Please," I say to him, not for myself. For Bruno. And
this is a serious mistake. Oh yes it is. To distract Mr. Indelicato from the exquisite pleasure of seeing Bruno's face
pounded to hamburger and his blood do a Jackson Pollock
number on the carpet is, on my part, a very serious mistake. A smarter woman would have tried to switch sides.
Jane Greer could have done it, or Gloria Grahame, as
easily and gracefully as changing a dress. I should have
slipped Bruno over my head, thrown him down in a heap
and walked on him, then said something witty to indicate
this shift in allegiances. I should have blown like a leaf
from one gutter to the next. Instead I said it: "Please."

"You fucked up one time too many," I remember my
stepfather saying as he banged my mother's head against
the mantelpiece. I hit him with a lamp that Brandy won
at Bingo, but I was only twelve. Jack didn't even turn
around, he was so intent on killing my mother, killing her
really dead this time. His eyes never left her face, which
was already turning purple. He batted me away like a
mosquito. He wanted to see it happen, in her face: to see
death creep into it, to see his buddy strut his stuff. By the
time the police arrived to tell us they never interfere in
domestic quarrels and would I please stop dialing 911 and
tying up the line, my mother had already lost consciousness.

"I saw his eyes," she told me later, from the stretcher.
"I saw his eyes, and I knew I was dead. There was nothing
human in them."

Mr. Indelicato's eyes are like that now. Fixed on *me*.

"Down, down," Mr. Indelicato commands, as if to a
rambunctious puppy. "Down." He points to the floor between his knees. I don't move fast enough, so someone

pins my arms behind me, pressing a knee into the small
of my back, pushing hard, and I go down. That's right.
Good doggy. But what a tasteless bone. Like something
dug up in the graveyard.

I gag, and there's pain in my shoulder, so intense it
shoots sparks across my eyes. Blinding at first, the pain
gradually fades, then resolves itself into a million tiny
stars. I try very hard not to gag again. I concentrate intently on not gagging. I remember Linda Lovelace and
relax my throat. I think of the sword swallowers I saw in
Paris, outside the Beaubourg. It is, after all, not that big.
It's the humiliation, really, that's making me cry, not the
pain. The humiliation, the laughter, the being watched.
Tears are streaming down my face. I gag again, feel hair
part from scalp. It would be so easy to bite down hard,
teeth instead of throat, to use the trusty white enamel. A
vampire bitch would wipe that smirk off. The bitch I
yearn to be would flood those ugly eyes with pain. And
die, of course, but *so what*. I can't even find the courage,
when it's over, to spit the bitter spoonful on Mr. Indelicato's shoes. I swallow. Mr. Indelicato zips his pants. I
fall forward on the carpet. I catch myself on my right
elbow. I can't feel my left arm at all. Mostly what I feel
is the carpet burns on my knees.

"You want her?" I hear Mr. Indelicato say from someplace far away. That Indelicato! What a host! I barely have
time to look at Bruno before it starts again. Hands lift my
skirt, not gently. Maybe if I ask, they'll get me a pillow for
my knees. The pain is making me slightly hysterical. If I'd
let Billyjim do this to me when he wanted to, maybe it
wouldn't hurt so much right now.

I remember seeing this white-haired cupcake being interviewed by a hairy submoron on some late-night cable
program in New York. He was naked and so was she. They

sat there, all opened up, thighs overlapping, on this set like an airport motel. I watched them the way you watch maggots in dead cats, or buzzards suddenly in front of you on the highway, too arrogant to fly even when you stop the car and sit on your horn. "You mustn't hate the buzzards, baby," my mother said with characteristic unselective goodness as I peeked at a pair of them through spread fingers, screaming, "Hit them, *hit them*, HIT THEM!" "The buzzards can't help being what they are," she said.

The mental midgets I saw on cable were a lot like those buzzards. "I just relax and expaaaand," the woman, a pornographic film star, said, when asked about her experiences with what's happening to me right now. There's no question that I hate her more in retrospect than I did when I first saw this program. A year ago, it made me *laugh*.

"And this has been done to you . . . many times?"

"Oh, many, many, *many* times."

I try to relax and *expaaaand*. It doesn't seem to be working so hot. I would scream if I could, but someone is using my mouth at present. Miss O'Shea's mouth is occupied at the moment, sir, would you care to wait? Miss O'Shea's mouth is taking a lunch, an *Italian* lunch. On the cheap acrylic carpet, my raw knees burn with each assault, like sliding into first on Astroturf.

"Look at that bitch go," I hear one of them saying. I assume this means I'm giving a credible performance. Behind me, one more faggot shoots his wad. I squeeze him out of me like toothpaste, like the little shit he is. They probably learn to fuck like this in prison. Every once in a while I hear Bruno, trying to make a comeback. I can't see him because I can't turn my head, which is firmly directed to the job at hand. I hear Bruno struggling to get up. I hear him go down a few seconds later. I wish you'd

254                                    Jayne Loader

stay fucking down, Bruno. Don't do it for me. I'm not paying any attention. I don't fucking appreciate it. I'm not even fucking looking. Someone else uses my mouth. Uses it, I guess, because it's there.

"Suck it, suck it, suck it," he says and I suck it, suck it, suck it. I am rejected, amazingly, by one of them as being too old, and in my slightly battered and come-soaked state, not desirable enough for the privilege of receiving his sperm. And a few minutes later the room is quiet. It's over as suddenly as it began. Nothing is moving in here at all. Nothing is alive. Nothing but the ugly echoes of male laughter and the metallic grate of zippers yanked hastily down and lovingly, smugly pulled up. And in the corner, Bruno's ragged breathing. I close my eyes.

Outside, in the corridor, the maids are delivering breakfast trays. Their carts make a cheerful rattle, their brisk knocks signal morning. For other people. The hotel smells like fresh-perked coffee. I throw up then, all over the hateful carpet. I throw up for a long, long time. I throw up every drop. I think it will never all come out of me, but it does. Immediately I feel better, purged of other people's evil. One more taboo to smithereens.

I try to get up, but I can't just yet. I try to crawl, but when I put my weight on my left arm, I notice it's not really functioning. It's just sort of hanging there, limp and loose in the socket, like overcooked spaghetti. I don't feel the arm at all. How interesting. I sit another minute, unable to move, trying to decide how to proceed. Trying to develop a strategy for getting myself out of this pool of urp, which is definitely starting to make me sick, and over to Bruno, to help him. And pretty soon I'm up on my knees, back straight. I rise up out of the vomit like a cobra from a basket, swaying gracefully. There is this wire attached to the top of my head, pulling me straight up, and

I walk like a ballerina across the floor to Bruno, who is still alive. There is no use describing his face.

When I kneel down and touch him, Bruno opens his eyes right away, like he's been waiting for me. The crusty scabs splinter and bleed. Bruno's face cracks, like ice on a pond that's not quite frozen yet. He looks at me through the blood and starts to cry. This is the worst part. He struggles out of his dinner jacket, then wraps it around me and tries to hold me, to comfort me. One more useless, gallant gesture. I start to cry too, but not for the same reasons Bruno's crying. It's just so fucking sad, all of it. We sit there for a few minutes, crying and bleeding on each other.

"It's all right. It's all right. It's all right," I keep saying, but it isn't, of course. Bruno keeps trying to say something too, through the mess they've left of his face.

I get up after a while and dial 911. Then I take all our money and jewelry and wrap it in a towel and shove it behind the toilet tank, hoping to suggest a motive for the carnage. All except for my wedding ring, which winked at me lasciviously all through the assault. That I throw in the bowl. The diamond sinks like a guilty witch. I flush and it vanishes instantly, just like my so-called marriage. "Marriage," as Lily would have said. The punch line to a dirty joke.

I gather some Percodans from off the floor, all I can find, and go back to Bruno and stuff them in his mouth like popcorn. One of the white things I pick up is Bruno's tooth. I realize this just before I feed it to him, then tuck it in the pocket of his dinner jacket.

Bruno is gurgling wetly at me, but I can't understand him at all. His eyes are desperate and pleading. His hands coil around mine like snakes. Then he stops trying to talk and takes his hands away and fumbles in his jacket for his gold Cross pen. He motions to me for paper, with the same arrogant gesture he uses for getting the check, but I don't get up, so Bruno turns around with effort and writes on the wall.

"You'll ruin the point, baby," I murmur as Bruno scratches on wallpaper. If Bruno shakes any harder, his bones will shatter like crystal, and I'll have to sweep up the shards. I croon soft words. I try to soothe him. The Percodan starts to take effect. Bruno turns around and taps on the wall.

*I never kill anyone,* Bruno's written, as preface to a whole lot more. He looks at me mutely, his dress shirt like a butcher's apron. After I read what he's written, he writes *NEVER!* again in big block letters, then underlines it twice, the pen in his fist like a dagger.

"Of course I know that, baby," I say. "I knew it all along." But I didn't. I really have to hand it to Bruno, though. He really had me going for a while. He really had my number. He pushed all the right buttons, pulled all the right strings. He played his part with panache, like a professional. He caught a cute blond mouse in her own little trap. He was in Toledo on business when Lily got killed by that hit-and-run driver and thought he'd make the best of a bad situation. He decided to play a trick. He never thought I'd actually fall for it, that someone so sophisticated could be so gullible! "You wear your cynicism like a pair of high heels that are too big for you," Bruno said one night in bed. He never thought I'd go to such lengths to *atone.* He kept wanting to tell me the truth, but he didn't know how. He figured if he *did* tell me, I'd leave him, since little Lulus only love killers, so he kept on pressing his luck. He played all the cards in his hand, my Bruno. Too bad he came up with a busted flush, and Mr. Indelicato, to call his bluff.

What's that you're saying? Who *really* killed Lily? Nobody *we* know. Some stranger passing. Some local psychopath. Kids in a stolen car. Some fool in a pickup truck, liquored up. It was an accident. She did it on purpose. She slipped, she tripped. She twisted her ankle and fell. Did she jump or was she pushed? Who *done* it? Who *cares.*

As we hold each other, crying and bleeding, I see the camera pull back, revolted by the sight of us, wrinkling its nose at our smell. We huddle against the wall as the camera dollies away slowly, repelled, but fascinated too, afraid to miss anything, any new small atrocity. The room is as big as a fucking football field when the camera finally stops. In the corner of the frame, Bruno and I are small and isolated, two flies on the wall with a spider offscreen. Insignificant. Alone.

We deserve each other.

WITHIN a few days, everything is under control. Luckily my right hand, the one I use for signing checks, is still functioning. I write the biggest check of my life to Mr. Indelicato, to cover most of Bruno's debt, and after it's written there really is no money left. The money wasn't endless, after all, just like Clemmy said. Mr. Indelicato, the ultimate whammy, took all my money away. As of today, I'm officially broke. Worse than broke: into Clemmy for more than most people make in years. But Clemmy's not complaining. He's executive producing for Touchstone. They're paying him lots of money. When Clemmy gives me his address on Dopey Drive, he's embarrassed of course, but *proud.*

Mr. Indelicato sends flowers. He really is sorry, it seems. He had no idea who I was, he tells me on the phone, or we could've handled it on a more businesslike basis.

"Why didn't you say you was somebody?" Mr. Indelicato complains.

"Instead of somebody's cunt?" I say sweetly. Mr. Indelicato sighs heavily. He doesn't like to hear women use language like that. Oh, fuck it.

"You didn't give me much of a chance," I say wryly. Mr.
Indelicato chuckles. He'll eat pasta on this story for weeks.
His expensive flowers go straight into the trash, but I keep
the bouquet of violets Rita sends, with an empty bottle of
Noche Cubano.

We lie to the police, I mean *I* do. Bruno is too stricken
to do any lying, and with his jaw wired up he has a good
excuse. I'm happy to spare him that, at least. I spare him
whatever I can.

"They black guys?" the cops ask me confidently.

"No, Polish," I say, staring at Officer Blaszczyk's badge.

"How could you tell?" he asks, looking hurt. *Because I
had to help them* is the reply that springs to tongue. I
suppress it with effort and shrug meaningfully, hoping to
suggest some unspeakable Polish perversion that only
Officer Blaszczyk and now I, unwillingly, know about. I
manage to describe three suspects in this brutal assault
that roughly approximate the cops who come to take my
statement. They leave my room grumbling, real pain on
their bulldog faces.

New Year's Eve is a slow night for news. The story
makes page six of the *Post*, page twelve of *Variety*, and
the front page of most of the local papers. After all, I'm
somebody, *an Academy Award nominee, the conscience
of the New Hollywood.* This turns out not to be so bad for
*me.* All at once my name is out there again, and people
respond much better to a crisis that can be measured, like
sudden arbitrary violence, than to the gradual withering
away of personality. In dramatic situations, they aren't
ashamed to offer help. They may all suspect I brought it
on myself, but no one will ever know for sure. It could've
been pure chance. I could've not *deserved* it. Like I heard
somebody say on *Policewoman* the other day, before Joan
Collins threw a hair dryer in her Jacuzzi, "The road to hell

is some kinda highway." Crisis gives people something tangible to respond to, to name, and a number of old friends do call. Emma Gomez, for example.

"You okay?" Emma asks brusquely. When I tell her I am, she chirps, "That's my girl," and the condolence-call part of our conversation is over. I tell Emma to get me work right away, any kind of work as long as it pays well, and Emma tells me very casually that her phone's been ringing off the hook. She waits a few beats for my reaction, then essays a small giggle. When I give back a tentative little giggle in reply, seeing the humor of the situation all at once, Emma starts guffawing hysterically and I join in for the first good laugh I've had since Billyjim died. It seems Emma is awash in these offers, a veritable checklist of the Great Rapes of History, from *Revenge of the Sabine Women* to *The Connie Francis Story,* from *Rashomon II* to *Ms. Temple Drake.* There are even rumors about a remake of Jane Wyman's rape classic, *Johnny Belinda,* starring Patti Davis. A great publicity angle there!

"Now don't sell Davis short," Emma cautions, generous to the core. "She's not *that* bad."

"Uh-huh," I say skeptically. "I'll do whichever pays the most. Get me as much money as you can." Emma is respectfully silent for a moment, in honor of one of life's little crossroads. Then she tells me exactly what she thinks that job is. Within forty-eight hours, I have an assignment to do the third rewrite of Bucky Cream's new picture, *Mr. One Hell of a Man.* This time Bucky's a bodybuilder who gets mistakenly transported to the future. It's kind of a time warp, see, and he has to fight these bad guys who have modern space weapons with nothing but brute courage, killingly funny lines, and a woman with pecs of her own egging him on. Bucky is threatening to pull out unless his dialogue gets funnier *fast,* and after *The Penetra-*

*tor,* Bucky *trusts* me. He asked for me *personally.* Touching, no? Uh-huh. The nights are cold, down Mexico way. There's a great rape scene in the picture, too. Emma says the boys in L.A. were wringing their hands over that one. "I told 'em no sweat, that you were a professional," Emma says, then chuckles. I'll be leaving for Cancun as soon as I'm out of the hospital.

"Thanks, boss."

"*De nada.* Besides, I owe you one."

"What do you mean?" I ask, really perplexed.

"Why, Freddy Pitluck!" *Uh-oh.*

"I meant to explain that—" I begin, but Emma cuts me off.

"Oh, Freddy explained it already. About how he saved you from the mugger. He's feisty, for a little guy," Emma says fondly. "You should've told me about that, *chica.* You must've been really upset."

"You and Freddy . . . *talk?*" I say cautiously.

"It's hard to have clients you don't *talk* to," Emma says cheerfully. "I've made more money on Freddy so far than I ever did on you. And his career's just beginning!"

"You signed him?"

"Signed him, sold him, he's already *out!* Number eighteen in hardcover, and climbing. Rastark got the option. We're bidding the paperback rights next week. Where've you *been?*"

"Ohio," I say.

"Well, get down to your local bookstore and pick up a copy. It's dedicated to *you.* I'll tell Freddy to send you an autographed one, when I see him."

"Emma! You don't . . . *see* him, do you?" Pregnant pause. Then:

"I never thought you'd be prejudiced, Anna Kate."

"Oh, I'm not. I'm not. It's not his . . . *size* that worries me, but isn't he just a little bit . . . *mad?*" More silence. "Emma?"

"Just because you write about insanity doesn't make you *loco,*" Emma says sternly. "You of all people should know that. You didn't think it was *real,* did you, Anna Kate?"

"Oh, no; no, of course not," I lie none too convincingly.

"It was a novel. You didn't think it was . . . *autobiography?*" Emma asks again, this worried tone in her voice. Worried for *me.*

"Why would I have sent him to you, if I thought that?" I lie, more confidently this time. Practice makes perfect! "Are you in love with him?" Say *no.* Emma hesitates.

"Well, he's funny. He's . . . *different.* Quite a handful in the sack. He likes *fat,* which is a relief! He's not the boyfriend who came from hell!" Then: "Fuck it. I might as well tell you. It's serious. I took him *home.*"

"And?"

"And it went *fine.* He even speaks Spanish. Daddy loved him! Daddy says Freddy looks just like the dwarf in that Velázquez picture. You know the one? With the little princess? 'Las Meninas'?"

"Uh-huh." Emma's dad's a professor of art history at UCLA. He's written about a zillion books on Velázquez. When Emma was eight, she was saying witty things about Velázquez to Michel Foucault and Roland Barthes, in *French.* Her dad's kind of disappointed by the way she's turned out: not because Emma went Hollywood, because she never got married. Now he's pleased as punch. "Everything reminds your dad of 'Las Meninas,'" I say.

Emma laughs, then tells me to get well quick, so I can make lots of money for both of us. Before she hangs up, she tells me somebody from Dick Clark's office called to invite me to guest on *The $100,000 Pyramid.* I say I'll think about it, then sneak down to the hospital gift shop and, sure enough, Freddy's novel is there. Freddy's taken those quotes from around the word "novel," and in a big way, too. "Move over, Franz Kafka! Here comes Fred Pitluck!" trumpets the blurb on the cover, excerpted from the *New York Review of Books.* Sure enough, it's dedicated to me: *To K.A.P.O'S.: Wake up and smell the coffee, sweetie.*

Bucky Cream calls the next day, to tell me how excited he is about our upcoming meeting. He has a sweet voice, kind of southern.

"Nobody told me you were from the South," I say provocatively. Bucky laughs and tells me he's from Foley, Alabama. Gee, he sounds young. Royce Browder's told him all about *me*, though.

"About Lake Placid?" I ask curiously. Bucky hesitates. "Come on, Alabama! Spill it!"

"Well . . . he said you were a fun chick," Bucky finally gets out.

"Oh, I am. I am. Poultry in motion."

"I'm looking forward to it."

"Likewise. You were great in *The Penetrator.*"

"I was great because you gave me somebody great to *be,*" says Bucky generously. And on this shameless note the Mutual Admiration Society of America, Hollywood branch, ends its January meeting. But there's more good news to come. Oh yes there is. Heinz Hunnertmark, who sent me into that tailspin in Cannes, calls to tell me he's changed his mind about the Melissa Reed bio-pic. The one he used to think was too depressing. As delicately as Heinz can possibly put it, he says there's a great publicity angle there.

Heinz has hard news too: They've caught Melissa's killer. He turns out not to be one of the lowlife teenage sociopaths Melissa was fucking so compulsively down in Mexico after all, but this rich English ne'er-do-well turned

mass murderer of women and little girls called Merlin
Sarno, who was killed last week after a three-day chase,
gunned down a mile from the border by twenty Texas
rangers. There won't be any rights problems on Merlin
Sarno's end, lucky for *us.* How did they tie him to Melissa's murder, three years ago? Easy. Merlin took *pictures.*

"This gives the story a certain *closure,* don't you think,
Anna Kate?"

"Yes, I agree. As long as it's still Melissa's story, not
Merlin's." I wonder if Merlin Sarno ever made it to Ohio.
Maybe it was Merlin Sarno who snuffed out Lily's light.

"A certain symmetry," Heinz is saying. "I like it now,
as a package." Heinz likes it so much he's optioned Melissa's letters for a measly five grand. Working title: *Melissa and Merlin.*

"Not bad," I say. I've got no choice but to deal with him
if I want to make the picture. I tell Heinz I want to direct,
and he agrees reluctantly, *in principle,* if I can keep the
budget under ten million.

"Maybe you should star in it too," Heinz says, then
laughs like a department store Santa. "Ha-ha-ha-ha-ha-ha-
ha-ha," he actually goes. He's joking, of course, but this
idea isn't half bad. "You've always been so good on television, Anna Kate." How true, how true. Already, I know
what I'll say to Johnny and Joan and David, when they ask
about the parallels between me and Melissa. I know exactly what I'll say when they ask me to compare our lives.
It's such a good line, and so true: *She's dead and I'm not.*
I tell Heinz to call Emma, to hammer out the gory details.
He's not quite sure what to make of me yet. "She's still a
little shaky," I imagine him saying over high-tab lunches
(I don't even know where the in places *are,* I've been out
of town so long). "But she'll be fine. She's a survivor,"
Heinz will say, savoring the water of the moment. "Anna

Kate always lands on her feet. She's a veritable fucking weed."

Before my fat cat hangs up, his voice gets low and insinuating. "You and I are going to make a lot of money together," he says.

Another nice thing about all the publicity is that I finally find out who Bruno is. I suppose I could have done it myself if I'd taken the trouble to hire a detective, but that never even occurred to me, I was so bamboozled, so *flummoxed*. But it didn't take the cub reporter stuck on the crime desk at the *Detroit Free Press* on New Year's Eve more than a few hours to ferret it all out.

Name: Bruno Bierbichler. One of the nurses explains that this means not just "beer drinker" but "beer guzzler." Doris works hard to make the difference clear, to make me see the humor of the Bavarian name. When I visit Bruno, I call him Herr Chugalug. From the foot of the bed, Doris and I sing the Roger Miller song to him, but Bruno can't manage a smile just yet. Age: thirty-eight. Parents dead. Never married. No dependents. "Mr. Bierbichler, a Manhattan-based banker, is taking an extended leave of absence from the Bavarische Landesbank in order to recuperate from the injuries suffered in last night's brutal attack." With his bad teeth replaced, his black roots touched up, Bruno will be a big hit in Hollywood, where I'm taking him, as soon as we get out of the hospital.

Heinz Hunnertmark's flack catcher calls and asks if there's anything he can do to help get me settled in L.A., where I'll be writing *Melissa and Merlin* after *Mr. One Hell of a Man* is finished. I ask him to find me a house, and presto! A sublease near Benedict Canyon materializes, not far from where I used to live with Clemmy. Even the address seems familiar. Maybe Clemmy and I went to a party there once. You see deer there sometimes, in the

evening. They come down from the hills to pose beside
the swimming pools. Little brown-speckled narcissists. I
wonder what they see in the chlorine.

Hey, speaking of Clemmy, he's got wedding bells in *his*
future too, just like Emma. He tells me the happy news
during our money conversation. Who's the lucky girl?
Why, Verity, of course. She and Clemmy really hit it off,
down in Mexico. Clemmy's a little bit awkward talking
about it. He thinks I still love him. He doesn't want to hurt
me. I tell him to give Verity my love. Long pause. Then:

"Verity doesn't like you anymore, honey," Clemmy
says with ill-disguised glee. "When I mention your name,
she foams at the mouth."

Despite or because of this, Verity calls five minutes later
with more wedding details. Since Verity doesn't have a
family herself, the ceremony's slated for Newport. I'm not
invited.

"I hope you *understand,* Katherine Anne," Verity says
with sham solicitude. "It just wouldn't be . . ."

"Yeah yeah," I say impatiently, before Verity finds the
word she's seeking: *fitting,* pronounced *fitten.* "How
about the Goodbloodes? Have you met them yet?" Verity
says yes. "How about *Mrs.* Goodbloode?" I persist. Verity's background is even more sordid than *mine.*

"Oh, Eliza?" Verity tosses off. "We get on like a house
afire!"

I could go home now, if I had a home to go to. There's
nothing much wrong with me really, except my arm. I
could go home at any time, but I decide to wait for
Bruno—who really *is* hurt, almost everywhere—to heal.
Every day, I sit by his bed and read to him. I hold his hand.
Emma sends one of her flunkies out to Bruno's condo in
Weehawken to arrange for its impending sale, and while
he's there he picks up and ships Bruno's records, so we
have something to listen to while we recuperate, and

every day it's the same old song. I try to get Bruno to
lighten up, to listen to some Schönberg or even Philip
Glass, but *Lulu* is what he loves, so we listen to that while
Bruno stares at me with tortured eyes. He's always loved
me, Bruno writes on the note pad he keeps by the bed.
Ever since the very first night.

I like it here in the hospital, and every time Dr. Wellborn talks about releasing me, these big tears start welling
up and I guess he figures I must still be in shock. The
hospital isn't crowded, and unless there's a major disaster
or plane crash or something I have a good chance of holding onto my bed for another week. Lucky Walter's insurance is picking up the tab. I'd be worried about Bruno's
bills, since he's been fired from the bank—a question of
embezzlement, his little charade was expensive, but I'm
paying that back too, bit by bit—and all the plastic surgery
my new love has to have, but the people from the Ren
Cen paid us a visit. *They* were worried too, about a law-
suit. Something about a defective door lock, imagine that!
A hotel in New York just paid out three hundred big ones
to a rape victim under similar circumstances. Even Connie Francis sued the Howard Johnson's, where *she* was
raped, before she went to the funny farm. I tell the lawyers we won't sue—no telling what a suit would *un-
cover*—as long as they pay Bruno's hospital bills, kick in
a few meager dollars to launch us in L.A., and treat Bruno
to a new face, *the very best money can buy.* I wonder how
much a new face goes for these days? It couldn't be *that*
much, since the lawyers leave smiling. While I'm here I
ask Dr. Wellborn for a complete physical. I'm as healthy
as a Percheron mare. My blood's nice and thin, too, probably because of all that alcohol. No liver damage, though.
Also, I don't have AIDS.

I read books and watch TV, new shows this time. They
don't have cable in Detroit General. Florence Henderson

does commercials for Wesson Oil now. Pat Sajak's gotten
kind of cynical. He referred to himself and Vanna White
as "Barbie and Ken" one day. Good thing we never met.
After watching *The $100,000 Pyramid,* I call Emma back
and tell her to turn Dick Clark down. It's far too hard.
   "What about *The New Hollywood Squares?*" I suggest.
Emma giggles, then promises to get right on it.
   I catch up on old friends, write letters. I listen to gossip
about other people and try to minimize the flow of it
about myself. When discussing the rape, I offer no details.
I refrain from confessing anything. *Weary and sad, but
bouncing back* is the impression I try hard to convey. I
trust absolutely no one.
   Chipper Donaldson shows up one day bearing gifts: a
pizza from Due's in Chicago, a VCR, and lots of tapes. It
turns out Chipper really did a job on poor Dixie Credit.
She gave him all her money, but that's gone now and
Chipper's had to come home, to extort even more from
his parents by promising to stay out of Wilmette, Illinois,
for yet another year. That's where Chipper was when he
read about me, so he stops in to cheer me up before
returning to France for one more season of pseudo-pov-
erty. In addition to a bunch of movies, including one of
mine, Chipper's brought a cassette of *The Robin Byrd
Show.*
   "You'll get a kick out of this," he promises, then locks
the door, turns on the video, and kills the lights. There's
this pretty young boy in red and black rubber harlequin
pants gyrating in Robin's signature video heart. His head's
thrown back, his tongue's extended, he's rubbing his big
cock through the rubber.
   "Ho hum," I say to Chipper. "Fag porn. Just what I
need, in *my* condition." Then I realize the boy is Johnny.
He's finally gotten into pictures, all right. Someone's fixed
his teeth for him, too. He sucks on his fingers, then his

nipples. I had no idea Johnny's tongue was so *long*. He takes off his pants and jiggles his soft-on around. He makes it go up and down, back and forth, round and round like a propeller, the way strippers rotate their tits. By the time Johnny dry-humps an elderly Cuban pornstar with third-degree cellulite on her buttocks and pulls off Robin Byrd's panties with his teeth, and a commercial for *Manpower!* magazine, published by First Hand Productions, interrupts the flow of soft-core action, I'm crying big pathetic tears and Chipper's trying hard not to smirk. Finally he bursts into strident guffaws. He laughs so hard he starts to wheeze. Revenge is *sweet*. I make him take the unclean tape and leave.

I wipe my eyes and put on *Last Chance for a Slow Dance*, which I've never seen. The two days I spent on Rodolpho's set were so excruciating I could never bear to. But the picture isn't as bad as I thought. There are some nice moments, some moments that remind me of what it was like, I mean Clemmy and me, when things were good between us. I especially like the part where Gerald–Clemmy teaches Betty Jo–*moi* how to talk right by reading Nancy Mitford to her in bed. Most of the good parts take place there, even though Rodolpho's made Betty Jo kind of a whiner and Gerald a charter member of the National Man-Boy Love Association. When the bad parts come on, I turn off the sound, but that doesn't do much good. One picture's worth a zillion words all right. I watch the bad parts silently. I watch my great love gasp its last. It's kind of nice, too, when it finally says THE END. I'm grateful to Rodolpho for being so old-fashioned, for tacking it on. There's a sense of closure, all right. Oh yes there is. Of bank vault doors slamming shut.

A number of other presents arrive in the mail: Brandywine sends me a 1986 Filofax knockoff, the one Meredith Baxter Birney pitches on the tube for $19.95. It's just as

nice as the original Filofax, just as useless, except it has this
fake lizardskin cover. I could never get away with carrying it in Hollywood. I write Brandy a thank-you note, then
shuffle down to the gift shop, buy a new card and sign it,
tape the wrapping paper back together, and give the
package to Doris, the nurse. When she opens it, she
thanks me effusively, with genuine tears in her big gray
eyes.

One day I get a card from my father, Rodgers O'Shea,
an antique card from Palm Beach, Florida, with a cartoon
of a skunk on it taking a bath. The skunk is scrubbing
himself really hard, it seems. He's surrounded by all these
vials and potions, by bath salts, B.O. Soap, My Sin Cologne, and violet talcum powder. The skunk has this frantic look on his face. IT'S HOPELESS . . . I'M STILL A STINKER!
the caption says. The back of the card says, *Get Well
Quick. Love, Dad.*

I get something from my mother, too. Not too bulky.
About three hundred pages. You saw it coming, right?
*Suuuure* you did. Is it any good? Come on now, be serious.
What's it about? Oh, *us.*

"The little girl was walking down the dusty road, kicking up dust," my mother's novel begins, "not doing much
of anything." Her book tells the old familiar story of Livia
and Roger, of young love falling apart in misunderstand-
ing and mistrust. But she tells *both* sides of it. She makes
both sides real. Love! Betrayal! Pregnancy! Abortion
. . . not quite, but almost. Whew! That was close. There's
this trip to the abortionist in Chicago with my father,
during which their love just leaks away. Daddy wants her
to have the abortion, but mother won't, so Rog just leaves
her there, in this fleabag hotel with this scapel-wielding
rummy thug.

My mother escapes the leering abortionist and gets on
a Greyhound bus heading south. A plastic ring from Ben

Franklin's transforms her into a Korean War widow. She's
so Southern and charming and witty in this section, making sense of the ebb and flow of life, its contradictions. Her
journey is filled with kind and helpful people—people
who are *wise*—as well as the occasional tormented villain.
It's a poor people's ship of fools, a Greyhound bus of fools,
and my mother's voyage on it illustrates as much as anything else how the poor take care of their own. All the
victories here are small ones. The biggest victory is my
mother's arrival in Texas, with seventeen cents in her
pocket, just in time to have a baby in the storybook town.

"I never wanted to be a mother," my mother writes,
about my birth. "Why is this happening to *me?*" she pro-
tests, right up to the point where I wriggle out of her,
covered in blood and slime, and the world changes. Everything is different all at once. It has been, and always
will be, worth it. In my mother's book, the baby girl is
born with eyes wide open. She looks at my mother. She
recognizes her. And even though I knew how that baby
ended up, tears were streaming down my face when I
finished my mother's novel. I saw all of it through her
eyes, saw myself newborn exactly the way *she* saw me: as
a baby no one could help but love, the triumph of my
mother's life.

Could anyone doubt after reading this small but perfect
novel with "classic" written all over it that the future
would turn out well for that woman and child, that the
two of us would have an idyllic, magical life? Not *me*. I
don't doubt it. I'll live forever as that baby girl, no matter
how many times I try to tell my own story, no matter how
well I tell it. No matter how many times I betray that early
promise or manage by the skin of my teeth to stop just
short of breaking it, my activities will only be footnotes to
my mother's book, about the birth of the daughter she
named—in a burst of inspiration and bravado—after the

woman whose books kept her company on the bus. My own attempts at self-definition, at carving out a snappy streetwise persona, at finding a voice, haven't got a prayer. My feeble attempt at grappling with this material—unearthed from the suitcase, grimly read, then shredded—sounds like adolescent whining, as grating and unmelodious as chalk on glass. What has the depth of docu-drama in my eyes is transformed by my mother into myth. Her Pascagoula is as shimmering as Oz. I remember it hot and sordid and dirty. I remember *mosquito bites.* Why do I always remember the bad things? There's this thing about me, my mother, and Katherine Anne Porter. I got her personal life, my mother got her talent.

I contain my bitterness with effort and dial my mother's number, to tell her how much I love her novel. Gosh, she's glad to hear from me. After she asks me how I am and I lie enthusiastically, she barely lets me get a word in edgewise. So much *news.* She already has a publisher, thanks to one of her friends from Yaddo. John Irving's writing a cover blurb.

"Katherine Anne! Can you believe it?" she asks.

"I'm not even a little bit surprised," I say genially. My mother's going to *New York City.* I offer her my loft, which I haven't been able to sublet, but my mother says no, they're putting her up at the Algonquin.

"The *Algonquin Hotel!* I'm positive to make a fool of myself, up there in New York," she says.

"They'll love you, Momma. Who wouldn't love my mother?"

"You've got that turned around, baby," she says softly.

"Uh-uh." This time she doesn't contradict me. Already she knows she'll do just fine. Her pleas for reassurance are just for my benefit.

"You'll be great, Mom."

"Oh, I know," she says cheerfully. Just tosses it off. "I love you, baby."

"I love you, too, Momma."

I'm crying when we hang up. This behavior continues longer than it should, I think. I wonder momentarily if it ever will stop, then remember the sequel. Cynicism stops the tears dead in their tracks. Will my mother be able to transform twenty years of screaming, bloody hell with Jack Hill into a similarly cheerful, uplifting, and poignant odyssey? Probably. Brandy will collude. She believes our family was absolutely normal, like *The Brady Bunch.* My mother will be able to pull it off, all right.

"Isn't it fun to be poor?" she used to chirp into my sulky ingrate's face. "Think how boring it'd be if you were rich and had everything handed to you on a platter." *"Fat chance!"* I'd scream. My mother loved to make do, really loved it. The realization that I could be so small, so worthless, as to begrudge my mother anything brings on a fresh onslaught of tears, but fewer this time. I'm about all cried out, I think, and ring for the nurse. With my best smile, I beg for the only all-purpose panacea I know: chocolate ice cream and 7-Up. But the ice cream isn't creamy, the 7-Up is flat, and the float is no better than the parts it's made with.

A few days ago, Walter sent me these flowers, these translucent white roses, to commemorate our dead love. They seemed repulsively sexual, as fecund as the jungle, their petals as white and silky as my thighs, with their tracery of fading bruises where Mr. Indelicato's henchmen held me. Last week, they were rich purple crescents, closed parentheses. The milk-white roses made me think of sperm, of all the sperm I swallowed that night in the Ren Cen and then threw up, of all the sperm I've swallowed in my entire life and not thrown up. White sperm, black sperm, Jewish sperm, Irish sperm, smart sperm, stupid sperm. Sperm from every country. Lots of Italian sperm, recently. Sperm from every state in the union. It's a fucking melting pot down there in my stomach. It's International Brotherhood Week, like a bad World War Two movie, where all the wops, kikes, playboys, micks, eggheads, and niggers get it together to fight Hitler. No one will ever come in my mouth again. Lucky Bruno doesn't like to. I woke up, Freddy. I smelled the coffee. I wonder why it took me so long, to learn how to throw things up.

Walter's roses smelled as phony as perfumed Kotex, and when they splashed against the wall like brains the nurse rushed in looking angry. Then Doris noticed my breakfast in a puddle by the bed, saw how hard I was shaking, how wet and white my face was as I banged my head against the headboard. That's what it's there for, right? She noticed how convulsively I was dry heaving, scanning my stomach for something else to throw up. I would throw up the soiled lining, if I could suck it out. Oh yes I would.

An orderly cleaned up the mess remarkably quickly, while Doris went off to find a doctor. One minute the flowers were there, draped artistically over jagged green glass, and then they weren't. They were gone, and *so fast.* Like magic. Nothing to see but shiny linoleum, shinier than ever before. Mess cleaned up. Everything wiped away, as if it had never been. The nurse came back. She held my hand. She sponged my face with a rough wet washcloth. Dr. Wellborn came in and smiled in typical phony fashion, took one look at me, and pulled out a hypo.

"It's all right," Doris said soothingly, pat-patting my hand, but it wasn't. "It's all right to cry, Anna Kate. You've been through so much. You've been so *brave.*" Dr. Wellborn nodded gravely. I laughed.

Doris has a crush on me, I think. I noticed it one day,

when she changed the bandage on my ass. She spent far too long rubbing the Unguentine in. Somebody used my butt for an ashtray. Did I tell you that? An *asstray.* But I don't remember it. Not even a little bit. It's gone, it's forgotten. I won't even be able to see the scars without a mirror. But Doris sees them. Her sooty lashes clot with tears. "Maybe you'll come see us in L.A., when we get settled," I told her. Doris thanked me effusively, then wrote down my new address in her Filofax knockoff: 10050 Cielo Drive.

"What's that?" I asked curiously as Dr. Wellborn got the needle ready. On the white tray table, it gleamed like Iranian caviar. Automatically, I tried to wriggle away. Doris held my arm effortlessly.

"Just a painkiller, Mrs. Light," Dr. Wellborn said.

"Don't *ever* call me that!" I said melodramatically. Then I realized I couldn't remember Walter's face. I *tried* to see it, but every time I thought of Walter, I saw Pat Sajak instead, spinning that fucking wheel. And it hit me that I might as well keep the only thing of Walter's I still loved. I'm entitled to it, as sort of a post-love souvenir. As alimony. It's a good name, don't you think, if I decide to become a movie star? A new name for a new life. Katherine Light.

"What is it?" I asked the doctor again.

"It's Percodan," Dr. Wellborn finally admitted. I stopped struggling and started to giggle. Dr. Wellborn seized the time and jabbed the needle in quick, seeing an opening, as it were, psychologically. I didn't feel the needle at all. It slid in like it belonged there.